# FOREIGN AND FAR AWAY

# FOREIGN AND FAR AWAY
## 2013

# AN ANTHOLOGY OF SHORT STORIES, NON-FICTION AND POEMS

SELECTED, EDITED AND COMPILED BY
WRITERS ABROAD

This collection copyright © Writers Abroad 2013

Copyright in the text reproduced herein remains the property of the individual authors, and permission to publish is gratefully acknowledged by the editor and publisher.

All rights reserved

No parts of this publication may be reproduced, stored in a retrieval system, or transmitted in any form of any means, electronic, mechanical, photocopying, recording or otherwise without prior permission of the copyright owner.

ISBN-13 978-1492762003
ISBN-10 1492762008

# Introduction

This is Writers Abroad's fourth anthology and takes as its theme foreign places, firmly grounded in a particular place such as a country, area, town, village, or building.

All the contributors are, or have been, ex-pats living in places around the globe. To reflect the 'international' status of our contributors we have chosen to represent that in the editing, therefore you will find that stories and articles have been displayed accordingly.

All proceeds from the sale of this book will go to Book Aid International. Book Aid International increases access to books and supports literacy, education and development in sub-Saharan Africa. They provided 543,280 new books to over 2,000 libraries last year alone and have sent more than 30 million books to partner libraries since 1954.
www.bookaid.org

Writers Abroad is a virtual community of ex-pat writers, living in all corners of the world. We are committed to developing our craft through constructive criticism and feedback, encouragement and a meeting of minds.
Thanks goes to all members of Writers Abroad who have contributed to this publication—in one way or another—providing their time and expertise freely. It has truly been a team effort.
www.writersabroad.com

©Cover Design and Production
By Vesna McMaster (WA member)

# Foreword

The American writer Eudora Welty believed that 'Every story would be a different story if it happened somewhere else.'

In this wonderful anthology of expatriate writing, her words are truer than ever. Within these pages are short stories, non-fiction and poetry from around the world; French angel-makers and tales of unrequited love born on the scent of Indian jasmine; Estonian memories and Amish lifestyles; tourism and ancient relics in the Himalayas and so much more…

As an expatriate writer myself, I have long been fascinated with the relationship between people and the landscapes they live in. Writers in general are constantly observing the world and for writers living abroad, the feeling of being an outsider looking in, the sense of difference, the desire to fit in and equally the pleasure or confusion of not fitting in can be great fuel for inspiration. Writing, after all, is stepping out of your comfort zone. Life abroad can be like this too.

My own story of a life in France began in 2002 in a grey-sky English downpour when my husband and I, along with our two young daughters, piled into an overloaded, ancient Renault Espace and said goodbye to the house we'd lived in all our married life. Our neighbours stood on the pavement huddled under brightly coloured golf umbrellas, waving us on. We pressed our faces to steamed-up windows, grinning, laughing. *Goodbye! Goodbye!*

Driving towards Dover we fell silent. The little girls slept, lolling together in that state of loose-limbed trust that only dozing children, cats and comatose drunks manage to pull off perfectly. I studied a French road map. The windscreen wipers hurried, lorries threw waves of waterspray over us.

We were heading for south-west France where the earth was bone-dry and the sun would be shining when we arrived. We were about to begin a new life in a new place…

The writings in this volume make me think of the same sense of mystery and clarity that my own experiences of life abroad have brought to me. They are all incredibly different but they contain certain themes. They are an exploration of how it feels to edge forwards without the light of familiarity to guide us, feeling our way, seeing the world differently, from the senses: from the heart.

And what better way of life for writers? The writer abroad after all, is surely unusually awake to the relationship between places and people. Perhaps this is why so many authors have long fuelled our fantasies about the particular romance and hardships of expatriate life. Certainly the writers in this collection carry on that tradition and I believe this anthology will delight any reader. As Alan Bennett said, 'Books are not about passing time. They're about other lives. Other worlds.' This volume is full of writing that examines the diversities, the similarities, the connections and misunderstandings of life. I am delighted to welcome you inside these pages, to ask you to read on and be transported by these tales of people and places…

**Amanda Hodgkinson**

Amanda lives in southwest France. Her first, multi-award-winning novel, *22 Britannia Road*, is a sweeping tale of love, redemption and hope in the aftermath of the Second World War. It has enjoyed both critical acclaim and commercial success. Her second novel, *Spilt Milk*, will be published in February 2014. www.amandahodgkinson.com

# Contents

*\* non-fiction*
*\*\* poem*

A Belly of Flies ................................................................... 1
A Cretan Celebration * ....................................................... 6
A Dancing Fool in Tokushima* ........................................... 9
A Gift from God ............................................................... 12
A Good Sense of Humour * .............................................. 17
A Mug, a Thug and a Cup of Coffee * .............................. 20
Africa for Softies * ........................................................... 23
Aliens * ............................................................................ 27
Altogether Rain: Altogether Dance .................................. 30
Amica del Cuore .............................................................. 33
Angel Child ..................................................................... 38
Angel Maker .................................................................... 42
Barnacles ** .................................................................... 47
Between the Mountains and the Sea ................................ 48
Beyond the Sea * ............................................................. 51
Borneo Nights ** ............................................................. 54
Casa Rossetti ................................................................... 55
Cold Stone Soup * ........................................................... 60
Coming Home ................................................................. 63
Coyotepe Fortress ** ....................................................... 68
Crossing the Road in New Delhi ..................................... 70
Danza Gitana * ................................................................ 72
Diaspora ** ...................................................................... 74
Did I Really Kiss the Removal Man Goodbye? * ............ 75
Dolma and the Golden Egg ............................................. 78
Down in Zhou Village ..................................................... 83

| | |
|---|---|
| Driftwood ** | 87 |
| Elephants * | 88 |
| Encountering the G8 Summit * | 91 |
| Excuse Me, Are You Real? * | 94 |
| Feel at Home at Perico's * | 97 |
| Fifty Minutes and Fifty Seconds * | 100 |
| Five Year Itch | 103 |
| Flat hunting | 106 |
| Floating World * | 111 |
| Flowers for the Lady | 114 |
| Flying Low * | 116 |
| Foreign Soil ** | 119 |
| Going Native | 120 |
| High Noon | 124 |
| Home is Where…? | 126 |
| Home James | 131 |
| Humanitarian Aid Worker ** | 136 |
| I Lived with the Arabs * | 137 |
| Incognito | 140 |
| Into The Moment | 144 |
| Knickers * | 149 |
| Le Choix du Roi | 152 |
| Living Will ** | 157 |
| Longhouse | 158 |
| A Land of Luxury and Wickedness | 163 |
| Mamasan | 168 |
| Manger, Manger Glorieux * | 170 |
| (Food, Glorious Food à la Française) | 170 |
| Mango Orchard at Chapai ** | 173 |

v

Meeting Abinaya * .................................................................. 174
Middle-Earth Sea ** ................................................................ 177
Missionary Dress...................................................................... 178
More Rakia for the Amerikanski * ....................................... 182
On Teach-Big Street * ............................................................ 185
One Percent............................................................................... 188
Postcard from Benares, India ** ........................................... 192
Pretty, Jittery Indian Girls..................................................... 194
Priorities * ................................................................................. 198
Queen for a Day * .................................................................... 201
Reaching out in Africa * ........................................................ 204
Saintes **.................................................................................... 207
Security...................................................................................... 208
Sensing Africa in Hong Kong ** ........................................... 213
Separated by a Common Language * .................................. 214
Sepilok Rainforest Virgin ** .................................................. 216
Sirocco........................................................................................ 218
Sisters of Mercy * ..................................................................... 222
Sunday ....................................................................................... 225
Sweet Shop * ............................................................................. 226
Taxi Rides with Aysha *.......................................................... 229
Tectonic Plate Shift * .............................................................. 232
The Beautiful Tent................................................................... 235
The Encounter ......................................................................... 240
The English Wall ** ................................................................. 242
The Interloper .......................................................................... 243
The Old Turkish Garden **.................................................... 245
The Other Paris *...................................................................... 246
The Road to Trail Creek Summit ** ..................................... 249

| | |
|---|---|
| The Surprise | 250 |
| The Tell-Tale Divided Heart * | 253 |
| The Temple of Isis | 256 |
| The VIP Latrine * | 259 |
| Upriver | 262 |
| Walking Barry Island Beach ** | 267 |
| Walking in the Afternoon II ** | 269 |
| Walking the Streets of Hong Kong * | 270 |
| When Only Rain Will Do * | 272 |
| Wild Dogs of the Middle Atlas | 275 |
| Worth her Weight in Gold * | 280 |
| Index of Authors | 283 |

# A Belly of Flies
## by Mikaela Nyman

It's horse racing day. We wake up to a sky bruised from excessive rain. A centipede, thick as my thumb, has tried to squeeze under the girls' sliding door and is slowly dying with its head inside and its tail still outside. The girls scream as it wiggles, causing me to charge into their room with a butcher's knife. At least Ezzy Kill managed to fumigate before the rain, leaving streaks of white powder like a cocaine perimeter around the house.

'Let's go!' The girls are yelping like puppies, pulling at my arms.

'Stop it!' I snap, pricklier than intended. Feeling offbeat after a night listening to the rain roaring and worrying about rising water levels in the lounge. 'Go and get your Dad.'

I chuck the knife in the sink and run the tap. Last time someone chopped a centipede they left the knife on the kitchen bench, unwashed, and I used it to slice pawpaw.

The roads are crammed with mini-buses shuttling people to and from the races at the edge of Port Vila, the Ni-Vanuatu drivers swerving to avoid the potholes, while the expats in their four-wheel drives drive straight through. The grass in the field where we park is slick with mud. Hopping out of the car, one of the girls slips and lands on her bum.

'That's that dress,' I say and she howls and wants to go back home.

'Do you want to sit in the car and wait for us?'

She shakes her head and I grab her arm. Pouting, she drags her feet as we leave the field. A sharp pain flares up in my shoulder. The old rotator cuff injury rearing its head. No one told me it would be dangerous to have children. A man with dreads waves out from a group of men sitting under a majestic *natavoa* tree with a carton of beers. Ben waves back and shouts, 'See you tonight!'

'Who's that?'

'The security guard.'

'Is he on tonight? He's drunk.'

'Just pretending.'

'You're unbelievable. If he's drinking now he'll sleep all night. Shouldn't you say something?'

Ben shrugs and walks towards the booming music and the white tents. At the other end of the field there's a string of huts knitted together from palm leaves and bamboo sticks. The sound system squeals before the MC regains control and starts announcing the upcoming events. When the music stops for a moment, we can hear the sound of a generator chugging away.

'Mummy, we want to go there!' Tugging at my skirt, the girls point at a Bouncy Castle.

About thirty children push and shove each other inside the castle. As I take in its frayed wobbliness, there's a scream of agony from inside. No adult seems to care.

'You're not going in there.' I start wading through the mud towards the castle. The girls howl with disappointment. Ben throws me an exasperated glance.

'I want to take some photos.'

'And leave them here? Do you see any adults around?'

By the time I get to the castle the screaming has stopped. No trace of the screamer. Children of all sizes and colours are bouncing and bumping into each other. Some are clearly over the age limit for this sort of entertainment.

'Look at those teenagers, they're drunk. Hey, get out, this is for *pikinini nomo*!'

The man running the generator looks surprised, then he grins. Ben takes off towards the makeshift grandstand, to be saved any embarrassment, I can tell. The girls are hunched on the ground, sulking.

'Great,' I say.

I grab their sticky hands and start pushing through the throng towards the white fence. String-band music struts across the field. The aroma of barbequed meat drifts from the huts, making our stomachs growl.

'Let's watch the races first,' I suggest. 'It's too early for lunch.'

'But I'm thirsty.'

'Me too.'

'Okay, you can share a drink. What do you want?'

We buy two soft drinks from a mama with a cool box filled with ice and head for the race track. In the shade of the white tents, those willing to pay, mostly expatriates, take their lunch at proper tables. Glasses of champagne cast cheery sunspots on pristine tablecloths. A waiter balances a platter with a tower of greens surrounded by white chunks. Chicken or fish? I squint, suddenly feeling an urge to know. Everyone underneath the awning seems content and happy to be envied. Not that I envy them, I assure myself. The crowd is growing by the minute. A man in a high-visibility vest walks past on the track side, tapping bare legs and hands with a stick.

'No sitting on the fence,' he says and I have to lift down the girls.

'But we can't see.'

'You will, just wait for the races to begin,' I assure them, craning my neck in an effort to spot Ben.

I think I see him with his arm around a plumber named Henderson, but then the crowd closes in and I lose sight of him. Why Henderson? I wonder. He did a shocking job on our water tank replacement, would have earned a kick up the arse, rather than a pat on the back, according to Ben. At least those shoulders didn't belong to Mrs Henderson.

The horses parade past us with jockeys in colourful jackets, a couple of them sturdier than any jockeys I've seen before.

'That's Gypsy! Look, Mum!' For once my eldest is excited.

I check the programme. 'Doesn't say so. Number five is supposed to be Lady Grey.'

'No, it's Gypsy. I know, I rode her last week.'

I don't believe her, but I can't stomach another argument. Minutes later the horses storm past, racing against each other, against the clock, against the clouds that are piling up at the horizon. The crowd is roaring, cheering for their horses, sweaty bodies pushing against us from all sides. I'm standing wide-legged, trying to create a safe haven for my girls. But it's impossible to resist the wave of excitement. We clap and scream until our throats are raw.

The horses line up, again and again.

'I'm sure that's Lady Grey, but the programme says it's Hurricane.'

'No, it's Gypsy,' my eldest frowns at me. 'Why don't you believe me?'

Out of nowhere Ben appears with his camera slung over his shoulder, beaming. With his scruffy beard and mud-splattered face he's like one of those war photographers emerging out of the fray. With my index finger I push up my sunglasses and wipe the sweat from the side of my nose.

'Are you part of the Henderson family now? The kids are hungry.'

'Man, they're all dressed up. You should've seen Mrs Henderson in black lace underwear and a feather boa.'

3

'Underwear?'

'Well, a short nightie that's not really a nightie, made of some shiny material.'

He throws back his head and laughs, without malice, oozing this crazy happiness that I've missed lately. He comes up for air, looks into my eyes and smiles. This time his eyes don't stray; he stays with me, even if the kids are between us and people bump into us. I feel a warm rush to my stomach. I'd forgotten how good it felt.

'Kids are fine. Let's watch the races.'

Ben takes up a prime position at the fence with his camera cocked. The horses thunder past, their hooves beating the ground, showering the spectators with mud. The MC's voice is crackling with excitement as he shouts out the names. The horses shift positions and his voice trips over the names as he tries to keep up. Far behind the others, a brown horse with a black mane and tail emerges in a stiff canter. Its coat glistening wet, streaks of foam on its neck and between the hind legs.

'That's his fifth race in a row,' Ben says, as he pushes his way back through the crowd, holding his camera above his head.

'Didn't realise they let them race several times.' I check my dog-eared programme.

'Different names, but the same horses that race over and over. All the riding clubs have contributed horses.'

'See?' my daughter says triumphantly.

I feel cheated. Just as I'm about to say something, the people around us start to mumble. It's like a breeze sweeping through a wheat field, the same message repeated, growing in intensity. Ben leans forward to catch the words.

'What are they saying?'

'Apparently one of the horses collapsed and died!'

The women next to me confirm that a horse collapsed on the finishing line.

'Come on, we should go,' I say.

'Why? The races are not finished yet,' Ben says with that look on his face that tells me I'm spoiling the fun.

'Kids need food.' I grab their hands and drag them through the partying crowd towards the palm leaf huts.

We buy sticks with skewered meat and sticks with warm watermelon and pawpaw from mamas in ballooning cotton dresses.

All of a sudden the sun is unbearably hot as it beams through a gap between purple black clouds.

'Let's go before it starts hosing down.'

Mud is squishing between my toes, making my flip-flops lethal. From a distance it looks as if our car is cornered by a jumble of cars and mini-buses. I wonder how we'll get out.

'Can we go and jump?'

The girls point towards a bunch of children jumping on a brown inflated bag. A couple of youngsters are comfortably propped up against the bag, listening to music, beer bottles in their hands. As we get closer, there's a loud farting sound as three children land on the bag at the same time. A swarm of black flies fan out like a halo around them. The children squeal. The girls giggle and tug at my arms.

That's when I see the hooves. The children are laughing, bobbing and bouncing on the sleek brown hide. I try to reel the girls back in. The smell of barbequed meat, mud and sweaty bodies is nauseating. The long, black strands of horse hair look like the hair of a woman lying on the ground. There's a crack from above. Then the rain starts to pelt down on animals and humans alike.

© **Mikaela Nyman**

Mikaela Nyman is a New Zealand writer currently living in Vanuatu, gaining insights into the challenges to sustainable development in Pacific countries. She holds an MA in Creative Writing from Victoria University. She's had short stories, poetry and non-fiction published.

# A Cretan Celebration *
## by Patricia Seman

Morning and the wind is blowing, a hot blast straight from the deserts of Libya. Palm leaves are streaming, crows rocked out of their roost in the eucalyptus trees, wheel and caw under a grey sky. Red sand amongst the dried leaves is strewn over the terrace and tiny green pellets, the miniscule beginnings of grapes, are ripped from the vine.

I go into the village to buy some eggs, into an atmosphere that clings and seeps into the pores of my skin. The wind is still blowing but the clouds are so dense that there's not a sign of movement in the sky. The sea is motionless; for the wind, with the force of its leap over the mountains that divide us from the south, sweeps across the water's surface without touching it. So, despite the reeds bending low in the valley, the rattling palm leaves, the tumbling of swallows in the updraft, there is a dead atmosphere. The sense of threat is enhanced by the boom and echo of jet fighters flying from the Nato base in Chania, high above the cloud cover, invisible.

By afternoon the wind has died down, the stifling heat subsided. The skies are clear. Fortunate, since this is a day of celebration in Greece when two of its most important saints are honoured: Constantinos the founder of Constantinople and its first Christian Emperor and his mother, Eleni. It's also the name day of all Constantinos's (Costas) and Elenis, and in Greece there are many. Name days are more important than birthdays in Greece and a fine chance for giving feasts and parties.

My next-door neighbour has a Costas and an Elena amongst her grandchildren, so in the late afternoon I go with the family to the tiny, whitewashed chapel dedicated to Ayios Constantinos and Ayia Eleni, which lies hidden in a narrow cleft in the hills on the other side of the valley. The chapel is so small that the service is held outside under a carved wooden extension surrounded by oleanders and sweet smelling pines. A table and a gilded lectern have been brought in especially for the occasion. The cantor, Kiria Irene, with her shock of white hair, bent double with age, leads us steadily through the service, while the priest in a fuss of robes and incense pops in an out of the chapel door swinging his censer. We leave with a chunk of sweet bread, blessed by the priest.

As an unexpected extra I am also offered a plastic cup full of *koliva*, prepared by the family of Archiroula, a woman of the village who died nine days ago. A brief memorial service has been tacked on to the end of this celebration of saints, the mourners gathered around the same table that held the round loaf of sweet bread.

*Koliva* is served in the Orthodox Church during memorial services. It's a mixture of boiled wheat, honey, sesame and pomegranate seeds symbolising death and the resurrection of the spirit. Like so many elements of worship in Greece each of these ingredients has a pre-Christian significance. Wheat symbolised the earth goddess Demeter, pomegranate seeds, Persephone queen of the underworld, whilst sesame seeds were believed to open the gates of consciousness.

Meanwhile we continue to celebrate the feast of life.

We are invited to coffee with Costas and his family, who run one of the local tavernas. We sit on the terrace outside his kitchen overlooking the sea and are served homemade biscuits and pastries and big slices of creamy cake.

That same evening on our way back from town, we stop off at one of our favourite restaurants. It's 9.30 and just beginning to draw in a steady stream of Costas and Elenis. They come in all shapes and sizes and all ages, together with their families and extended families. Small babies with the latest in baby-chic headbands, little girls in sparkles and frills, stern patriarchs, heads held high, striding in at the head of their clan.

After a day of indulgence we eat modestly, eyes drawn to the kitchen. A party has just come in and obviously started ordering. Trays of food pass by us, all headed for the same long table, the first bearing jugs of local red wine, then a tray stacked with plates of *dolmathes*, then one of grilled aubergines sprinkled with sheep's cheese, then one of *keftethes*—tiny mint-flavoured meatballs. And so it goes on, tray after tray carrying plates and plates of *kalamares*, lambs' liver, fried potatoes, potatoes roasted in olive oil, broad beans crushed and soaked in olive oil, butter beans baked with fresh tomatoes, swimming in olive oil, beef in red wine, succulent lamb, one solitary sheep's head.

The food here is fresh, plentiful and irresistible and to sit at a table with good food, good company and a steady flow of wine and conversation, all without measure, is one of the core pleasures of Cretan life.

As we leave, the procession of loaded trays continues. It's gone eleven and cars are still drawing up, unloading families; toddlers and babies in pushchairs, grandmothers leaning on the arms of their daughters, women from the villages dressed in their best, the groomed young men.

For some the evening is just beginning.

© **Patricia Seman**

Born in the U.K., Patricia Seman lived with her husband for several years in Crete where both her children were born. She is now an English teacher in Amsterdam.

# A Dancing Fool in Tokushima*
## by Leanne Mumford

*Dum de dum, dum de dum*. Large drums, small drums, *shamisen*, gongs beat a rhythm. In every *ren* troupe parading musicians drive the dancing. Bamboo flutes hurl the melody. *Tweedle eedle ee, tweedle eedle ee*. The familiar motif skips through my head. My limbs stir to the beat, though they have only ever tried this dance privately at home. As an eight-year old I was a lumbering clod of a ballet student while graceful dolls half my age and size glided around me. I've avoided dancing in front of anyone since.

*Obon* is the time in Japan when families gather and honour the spirits of their dearly departed. Throughout the country it is associated with circular *bon odori* community dancing at local shrines, temples and parks. Tokushima is different: its *Awa Odori* is a major annual festival that takes over the city during four days in August. After my first visit fifteen years ago I vowed to return one year at festival time.

My personal encounter with *Awa Odori* finally began when I arrived before six-thirty this morning. The information booths by the bus terminal were unstaffed. A few bedraggled people wandered about, left over from the previous night's festivities. I hung around as queues formed to buy tickets to the spectator stands. I joined one. By 9 a.m. it was already stifling in the shade. Someone handed out *uchiwa* flat paper fans with a sponsor's logo. Outside the station musicians struck up the tune, accompanied by parading dancers. A deep feeling of connection momentarily flooded my body and spontaneous tears leaked into my eyes. I bought a ticket for six o'clock so I could take to the streets later.

The long temporary stands beside the Aibahama stage are packed with families. For two hours troupe after troupe of dancers perform *Awa Odori*. Each troupe can be distinguished through the colours and patterns of their cotton *yukata* and short *happi* coats. All the musicians and dancers, women, men, young, old, wear white *tabi* socks. Everyone looks immaculate despite the heat. They all move so eloquently.

Only young women doing the women's dance wear sandals. The heels of their high wooden *geta* never touch the ground as they stab toes at the bitumen. Hands elegantly scissor the air over their folded-in-half straw hats. Arms never sink below shoulder height. I marvel at the tight formations of young women dancing with such precise grace.

Boys and girls join their fathers, older brothers, uncles and neighbours crouching low in the dynamic men's dance. Some vigorously wave *uchiwa*. The fittest men carve intricate patterns in the air with slender paper lanterns. Printed cloths cover their heads, knotted below noses. Lacquered or plain wooden *inrō* cases dangle on cords from waistbands. Now and then a grandfatherly man shows off his finesse or comic timing. Pairs of acrobatic youths dash and leap and turn in spaces between wheeling lines of dancers. All dance with finely honed life-affirming passion.

The announcer sitting in front calls the last troupe. People pour from the stands to make way for the next tranche of paying spectators. Night has fallen. I push through crowds to the riverbank. I want to see wilder dancing. On the last night of the festival I want to feel its famous unbridled spirit.

A sultry quilt of noise and humanity drapes the centre of Tokushima. I read somewhere that more than a million visitors come over the four days of the festival, making it difficult to secure a hotel room for even one night. Thousands dance in hundreds of *ren*.

Metal clangs on metal at the *yaki soba* fried noodle stalls. The crowd exhales beer breath. Brown sauce sizzles on grilling corncobs. Laughter. Trilling mobile phones. Stallholders sing out for customers. Cigarette smoke mixes with cooking smells. Drink cans rattle against ice. Breathless air. A motorboat chugs through the odorous multicoloured river. Excited shouts. People push past each other like hungry koi carp in a too-small pond.

There is intoxicated street dancing on the bridge. Low stands line the Motomachi stage close to the station. Whole city sections are closed to vehicles and awash with bodies. I try to watch from a pedestrian overpass, until a policeman moves me on. I stand on the kerb. Troupes pass endlessly. A student *ren* from a swimming club, I can tell from by their non-traditional overarm movements. Dancing cows with *Tokushima Holstein* in English letters on their black and white *yukata*. Small children concentrating out in front, older siblings and parents following. Earlier I saw a bunch of dancing amputees, each with one artificial leg. It seems that anyone can have a go.

The music quickens and slackens. Potent chants and vigorous responses bounce off the nearby buildings.

*Hayaccha yaccha ,*
*yoi yoi yoi yoi,*
*erai yaccha erai yaccha,*
*yoi yoi yoi yoi.*
"*Yoi, yoi, yoi ,yoi,*" I hear myself calling under my breath.

Dancers and musicians spur each other on. *Yattosa yatto yatto.*

I came here from my temporary home of Yokohama by the Eddy overnight highway bus and I've hardly slept since yesterday morning. There's an air-conditioned hotel room waiting for me just around the corner. I'm tired, but not yet satisfied.

Near the bridge people loosely orbit a small posse of stationary musicians. A yellow banner with the English text *awa connection* rotates with the crowd. Some dancers wear flapping, sweaty *yukata*. Most are in street clothes, holding *uchiwa* fans aloft. Everyone moves fluidly, but without the precision and grace I saw earlier. My body remembers the joy of rhythmic movement. I curl in. Dancers part. Grin at me. The balls of my feet shuffle forward. Knees bending slightly, hands flapping to and fro above my head, I dance *Awa Odori*.

As the chant says:

*Odoru ahō ni, miru ahō, onaji ahō nara odorana son, son.*

A fool dancing, a fool watching, if you're a fool either way, not dancing is a loss, a loss.

## © Leanne Mumford

Sydney-based Australian Leanne Mumford previously lived for a total of three years in Japan's greater Tokyo area. She is working on a memoir, and writes English Language haiku, some of which have appeared in *A Hundred Gourds* and *Paper Wasp*. http://lemumford.id.au/

# A Gift from God
## by Gillian Brown

Her mother called Amber's eyes 'a gift from God'. One was greengage-coloured; the other dark as chocolate. She could mesmerise the stallholders, and before they could blink, a flat Berber loaf or a handful of sticky dates would be in her pocket. Her sparrow-like figure, with her spiky hair and gamine looks, was a familiar sight around Casablanca's marketplace. She knew the streets blindfolded; where to run, and where the police were. But it wasn't enough. Not for her sick mother. Not for herself.

Today, like every day, she walked back barefoot from the well, her fifteen-year-old frame straining beneath the weight of the water-jar on her head. Her ever-watchful eyes spotted a magazine in the gutter. Remembering her reading lessons at the mission school—a punishment for pick-pocketing—she crouched down and snatched it up. She stuffed it up her shirt and hurried home.

On her way through the slum, she caught sight of a newborn baby tugging at its mother's breast. Its tiny fist punched the air, whilst flies sucked the moisture from its eyes. Amber hurried on.

Her mother's face lit up as she arrived. Amber aimed a kick at a scavenging dog and placed the water in the shade of the tin awning. She'd read the magazine later, she told herself, and handed her mother a clay cupful of water.

'What was our village like?'

Her mother smiled. 'In the distance were mountains, and at night the sky shimmered with stars. Flowers sprung up in the desert after it rained.' She sighed. 'Then the drought arrived. For three years we prayed for it to end. The rain never came.'

Soon after their arrival to find work in the city, Amber's father had died, leaving her mother and herself to fend for themselves. Stealing from the markets wasn't enough, now that her mother was ill. She needed medicines and proper care. Amber knew something had to be done.

As soon as her mother drifted off, Amber pulled the glossy magazine out from her shirt. She gasped at the images and ran her fingers over the sequined dresses of the movie stars, imagining herself silky-skinned and with perfumed hair. Turning the page, something caught her attention. But just as she started to decipher the words, a choking cough bent her mother double. Amber slid the magazine beneath some cardboard sheeting and handed her a drink. The magazine could wait. Remembering more pressing problems, she jumped up. 'We need food, Ma.'

'Keep away from those bad boys.'

Amber knew who she meant. Pimps had started pestering her, offering her money. Some of the street kids took the easy way out.

As Amber hugged her mother, she felt the bones beneath her skin. But she mustn't cry. Or remember how beautiful her mother used to be. Crying didn't bring food. She pulled away and ran off.

'Don't be long.' Her mother's voice trailed after her.

She headed for the central medina. She'd overheard a beggar boasting about the fortunes she earned from tourists there. A pink wedge of watermelon dripped with juice on a market stall, but she resisted and raced on, past the food-laden stalls and the aromas of bubbling tajines that made her faint with hunger.

As she ran, pictures from the magazine filled her head. She touched the red frayed shirt that stretched over her newly-formed breasts. Catching her reflection in a shop window, she brushed the skin of her cheek with the back of her hand. It was soft to touch. And then, of course, there were her eyes.

But she must get on. The cruise ships would already have disgorged their tourists. They'd be heading for the medina, pockets brimming with cash.

As Amber approached, a tall boy scowled at her. 'Hey! Where are you going?'

He was good-looking, except for a jagged scar that cut down his cheek.

'And who are you?' Her voice was steady, but her bottom lip quivered.

'I'm Hassan. If you're thinking of begging here, girl, forget it.'

Amber stuck out her chin. 'I'm not "girl"! My name is Amber.'

He laughed. 'Most girls your age find other ways of earning money.'

She opened her mouth to answer back, then remembered she was here to make money for her mother. She turned her eyes on him. 'Please!'

He hesitated, and then—to her amazement—shrugged. 'Stay over there,' he said, pointing away from the medina, far from the precious tourists.

13

Amber took advantage of the other street boys' admiring glances, and inch by inch she crept closer. Soon she was inside the medina. She quickly learned the exact look and just how cheeky to get. She saw how tourists smiled in satisfaction when they put money into her outstretched palm. Tourists were soon begging *her*. 'May I take your picture?' She posed in front of pyramids of golden saffron or pale green henna, and smiled. Click. Click. A timid hand. The money came easily. This was better than stealing.

Once the tourists had all gone, Amber jingled the coins in her pockets. But the sun had set and her mother would be anxious. She must get home.

Soon they'd be rich!

As she rounded a corner, two boys ambushed her. One twisted her arms behind her back, whilst the other emptied her pockets. 'Hassan says don't bother coming back!'

She cursed Hassan, and with a hanging head, made her way home. When she got there, there was no sign of her mother. 'Where's Ma?' she screamed, rushing over to their neighbour's shack.

The woman grasped Amber's hands. 'I'm sorry,' she said. 'God has taken her.'

Tears gushed down Amber's cheeks. 'I should have been here. I left her alone all day.' She choked on her sobs. 'For nothing.'

'Everything happened so fast. But she wasn't alone,' the woman said. 'I saw she was troubled, losing breath, so I went to comfort her. Then she became animated and I could see she wanted to tell me something.'

'What?' Amber grabbed her arm. 'What did she say?'

'She said, *Amber has a special gift. Tell her to use it.*' The corners of Amber's mouth trembled. The neighbour continued. 'After that her face relaxed…and she was gone. I tried to make the authorities wait for you. They just laughed, and sneered. 'If you want to pay!'

The woman reached inside her dress and held out the celebrity magazine. 'She asked me to give you this.'

Amber clutched it to her chest. Her mother must have found it and looked at the pictures. For just a moment, had she shared Amber's dreams?

She sighed, then prostrated herself on the hard packed earth where her mother had sat, as if to touch her one last time. Her high-pitched moans drew a crowd. She lay in the same place for days, occasionally accepting a scrap of food or some water. There was a hollowness inside her, much worse than hunger.

Finally, the neighbour tapped her on the shoulder. 'She is in paradise now.'

She was right. It was time to take care of herself.

As she sat up, the magazine fell open at the announcement she'd glanced at earlier. With a silent thanks to the nuns who'd taught her to read, she pored over the words: 'Film Extras Wanted. Casting 9 a.m. Monday. Casablanca Central Medina.'

She leapt to her feet. It was Monday today! What time was it? Only sunrise. Trembling with excitement, she rushed off to the well. She scrubbed her face until it stung and washed her hair. If only it would just lie down, on this, the biggest day of her life.

Panting, she reached the medina. A crowd of hopefuls had gathered, in their best clothes. As she looked down at her patched shirt and bare feet, her confidence drained away. She looked nothing like a film star.

A man in a suit, buttons bursting and his hair red with henna, got out of a shiny car. He took in the crowd, and then selected some kids at the front. Amber, standing behind, tried in vain to catch his eye. Her stomach roared with hunger. Her heartbeats slammed against her chest and her palms felt clammy. With her mother's last words ringing in her head, she raised herself up on tiptoe. It was then she noticed Hassan. His mocking look only made her more determined. She turned away and fixed her gaze again on the man in the suit.

Just as she was giving up hope, a fat finger pointed in her direction. 'You,' the man said. Amber tensed. 'Yes, you with the eyes!' he boomed. 'Over here. The rest of you can go.'

The sun pressed down. Her head swam. As she stepped forward, she sensed Hassan's glare on her back. But he couldn't touch her now. She was floating on air. To make sure it was real, she pinched her arm until it hurt.

Then, from the corner of her eye, she spotted a tourist bend down across the street, his jacket flapping and a bulky wallet half spilling out of his inside pocket. She started to run. She needed to be quick. *No, Amber, not now!* Was that her mother's voice? She hesitated, and the tourist straightened and sauntered away.

As she pushed back through the thickening crowd, she caught sight of the fat man in the distance, looking around. Then he shook his head and got into his car. The window rolled down and his hand smacked the side of the limo. She shouted, 'Wait!' but the driver pulled away. Half a dozen wide-eyed kids peered out of the back window, grinning.

Hassan sidled up and laughed in her face. She glowered at him until his Adam's apple twitched and he backed off. Dragging herself home, her mother's words kept going round and round inside her head. *Amber has a special gift*. Yes. She must use the gift God gave her, she thought. Her footsteps lightened. And next time she'd get it right.

## © **Gillian Brown**

Gillian Brown, a Scot living in France and a member of Writers Abroad, writes travel articles and short stories for magazines. Her stories have also been published online and won and been placed in competitions.

# A Good Sense of Humour *
## by Anne Wilson

I was passing a communal rubbish bin when I saw a head and shoulders sticking out, braked the car and backed up to rescue her. She had lost her arms and never had any legs but her head and torso were undamaged—what a find!

Having already cleaned and painted the lock-up that was to be my second-hand shop, for 'Designer Wear Only', I was on my way to dress the window before opening the very next morning. My new mannequin took pride of place. This could only be a lucky omen.

However, the people I subsequently had to deal with were a very diverse lot, being of various nationalities and having very different attitudes to my business.

I was in Spain, on the Balearic Island of Mallorca, and had failed to realise that Spanish people have no respect for anything with second-hand status. This was perfectly demonstrated by my first Spanish clients, a middle aged, professional-looking couple.

She ignored my greeting and wafted about haughtily before saying something to her husband then leaving the shop. He indicated, in good English, that he wished to buy a beautiful, French, designer two-piece. I wrapped it carefully in tissue paper, after removing the price tag, which I placed to one side on the counter. He then picked up the wrapped garments, threw a few loose coins on the counter and walked out, ignoring both the label and my protestations. He rejoined his wife, neither of them looking over their shoulders as they walked off down the road.

All my stock was on sale or return to the owners so I had to pay for the garments in addition to feeling angry and humiliated. Both the 'customers' and I knew that the local Spanish police would not have supported my case.

I discovered that a sense of humour often saved the day and this was especially true with my British customers. One lady brought in the contents of her wardrobe for me to sell and confided she was saving up to treat herself to breast enhancement surgery. Before I had time to think, to my utter horror, I heard myself say, 'oh what a good idea, tits for tat'. Thank goodness she was British and we both burst out laughing.

17

However, my sense of humour was taxed to the limit when I opened up one morning to discover a makeshift bed had materialised between racks of clothes in the already cramped stockroom. In addition, an assortment of men's toiletries was arranged on the shelf above the hand-basin in the little toilet. There was no one about. I locked up again and went in search of the agent through whom I had leased the premises.

It transpired that the female owner, who went by the name of Puri, short for Purification, had a cousin living on the mainland who came to the island each summer season to work as a waiter in a nearby hotel. He couldn't afford rent so she gave him a key and allowed him to sleep at the back of the shop. No mention had been made of this extremely unconventional arrangement when I signed the lease but, once again, I knew that the police would take no interest in my side of things and I was expected not to mind. I returned to the shop and rearranged my clothes racks to hide the bed.

Disruption was minimal; the bed was made each morning and all that remained of the waiter between shifts were the mingled smells of toothpaste and strong aftershave. Our paths never crossed and I never once met my lodger all that summer. I think I was secretly disappointed that he didn't make himself known and must have felt no curiosity about me. One morning, as the season drew to a close, his collection of toiletries disappeared and the bed was folded against the wall. I had the lock-up to myself again. I hoped he had had a good summer.

There were unhappier lifestyles. One customer, who begged knock-down prices, had sold her guest house in the UK to purchase an apartment on the island but, duped by an unscrupulous estate agent, she had failed to notice a couple of missing noughts on a confusingly long number of pesetas. Ashamed to return home, where she was disowned by distinctly unamused relatives, she had been reduced to living in one room with her three parrots and two budgies.

In the heat of the summer, I closed my shop and took my son to ride on the train that runs from the centre of Palma up over the mountainous terrain of the Serra de Tramuntana. The train is German built with sturdy carriages and, although the service provides cheap public transport, it is a wonderfully scenic ride for visitors and locals alike.

Two lanky young men with backpacks collapsed in the seats opposite us like a couple of rag dolls, their skin and clothes wet with perspiration. One eased off his hiking boots and positioned himself, legs across the table and feet half out of the fully open windows. He promptly fell deeply asleep.

The smell from his damp feet was overpowering and very quickly became a subject of discussion throughout our entire carriage. His companion had also fallen asleep and no one seemed sure how to deal with the situation. As grumblings on the subject travelled up and down amongst the passengers, a young Spanish girl alighted from the train when it stopped beside a level crossing. A rather smart-looking saloon car was waiting to pick her up but, from the train, we saw her first speak briefly to the driver, probably her father, who handed her something. She ran back to our open carriage window, reached in and stuck an adhesive air freshener beside the offending feet before the train began to move again—at which point the whole carriage clapped and cheered.

I loved how, given the right circumstances, humour can transcend language.

© **Anne Wilson**

Anne Wilson now lives in the UK but her years spent living on the Spanish island of Mallorca have inspired most of her short story and memoir writing. Anne's first novel *Here be Dragons* is now available. www.authoranne.co.uk

# A Mug, a Thug and a Cup of Coffee *
## by Chris O'Neil

'I'm starving, Dad,' Jake wailed from the back seat, his younger brother nodding in agreement.

'Did you read that sign, boys? We've arrived.' My son-in-law, Jeremy, stopped the car.

'But there's nothing here.' Cody folded his arms and sighed. His bottom lip stuck out a little further.

'Let's feed them first and explore later.' The Wise One, my daughter, pointed to a small cafe across the road.

Minutes later and with food ordered we sat outside in the winter sun. The cafe we had chosen was right beside the south-west highway which is the main road from Perth to the far south coast. The highway passes right through the middle of the tiny town of Balingup.

Don't imagine for a moment that we sat there breathing in traffic fumes or were unable to hear ourselves speak as cars roared past; it was, in fact, quite the reverse. A dog barking in the distance, the sound of two willie wagtails squabbling over a piece of bread and a kettle whistling inside the cafe was a noisy as it got.

'Here we are.' A man with long hair, tatts and dressed all in black approached our table.

He put down the biggest BLTs, real works of art, garnished with gourmet lettuce leaves and paper-thin slices of tomato. If the kids' mouths were watering at the sight of these, I felt the same when he returned with the coffee, even the steam lifting and curling from the cup smelt good.

'You must be the thug,' Jake said.

My daughter's eyes widened. She opened her mouth to say something when the man replied.

'Yep, that's me!' He smiled and put down our meal. 'Are you here for long?' He bent to shoo away the willie wagtails.

'Just a week. What do you recommend to do round here?' Jeremy asked.

'Balingup might be small, but we have a lot going on. Depends what you like really. See that shed over there?' He pointed to a large building in the distance. 'On Sundays some of the towns folk get together to make costumes for the Medieval Festival which is held every year in August. They practice jousting, make costumes and they reckon they always need a helping hand so they welcome visitors. They might even make you a cup of tea if you're lucky.

'I reckon you will have heard of the Bibbulmun track, well, there's a sixty kilometre section that runs from here to Donnelly River Village and trust me: you'll see some amazing jarrah, marri and karri forests. Enormous trees to climb along the way too, boys.' He grinned at Jake and Cody who were watching him intently as they finished their lunch.

'It says here in my guide book, the Bibbulmun track is a one thousand kilometre walk from Perth to Albany through the bush and even though it can be walked in sections, we might leave that for another day.' I held my breath and hoped my grandsons had missed the bit about climbing trees.

My daughter got up to pay the bill.

'Sorry about my son calling you a thug.'

The man laughed, his long gingery curls shaking about his shoulders. 'Reckon he read this.' He indicated a sign on the wall. 'A Mug, A Thug and a Cup of Coffee.'

As if on cue, a lady dressed all in black appeared from the kitchen behind the counter. 'I'm the mug actually because I do all the cooking!' She waved her hand proudly towards the glass cabinet that displayed the best looking vanilla slices, rocky-road bursting with pink and white marshmallows and chunky chocolate brownies. 'Make all my own pastry too.' She glanced at the enormous sausage rolls and pies on the shelf below.

'It looks so good, I'm sure we'll be back.' The Wise One picked up her change.

Minutes later we were walking up the main street of Balingup. For a country town with a population of just over six hundred, there were several cafes, an antique shop, a pub, and a second-hand bookshop which also sold gloves and socks... it does get very cold in Balingup as we discovered one minus-five-degree Celsius morning. A wonderful shop called 'The Tinderbox' that makes every kind of herbal cream, lotion or potion to cure all sorts of ailments became our favourite store. Time passed quickly as we drifted around their beautiful earthy shop and lifted the lids on their blue glass jars and sniffed this and dabbed on that.

Our last day in Balingup arrived all too quickly. The acres of rolling hills and fields that I gazed at each morning from the kitchen window were shrouded in mist that day and the smell of log fires burning in the valley filled the air. It was winter and wonderful and no-one wanted to go home.

After the cases had been safely stowed in the car and the house tidied, Jake followed his father outside.

'Dad, this has been a great holiday but there is one thing Cody and I would like to do before we leave.' He looked at his father as if expecting him to mind read.

'All right, as long as it won't take too long. What is it you would like to do?' Jeremy asked, blissfully unaware of the trap his sons had set.

'Could we have lunch before we go?'

'But we'll be home by midday; surely you can last three hours?' Jeremy picked up the car keys.

Convinced his powers of persuasion were superior to his older brother's, Cody began, 'Well, my tummy is rumbling Dad and I know Grandma wants a cup of coffee. I heard her tell Mum that the coffee at the Thug's place was the best she had ever tasted. You wouldn't want to disappoint her, would you?'

© **Chris O'Neil**

Chris O'Neil, originally from England, is a Sydney based writer. A member of Writer's Abroad, she divides her time, not always successfully, between six children, two grandchildren, a long-suffering husband and writing. Her novel remains a work- in- progress.

# Africa for Softies *
## by Susan Eames

The empty road shimmered under an uncompromising sun.

I glanced at my husband. 'Can't be too far now,' I said.

'Good,' he replied.

We lapsed into sweat-soaked silence again. I cradled my road map like a security blanket, contemplating the circumstances that led to us being on this desolate highway.

We had bought a Motorhome to tour Europe. I should have known better. My husband always pushes boundaries. When we reached Spain he instantly wanted to do something more adventurous.

'Let's go down to Morocco,' he said.

'In a Motorhome?'

'Why not?'

'Well, it's Africa.'

'Africa for softies.'

'And you said you hated Morocco when you went there.'

'That was years ago.'

'They called you a Hippy and made you cut your hair.'

'It grew again.'

'You were propositioned by a prostitute veiled in a *burka*.'

He laughed. 'She scared the life out of me.'

'Someone pulled a knife on you.'

'I was young and headstrong.'

'Now you're old and headstrong.'

He smiled, sly-eyed. 'There'll be wildlife.'

'D' you think?'

His smile deepened, knowing he had dangled an irresistible carrot.

It was June. Morocco would soon become unviably hot. I did some rapid research. Moroccan drivers were allegedly maniacs but to my astonishment, the country was Motorhome friendly. The trip was on.

I chose our first campsite on the Atlantic coast because it overlooked a lagoon known for its nesting flamingos. We took a boat trip to see the flamingos, only to learn they had already migrated. Our guide spotted three tardy birds on the horizon, barely visible through binoculars.

The trip was pleasant enough. Men fished from colourful boats. Women waded neck deep in the water, probing the seabed with their feet for mussels. Clusters of gulls huddled on sandbanks like refugees. Light gusts of wind dispersed their forlorn cries and the ammonia sting of guano. But I wanted more dramatic wildlife sightings than this.

We left the coast and comfort of the motorway to put my husband's driving skills to the test. My research about maniacal drivers was accurate. *Inshallah* that anyone completes their journey safely in Morocco. Yet we settled into the crazy rhythms of the roads.

Storks soared on the heated air, silent as phantoms. Little egrets gathered in fields of grazing cattle. The egrets stalked the cattle in their elegant, measured way, deftly side-stepping clomping hooves as they plucked insects from the disturbed earth.

Whilst happy to see storks and egrets, I had already seen their cousins in Spain. I wanted truly foreign exotica, endemic African animals, not flibberty gibbet birds with no compunction about crossing continents.

In hot arid conditions, wild animals seek reliable water sources. I picked an isolated overnight stop by a lake. This entailed a tortuous drive down a track more suitable for donkeys than Motorhomes. The location was stunning but stark and with no sign of tracks or droppings, my hopes of wildlife encounters died. My husband lent his hacksaw to a deaf/mute fisherman. By way of thanks, the fisherman mimed a triumphant catch of a 'big fish' for us before rowing off with his newly sawn paddles in a precarious toy-sized rubber dingy.

'Sign language is an amazing thing,' said my husband.

I replied that a dead fish, even a freshly caught one, wouldn't count as a wildlife sighting.

Near a waterfall in the Atlas mountains we eschewed the tourist trail to explore an area crosshatched by ancient olive trees. Surely we'd find something in these hushed groves? In a glade skeined by ribbons of sunlight we found a carpenter bee on a thistle.

'Hardly thrilling,' I said.

Much as we love the unfrequented places, we couldn't completely ignore Morocco's iconic cities. In a secure though pungent location in Marrakech, we were directed to park beside a lean-to bulging with sacks of garlic. The owners lounged in the shade waiting for business. We gave the 'garlic men' French walnuts in exchange for tiny glasses of teeth-clenchingly sweet mint tea. In the midst of this roaring city I was amazed to see storks nesting on an antenna. The youngsters clacked their beaks in noisy anticipation every time an adult glided in. Although enjoyable to watch, I wanted more.

We looped back to the coast. Time-warp Sixties-style surfer dudes claimed the windswept beaches and tested their prowess in the crashing seas. We watched them from the sanctuary of beachside cafes which served spicy chicken *tagines*, scented with olives and preserved lemons.

The area teemed with domesticated camels. Where were the wild ones?

We found a gecko in the shower block. It stared, unblinking. Too small! Too ordinary!

We would have lingered but the wind defeated us and we nearly lost our aerial. My husband secured the loosened fitting before the aerial could frisbee off and decapitate someone.

In a barren red and ochre land flanked by fractured mountains, I dozed and fantasised about antelopes. Instead we found a chap buried up to his chest in the sand to treat his rheumatism.

Now, over halfway through our journey, I was resigned to not seeing any exciting African wildlife in Morocco. I checked my map for the umpteenth time and peered ahead. The baking road melted into mirages. It felt like we were travelling towards the void. The heat lapped my face. Were we lost?

Our campsite eventually materialised. Being late in the season, we were alone. As my husband manoeuvred onto our pitch he suddenly pointed.

'Look!'

A small tortoise was mincing along on tippy-toe claws. We tumbled out of the Motorhome

The tortoise halted at our approach. He first retracted then tentatively stretched his old man's neck. He wore a textured shell of black and amber. His eyes were like tiny black glass beads.

I realised I had been missing the point in my quest. Wildlife encounters come in many guises and they're all special. This tortoise was not large: not exciting or glamorously dangerous, but he was a wonderfully foreign wild creature and he was all ours. He would do.

© **Susan Eames**

Susan Eames left England over twenty years ago to explore the world. She has had travel articles and short fiction published on three continents. Susan continues her vagabond lifestyle, flitting from Fiji to Europe and the places in between.

# Aliens *
## by Vesna McMaster

In common with an increasing mass of humanity in this mixing, shrinking world, I don't really come from anywhere. I just growed, like Topsy.

In this predicament, surroundings can seem relentless. Nowhere to run and hide, nothing so familiar that mores and customs are never questioned, simply worn like a hardy waterproof. Humans crave the easy carbohydrate of mono-culture, the refined sugar of knowing where you belong—sweet words in your mouth, filling your stomach with warmth.

But we move about these days, our legs far outrunning our minds. We have mixed families and are perpetually on Skype. I keep a special book with all the addresses I have lived at since leaving the last house I shared with my parents (itself the end of a scattered dozen or so that I can recall), because 'they' ask these things sometimes when you apply for official documents. The current tally is 22. I am 42 years old and still shifting.

The other day, one of our children (age 8) comes out with the random question of 'Have you ever been to Poland?'

'Yes, I was born in Poland.'

My partner spins round, half-chopped onions scattering in an astonished arc.

'How come you never told me you were born in Poland?' he demands, with the indignation of just discovering he's been diddled out of a tax rebate.

Why would I? It's not a stand-out feature, salient, defining. It's been absorbed and translated within the general package of Me-ness but doesn't need explaining any more than a stew needs to separate out all its ingredients while being served in a bowl.

Sometimes, one Serial Migrant (which is what we are) will bump against another. The 'tells' are light but unmistakable. An unwillingness to elaborate on origins in a casual introduction, a skin colour that jars with an accent, resignation in the gaze—acceptance. They nod, exchange unspoken condolences/congratulations, and move apart. Space is needed.

Life is hard for such children. Young bones compiled from calcium from so many different breeds of cattle cause growing pains.

Personalities and opinions in an unformed, amorphous state wobble without support, thrown from one mould to the next until the original intended form is barely discernible. They struggle to stand without support of an accepted culture, and wonder if they'll ever be fully formed as they stand before adulthood.

Then they start to let go, realising that they will never have that one place where they are safe: the place they've been trying to create with such desperation. They straighten up and find (with astonishment) they can stand. They are a little like those sci-fi monsters who absorb strength, appearance or other intrinsic attributes from their human hosts to acquire an undefinable polymorphous anonymity. A uniqueness carved from a host of typicals. This shape-shifting ingests the foreign particle, digesting, utilising, neutralising.

On the bus home from Junior High as I sat chatting to my friends, strangers would often stare at us without restraint. Sometimes their bafflement forced them into a direct question.

'Are you Japanese?' they would blurt out.

'No.'

'But you are speaking Japanese. Why are you not speaking like a foreigner? You don't *look* Japanese.' Again, there was that diddled-out-of-a-tax-rebate ring to this last.

'Because I live here.'

'Oh,' they would say. Then they'd retire back to their own private space to consider the implications of such encroachment on the natural order. Reminiscent of a child's expression on first learning how much space the atoms of seemingly solid matter consist of. A re-focus, a silence. My friends would suppress a giggle and be a smidge self-conscious for a few minutes.

I am a sci-fi alien. Under the freckled skin, bones morph and glide in visible bumps, changing my shape to fit into any crevice, lodge on any outcrop. I have prehensile toes to grip the branches of trees and leap off again in one spring. I have rudimentary gills and a skin that absorbs oxygen from the water so I can survive in tidal estuaries, burrowing into the salt mud and feeling it cool on my sides. I can clamber up sleet-whipped cliffs with clattering hooves, safe inside wiry fur, and relish the desolate echoes that drop down the ravine. It is not odd that some people stare.

Strange is familiar. Foreign is home. In this oxymoron of linked disassociation, I am a paradox of exotic familiarity—unique in a completely similar way to millions of other inhabitants of this narrowing planet.

## © **Vesna McMaster**

Vesna is a peripatetic Brit currently living in Australia. She has published a book of short stories as well as numerous stories, poems and articles in competitions, anthologies and publications. www.vesnamcmaster.com

# Altogether Rain: Altogether Dance
## by Anton Agar

The storm washed away the long, crackling days of August and early September as it rumbled through the valley, its spectacular lightshow bouncing off the mountains.

Lothar the Dutchman was summoned by a primitive force. He stripped off his clothes and stepped outside, wild-eyed like a celluloid Van Gogh. In fact, he was German but—new to the neighbourhood and a determined recluse—everyone assumed he was Dutch. As the thunder cartwheeled through the night and the rain intensified Lothar danced in celebration of a greater force at work. He was in his garden but Françoise saw him from the window.

'The Hollander's out there naked.'

Who could blame her surprise?

Yves frowned, searching for an appropriate response. He kept his yawn undercover.

'I…'

The lightning that briefly lit Lothar was gone again and Françoise struggled to make sense of this new image in her mind. She knew foreigners could be strange, barking mad even, especially round here, but naked in a teeming downpour?

'He's got nothing on. He's dancing. In the rain.'

Yves thought, Gene Kelly, and wondered if Françoise was dreaming. Or was he dreaming? He thought of a handsome man, athletic, leaping onto lampposts, and watched the outline of his wife's body in the glow of her cigarette. Then the lightning forked again and he saw her crane forward for a glimpse of the male nudity that danced through her dreams. Or his dreams. Her T-shirt rode up and he glimpsed the shadow between her buttocks before the light was gone again.

'Come back to bed.'

'He's out there without a stitch on.'

She was stretching through the window now and he heard her giggle. He hadn't heard that for a while.

'Shall I call out? Nether-lander…'

He thought she was being quiet, just a little singsong, but she was facing away from him and leaning into the storm, so he could be wrong. Maybe the stranger—if there was a stranger—would hear her. He was awake now.

'Ne-eth-er-land-er.' Singsong.

'Come in.'

'I want to see the Dutchman.'

She giggled again, sounding younger, 'In the nude.'

More lightning. The storm was right overhead and she pushed herself against the deep window ledge and pointed her backside up a little more as she leaned out. Yves stirred, thought about her, thought about the naked stranger, swallowed, and pushed the sheets away. He joined her, pressing into her rear and felt her wriggle into a comfortable place, sensed her smiling. Neither of them spoke, but they watched the storm flash and heard it trundle around the mountains, like a giant rolling rocks. When she turned she helped him pull the T-shirt over her head and let it fall.

On the bed he thought briefly of Gene Kelly, and his wife, and Lothar, and himself, and their quiet valley banging away. Periodically the storm illuminated the room, charging their lovemaking until they were spent and lolled onto their backs. The riot outside continued and they listened to its retreat until they drifted into sleep.

The last thing she said—murmured—was, 'We didn't use anything.'

He was too tired to say much, but surprised them both. 'Good,' he murmured back.

Lothar was spent too. Liberated from the expectations of home he had danced raw in his garden, and more daringly, down the little road that led to his few neighbours' houses. Water streamed off his happy, fat body and he was cold now but as he pushed the gate open he was ruder than he could ever remember. He thought of a new life, here in the valley. And he remembered his own country and loved it more than he had when he lived there.

On the bed, Françoise wondered if she would have to give up smoking. Inside, something was growing. Things were changing—again.

© **Anton Agar**

Anton Agar lives in southern France. Born in the UK, he was a journalist and screenwriter, published and produced in the UK and France. His crime novel, *Idiot Banana*, is the first in a series set in and around Marseille. http://antonagar.zohosites.com

# Amica del Cuore
## by Kimberly Sullivan

When people asked how we met, we'd look at one another with a sly smile. Then either Giulia or I would say, 'We both fell for the same guy.'

That was twenty years ago, when I first arrived in Rome.

Growing up, my family's idea of an exotic vacation was an annual Mecca to the Poconos. An impossibly glamorous holiday in their youth, my parents clung to the mistaken notion that it still was. Each summer they dragged my brother and me to the same faded lodge filled with geriatric crowds playing Bingo.

Wednesdays were Italian Nights, complete with Frank Sinatra and Tony Bennett wannabes. My brother and I kicked one another's shins under the checkered red-and-white tablecloths, our heads low over our overcooked spaghetti, rubbery meatballs, and Kraft parmesan cheese.

Yet it was during one of those dismal Italian Nights that I first decided to live in Rome.

When the stage show mercifully ended, I watched in fascination as Gregory Peck and Audrey Hepburn raced around Rome on their Vespa scooter. My eyes grew wide as they placed their hands in the *Bocca della verità*. Rome, I convinced myself, was where my life would begin. My Roman Holiday.

That decision carried me through my awkward teenage years. Money from waitressing stints and babysitting was all squirreled away for my Roman life.

I was the first in my family to attend college, commuting by bus into Pittsburgh each day from my parents' rural home. Living in the dorms was never an option. I didn't make friends. The few dates I went on were disastrous, but I repeated to myself it was better that way. The perfect guy would only keep me in Pittsburgh.

After graduation, my mother cried when I turned down an offer with the local electric company and told my father and her about Rome.

The days before my departure were strained, but my heart soared as I boarded the plane to my new life, to the fantasy I'd constructed in my mind.

Soon enough, the fantasy faded, but I couldn't declare defeat. So I stubbornly stuck it out, alone in a chaotic city.

I had no job, no friends, I didn't speak the language, and my savings were dwindling fast. I dressed like a girl from rural Pennsylvania, making me an alien in my new city. I smiled too much and was too eager to please, ripe for the picking. Roberto knew an easy target when he saw one.

My rounds at the language schools finally proved successful. I spent my first day of work shuttling between lessons, ignoring the bemused looks of fashionable Italians taking in my slouchy college clothes, sneakers, and the poodle-curls of my permed hair. I deflected their scorn with forced enthusiasm.

With money in my pocket but my spirits low after my first day of work, I sat at an outdoor table at the *Campo de' fiori* and ordered a glass of Novello, the cheapest celebratory drink on the menu. I toasted my success, but my smile, as I surveyed the crowd mingling on the piazza, was forced.

A shadow fell over the table, and I looked up to see a tall man in dark sunglasses. He wore Levi's, a blue shirt stretched tight across his broad shoulders, and a pair of shoes that probably cost what I'd earn in four months.

'*Americana, vero?*' he said as he sat down beside me, unhindered by the absence of an invitation. That's the best he can do? I might as well have had the Stars and Stripes tattooed across my forehead. But sarcasm never crossed my lips; my rural upbringing and naïve politeness towards strangers kicked in. I smiled and said yes, even apologized for not speaking Italian.

He took off his sunglasses. Tall, dark, and handsome. I loved how he spoke with his hands, the lilting sound of his Italian when he ordered us more wine. Finally, someone in Rome even knew I existed.

From then on I was hopelessly in love with Roberto. My transformation from blushing virgin to willing partner was rapid. Roberto filled my thoughts when he was away, but even my obsessed brain admitted that his visits were increasingly rare.

One lonely evening, I broke his rule—I called him.

'*Pronto,*' said a nasally, slightly whiny voice that some Italian women manage to perfect. So there was someone else, something I'd always suspected. I should have hung up, but instead I asked for Roberto in my horrendous Italian.

'Oh, for goodness' sake,' said the voice in English. 'You must be that *americana*. We need to talk. Meet me at the Enoteca on Via Panisperna at seven tomorrow. Ciao.'

I stared at the phone in disbelief. The other woman had summoned me, but I'd never meet her.

My resolve dissolved quickly. The Monti wine bar was filled with rows of bottles. The wooden tables were cosy, the clientele fashionable. I scanned the room. How would I find her?

My gaze fell on a stunning woman sitting alone. She sipped her wine, her face slightly turned from me. I took advantage to observe her silky blouse, revealing just enough cleavage to be seductive, not desperate. Her tailored pants draped beautifully over long legs, falling to the perfect point on expensive shoes. I sighed as I looked down at my own haphazard wardrobe choices, ready to leave before she noticed me. Too late. She acknowledged me with a nod, and waved me over.

I approached her, attempting to look more confident than I felt. My ears burned as she looked me up and down, Italian-style, dismissing the competition. She stood as I reached the table, showing her enviable figure off to perfection. I wasn't the only one to notice.

'I see the eighties are alive and well in Pittsburgh. Nice to meet you, Jamie. I'm Giulia.'

We sat. The waiter sprinted over the moment Giulia acknowledged him. He appeared eager to serve her, as I imagined most men were. I may as well have been invisible.

'White or red?' she asked.

'Red.'

She ordered Barolo without consulting me, and I wondered how I'd afford my half of the bill. We sat in awkward silence before she spoke.

'So, Roberto.' She dug a cigarette out of her purse, lighting it and taking a drag, a dead ringer for a 1950s Hollywood diva.

'Yes, Roberto… my boyfriend,' I said, with far more conviction than I felt.

Her laugh was throaty, sexy. 'Poor Jamie. I needed to see you for myself. It's exactly as I suspected. You need to be warned away from someone like Roberto.'

My eyes narrowed. 'I suppose I do. You want him all to yourself, better to have the competition out of the way.'

She observed me closely, sizing me up. '*Sei ridicola.*' She smoked her cigarette again before continuing in an authoritative voice. 'Roberto is not boyfriend material. And you're clearly not in it for fun. You're setting yourself up to have your heart trampled by an expert.'

My face tensed in anger as I observed this vision of perfection, with her elegant hair and stylish clothes, her long slim fingers stroking the stem of her glass. She was laughing at me, the stupid farm girl, who dreamed of remaking herself in Rome. A tear slipped from my eye, then another.

She reached across the table to hand me a handkerchief, the old-fashioned fabric type. I dabbed at my eyes.

'Jamie,' she said gently, reaching across the table to pat my hand. 'You'll be eaten alive by the men here unless I take you under my wing. Forget Roberto. He's a *cretino*. You'll find the right man for you, believe me.'

That's how our friendship began. Roberto was a cretin, but he's how I met my *amica del cuore*. My friend of the heart. My best friend.

Giulia did take me under her wing. She taught me about Rome and its bewildering cultural differences. She introduced me to her friends—the impenetrable cliques in Italy who've known one another their entire lives. She brought me to her hair stylist, who rid me of my poodle curls. She taught me to smile less and be less eager to please. Giulia gave me direction. I took out a loan and enrolled in LUISS University, earning my MBA and finding work as a consultant.

Giulia needed me, too. I comforted her when her father died, when she cried over frequent heartbreaks.

We vacationed together at her uncle's villa on the Tremiti islands. It was there I met my husband, Teodoro. Giulia saw him first.

'Look at the blond who keeps glancing over. *Un ragazzo per bene.* He's got "Jamie" stamped all over him. Go meet him.'

Teodoro and I spoke on that beach, overlooking the crystal blue waters and the imposing, medieval San Nicola abbey-fortress on the island just beyond.

Teodoro and I married two years later. Giulia was our witness and the godmother to our first child, Lorenzo. Her son, Andrea, was just six months younger, but the relationship with his father didn't last.

Now, years later, I look down on this face I know as well as my own. I see how it's been ravaged by the chemo, by periods of hope during remission that are dashed by test results. We're at the end now. I know it and Giulia knows it.

Giulia's in tremendous pain, but she needs to talk to me, and to ten-year-old Andrea. Giulia's mother will raise Andrea, but she's asking me to be present in his life, to tell him about his mother.

'Mamma will make me into a saint. No boy wants to remember a saint. Tell him everything … the good, the bad, the ugly.'

I kiss her forehead and stroke her cheek. 'I'll tell him everything. Thank you for being my *amica del cuore*, Giulia. I'm lucky to have you.'

I fight to stop the tears. Andrea needs to see me strong. I kiss my friend and see the peace in her face as our eyes meet for the last time. My friend of the heart.

© **Kimberly Sullivan**

Kimberly Sullivan is an American living in Italy. She's also enjoyed being an expat in Austria, the Czech Republic, France, and Germany. Kimberly's short stories have been published in journals and anthologies. kimberlysullivan.wordpress.com

# Angel Child
## by Mary Davies

I can't help laughing, though the joke is about angels and makes me look stupid again. My step-son is funny, but he doesn't believe in angels and he thinks I'm a bit screwed up because I do. Though he uses humour to put me down, it isn't because he doesn't love me. After all, he's the one who insisted on my migrating to Australia when his father died. He said he wasn't going to make another half-way-around-the-world trip to bury me.

There's no malice in his teasing. Cory does it to make me laugh. We've always laughed a lot and he doesn't like it when I'm away with the fairies, as he puts it. Every time I try to say something sensible he turns it into a joke. They all do it now. His wife, Joyce, is a lovely woman but she has an inferiority complex and needs to feel important. Well, she would, seeing that she's married to Cory. And their daughter, Julie… God knows what she needs. A clip around the ear, most likely.

The trouble is I'm deaf. We all have a good laugh when, 'I'm not going to sit near Tom tomorrow,' turns out to be, 'I'm not going to Sydney tomorrow.' But then Cory gets me some new hearing aids and starts nagging me. 'Put your deaf aids in, you silly old bat,' he says. It's strange; they turn you into a character that's not like you at all, and then get annoyed when you step out of it.

I suppose I do have a short-term memory problem, but it's not as bad as they make out. I always remember to take my pills and I write down every doctor's appointment in my diary—although I do forget the podiatrist sometimes. And Joyce tells me I've forgotten how to cook.

That's why I'm here on this holiday with the family. Joyce won't let me stay at home on my own. But I'd rather be there. It's literally a pain, not being close to a lavatory sometimes. Ayers Rock doesn't have a lavatory and though they have one on the coach they don't let me use it.

We start out in the middle of the night, so that we can see the sun coming up. But it's weird. Crowds of people are standing here, silently waiting for the dawn, and they're all looking at the rock. 'You're looking the wrong way,' I say, worried that they'll miss the sunrise. Cory has a good laugh, and then I see that the rock is changing to a lovely red colour.

We get back in the coach and move on to a hotel in Alice Springs. The family wants to see some caves. Luckily, the guide says that the climb will be too much for me, so I get to stay in the hotel. When I get bored, somebody suggests that I take a taxi to see Alice. I wonder who she is, then see a post-card on the reception desk and remember.

I like Alice Springs. The main street has wooden pavements like in old cowboy movies. It's close to the hotel so most people walk there. But I have the taxi because the road to Alice is uneven, and there are no buildings or trees for shade.

I walk up and down the main street. But there are groups of aborigines everywhere, drinking and making an awful noise. I go into a shop to get away from the noise and they tell me it is Thursday, when the aborigines get their pension and drink themselves silly.

I'm walking back to the taxi stand, feeling a little tired, when I notice that there are some aborigines following me: two women and three children. They don't look drunk, so I walk even slower and let them pass. As they do, the youngest child, a toddler with a cheeky face, grins up at me. I grin back and wink at him.

It's the wrong thing to do though, to let them pass. When I get to the taxi rank the aborigines are already waiting there; and then a white couple, walking fast to get ahead of me, joins the queue. The large woman shouts at them. There's nowhere to sit and no shade.

When the taxi comes it goes straight past the aboriginal people and picks up the white couple. The aborigines are very angry and the large woman with the toddler shakes her fist at the taxi and at me. But I tell her it's not my fault.

I worry about the taxi. When it comes back again, is the man going to drive past the others and pick me up? If he does, they will be furious. It's not fair; they were first in the queue. But if he takes them next, how long will I have to wait in the sun for him to come back?

It is a problem. What can I do? Can I walk to the hotel? No, it is too hot and I'm too tired, and I would have to walk past the woman who shook her fist at me. So I walk the other way.

I walk for a long time, resting now and then in the shade of a tree, through streets that are all alike. Then I come to some grass by a stream. I sit on the grass and without taking my shoes off, because it hurts to bend that far, I dangle my feet in the water. I smile, wondering what Joyce would say. The water is soothing. I sigh as I lean back against a tree and have a little nap.

I wake because something is tickling my cheek. I wave away a long blade of grass and hear a deep chuckle. The toddler who grinned at me climbs onto my lap. He tickles me again with the piece of grass and then falls asleep.

I'm worried. Soon it will be dark and this child should not be out alone in the bush. I wake him and ask him where he lives, and he points down-stream. I carry a long scarf in my handbag because the nights are often cold. I wrap it round him and around my shoulder and middle like I used to do when Cory was little.

I walk slowly in the direction the child has pointed out and soon see the light of fires, close by. I stumble when I walk over the rough ground, but because I am carrying this precious boy, whose cheek rests so trustingly on my chest, I am very careful.

I walk until I think I can't do it anymore. But somehow I still manage to keep going. People surround me but I only vaguely realise they are there. I am exhausted and the child is weighing me down. Yet I can't seem to stop walking. The large woman who threatened me at the taxi rank tears the child from my arms. She sinks to the floor, hugging the toddler and howling like a dingo. I fall to the ground too.

Gentle hands pull me up and sit me on a chair by a fire. A cup of something pleasant is held to my lips. I drink thirstily and feel better. When I open my eyes I see the big woman, sitting beside me with the toddler on her lap. She smiles, gestures to the child and says, 'Thank you.' I nod and hold out the cup.

Three women vie with each other to fill it. I laugh drunkenly and say, 'My cup runneth over.' They all laugh too. We talk. Though I have been living in Australia for twelve years, I have never talked to an aborigine before—there are none where I live—and I am surprised that their English is so good.

They ask about my life and when I answer they hang on every word, as if I was a wise woman. It has a more potent effect than what I am drinking. One of them brings me a meal and I realise I have not eaten all day and am ravenous.

We sit in the firelight talking about putting the world to rights. The big woman, Maya, tells me they are of the Aranda tribe, the traditional owners of Alice Springs, and she talks about the

Dreamtime. They tell me stories about how the sun was created and why the crocodile rolls in the river.

Later, they dance. At first they all go round and round; men, women and children, skipping and hopping in time to the didgeridoo music. I jig with them for a while, laughing and clapping as they are doing. Then the women and children sit down and men burst into the natural arena, all in a line. They dance proudly, shaking their clapsticks and stamping their feet. They are a little frightening because they don't smile. I drink some more and go to sleep, feeling very happy.

The next day I wake up in an ordinary bedroom, and am surprised I don't have a headache. Maya is sitting, watching me. 'You are in my home,' she says. 'That place where you found us is where we gather for ceremonies or just to talk.'

The toddler comes into the room and jumps on my bed. We cuddle and I feel good. So good that when Cory gives a rap on the door and marches in, full of righteous indignation, I laugh at him.

'Why didn't you come back to the hotel last night,' he says. 'We were worried sick.'

I can't remember why, but I don't tell him that. 'I had a marvellous time,' I say. 'Sitting by the fire and listening to their stories. And we danced.'

'Your friend here guessed you were staying at the hotel. She telephoned and I came over. But by then you were fast asleep.' He smiled. 'And when they told me that you'd rescued a child…' He tickled the toddler's tummy. 'Is this the one who went walkabout?'

When I nod, he says, 'I'm proud of you, you silly old bat.'

I don't tell him that the angel child rescued me.

© **Mary Davies**

Mary has had one craft book published, won two M & B competitions and came second in a novel competition adjudicated by Katie Fforde. She has also had four short stories published in anthologies on the internet.

# Angel Maker
## by Vanessa Couchman

'Better dead than unwed. That's what I say.'

*La Mémé* rapped her cane on the stone flags. 'In my day, the father married the girl or she got packed off to the convent. Then the brat was adopted and everyone forgot about it. People will point at us in the streets. What were you thinking of, you stupid girl?'

Arlette's skirt moulded her rounded stomach. Her ears burning, she looked away from the heat of her grandmother's glare.

'This doesn't help, *Belle-Maman*,' *Mère* said as she clattered the crockery in the shallow stone sink. 'And things aren't the same as they were in your day. This war is changing everything. Of course he would have married her if he hadn't joined up. We don't even know if he's aware of it yet. Arlette's written to him, you know. She's just waiting for a reply.'

'Pah! It's a pity my Emile isn't here to teach that rascal a lesson. He'd marry her then all right. His own apprentice—what a nerve! But my son had to be one of the first to join up. That's just like him, putting other people before his own. And what if the boy gets himself killed up there?'

With a sharp intake of breath, Arlette grabbed the terracotta pitcher and slipped out into the courtyard, her eyes stinging. She sucked in the freezing air and wiped her face with her sleeve. She dropped the bucket into the well, rattling the chain to make it take in water, and then filled the jug from it.

*Mère* had found out earlier that day when she discovered Arlette being sick behind the hen-house. It was a wonder she had not guessed before, when Arlette had jumped up from the table gripped by nausea.

She leant against the well, staring at nothing, ignoring the cold that chafed her fingers.

Claude had attracted the gaze of all the village girls, like metal to a magnet. Long days spent pounding iron at the forge and calming the horses and oxen while Arlette's father shod them had broadened his shoulders and pumped up his muscles. He flashed the girls his easy smile but walked out only with Arlette. Throughout that arid summer, while the grass scorched on the plateau above Cahors and the nights blazed with stars, they wandered the lanes hand in hand and talked of the future after his apprenticeship.

On the night of the village *fête*, the bonfire lit up the stone Mairie and the church, on opposite sides of the market square. They all danced the traditional *bourrée* to the strains of *musette* and violin. Their clogs raised dust from the beaten earth, which mingled with the sweat of their bodies. He pressed her close and her heart danced too.

'You're much prettier than the other girls,' he whispered in her ear.

Later, in Bouyssou's barn, they lay in the sweet-scented hay and moved together to the rhythm of the dance.

A fortnight later, the crazed church bell sounded the end of peace. And then he was gone, with a tight embrace and a light in his eyes. The August heat crushed the soundless village, stripped of men. The fires of the forge died and the ringing of metal ceased as Arlette's father left too.

Autumn advanced and the oak trees turned flame-coloured. Arlette wore thicker clothes that concealed the swelling at first. She wrote to Claude with the news. Every day, she looked out for the postman. Every day, her heart plummeted when he brought nothing. Perhaps the mail didn't reach the Front. Père sent *Mère* occasional terse missives, revealing little. He could not say where he was.

'Read it to me once more,' *la Mémé* would command *Mère* yet again.

Arlette confided in her best friend. 'Oh, Simone, what shall I do? If I can't get Claude to marry me, *Père* will throw me out when he knows.' She covered her face with her hands.

Simone put a hand on her arm. 'But why didn't you make sure he was careful?'

Arlette raised her tear-streaked face. 'What do you mean? I didn't think you *could* get pregnant the first time.'

Simone shook her head. 'Where did you learn that? Of course you can.' She paused. 'I think you'd be better off getting rid of it. Then if he does marry you, you can still have plenty more if you want.'

A chill rippled down Arlette's back. 'Get rid of my baby? I don't know if I could do it. And how? I've no money for a doctor.'

'You don't need a doctor. My mother had 10 children in as many years and was worn out by the time she was 30. And she almost died when Jean-Pierre was born. So when she learned she was carrying the eleventh, she went to see *Mère* Delpech. And we stayed at 10. But you mustn't tell anyone.'

As dusk fell, her heart hammering, Arlette pushed open the door of *Mère* Delpech's tiny stone cottage, set apart at the edge of the woods. When she was little, her mother would say, 'If you don't behave yourself, we'll fetch *Mère* Delpech to you.'

'Well, you're not the first. And you certainly won't be the last. You young women, you never learn. Heads turned by a handsome face,' *Mère* Delpech said. She rummaged in the oak *buffet* and handed Arlette a squat bottle filled with a viscous liquid.

'What is it?'

'I call it the Angel Maker. Drink that and your worries will be over.'

Arlette handed over eggs and goat's cheeses in payment.

She hesitated but her father's image loomed, so she drank it down, gagging at the bitter taste. Half an hour later, she thought she would bring up her stomach, so violent was the vomiting. Her head spun and her limbs dragged. But the Angel Maker did not live up to its name. She jumped from rocks and lifted heavy weights but the intruder clung on.

Now *Mère* knew. And she had told *la Mémé*.

Arlette sighed and picked up the pitcher with numb fingers. The baby kicked. Arlette smiled at the stirring life within her. Part of her was glad the Angel Maker had failed. But this war that was supposed to last no more than a couple of months was dragging towards its first Christmas. And still no word from Claude. She lifted the latch and entered the living room, lit only by the glow from the embers. *La Mémé* had already retired to her small bedroom next door.

'*Mémé* wants me to write to your father and tell him,' *Mère* said, raking the ashes. 'I think it would be better not to give him something else to worry about. It must be bad enough being in the war. But you know what *Mémé's* like when she's in that mood, so I didn't argue. By tomorrow, perhaps she will have simmered down. Then we'll decide what to do for the best.'

*Mère* stood up and their eyes met. Arlette managed a weak smile. *Mère* shook her head and went to her room without a word.

The next day, her grandmother ignored Arlette's whispered, 'Good morning, *Mémé*' and installed herself in her chair by the massive fireplace. She took up the family almanac. The words were meaningless squiggles but she never tired of the illustrations of calamities.

Arlette put on a heavy cape, picked up the basket and stepped out into the alley that led to the market square, overshadowed by close-packed houses. Every Tuesday before the war, the place had thronged with stallholders and bustling housewives. The stone arcades echoed with hearty greetings and banter. Now, a handful of stalls presented meagre offerings as women struggled to keep the smallholdings going. Whispered conversations had replaced the hubbub.

Two women broke off their discussion to look at Arlette but turned away when she glanced at them. She bit her lip. Simone had said that *Mère* Delpech was discreet but maybe someone had seen her.

Her basket only half filled, Arlette walked back up the alley.

'There's a letter,' *Mère* said, holding up an envelope.

Arlette dropped the basket and turnips rolled along the floor. *La Mémé* tutted. Arlette took the letter, ripped it open and squinted at the unknown handwriting.

> *Dear Mademoiselle Viguié,*
> *Private Claude Authier has asked me to write to you since he is at present not able to do so. He was seriously wounded during the Battle of the Marne and has spent the past three months in hospital. He has made a good recovery but has only recently recovered his speech. He will be discharged in two days' time and will return by train to Saint-Martial, where he looks forward to seeing you again.*
> *In view of his injuries, he will need help to adapt to daily life, but I am sure he will achieve this with your support.*
> *Yours sincerely,*
> *Sister Claudine Bourcier*

Arlette frowned. What injuries? A chasm opened in her stomach. And there was no mention of her letters. But he was coming home and they could marry and be happy.

'Well, what does it say, girl?' *la Mémé* asked.

'Claude was wounded but he'll be coming back in a few days' time.'

'Now we've got him,' *la Mémé* said, rubbing her hands. 'Better start preparing for the wedding, Christiane, but it'll have to be a quiet affair given her…situation.'

*Mère* just nodded.

The following days crawled past. Each time Arlette looked at the pot-bellied clock, the hands had barely moved.

She walked to the station under leaden skies to meet the daily train. An icy drizzle coated her clothes. A few people huddled on the platform. The train wheezed into the station and smut-laden steam pumped into the bitter air. Arlette held her breath as doors banged and embraces took place around her.

She glanced at the last carriage, where the stationmaster was helping someone off. A man leaning on a crutch, his empty right sleeve tucked into his pocket, struggled to get his balance on the platform. He had Claude's chestnut curls. Arlette's heart stopped.

He looked up and turned his half a face towards her.

## © **Vanessa Couchman**

Vanessa Couchman is a Writers Abroad member living in southwest France. She runs a copywriting business and writes magazine articles about France. Her recreation is writing short stories. She has finished a first novel and is writing a second. http://vanessafrance.wordpress.com

## Barnacles **
### by Tracey S. Rosenberg

A small cluster stewed in the sea of my palm.
They were shell-like, not shells, wary,
as if prepared to be scraped, thumped
by weeds and grit and endlessly watery overturnings.

When they're single lumps, barnacles flail
lost in the ocean, or cling
to rasping wisps of seaweed.

If a dozen or so find each other
they clump like buns,
each with a bite snatched from its middle.

Great groups form a hard rippling carpet
overtaking any surface it can grasp.
These squinting accretions cripple ships,
forcing vessels over and up
like a tumbled lady
distraught at the loss of protective petticoats.

I wanted to hurl them back,
let them lead submerged Pacific lives.
They would meet others and grip their own kind,
unable to resist growth,
banding together to destroy.

Instead, I rinsed my little group,
leaving them to dry on a clean corner of my desk,
a huddled touchstone,
complete.

## © Tracey S. Rosenberg

Tracey S. Rosenberg is American and now lives permanently in Scotland. She previously lived in England, Ireland and Romania. Her poetry pamphlet *Lipstick is Always a Plus* is published by Stewed Rhubarb Press. http://tsrosenberg.wordpress.com

# Between the Mountains and the Sea
## by Nina Croft

'I only came on this stupid holiday because I felt sorry for you.'

Amanda didn't answer, just strolled on up the steep track, the sun warm on her back, the air crisp and fresh, chilled by distant snows and heavy with the scent of wild lavender and thyme crushed underfoot.

Ahead, the rest of the group was almost out of sight. Beside her, Kelly was breathing hard, her pretty face turning a lovely shade of puce as she tried to keep up.

'I mean,' Kelly panted, 'everyone knows you don't have any real friends. How sad is that?'

Pretty sad, Amanda acknowledged silently. Then smiled as she realised that she didn't care anymore.

'But sorry or not,' Kelly said coming to a standstill, 'there is absolutely no way I am going up there.' She pointed up at the snow-capped peak of Mulhacen, looming stark against the blue sky.

Amanda wasn't really surprised by Kelly's complaints. After all, she had been purposefully vague about the details of the holiday, saying only that they were flying to Malaga and leaving the rest to Kelly's imagination. But then, if she had explained what was actually involved, Kelly would have turned her down flat and that would have spoilt everything.

'Though it's hardly surprising that you don't have any friends, considering...'

'Considering?'

'Well, you know...,' Kelly lowered her voice. 'Considering you've been in prison.'

'It was a young offender's institute.'

'Whatever.' Kelly shrugged. 'Anyway, the girls are just a bit scared of you, even though I told them that it couldn't have been anything *really* bad or they wouldn't have let you out.'

'This was presumably after you told them about it in the first place.'

'Yeah well...' Kelly glanced away, actually looking slightly discomfited. 'They had a right to know they were working with an ex-criminal.'

'Just as a matter of interest, how did you know?'

'My mum told me. She knows a man whose sister works with a woman who went out with your uncle. They didn't know the details though. Mind you, my mum says they let kids get away with murder these days.'

'Really?' Amanda murmured.

She had seen the competition in a magazine on the same day she'd discovered that Kelly had told the entire office about her past. 'Win a walking holiday for two in the beautiful Alpujarras,' she had read. But it was the photographs that had caught her attention; all those high mountains and deep, jagged gorges. When she had received the e-mail congratulating her on her win, Kelly had been the one person she had wanted to ask.

'You're trying to tell me there are no hard feelings about this promotion, aren't you?' Kelly had said when Amanda had made the offer. 'But really, Mand, did you honestly think they'd give the job to an ex-criminal?'

'No,' Amanda had replied.

They walked on. The sun was warm and bright, the landscape dazzling; lush green splashed with the scarlet of a thousand poppies. Amanda realised she had fallen in love with this land that lay between the high mountains and the sea and for the first time in years, she felt at peace. She had been trying for so long to fit in, to be a 'nice' person. It was a relief to finally give up and accept that it just wasn't working.

The rest of the group were now out of sight and up ahead lay a narrow bridge over a deep gorge.

'Look,' Amanda said, 'I'd like to see the view from that bridge, then we can go back to the hotel. Have a jug of Sangria or something.'

'Thanks, Mand, 'cos this is ruining my Reeboks.'

The view from the bridge was spectacular, like being on top of the world. Far below Amanda could hear the jangle of bells from a herd of goats. She searched the area, but the shepherd was nowhere in sight.

'What are you staring at?' Kelly came to stand beside her, peering over the edge.

This was going to be too easy, Amanda thought, hesitating. Then, just as she was about to make her move, Kelly slipped under her arm and shoved.

Utter disbelief engulfed her as she teetered on the edge.

*This wasn't the way it was supposed to happen.*

49

'Sorry, Mand,' Kelly murmured. 'But I couldn't let you do it. And really, you would never have got away with it. Not with your record.'

Then Amanda was falling, down and down into the deep and jagged gorge she had so admired.

© **Nina Croft**

Nina Croft grew up in the north of England. She travelled extensively when younger, but has now settled to a life of writing and picking almonds in the mountains of Southern Spain. Meet with her at www.ninacroft.com

# Beyond the Sea *
## by Elisabeth Howie

It begins with a sound. A battling against the sides of my 1988 Nissan Vanette. I am rocked gently awake like a boat on water. I have noticed during my time here that wind seems to be omnipresent like wine and fruit regions, they go hand-in-hand.

A patch of sun shines through a crack in the old van's curtain, warming my face. It's a December kind of heat in here, enough to have you shedding your clothes and longing for the fresh embrace of water.

The night had smelt of the ocean even though I had been locked up tight, nestled inside my sheets, musty curtains drawn as far as they can go on their flimsy wire railings, a few cracks here and there. Its scent surrounded me in its bubble, mingled with rubber and board wax and sun cream. The smells of summer.

I pop the rear door and all I see is sand and sea and a rather large tree with brilliant crimson flowers, a *Pōhutukawa*. I remember them well from my youth. A coastal evergreen tree renowned for its stunning colour and ability to survive perched on rocky, perilous cliffs. Its strength and beauty has found a significant place in New Zealand culture, regarded as a chiefly tree, *Rākau Rangatira*, by Māori.

This ebb and flow of the day in Vanette quickly becomes a way of life. I wake with the sun, pop open the rear door and find myself in a new picture. In my mind, I capture and frame it, sometimes freezing it and wishing I could stay in it forever, sometimes hungry to move on to the next.

Driving up Highway 1, I can intermittently see ocean on either sides. To the left 90 mile beach, and to the right, Rangaunu and Great Exhibition Bay. I'm heading to the Cape—Cape Reinga, *Te Rerenga Wairua*, the place of the leaping.

What I love about it here, and in so many places in New Zealand, is that it feels so uninhabited and everywhere you look the scenery is so diverse. In one direction you might see the ocean and hulking great sand dunes, and in the other thick forests with giant *Kauri* Trees or man-made pine trees, to an abundance of exotic looking flora; Agave, Palms, and Yukka. You feel as though you have stepped into your own little world; a Utopia of sorts; endless possibilities in every direction; a place where no-one is, but you.

51

As I wind my way up to the Cape the sun is starting to peek on the horizon, warm colours burst from the ocean line. It's dusk. The quilted grey skies have passed, replaced by reds and oranges and golds. When I reach the top and step out of Vanette, I am almost hit by a number of feelings. I see the ocean and the colossal sand dunes of 90 mile beach. The cool breeze whips my hair around my face and I feel something. A strangeness, like stepping outside of my body, something ethereal and almost unworldly. This feels like a place of wholeness, a place where one comes to fit themselves back together. An ending and a beginning.

I walk down the snaking path to the lighthouse—the end of the road. Here, under the watchful gaze of the wind-whipped Cape Reinga lighthouse, the Tasman Sea and Pacific Ocean meet, colliding in a fit of fury and spitting salty spray as they battle for dominance like two sides on a battle field. And, although you can see this blatant roughness as the seas meet, there is a stillness and peacefulness, as if I am the only person left in the world. I am at land's edge. One more step and I might tip over.

As I am pondering this a Māori couple walk into my line of vision. I am overcome with the urge to know more, I want to know the stories behind the Cape. After sidling my way over, Amiria and Hemi tell me that the surroundings I can see is the Aupouri Forest, a Narnia-like place where bands of wild horses roam free. They tell me that the name of the Cape comes from the Māori word *Reinga*, meaning the 'Underworld'. Another Māori name is *Te Rerenga Wairua*, meaning the leaping off place of spirits. I learn that for Māori, Cape Reinga is the most spiritually significant place in New Zealand. It is here that after death, all Māori spirits travel up the coast to the gnarled *pohutukawa* tree, reputed to be over 800 years old, on the headland of *Te Rerenga Wairua*. They fall away into the underworld, '*reinga*', by sliding down a root into the sea below and are said to surface again on *Ohau*, saying a last farewell before reaching their final resting place in the ancestral homeland of *Hawaiki*.

The sun is setting and the sea is ultramarine blue, my favourite colour. A deep, vibrant, pure blue. I tell my new friends that the name 'ultramarine' comes from the Latin 'ultra' meaning 'beyond', and 'mare' meaning 'sea'—beyond the sea. It seems fitting. They smile.

I tell them there is nowhere else I'd rather be, nothing else I would prefer to be doing. I am standing at the edge of world, the smell of the ocean loaded in the air. I can almost see the earth's curve and the water's veins. It reminds me of how wild and lively and vulnerable the world is—how full it is of places whose nature we will never gauge in a lifetime. Places that I am yet to see and feel. I have my bearings. And if my spirit flies up this way when I die, finding the ancient *Pohutakawa* tree, I'd be happy.

## © Elisabeth Howe

Elisabeth dreams of adventures in faraway places. She holds a Masters of Communication and loves writing, books and the changing of seasons. She eagerly anticipates the next chapter of world exploration with her new little family of three.

## Borneo Nights **
### by Valerie Cameron

I remember those Borneo nights,
sweating tiles, bougainvillea scraps
pasted on the verandah,
delirious croaking frogs after the rains.

Clacks of mahjong and laughter
curl round my yard like smoke,
moonlight on limp palms,
a land below the wind.

Fighting cocks sleep
in black-feathered night;
a fat man under a tree
wraps notes in tin foil.

At the Sentosa hotel,
Germans drink brandy with Chinese,
eat ginger crab off blue plates,
lost in swirling mists of a hundred dim sums.

A night of whining insects,
restless half-sleep twirling damp sheets.
A monitor lizard lurks in a drain,
his eye a headlamp.

**© Valerie Cameron**

Valerie has been teaching overseas for 30 years in Borneo, Sri Lanka, the Middle East, Europe and latterly North Africa. Following a two-year posting in post-revolutionary Egypt, she has relocated to peaceful Dahab on the S. Sinai coast.

# Casa Rossetti
## by Taylor Jennings

The day I sprained an ankle slipping on the gravel path leading to Dracula's supposed castle in Transylvania was a lucky day. Lucky because I wound up recuperating in my friend Ruxandra's home and learned the secret of the part of Bucharest known as Little Paris.

I'd known Ruxandra since 1989 when we, as fellow journalists, covered the exciting days of a bloody revolution that ended with the televised execution of one of Europe's most brutal Communist dictators.

Thirteen years later I returned to write a story about a local tycoon's project to transform Castle Bran, the reputed home of Vlad the Impaler, into a million dollar Dracula theme park for tourists. Not the most popular idea among many Romanians and it was never built. But at the time it was an irresistible story for the foreign press.

We arrived at the nearby medieval town of Brasov in Ruxandra's battered *Dacia* and walked the rest of the way to the castle. Perhaps because we were talking and not looking where we were stepping, as women are wont to do, I suddenly found myself on the ground and unable to right myself.

'It doesn't appear to be broken,' Ruxandra said, gently manipulating my ankle without causing me to wince in agony. 'Hold on to my arm. If you can walk I think we should go back. You must come and stay with us at Casa Rossetti instead of that awful hotel.'

I started to protest but she waved me off saying it would be easier to work together and that we would return to Castle Bran when my ankle was better. I knew it meant Ruxandra would be playing nursemaid but the pain and swelling was getting worse and I had no objection to staying several days in the house named after my favorite romantic poet in a part of Bucharest I had read so much about.

After a brief stop at my hotel, we threaded our way through an ominous landscape with no street lighting and no sign of human life apart from feral dogs. Suddenly before us loomed a vast and empty lot, paved in concrete and lit up by stadium lights as if for a nighttime game.

This was the beating heart of Little Paris. Beautiful villas once lined these streets, streets with ancient names like Besarabia, Romulus, and Labirint. They were destroyed during the 1980s to make way for high-rise apartment buildings for government officials and visiting Soviet dignitaries.

Against the night sky, I barely made out some empty mansions that had escaped that fate, several with Ionic columns, fanciful balustrades and ornate grillwork, standing forlornly next to vacant lots.

'They're mostly inhabited by gypsies now.' Ruxandra said as if reading my thoughts. 'No electricity, no running water, no roofs. They build fires in the courtyards and burn trees, furniture and floor boards.'

We stopped in front of a rusty, iron gate and I looked out at the crumbling façade of a once beautiful turn-of-the-century building with an overgrown garden of weeds in front.

Ruxandra jumped out to give me her arm, looking furtively up and down in what I imagined was a reflex from the bad old days. Her husband, Florian stood at the top of the steps, a tall man with wild frizzy hair silhouetted against the dimly lit hallway.

'You are late,' he said as he embraced his wife. 'I was beginning to worry.'

Ruxandra introduced us, recounting my accident and he raised my hand halfway to his lips in the old Central European manner. 'Welcome to Casa Rossetti.'

I limped after them into a book-lined room where colorful throws and elaborate, fringed shawls disguised threadbare sofas and chairs that had seen better days. Heavy drapes were drawn across the windows and a fine fragment of lace was carelessly tossed over a torn lampshade. The Eastern European half-watt lighting created a warm, inviting ambiance.

Ruxandra went into the kitchen and quickly boiled up a poultice of local herbs. Soaking an old handkerchief in the cooling mixture she wrapped it around my ankle and propped my foot on a leather ottoman under the dinner table from where we didn't move for the next several hours while they told me the story of Casa Rossetti.

After a brief period of relaxation in the 1970s, Ceausescu had used the devastating 1977 earthquake as an excuse to demolish entire neighbourhoods to build his gigantic Casa Poporului (the People's House) and create a city along the lines of what he'd admired in North Korea.

'We decided the trick would be to allow the exterior of Casa Rossetti to deteriorate so as not to attract the notice of envious neighbours or the Securitate and since I had been removed from my job at the university, it gave me something to do.' Florian gave a wry smile.

'Does that mean there are other homes like Casa Rossetti here in Bucharest, hiding behind closed doors?' I wanted to know.

'Probably but who knows?' Ruxandra answered. 'We don't have many friends any more, you see. We lost the habit of inviting anyone to our home. For so many years no one trusted anyone and no one wanted others to see how they lived and perhaps become envious.'

'I carried huge bags of debris across the city in the dead of night so the neighbours wouldn't get suspicious,' said Florian. 'We thought we had succeeded.' A look flashed between them.

One unforgettable day Ruxandra received a notice in the mail announcing that her family's two-story villa had been scheduled for demolition by the end of 1989.

'First, they sent you an official notice of the scheduled demolition and if you failed to vacate, they cut off your water and electricity.' Ruxandra drew hard on her cigarette. 'If this didn't force you out, a huge claw-like crane would appear one day without warning in front of your house to tear down the front gate and rip off the roof, baring the house to the elements. If it was summer perhaps you could survive for a few months but in winter, with snow and sub zero temperatures, it was impossible.'

'Remember old Septimiu?' She looked at her husband who nodded. 'He refused to leave his home. They found him in his bed frozen to death.'

I listened in stunned silence while Ruxandra talked and Florian stared at his empty plate.

'Some people only got a 24-hour warning, others a couple of months, as in our case, which gave us time to agonize and imagine what the future would be like in the collective tenement we would be assigned to somewhere in the suburbs.' She paused to light another cigarette.

'Casa Rossetti was scheduled for demolition in December 1989.' Florian said with a huge sigh looking up at the ceiling.

'You mean it was saved by the Revolution?' I was incredulous.

'At the eleventh hour.' Florian and Ruxandra beamed at each other and she jumped up from the table.

'Come. We'd like to show you the work we did during those terrible days.'

We'd had drunk more than a few glasses of potent *tuica* which had eased the pain in my ankle but I was grateful when Florian took my elbow as we negotiated the stairs.

Ruxandra threw open the door of a large unused room. 'You must stay in my mother's old room until your ankle heals.' Ruxandra swept her arm across the room. 'This is what the house was like in her day. We've kept this room as it was in memory of her and of better times. You are the first non-family member to see it.'

In the dim lighting, I saw several large gilt-framed paintings hanging on damask covered walls and threadbare oriental carpets on the worn parquet floors.

'We'd like to have a guest, especially one from abroad,' Florian said, turning toward a long shelf of books. 'As you can see, we are good armchair travelers. Before, it was forbidden to travel and now we can't afford it. I want to hear all about those cities you know: London, Paris, New York.'

My eyes wandered over the author's names: Bruce Chatwin, Patrick Le Fermor, Laurence Durrell. Many were in English, a few in French, most in languages I couldn't read: Romanian, Greek, German and Russian.

'Well, that's settled then,' said Ruxandra, not waiting for my response and tossing an eiderdown encased in a crisp white coverlet onto the bed.

'Do you know why Florian and I want you to stay?' Ruxandra asked, handing me a pillow.

I shook my head.

'Because no one in our generation has friends anymore. That's Ceausescu's real legacy. We still don't trust each other and can only be friends with foreigners.'

I thought we had all probably had too much wine and *tuica*. But she went on.

'That old woman next door, you may have noticed peering out at us when we arrived?'

I shook my head again. I hadn't noticed.

'She used to be my mother's best friend. I played with her children. Sometime in the mid 80s Florin and I discovered that one of her sons was a Securitate agent. Either she or her son denounced us for trying to improve our house; for daring to better our neighbours!'

'You mean Casa Rossetti was scheduled for demolition because of your neighbours?' I was aghast.

'It's not an unusual story in Romania,' Ruxandra said bitterly. 'It probably would have happened anyway. Neighbors denounced neighbors and friends, even family denounced each other every day.'

'And that won't change,' Florian interjected, 'until our generation is dead and in our graves.'

## © Taylor Jennings

Pamela Taylor writes under the nom-de-plume Taylor Jennings to differentiate her fiction writing from journalism. She has lived and worked abroad for over 25 years in London, Paris, Sarajevo and for the past 10 years, Geneva

# Cold Stone Soup *
## by Alison Stewart

I was born with a caul, which the nurse brought my mother in a jar. It was so repulsive my mother hastily sent it away, only learning later that though hideous, it was a lucky object. I burst caterwauling into Grey's Hospital labour ward in Pietermaritzburg around the same time that J.G. Strijdom was succeeding Daniel Malan as Prime Minister. Strijdom proclaimed, 'Either the white man dominates or the black man takes over.'

His words delivered a bitter sentence to all South Africans. Not that I suffered materially. I was, after all, white and therefore lucky, caul or no caul.

My family has drifted around the world, washed up on first one continent, then another. I happened to grow up privileged in 'white' South Africa. All I did was live there but belonging was never a right. When your country does harm, it diminishes everyone. Yet as my family prospered in Africa, it experienced its own kind of disintegration. Eventually, I saw that Africa did not want me and so I left and came to Australia. But Africa still encased me and because of this and for a long time, I no longer belonged anywhere. I spent years looking over my shoulder at the home I had left, while the land I had come to retreated into the distance. It's different now, but the Africa of my flawed childhood, full of sublime ignorance, remains with me, welcome or not:

It's time for our summer outing to St James. We walk in crocodile to Rondebosch station where we sit on whites-only benches before boarding the whites-only part of the train which runs from Cape Town to Simonstown. We have buckets, and *takkies* (sandshoes) for negotiating the rock pools. The colourful beach huts line up against the back of the beach underneath the railway line and they tremble when a train roars through, but the beach is ours for the day, except for the odd maid in uniform supervising a small white child.

Unlike most of Rustenburg Junior School's Standard Two class, perhaps those maids are aware of what's happening in the big wide world. Perhaps as they dig holes with the small master's spade while holding the miniature Ceres fruit juice drink, they occasionally gaze across to a misty Hangklip and contemplate the fact that Nelson Mandela, Walter Sisulu and fifteen other ANC leaders have just been charged with treason.

What does this mean for their future and that of the young master who, bum up, tunnels down through the whites-only sand? The question occupying my mind on that balmy day is what manner of creature inhabits the rock pools?

I peer in and see shoals of tiny fish, sea anemones that contract when you prod them, lank and slimy seaweed and my favourite—shells. Shells that now litter the abandoned trails of my life. Away from the sea, they lose their colour, attract dust and eventually crumble, but each tells a story of the beaches I have tramped in search of, I'm not quite sure what.

My bucket quickly fills up with these miraculous accretions of sea animals, pink and brown, bumpy and smooth, green and doughnut-like, fan-shaped and spiralled.

When the bucket is full, I pronk from rock pool to rock pool in my non-slip *takkies*. Vanessa Sterling has already fallen on her bottom and now sheds some self-pitying tears in the lee of a beach hut. I am agile, however, and hop from one dry bit to another. Finally I reach the outermost rock pool before the sea slips away to waves and kelp.

'Not too far,' the teacher calls, but I am careful to keep my back deafly to her.

What is in this one? I squat to see—nothing much. I look up. Across False Bay is Seal Island. Looking further along from Muizenberg, the long beach becomes mistier and there are no more colourful beach huts. People live behind those far sand dunes, my crocodile partner Elise has told me.

'Poor people,' she says darkly as we walk under the railway line.

This thought hasn't occurred to me. I'm too concerned with listening for a train which might collapse this tunnel under which we are scuttling.

'They have no lights and no toilets,' she adds. 'And no real homes. Our maid told me.'

'How does she know?'

'She lives there.'

'But it's by the sea,' I say hopefully.

'She says the wind howls all night long. She says the sand comes in through the cracks in the walls which are made of paper and pilchard tin cans so they can't warm themselves up.'

Do I really want to know all this on my special outing to St James? I skip off down the white sand, do a cartwheel and am chastised for revealing my large bloomers.

But now that my bucket is full and the rock pool appears empty, my gaze is drawn to that misty distance where poor people allegedly live. What do they eat when the wind howls and the sand pours in through their paper and canned-pilchards walls? I look into the rock pool. This is what they would eat—cold stone soup. I scoop some up.

'Are you going to drink that?' Mary Harrington-Fleming stands over me, appalled.

Is it a juvenile sense of guilty good fortune that causes me to snuggle in my bed on a wet winter's night watching the heavy rain clouds boiling over the top of Devil's Peak and down towards my bedroom window? I'm here in my warm bed with my eiderdown and hot water bottle. Up there in the mountain however, homeless *bergies* (mountain people) live.

Did this comfy snuggling, this rock-pool observation, reflect a fledgling shiver of awareness? Was this when critical thinking began?

I can't rightly remember. More than likely, I rolled over and went to sleep.

© **Alison Stewart**

South African-born Alison Stewart emigrated to Australia in her 20s after the Soweto riots. She writes fiction, young adult fiction, non-fiction and travel journalism. This is an extract from her unpublished memoir, *Cold Stone Soup: An African Childhood*. www.alisonstewartwriter.wordpress.com

# Coming Home
## by Alyson Hilbourne

Maureen glanced into the kitchen on her way to answer the front door. She caught sight of a piece of paper by the kettle. She frowned as she twisted the door handle. Was it a note? And where was Robin? Why couldn't he answer the doorbell? He knew she was working in the garden. She gripped the trowel harder. She had half the border to weed and the roses to deadhead. Why couldn't Robin deal with this?

'Mrs Monks? How nice to see you.' A smartly-dressed woman thrust a hand out towards Maureen, who wiped her palm on her trousers before making contact. 'I've come to invite you and your husband to the annual dinner dance.'

Maureen's hand was enclosed in a firm double-handed grip. A grasp with no escape.

'Thank you,' she said, 'um, Mrs ...'

'Franklin, Mrs Franklin. We met at the shop last week. Had a little chat about the Far East.'

The woman moved closer, into Maureen's space, as if the Far East was a secret between them. She was plump and her face had a healthy rosy glow reminding Maureen of sun-ripened tomatoes.

"Oh, yes." Maureen peered back into the hall for Robin. "I'm working in the garden. Would you like to come through?" She gestured, turned and led the way without waiting for the woman to reply.

'Oh my! What a charming summer house.'

Mrs Franklin had stopped and was staring at the wooden *sala*, which had pride of place in the middle of the lawn and flowerbeds. Maureen frowned. She thought back to *salas* in Thailand. The outside pavilions varied from exquisite carved wood palaces to rickety thatched bamboo structures. They served as waiting places by the road or canal or meeting places for the village. They were somewhere to sit out of the sun and rain. They were centres of communities seating families or groups. They were not summerhouses.

'Did you bring the whole thing with you?'

Maureen nodded.

'It must have been wonderful living somewhere so interesting.' Mrs Franklin babbled on.

Wonderful? Maureen pictured the Bangkok streets, grimy, hot, crowded with cars, the pavements spilling over with stalls and pedestrians. Getting anywhere on time was a juggling act. The traffic was stationary half the day, the skytrain and underground coverage patchy. The canals stank of mud and rotting vegetation. Cooking oil smells wafted along the roads. She hadn't thought it was that wonderful although they had been there nearly twenty years. She was happier now. In England. In her garden. She could smell the buddleia and the loudest sound was the hum of bees. She wished Mrs Franklin would leave so she could finish weeding and get on to the roses.

'I am very happy here,' she said.

'But the beaches, the food, so exotic … don't you miss it?' The woman's voice rose in query.

Maureen thought about the food. Hot, spicy and frequently of poor quality. It was still the same if they went out into the country although in recent years the influx of visitors and smart hotels had improved things.

The beaches however, had been nicer before the tourists came. When they first arrived they could find fishing villages untouched by the twentieth century. Now the sand was lined by big hotels or overpriced cutesy thatched bungalows where westerners paid more for a night than the staff earned in a month.

'And I expect you had servants and a fine life with your husband's job.'

Where was Robin? Why had he left a note? Had he gone out somewhere?

A tiny tug of unease bothered Maureen but she smiled at her visitor. There was no point in explaining to Mrs Franklin what life had been like. People thought because you lived abroad it was one enormous holiday. They forgot that you still needed to shop, and cook, and do the laundry, just as you would wherever you lived. They didn't understand that mostly evenings were made up of boring dinners, with excessively long speeches, shifting restlessly in uncomfortable clothing in the sticky climate, whilst shaking hands with people who spoke little or poor English.

Then just as she started to feel comfortable, friends left, people were uprooted and sent off round the world, coups or disasters scared people away, so that she learned to put up barriers and not become too attached. Her days were long and the hours lonely when Robin was in the office.

And Robin was in the office often. Maureen felt an uncomfortable prickling at the backs of her eyes. For years she'd longed to be back in England, have a house, have a garden. But she'd been a dutiful company wife, although the experience had dulled and tarnished her like a piece of unused silverware.

'Would you like a cup of tea?' Maureen asked, anxious to escape inside.

'Lovely,' said Mrs Franklin gazing at the *sala*. Maureen left her running a hand over the teak wood, gazing at the carved fretwork on the underside of the roof. She had insisted on shipping the *sala* back, for the garden she knew she would have. The one she'd been planning for years, she now realised. Inside, the house was quiet. After the brightness in the garden, Maureen blinked several times to adjust to the light in the kitchen. On the counter, quite alone and out of place, was the sheet of paper. It was weighed down by something that she couldn't quite identify.

She moved closer.

It was a ring. For a moment Maureen's brain refused to recognise it. The hair on her neck and arms rose.

Robin's wedding ring.

She moved round the spot on the counter where it lay, as if avoiding it would delay the inevitable. She filled the kettle at the sink and moved carefully to plug it in.

Only then did she take a deep breath and pick up the typed sheet of paper. How typical of Robin to type her a note, so there could be no misunderstanding.

*I am going back to Thailand.*
*The house and what is in the bank account is yours.*
*I have everything I need there.'*

Maureen flinched as a wave of heat rolled over her. She pressed a hand to her head and steadied herself on the counter. Once the immediate dizziness passed and her head cleared, she realised she wasn't really that surprised. That he'd gone today was perhaps a shock, but not really a surprise.

Leaving the kettle to boil she slowly climbed the stairs to their bedroom. A depression on the bedcover suggested a bag or case had been lying in the space. She opened Robin's wardrobe. Several empty hangers rocked gently in the rush of air. His suits still hung there. She supposed he wouldn't need them again.

As she wandered downstairs she heard the kettle whistle. She threw a teabag in the pot and put some cups on the tray. She assumed he was on the way to the airport now. He must have planned this for some time. Robin wasn't one to do things on the spur of the moment. The surprise to her was really that he'd come back to England at all and that they'd had gone through the pretence of making this a home.

She'd known about the woman for a few years. The latest of several that she had tried to ignore. Friends had told her about the child. The child was a new element. Something he'd managed to avoid in the past. Perhaps that was what pulled him back to Thailand.

As she carried the tea tray out into the garden, Maureen couldn't help wondering if things would have been different had she and Robin had children. He said he didn't want any, and she didn't care either way, so it hadn't been a difficult decision.

He must have changed his mind. When she'd been told the news stuck in her throat like dry bread. She'd wished they'd had children after all. Children would have given her some purpose for all those years abroad.

Now however, she had a purpose in the garden and he was welcome to the sleepless nights, temper tantrums and homework assignments. He would be another elderly western man wandering Bangkok with a young Thai girl on his arm pushing a buggy with a mixed-race child. If that was what he wanted she wished him happiness.

Mrs Franklin rose to help with the tray as Maureen carried it across the lawn.

'This is just a wonderful summer house,' she said. 'It sets off your garden perfectly.'

Maureen nodded. She'd planned the garden round it so there was a good view on all sides and the sunset could be seen over the flowering borders with the bushy white buddleia to give an evening scent. This was what she wanted. This was what she'd dreamed about for years.

She leaned back against the railing of the *sala*, teacup in hand and surveyed her garden kingdom. She was happy. She didn't mind about Robin. She would check with the solicitor in the morning, but she was sure Robin would have left her well provided for. He wouldn't like a scandal. Everything would be tidy. She could get on with what she cared about. The chrysanthemums needed tying up. They had become too long and rangy. Another job for tomorrow. She smiled.

There were no regrets. A stage of her life was over and done with. She'd come home.

'So I came to ask if you and Mr Monks would be able to come to the dinner dance in aid of the village hall repairs.' Mrs Franklin said. 'It's the evening after the flower show and I'm sure you'll be entering things for that.'

Maureen hadn't thought about it. But perhaps she would. She needed to make some friends in the village.

'I'd be happy to come,' she said, 'but I'm afraid Robin won't be able to. He's had to return to Thailand. Some interests to attend to … he won't be home for a while.'

© **Alyson Hilbourne**

Alyson has lived in several countries in both Europe and Asia and prefers to be where the sun shines. She writes short stories and travel articles and has been published in magazines, anthologies and on the Internet.

# Coyotepe Fortress **
## by Diane Kendig

*Here in Nicaragua, we are living from one minute to the next, and the future waits on another roll of the dice of history*—Julio Cortázar

You're back now, blinking in the yard,
seeing spots, while Wanda, pregnant and planning
to return to Minnesota, shouts how repression happens
overnight in Latin America. Carlos, the father,
argues no, not here, never again.
'Don't crap out, Carlos,' she warns quietly
to the skies, not to his face. Below lies
the road where Coyotepe rises sun-blind white
over Masaya, reigning over the vista of farms
and the volcano the conquistadors called,
'the mouth of hell.' You usually climb and pose
outside the bulwarks, your head in the sky,
your back shouldering the hills, and once there,
you enter and clamber the ramparts and watchtowers
for new angles. At your back, like an old lady
hunched over her cards, the guard station hunkers,
painted pink by the Boy Scouts in the eighties,
then left to graffiti and dust. Most visits
you go no farther, but since your friends
brought a flashlight, you enter the tunnels
riddled with dark holes—'pipped to heck,'
a Brit on a tour remarked—and walk
to the chambers stripped in the lootings ages ago
for bars, plates, and metal fixtures.
Just the last time here, you descended and dipped
the beam along the walls where screams used to echo
and echo, the light sliced into the cells, widened
on the inquisitional space where now, in this minute,
it filters through a new iron gate, then slams and reflects

against many glinting doors, and you see
the fresh-black paint stenciled above the first door,
as everyone's breathing stops, and a fist
fills your chest and flicks open,
more figures flashing up down the hall.

© **Diane Kendig**

Diane Kendig has worked as writer and translator for 40 years, authoring four poetry collections, most recently 'The Places We Find Ourselves'. The poem 'Coyotepe Fortress' comes out of her teaching in Nicaragua 1991-2. She blogs at 'Home Again' http://dianekendig.blogspot.com

# Crossing the Road in New Delhi
## by Margaret Challender

'Let's get a rickshaw', Annette said. Her voice was decisive, but her eyes gave away the doubt she felt. Could we really be this inept? Two grown women unable to get across a road without help—without paying for help? How had it come to this? Our Indian adventure had started with such promise. Club-class comfort on the flight over. An efficient welcome from dependable ex-pats. We relished every sight, sound (and to a lesser extent smell), but nothing had prepared us for the effects of the heat.

It shouldn't come as a surprise, should it, that India is hot? But European summers do nothing to prepare you for the heat of the Indian city. The heat drained us of energy and sapped our mental resilience, leaving us unable to function, to make simple decisions or to trust our own judgment.

We found ourselves retreating from 'the real India', finding sanctuary in cool hotel lobbies, like a pair of *Raj Quartet* spinsters, wilting in wicker chairs, cotton dresses clinging to pink flesh, sipping a *chota peg* or a *nimbu pani* served by a neatly-turbaned waiter.

So there we stood, in the mid-afternoon sun, gazing across Jan Path as if it were a crocodile-infested river rather than a dual carriageway. The travel agent's office we were trying to reach was barely 15 metres away. We could not get there. There was a network of subways further up the road, at Connaught Circus, but that was a 15-minute walk away. To walk for half an hour, running the gauntlet of the street hawkers and amputee beggars was more than we could contemplate.

We made the decision. We hailed a rickshaw. Annette pointed to our chosen destination and, already seasoned in this sort of transaction, agreed a price in advance. One minute later we got out. I'd like to be able to say that the driver was amused at his English passengers' eccentric request, but he didn't give us a second glance after setting us down—he just guided his rickshaw deftly through the lanes of traffic and was gone.

I wanted to weep. Annette was suddenly chipper and rallied me. We had fallen into a sort of bi-polar relationship in terms of our moods. When one of us was low and brittle, the other would display a sort of febrile efficiency. We grew dependent on one other for a sense of equilibrium. Freud would have labelled us hysterical. I blamed the heat and lack of sleep, but in hindsight I think the anti-malaria drugs may have had something to do with it.

## © **Margaret Challender**

Margaret worked as a translator throughout the 1990s and has lived in Granada, Spain and in New Delhi, where she studied Punjabi. She now teaches English to international students.

# Danza Gitana *
## by Christine Nedahl

The passion of flamenco echoes through the strings as Juanma Torres, intensity etched in his face, urges the instrument to crescendo. The singer, Vicente Gelo, tendrils black as the night sky falling onto his handsome, glistening face, begins a slow handclap. The rhythm is unhurried yet pointed. Gradually, the strike of palm on palm increases until both men are as one.

With unexpected suddenness, his voice intersperses with the music, the sounds and words melodic and penetrating at the same time. They tell of a past full of the fire of life—love, desire, rage, sorrow, hope. All the emotions of human existence pass across their faces, fleeting, rapid and powerful. They are baring their souls.

Nerve ends tingle as your heart and mind experience the strange assault on your senses. Just as you think you have feasted on each musical sentiment possible, the dancers grace the stage. Maribel Ramos and Felipe Mato stand before their audience, every fibre of their being electric. The movement begins and the small auditorium resounds to the click, click of shoe on wood. Their bodies are fluid—magnetic waterfalls attracting, repelling, parrying—until the sensual climax is reached.

The spectators shout for more and the sapped performers find a surge of adrenalin to fuel another tune, another song, another dance.

At the *Museo del Baile Flamenco*, Cristina Hoyos has made her vision reality. These family-oriented premises belie a steely professionalism. Señora Hoyos' museum and school of dance, dedicated to flamenco, is the only one of its kind in the world and within its walls a piece of spectacular history is preserved for the modern world. The dance teacher, Victor Bravo, is as renowned for his own skill on stage as in the studio. Victor often personally greets the audience of the night or will be at the exit to thank them for their patronage.

Seville is Andalucia's largest city and tucked away in a narrow, winding side street, much like a hundred others in *barrio* Santa Cruz, is this prestigious venue.

If you fail to seek out this hidden gem, you will miss the opportunity to feel the passion, to be one with the Andalucian *gitanos* who bequeathed their brand of folk music to the world.

© **Christine Nedahl**

Christine Nedahl is a member of Writers Abroad. She has been published in four anthologies and online. She has two novels written both of which are in that ethereal state called 'editing'.

## Diaspora **
### by Susan Carey

My spade cleaves a hillock of soil.
Deranged worker-ants scramble
across her headstone,
rhythms disrupted, beats broken.
They must move on, build a new colony.
My hands flatten the ground, robe it in grass.
Plant primroses; join with the earth,
grave-dirt under my nails, drawing closer.

Tractor tyres ooze red mud
onto the road, splatter a minibus
full of Ukrainian pickers.
Gang-masters run the potato harvest
now no locals will bow low
to dig England's buried treasure.

Kestrels wheel in the sky
above my old home.
Summer guests have fled.
The kissing gate closes behind me.
I'm already on my way,
Walking along a foreign street,
red earth stuck to my soul.

© **Susan Carey**

Originally from Herefordshire, England, Susan currently lives in Amsterdam and teaches business English. She writes short stories, flash-fiction, poetry and the occasional novel. Some of her work has been published online and in print. http://amsterdamoriole.wordpress.com

## Did I Really Kiss the Removal Man Goodbye? *
### by Frances Johnson

Yes. He was the bully beef type, cheeky and wore builders bum trousers.

'I'm Harry. I'll have you packed up in no time,' he said when he arrived at my house. He had a jolly smile on his face.

Harry packed my dismantled drum kit with loving care. He'd once been in a band, he told me. Harry wrapped every wing nut and key clamp, cymbal and stands in brown paper, and packed them tightly into the crates so they wouldn't get damaged. My patio furniture was the only other 'must have' item that was coming with me. What need had I for items such as gardening tools and winter woollies where I was going.

When the aeroplane circled making its approach towards Alicante airport in Spain, my stomach curled around another life-changing experience about to start, coupled with my anxiety of flying. Once the mechanical vibration of the undercarriage disengaged and the wheels juddered as they hit the tarmac, the aeroplane taxied along the runway and then stopped. With a relieved outtake of stale breath, and a silent prayer to the Almighty, my white-knuckle ride in the claustrophobic cabin was over.

Stepping off the metal staircase and pacing along the tacky tarmac caused by the blazing heat, reality hit me square in the face. No more would I be hiring a car here and spending two weeks out of fifty two at a Spanish holiday resort working on my sun tan. My new life as an expat was starting today. There was no going back now.

I landed on Spanish soil in June 2007. My lifestyle would be regulated by the residue from the sale of my house, and an endowment policy due to mature in five years. I had no shackled mortgage on the brand new apartment with white goods and furnishings included. The plot afforded me room to have a swimming pool. I mean, why live the dream without one? And finally the pink icing around the doughnut, a line dance class operating in the nearby village. I had to pinch myself.

June was hot, July was hotter and August was scorching. Thank heavens for the swimming pool to cool me down! At least I had the good sense to have brought my patio furniture to make the shaded area complete. But the plot was larger than I had anticipated. This meant that the blank canvas of builder's rubble that bordered the pool had to be landscaped. I had given all my gardening paraphernalia to the council for their allotments. So I spent a small fortune recouping my losses on rakes, trowels, spades and a wheelbarrow. Palms, yuccas and fruit trees followed along with several tons of gravel. My drum kit still hadn't been assembled; it was far too hot for that nonsense.

Every morning at eight, I would be woken up by a man who sold bread and eggs hooting his horn from a white van. This time was also announced by the local cockerel. How considerate. The shepherd with his herds of goats and sheep was a surprising spectacle to see at first. His munching livestock crossing the arid landscapes seemed so removed from reality. The cow bells alerted me to this biblical of crossings on balmy evenings too.

The Cabrera Mountains were my ever changing horizon that never disappointed me. I looked out at them every morning from my apartment and they would greet me in their dressed greens and browns. As sunset faded ebbing towards evening, they could take on a pinkish hue. Sometimes, rain swollen clouds might circle the contoured peeks, and then they could resemble something akin to the Himalayas, a conjured up vision of a Shangri-La in my imagination. How idyllic.

The village down the road offered everything I was looking for too. With its narrow streets, white washed houses, hanging bougainvillea and scented jasmine; it had a quaint charm that I warmed towards. There were shoe shops here, dress shops, hardware stores, tapas bars, a hairdresser, post office, doctors and a local market once a week. By frequenting these places my Spanish would improve.

I have a comfort zone of English minded friends.

'The Rover does a lovely Sunday roast, dear.' I was told.

'I get all my groceries at Mercadona,' said another.

'Iceland has just opened in Vera.' I had been informed.

'They do a cheap pint at the Spot.'

Don't get me wrong. I do like my fish and chips. I do like my cooked breakfast. And I do look forward to my Sunday roast. I like a glass of Guinness, too. After all, I can't forsake my English lifestyle that has been my mind set for fifty five years, and go cold turkey on tapas and paella. But my attitude out here is slowly changing.

You see, I'm not tied to time anymore. It took me a while to accept that I didn't have to rush to the local supermarket, because another pressing chore was waiting for me at home. The village market supplies me with fresh produce which I can pick and choose at my leisure. Shopping for daily items is never a chore in town, either. I have a cup of coffee when I'm done. Sit in the shade and watch the world go by with an acquaintance. The Spanish have word for this slower pace of lifestyle…tomorrow.

So yes, I did kiss the removal man goodbye. I wanted to thank him for packing away my old life.

By the way, my drum kit went off to a car boot. I don't need my stress reliever any more.

© **Frances Johnson**

Frances Johnson was born in Wiltshire in 1952. Her poems and short stories have appeared in several newspapers, periodicals and anthologies. She is currently running a line dancing class with her twin sister in Spain.

# Dolma and the Golden Egg
## by Mary Manandhar

'Namaskar.' Dolma's father, Pemba, greeted the uniformed officer at Namche Bazaar police post.

'Well...?' the policeman mumbled, without looking up from his newspaper. A lean, angular-faced Brahmin from the Indian borderlands, his displeasure at being posted to the Everest region with its thin air, snow-frozen fields and its unwashed, carnivorous mountain people was common knowledge. The ever-increasing swarms of unruly foreign trekkers and mountaineers passing through were also not to his taste. But they were the only ticket to any sort of viable economy in such a desolate place. In these remote Himalayas, he had to admit, tourism was the goose that laid the golden egg.

'I have something to report from Dhampoche,' Pemba announced self-importantly.

'Really?' sneered the policeman, head bowed in the crumpled pages of last week's Kathmandu Post, booted feet crossed over each other upon a file-strewn desk.

'Someone has tried to steal the yeti scalp relic in the *gompa*!'

This came out of Dolma's blurting mouth before she even knew she was speaking. Her father swung round and cuffed the back of her head.

The words, rather than the cuff, caught the officer's attention. He studied the young girl, about seventeen, wearing traditional dress. Her black hair plaits were intertwined with red cotton ribbons ending in tassels dropping below her aproned waist. The cheeks in her moon-round face were wind scoured. Her father stood over six feet tall, in a long-sleeved overtunic, felted boots and turquoise earring hoops: a Khampa tribesman from Tibet. This was a man to be handled with care. Khampas had a fierce reputation and a tendency to foul tempers and desperation borne from empty pockets. This one was agitated and smelt of liquor.

The policeman reached for notepad and pen.

'Sit,' he commanded, with an imperious jerking back of his head so that his chin jutted out like a pointer in the direction of a rickety chair. 'Continue'.

'My name is Pemba Gyaltzen. I am the *gompa* guardian of Dhampoche. This is my daughter Dolma.' There was no other chair for Dolma so she stooped, as if hiding, behind her father.

He continued: 'I took the yeti scalp relic out of its box as usual this morning in case any foreigners might ask to see it. Then I went home to have my meal. When I returned to the *gompa*, the yeti scalp was … GONE!' Pemba ended with a shout. His clenched fist hammered down onto the desk as his chair wobbled precariously beneath him.

'*Harey*! This is a serious situation,' exclaimed the policeman, now leaning forward with interest.

'There was a tourist group in Dhampoche at about that time,' Pemba went on. 'So I summoned the villagers and we chased them, with some throwing of stones, back into the *gompa*. I locked them inside. I have come here for justice. I want you to search their bags and arrest the thieves.'

The policeman sprang to his feet.

'I will arrange a squad,' he announced. The energy with which he left the room betrayed a certain relish at this news from Dhampoche.

Within minutes, a troupe of eight policemen, armed with long *lathi* sticks and holstered pistols, clattered up to the police post door. The order was given to march north up the valley into the day's fading light. Like the policemen, Pemba looked excited and eager. In contrast, Dolma's downcast face registered something quite different.

Much earlier that same morning, Dolma's day had started with her usual chores long before sunrise. She had collected firewood and water, and tended to the yaks. By mid-morning, she was churning yak milk into butter in a tall wooden cylinder, decorated with embossed brass hoops. She pounded the slat-ended pole down hard and twisted it around between her palms. Then through the open window she noticed an approaching gaggle of tourist women hiking into her village, shouting and prancing as they passed by the burial *chortens*. They wore sleeveless vests and half-pants like common lowland porters.

'Why don't they wear long pants?' Dolma and her friends had often wondered. 'It's not as if they can't afford the cloth.'

The women came to the water standpipe and began to wash off sweat and dust. They splashed each other liberally. With no respect for the water, they left the tap running. Wasted overflow shimmered away in dark ribbons, fanning out down the path. Several women rolled up their vests and tucked their half-pants up between their legs, leaving thighs and midriffs exposed for all to see. Dolma's mother folded in the window shutters.

'They may be rich but they have no shame,' she hissed. 'They show their flesh like Bombay whores.'

Dolma agreed. Westerners generally were unappealing, bad-mannered and intrusive.

The women approached Dolma's house to ask for an overnight room. Dolma's brother, Mingma, was all smiles.

'Yes please!' he smarmed. 'Lodging and fooding here.' He sounded to Dolma like a fool with his strange words.

Coming inside, one of the women tossed a biscuit packet wrapper into the hearth, in what to her was an innocent and casual act. Not so to Dolma. For her, this was soiling the life-giving fire, polluting the smoke that would now spread over the village, breathing on people and livestock, contaminating the prayer flags. Dolma resented these women with their plucked-chicken-pale skin. She hated their way of looking you straight in the eye. She had seen women like them on the TV screens in town—half-naked, spreading their legs, rubbing hands down the outline of their breasts. Disgusting. If she behaved like that, she would be soundly beaten and flung into the yak dung pile. Her father might even take his knife to her hair plait and smear her face with red chilli powder.

Mingma showed the trekkers into a back room sometimes used for tourists staying overnight. Seeing Dolma at the butter churn, one woman asked, Is that your wife?

'No, no. Not wife.' Mingma's laugh was high-pitched. 'That is sister. She is too stupid for school. Too ugly for husband!'

Dolma saw all eyes upon her. She felt the red burning up her cheeks. She threw down the butter churn and left the house at a run, passing quickly through the village and coming finally to throw herself into a forlorn heap on a high grassy spur. Above the hurtling glacial waters of the Dudh Kosi, the mountains rose steeply. South-facing slopes still blushed pink with rhododendron blooms. Along the trail below, tiny figures were making their way along contouring paths: trekkers, porters and yak caravans carrying food, fuel, and climbing gear. There was a reverberating rat-a-tat of a helicopter in the distance.

In that vast landscape, Dolma felt small and alone. Her thoughts turned to her neighbour's son, Tenzing, who had recently left for the city. She remembered how they had danced together at festival times, taken walks along the river, played cards by the fire. She recalled the gaze of his dark almond eyes and the feel of his muscular body. But then she felt a newer feeling, the pain of rumours circulating that he had joined a trekking company. He had been seen late at night in the alleyway 'dance parlours' of Kathmandu. Dolma was convinced he was bewitched by immoral city women and foreigners arriving daily on huge planes. She was sure that he would never come back to her. She wished she lived in a valley where there were plentiful crops, an easy climate and no famous mountains so foreigners need not come and Tenzing need not leave and life would stay tranquil and calm.

She thought of her house filled with the alien clamour of the trekking women. By now, they had probably washed their inner garments and left them to dry over the balcony of the house, bringing more shame. They were likely parading immodestly in front of the household gods and *thangka* paintings. They'd probably touch things they shouldn't with their left hands. Some of them were probably even menstruating so they shouldn't even be near the kitchen hearth at all. Mingma would be leering, excited by exposed thighs, undulating cleavage and gold-blonde arm hair in such close proximity.

Dolma sat for a long while, until she saw the shadows moving across the valley as the morning passed. She thought of her chores, her mother's judgment and her father's temper, and so returned slowly to the house, passing along the *gompa* walls. She noticed that her father had left the *gompa* door unlocked. He was probably off drinking millet beer *chang* with the yak herders.

Soon after midday, Dolma was back at home and had resumed the butter churning, but more sedately than before. A faint smile pushed up her cheeks as if she was distracted with some amusing thought. She hummed to herself, in time to the rhythmic pounding. She twisted the churning pole almost tenderly.

Eventually, and with their usual noise, the trekkers emerged from resting in the back room. They ordered lunch of buckwheat pancakes with apples and honey and some masala tea. Then they announced they were going to see the yeti relics at the *gompa*. With her parents and Mingma nowhere to be found, Dolma told them that the *gompa* was unlocked and that they could let themselves in. She said that she would go and find her father so he could assist them. The women set off for the *gompa*.

Dolma put down her butter churn handle. She also left the house, shadowing the women through the village, but keeping her distance. No one would have noticed her slipping into the *gompa* behind the tourist group as they entered the inner hall. No one would have seen her hidden squatting, like a secret in the shadows. No one would have identified that small bundle she was pushing into the top of one of the rucksacks left in the porch.

As the trekkers explored the dark interior of the *gompa*, their laughter and chatter seemed to Dolma like a gaggle of wild birds arriving to feed at the lakeshore.

Tourism may be the goose that laid the golden egg, she thought, but it also fouls its own nest.

© **Mary Manandhar**

Mary Manandhar is an English woman now working in Bangladesh. She has spent 25 years abroad, including 12 years working in Nepal. Before moving to Dhaka a year ago, she lived for 10 years on the west coast of Ireland.

# Down in Zhou Village
## by Cathy Adams

Conversations took forever because Liu had to translate everything Molly said. She picked up about one word out of seven, less if it was Liu's grandmother talking. Nai Nai spoke as if she was chewing on something all the time, and she frequently stopped so that she could spit on the ground. Molly tried hard to keep her eyes off of Nai Nai even if the old woman was saying something directly to her.

'Tell her I'm sorry about the dog,' said Molly.

Liu smiled, a little painfully. 'She knows,' he said.

'It's just, it's just that things are different in America with dogs. They're like our babies. We pamper them.' She wanted to say more, but nothing she could think of to say seemed to make the situation any better. The dog's carcass was still in the yard. Molly could see its brown paws jutting from behind the water tub where Liu's mother had dropped it after she retrieved it from the road. Every so often Nai Nai would gesture at the dog and say something. Molly understood *tong*, which meant soup. Liu's mother would glance at Molly, then shift her eyes to Nai Nai and say something that Molly was sure meant 'not now, Grandmother. Wait until the stupid American leaves and you can do whatever you want with it.'

'I feel like such a terrible guest,' said Molly. 'I had no idea that was going to happen. We take our dogs for walks all the time. I should have asked. I'm just so sorry.'

'I know,' said Liu.

'I didn't know those little carts could go that fast,' said Molly. 'I mean, he didn't even try to slow down.'

This time Liu just looked at her with that same pained expression and said nothing.

'People look out for dogs in America,' said Molly.

'You are not in America,' said Liu, his voice a little lower and softer than it had been.

Molly sank down on her stool, her stomach roiling with guilt and tension as Liu's mother got up from her seat to start their lunch. 'I meant what I said about getting her another dog. I know it won't be the same dog, but I will get her a dog.' She leaned forward on her stool, her words hanging dramatically before her as if she had promised to find a child's killer or bring justice to a village of peasants attacked by warlords.

Liu's mother was bent over a cooking fire under the shed next to the now empty dog pen. She gently stirred noodles in a deep pot of simmering water. On a low table next to her, flies lit on a mound of chopped green vegetables in a plastic bowl. Next to it sat a pot of reheated chicken cooked in a kind of brown sauce with onions floating on top that was momentarily too hot for the flies to make a playground in. Another bowl held a mound of something brown, and Molly thought for a moment that the contents were moving.

Nai Nai sighed, said something in Molly's direction and then coughed up a ball of phlegm at her feet. The rich blue, fuchsia, and purple knit cap of textured cotton that Molly had given her sat on her lap. Every so often the old woman would notice the hat was there, finger it, and then announce something unsatisfactory about it.

Why so many colors? Liu had translated when Molly presented the gift to her that morning. Did they run out of thread?

'It's supposed to look that way. It's from Etsy,' Molly said in the too loud voice she had promised herself she would not use when speaking to people who did not understand English. 'Very nice. Made by artist,' Molly added, pointing at the hat.

'She thinks you give her an old hat made of leftover thread pieces,' said Liu.

Molly tried to smile. 'Next time I'll shop at Walmart.'

Liu's face brightened. 'Walmart is very good. We go to Walmart once in Zhengzhou. They have many refrigerators, washing machines, and televisions.' He held his hands out excitedly in approximation of a large box.

'Those are nice, too.' Molly nodded her head, grateful no one was talking about the dog anymore. It had been a good idea, she thought. Take the dog off the pole his chain was attached to and go for a walk in the neighborhood before anyone was up. The man in the cart who had careened around the corner was on the left side, and he was going so fast there was barely enough time for Molly to get herself out of the way, let alone the dog who stood transfixed in the path of the red motorcycle engine that in a split second left him lying in the street, broken and bleeding from the mouth. The man's yelling and arm waving had brought not only Liu, but the neighbours and some nearby workmen from a construction crew who stood grinning at the *Meiguo* who stood by stupefied with a rope in her hand attached to a now dead dog. 'It was supposed to be kind,' Molly whispered. No one heard.

The courtyard door opened and a squat looking woman with a big smile stuck her head inside. Liu's mother waved her in and said something in greeting as she dropped the contents of one of the bowls in a shallow cooking pan that popped with grease.

'This is our neighbor, Pengpeng,' said Liu. 'She has never seen a foreigner before.'

Anxious for a chance to make a good impression on someone who had not seen the debacle with the dog, Molly stood up, said her name slowly and stuck her hand out as Pengpeng stared down at it. In an instant Molly realized her mistake and shoved her hand in her pocket. The smile never wavered, and Pengpeng immediately began pointing at Molly and speaking in high, rapid Mandarin to Nai Nai. Molly made out the words *'you diar pang'* and *'Meiguo'*—a little fat and American. Molly instinctively put a hand to her chest and forced a polite smile. Still talking and smiling, Pengpeng nodded back at her and then gesticulated toward the dead dog next to the water tub. The profuse smiling, nodding, and waving toward the corpse gave Molly a queer feeling that Pengpeng was more excited about the implications of the dead dog than the fat little foreigner before her.

Liu's mother spoke up and flipped her hand toward the table and mismatched stools surrounding it. Molly made out *'chi fan'* and knew it was time to eat. Pengpeng hawked up a big blob of phlegm and deposited it in the dirt in front of her, much to Molly's disgust, but she didn't let her eyes drop, and she kept up her polite smile that was now embedded in a hard knot of quivering muscle around her mouth.

Bowls of chopped greens, noodles and chicken filled the middle of the table and smaller bowls of *mifan* had been placed at each seat. Molly was reaching for a set of chopsticks when she caught sight of the bowl of crunchy winged, golden fried locusts staring up at her with reddish brown eyeballs. Liu took one between his chopsticks, dipped it into a dark purplish sauce, and bit through the thorax.

'Best part,' he said, chewing the head. 'You try.'

Molly felt something in her jaw, a flutter, a spasm, and realized that her smile had frozen so hard she could not relax her mouth. Pengpeng and the family were busy reaching across the table, taking bites from the bowls with their chopsticks and happily munching while they talked. Still holding the hat in her lap, Nai Nai was pushing bites of green into her toothless mouth. Liu's mother grinned and gestured over the food with her chopsticks as she said something to Molly. The smiling, the crunching, the laughing, the reaching, the spitting, and the squatting on tiny stools on a warm day around a table with family made her think of July 4th at her grandfather's farm in Wisconsin. They would eat a lunch of hamburgers and boiled corn from her grandfather's garden. After the meal he would slice a watermelon still warm from the afternoon sun where he cut it from the vine less than an hour before. They drank Coca-Colas and fished for bass in the pond behind her grandfather's barn where he stood in the doorway waiting for the children and grandchildren to bring their catch to him. One by one he would nail the fish to an upright board, rake the scales off with his knife, and then gut them before tossing them into a bucket of water. His barn cats swarmed the open door and leaped to catch the heads he tossed to them. At the end of the day her grandmother would dip the fish they had caught in egg and corn meal and fry them up in a deep iron skillet on the stove. The whole family ate fish, coleslaw, and mounds of hushpuppies at the backyard picnic table as the sun descended over the pond.

Molly felt enormous tears welling up in her eyes and she wanted to say something to each of them. She wanted to thank them for something but she could not think of what. She wanted to hug Liu for explaining her words all day and Liu's mother for cooking their lunch and then push the knitted hat onto Nai Nai's head and tell her she was lovely. She quickly wiped away the tears that splashed onto her lap.

'I really am sorry,' she said, but they just smiled and continued eating. Reaching into the bowl with her chopsticks, Molly took out a plump locust, turned it over and looked at its tiny dead eyes. How lucky you are to feed this beautiful family. Biting through the middle, she chewed the crunchy warm head and swallowed. 'Delicious,' she said, and took another, and another, and another.

© **Cathy Adams**

Cathy Adams' novel *This Is What It Smells Like* was published by New Libri Press. Her short stories have been published in *Utne*, *Steel Toe Review*, and *Relief Journal*. A native of the USA, she now writes in Xinzheng, China. http://adamsjackson.tumblr.com/

# Driftwood **
## by Marilyn Hammick

The East Pacific Highway, last light
on Napier's cliffs, piebald sheep
grazing land that straddles
the Australian and Pacific plates, then
Picton, Queen Charlotte Drive, Governor's Bay,
to Havelock for lunch where I learn
how to eat mussels from italicised instructions
on a fish-netted poster.

*Take the first one out with your fingers,
then use that shell like tweezers,
just pull, no forks.*

My destination, Nelson, supper at *The Boat Shed*
whitebait, snapper, local *Sauvignon Blanc*.
I choose carefully, no opportunity now
to taste a second entree, no
how's yours, mine's fine, no
order for *pannacotta* and two spoons,
no discussion about how much to tip.

You prop your book on the napkin ring,
eat without conversation; after a while it becomes a habit.

## © Marilyn Hammick

Marilyn's poems emerge from geographical and emotional journeys across bumpy and blessed borders. She writes and reads poetry while travelling and at home in England and France. Her poetry often recalls a childhood in New Zealand and years living in Iran.
http://glowwormcreative.blogspot.co.uk/

# Elephants *
## by Pamela Barick

It was May 1964 in Kodaikanal, India and I was nine years old. The Dads were up from the plains and the hill season had begun. A month before, in April, the Moms had arrived and taken us out of boarding school and now we were all on vacation for three weeks.

During the season plays were performed, which everyone had been preparing throughout the year: Shakespeare *Henry IV, Part 2*, Gilbert and Sullivan *The Gondoliers*, *The Pirates of Penzance*, musicals *Oklahoma!*, and opera *Amahl and the Night Visitors*. The adults from our mission would meet and family events would take place, like the picnic where a wild pig that one of the Dads had shot was cooked for us all in a fire pit.

While at boarding school we were not allowed to leave the compound without an adult chaperone, so going to the local bazaar with our parents was a big event. We would buy Bombay mix and sweets to eat while roaming the small streets crammed with tiny shops full of exotic wares. My favourite was one that seemed to sell everything - food, fabric, furniture, lamps. Then, way at the back, were the toys and the magical world of glass animals. I would save up my allowance and spend a few rupees on a small green rabbit, a blue peacock with its tail feathers open, a miniature hen with her tiniest chicks. My special favorite was a pink and white marbled elephant, thumb-sized, his trunk raised high, trumpeting his presence to the world. He was the largest creature in my collection, but still small enough to get lost behind the hairbrush on my dresser.

I bought the elephant later that summer after a day trip with my parents and several others from the mission. We went down to the plains to the city of Madurai to visit the temple, which is one of the most beautiful and impressive in all of South India. Having researched it since I now know it is dedicated to the goddess Meenakshi, an avatar of Parvati and consort of Sundareswarar, who again is an avatar of Shiva. Madurai temple is very old and covers about 45 acres. It contains gate towers known as *gopurams*, courtyards, shrines and a temple tank.

But this is all adult knowledge. Then I was a small child and now my memories are 49 years old. At the time I saw it as a large and marvelously strange place, a huge complex with towers so high you almost fell over backwards craning your neck to take in all the painted figures. My Dad said they were statues of all the Indian gods and goddesses. I was shocked. How could there be so many gods? I thought there was only one.

We walked through the main gate into the temple grounds. First there were courtyards, hot and smelling of dust and cow dung. Then we continued through long dark corridors full of statues, carved columns and painted ceilings. There were niches lit with oil lamps holding colourful images worshipped by women in bright saris.

I remember the place as calm and cool after the heat of the courtyards. I'm sure though it was busy and crowded, as over 15,000 people visit it each day. But that is not how it seemed to me. I found it mysterious and full of wonders. Like the elephant in one of the corridors that had flowers and designs painted on his forehead and trunk. It was attended by two men. The first man took rupees from the pilgrims, who would stand and bow before it, while the other would speak to the elephant, instructing it to touch the pilgrims' brows with its trunk in blessing. Sometimes a young boy would be placed on the elephant's back for a short walk backwards and forwards. I was fascinated.

From there we went into a courtyard that was hot and dry and almost empty. At the far end stood one lone elephant, chained by his feet to the wall. Another chain around his back leg was driven into the ground with a spike, and no-one stood near him. Hanging his head low he pulled at the chain, first to one side and then to the other, left, right, left, right, left, right, over and over and over. Sometimes he would shake his head, swing his trunk back and utter a loud cry, still swaying from one foot to the other.

I was transfixed. I stood watching him for as long as the grown-ups would allow. They, too, were mesmerized by this disturbing, repetitive behaviour. Why was he acting this way? We were told he had gone mad and killed someone, but because he was a temple elephant, sacred to the gods, he could not be harmed. So he was chained and fed and kept alive in this courtyard, where he could not hurt anyone ever again.

A year later we returned to America, but from the time I bought my pink glass elephant right up until I left home for college I kept my collection on my dresser, patiently lifting and dusting each one every Saturday when I cleaned my room.

## © Pamela Barick

Pamela Barick is a writer and visual artist currently living in the Netherlands. The older she becomes the more she realizes how much her youth spent in India has influenced her creative work.

# Encountering the G8 Summit *
## by Dianne Ascroft

I slowed down as I approached the short queue of traffic that had come to a standstill on the outskirts of Enniskillen. Two police officers stood beside a white van at the front of the queue, talking to the driver. More than a dozen officers from forces throughout the UK, drafted in to help with the security operation for the G8 Summit in Northern Ireland, lounged beside four armoured Landrovers parked in the layby next to the checkpoint. The officers from the Police Service Northern Ireland were recognisable by their regulation green peaked caps while members of other forces wore blue baseball caps emblazoned with G8 insignia. Despite the unusually warm weather that June weekend all the officers sported flak jackets. Their batons and handguns, strapped to their belts, looked heavy and cumbersome.

As I watched, the van driver got out and opened the double back doors. The officers glanced inside then, smiling, they motioned to him to close the doors. When I approached the checkpoint one of the officers peered through the driver's window at me, nodded courteously and waved me on.

I continued into Enniskillen, passing five police Landrovers parked in a row on one of the stone bridges leading into the town centre. The back doors of the vehicles were flung open and officers lounged on benches inside or stood on the pavement beside them, chatting. The drive from our farm into town had been quiet as many people were staying home to avoid possible traffic congestion or disruptions due to protests. Few cars were on the road and every third vehicle I met was a police cruiser or armoured Landrover. I hadn't seen so many security forces vehicles in years. The streets in town were also deserted except for foot patrols, in twos or fours, sauntering along, relaxed and cheery.

A huge white vehicle, like a windowless mobile home on wheels, lumbered past me as I got out of my car in Enniskillen Museum's parking lot. The protrusion on the top, like a tank's gun turret, marked it as a water cannon. I wondered if it would be needed as the few tents pitched in the park where protesters were allowed to camp indicated that they had not arrived in the numbers that had been anticipated.

Hurrying to the Craft Fair book stall I had volunteered to man, I strode through the Museum grounds, rounded the corner of the Inniskillings Regimental Museum's grey stone cavalry stables, and almost collided with yet another police patrol. I froze, expecting a cold stare at best, but they stepped aside to let me pass, greeting me pleasantly. As I passed them I remembered a very different encounter I had with the security forces two decades previously.

One evening soon after I arrived in Belfast, I was enjoying an Irish music session in a city centre pub. The music was lively and I lingered over my drink until the barman called closing time. I heard the clock on the mantelpiece strike eleven o'clock as I went down the stairs and out of the side door. It was a cold, starless winter evening. I pulled my coat around me and hunched against the chilly air, staring at the ground as I stepped out into the narrow street. A shadow wavered in front of me. I glanced up and stopped dead. I was looking into the mouth of a rifle. I followed the line of the barrel up to the thin, boyish soldier holding it and waited. He held the rifle steady and, watching me through the gun sight, his expression never changed as he said 'Good evening' in a thick Liverpudlian accent. I almost laughed at the incongruousness of that accent, which invariably sounds questioning and friendly. Not knowing what else to do, I returned his greeting and awaited his next move. I became aware of several other soldiers crouched in the doorways of buildings nearby, their forms blending into the grime-darkened bricks of the industrial city's old warehouse buildings. After studying me for a moment, the young soldier gave a hand signal and the other men ran from the doorways, crouching low and moving silently, to continue their patrol along the street, leaving me staring after them.

During my first few months in the province I grew accustomed to heavily armoured police vehicles patrolling the streets, their occupants hidden from view, and military foot patrols racing through residential estates, training their weapons on passers-by they encountered. I found that the security forces treated every civilian with cool suspicion and, when we met face to face, I got used to their reserve and wary, appraising stares, despite my open smile.

My encounters with the security forces during the G8 Summit this summer were very different from the ones I had when I arrived in Northern Ireland more than two decades ago. From my vantage point at the Museum book stall, I watched police patrols roam the grounds, stopping at stalls to admire the crafts on display and chat with the traders. One officer promised a jeweller that he would return to buy a necklace as a gift for his wife at home in Birmingham. Other officers laughed and joked with the traders, chatting about their home towns and what tourist sights they had seen in County Fermanagh. Officers from the local force were equally genial and relaxed.

During the last two decades peace has crept into Northern Ireland and the police have traded their armoured vehicles for patrol cars and walking the beat. The sight of huge numbers of armoured vehicles arriving in the county for the G8 Summit awakened uneasy memories of the past for many people. But this turned out to be a very different security operation: professional and thorough as always but without the tension that once surrounded interaction between the security forces and the public. Northern Ireland is moving on.

© **Dianne Ascroft**

Dianne Ascroft, an urban Canadian who has settled in rural Northern Ireland, writes both fiction and non-fiction. She has released several e-books and online she lurks at Writers Abroad and www.dianneascroft.wordpress.com.

# Excuse Me, Are You Real? *
## by Epp Petrone

'Look!' Papa yells. He's excited.

Here they are, indeed. In between the rows of cars, there's a horse cart where two men with beards and black clothes sit. They are talking and don't pay any attention to the people gawking at them from the cars. They are used to us tourists.

When we turn the corner, we spot houses that look different. No more whale-shaped weather vanes or cat-shaped welcome signs. Instead, we see simple box-houses and laundry hung out on strings between poles. This is where the Amish live.

'It's just like my home,' I tell Mama, my husband's mother. 'In Estonia, most people hang their laundry outside.'

Mama looks at me with disbelief. I can see those two extremes residing in her: the consumer and the romantic soul who adores everything old-fashioned. She doesn't ask me if clothes dryers are not sold in Estonia. Instead, she says, 'I also like to hang a shirt to dry in our yard sometimes. The smell is completely different.'

I don't ask her why she uses an electric dryer at all when she has a large yard. I do mention something else. 'In dryers, clothes wear thin a lot faster...'

'That's true, Mom,' Justin interjects. 'When we were living in Estonia and drying our clothes outside, all of them stayed intact, no holes, can you imagine?'

That's how this conversation ends. These never asked and never answered questions remain here in the conditioned air, not causing any arguments, but bringing up the obvious: I am from a world that is different. I am the Amish for them.

While waiting to cross the intersection, we see another cart. At the reins, there's a woman wearing a long dress, an apron, and a white cap on her head, with a gaggle of kids in the back. The girls are wearing caps and the boys wear straw hats. The sight is so sweet. I understand perfectly why tourists come here.

But I do feel sorry for that romantic-looking horse who is switching from foot to foot on the hot asphalt. How can those creatures in front of the cart, and inside, manage to even breathe among all those fumes from the cars that pass them?

'Whoever it was that forbade them from using electricity and cars must have been a masochist,' Papa moans, watching the carriages. 'I wouldn't wish it on my worst enemy!'

Papa, have you thought that if the Amish didn't have to stop at red lights and in traffic jams, if they could keep moving, like they used to in the past—as we all did in the past—they wouldn't be as hot? They could catch a nice breeze. But I only think these thoughts. I don't say anything.

In the center of the town, we see the local superstars—a family of sheep with their lambs. I pet the lamb, and Papa jumps to rescue. 'They could bite! And they could carry bacteria!'

There are, in fact, notices up on the fence affirming his suspicions. I see. If a sheep bites us, we won't be able to sue. Although during all of my childhood adventures in the countryside, I never saw a sheep that bit.

And next to the sheep stands a plastic cow with rubber teats that excrete water mixed with white dye. This way the tourists can try their hands at farm work.

We drive through a desolate area, where a lone Amish farm sits beside a giant shopping center, all this by a highway that used to be a country road. At last, we arrive at the cultural center. Justin and Papa announce that they'd rather nap in the car. The humming air conditioner and the ticking gas meter bother me, as we slip away with Mama to go see an hour-long show.

'One time, I was walking down the road, a car stopped by me, the windows were rolled down and the people asked me: 'Excuse me, are you a real Amish?' said a man in the film. 'I told them I'm a fake one; the real ones are down the street!'

Or another story: 'I was working when a car drove up, a woman walked out and asked me, 'What does it feel like to live a life this strange?' I didn't know how to answer. She's the one driving around in a rumbling metal can, living a stressful life in a city somewhere, yet she's the one asking me what it feels like to live a strange life?'

After the program, we drive down a country road. The landscape reminds me again of my childhood. I think back to how we used to go milk the cow with my father and how I was planning on living on a farm when I grew up. Life did take a different turn, but I still remember that feeling of peace. The child of a banker will never feel the same satisfaction that a child on a farm will get from going to work with her father.

We drive on at a quiet pace and wave to the Amish people working in the fields, who cheerfully wave back.

I would love to stop here and step into one of their homes, to tell them that all of America should be sent here, for reeducation. But right now any further communication with the Amish would be impossible, because Mama and Papa are eager to get to dinner.

'For the goodbye, listen how the corn grows!' Papa announces.

This is one of their rituals. Every time they visit the Amish, they stop the engine for a moment.

The windows slide down. Corn fields rustle along both sides of the road. I fight the urge to open the door and run into the field. Justin would run after me. And then we'd live here forever.

'Whew!' says Mama. 'Enough! Without the conditioner, it is way too crazy here!'

## © **Epp Petrone**

Epp Petrone is an Estonian author, journalist, and publisher, who has lived on and off in the US for the past 10 years. She currently lives in Estonia with her husband, the author Justin Petrone, and their three daughters.

# Feel at Home at Perico's *
## by Andrea Isiminger

My pace quickens. I am desperate to be rid of the traffic noise, crowds of shoppers and hot mid-day sun on Madrid's famous Calle Gran Vía. Upon reaching a cross street, my mood lightens with the drop in temperature. Slowly weaving through tourists trying to choose a shaded table at a sidewalk café, I finally begin to examine my surroundings.

A respectable distance from the Tryp Cibeles Hotel, several women are lounging in the shade created by one of the buildings. A couple more ladies chat quietly underneath a tree. Only one wears the usual uniform of mini skirt and ultra-high heels. The others sport brightly patterned stretch pants—their neon advertisement of what's for sale. Business sense dictates that the lighter-skinned working girls get the shade. The exotic women, who are the color of melting dark chocolate, are posted on Calle Ballesta where I am headed.

Four years ago a move was made to clean up the street business in this area known as *Triball*. The over-priced shoe store I turn my attention to is a small testament to this effort. An old man, selling packets of tissues and ranting against the economic crisis, startles me away from my window shopping. One with the neighbourhood, he is the same dusty color as many of the buildings that have seen better days.

I idly watch him shuffle past the ebony ladies until my eye rests on a familiar figure in a vibrant teal-trimmed sundress. My friend Linda is already at the restaurant, waiting under *Casa Perico's* cream-colored awning.

*Casa Perico* restaurant really was Perico's house; he was born there. His parents opened the restaurant in 1942, and his older sister Angelines (Nines) joined the business full time at the age of 12, shortly after their father died. The building assaults your vision like the wildly decorated refrigerator of a proud parent. More than 50 framed articles are scattered across the dark brown façade. It's a quick preparation for the décor inside.

Memorabilia from over 70 years is crowded into every available space. Siphon bottles march to infinity over the bar, while on the bar sits a large glass container shaped like a bee hive. My fingers itch to turn the spigot to see if the mysterious dark liqueur inside flows like honey. We are seated at a table where child-sized versions of the costumes worn during the May festival of *San Isidro* hang on the wall. I haven't turned my attention to my menu yet since I can't stop staring at an odd grouping of empty wine bottles whose necks appear to be angled right into the wall. I am half-way out of my chair to go investigate when Linda grabs my wrist to pull me back down.

'Is that him?' she whispers. The slight toss of her head indicates the white-haired gentleman in the crisp blue dress shirt who is greeting two distinguished male diners at the entrance.

Linda hands me a photograph she took when we were in *Casa Perico* for our first meal six years ago. I understand her confusion as my eyes flit from the photo to the gentleman and back again. If that is Perico, he magically appears younger and thinner. Then Nines bustles out of the kitchen looking radiant in red and sporting a spotless white pinafore apron, just as she did six years ago. Not a brown hair on the head of this 74-year-old woman has changed.

I feel just as I do when I am transported in a dream to a particularly wonderful event of my childhood. The rational part of my brain tries to break through and remind me that I am no longer eight years old, and it is not Christmas or Easter or my birthday. But my pleasure centres kick that thought to the side and allow me to enjoy the moment, however brief, where I feel safe and cared for. Linda and I are both expats who consider Spain our home. However, our extended families remain thousands of miles away in the US. Somehow *Casa Perico* fills a void and warms us with a nostalgia we can't quite explain.

The waiter appears, and I surprise myself by ordering *pisto*, a dish I often prepare. A simple medley of sautéed onion, pepper, eggplant and zucchini, the vegetables are simmered in a tomato sauce and topped with a fried egg if you wish (and I do). Without a doubt, it will be followed by the veal *scaloppini*. Six years could not lessen the memory of the unadorned perfection of this dish.

Our piping hot first course arrives. Linda digs into her *panaché de verduras*, and I take my first bite of *pisto*. It is wonderful and somehow so much better than mine. I wish I could say there is a secret ingredient hiding in Nines' recipe. If I could tear myself away from my plate, I would slink out the door and down the block to throw myself on the mercy of the new cooking school I noticed. I am a novice. It is obvious why articles have touted Nines as *la mano de*

*Madrid* (the hand of Madrid) and why *Casa Perico* is one of the last bastions of comfort food *madrileño* style in the city.

After lunch, we present a pleased-as-Punch Perico with the photos from our first visit. A diner at the next table kindly offers to take a new one of our foursome and email it to me. All these strangers feel like one happy family as someone else passes me a pen so I can write down Nines' recipe for *scaloppini*.

Finally we are treated to a tour of the back room used for private card games and for hoarding more memories. That is when Perico drops the bomb—he is thinking of retiring. My friend rests against Nines' arm for support. Nines shakes her head; it's obvious that retirement isn't part of her plan. She firmly tells Perico to put away the paintings he has taken out to show us before someone trips over them. Will she always have the last word? We certainly hope so.

© **Andrea Isiminger**

Nothing pleases Andrea Isiminger more than culinary discovery, except perhaps producing a good piece of writing. She was honored to be 2013 winner of Transitions Abroad's Expatriate Writing Contest. In 2012 she contributed to the Writers Abroad anthology *Foreign Encounters*.

# Fifty Minutes and Fifty Seconds *
## by Claudia Landini

It took them fifty minutes and fifty seconds to demolish my neighbours' house. It happened on a bright Tuesday morning that had started off as an ordinary day. The quiet of this peaceful neighbourhood was suddenly broken by machine noise. From my window I saw an unusual number of people walking into my garden. They sat on chairs and stones, as if settling down to watch a movie. My landlord explained that the border police had just demolished a shack where my neighbours kept their tools, and they were now going to tear down the house where part of the family lived.

All this in itself was not unusual: since 1967 under Israeli rule Palestinians have not been allowed to build or extend their premises without a permit from the Israeli government, even if they own the land. Out of 100 permit applications per year, only 5% are accepted. The remaining 95% can chose to reapply, not to build, or build without a permit, which is what most Palestinians do, since families grow, couples get married, children are born, and they must be accommodated somewhere.

My neighbours had built an extension to their home twelve years ago, after waiting ten years for a building permit that never arrived. They were living peacefully in this white stone house facing the Old City of Jerusalem. The old grandfather, an adorable man, worked at the Gethsemane gardens on the Mount of Olives. We often gave him a ride to town, and chatted about his past life and present difficulties. His grandchildren, a bunch of lively and smiling rascals, always greeted me when I passed by their house on my way to town—I usually stopped the car and joked a bit with them, in my few words of Arabic.

When the border police arrived to demolish their home, my neighbours were taken aback. The usual procedure is that a government paper is issued and delivered to the family a few days before demolition, allowing them to empty the house and organize the collection of rubble—if the spot is not cleaned within three days after demolition, they'll have to pay a huge fine. In their case, no paper arrived. They woke up that morning as every other day, not knowing what was in store for them.

From my window I observed the men in yellow and orange fluorescent jackets taking out every item from the house: beds, tables, chairs, a washing machine. Every piece that was set on the ground in front of the house spoke of the family's life—toys children played with, the cradle of the last born, the TV set around which the family gathered at night.

Policemen were everywhere: in front of the house, on the hill, on horses, on foot, in their jeeps, down the road—it was like a war scene. The two bulldozers were parked by the house and they turned the engines on from time to time, as though they were impatient to start the job. Members of the family were talking to the policemen, others were calling the lawyers, others simply sat in my garden, staring ahead. Women cried and children jumped around.

I joined the group in the garden. We stuck together trying to overcome the sense of unreality developing around us: were they really going to demolish the house? Would the family really be without a roof by night? Coffee and coke was distributed, phone calls filled the silence, journalists took pictures.

Then the bulldozers started. Like prehistoric animals they approached the house, and with their long necks started tearing it down piece by piece—the window, the balcony, the main wall. We just watched, powerless. It was like a movie scene, a nightmare, a circle of Dante's inferno. I had to remind myself that this was nothing more than the act of human beings, who also have a house and a family to return to. Men had issued the demolition order, men were manoeuvring the bulldozers. After fifty minutes and fifty seconds the house was no longer there. The bulldozers parked beside the pile of rubble and turned their engines off, bending their necks like animals exhausted after a fight. Everything was silent while the dust settled.

I was shaken to the bone, tears flooded down my face. I, who will most probably never see my house torn to pieces under my children's eyes, was trying to imagine what it must feel like to walk on the rubble of the walls that once contained your joy, your love, your life. I was desperately trying to find a reason for all this, a meaning that could help me come to terms with this overwhelming event.

My neighbours immediately started cleaning up, cutting all the iron bars which dangled sadly where once there were concrete walls, taking out pieces of protruding cement. They worked all night. The morning after, still not wanting to believe what had happened, I took my car and drove past the debris. And there I found the meaning I was looking for. The remaining wall of the house had been cleaned, and decorated with a mirror here, a painting there. A piece of remaining floor now hosted stools and a small table around which men were drinking coffee. A huge Palestinian flag waved in the light breeze. The area around the house was clean and neat. Everything spoke of resilience, resistance, and love. I was overwhelmed by a sense of joy and hope—joy for having crossed such inspiring human beings in my life, hope for a better future. One of the men saw me and stood up. I pulled down my window, smiled, and gave him the thumbs up. He smiled and raised his thumb in return. They destroyed their house, but not their dignity.

© **Claudia Landini**

Claudia Landini is Italian and has lived abroad for 24 years, in Africa and Latin America. She is currently based in Jerusalem. Cross-cultural trainer and coach, she is the founder of www.expatclic.com, an international website for expat women.

# Five Year Itch
## by Christine Nedahl

I gazed at the *finca* lovingly.

The sun tinged the white walls a warm pink, and a light breeze gently swayed the leaves in the surrounding orchard. I sighed. It was perfect but for one thing—Ben had gone. I'd better get used to it. He'd made it clear he'd not be back. How easily five years had slipped by. Would I have been any wiser if I could turn the clock back? Probably not. I gave a wry smile. I first set eyes on him at my twentieth birthday party. Francisco had brought him along to the bar-restaurant in the village. A birthday is always a good excuse for a *fiesta* here in Spain.

'*Él no tiene muchos amigos aquí, Claudia. Es nuevo al pueblo.*'

'*Claro. No hay problema.*'

I'd smiled and lifted my hand to the newcomer.

The night passed in friendly banter. Ben, the new guy, joined in the conversation with his limited Spanish. A few in the group had a smattering of English and the party was a success.

I bumped into Ben two days later in the village shop.

'Like to go for a drink?' he asked and the rest is history, as they say.

Tall, fair-haired Aussie Ben. He'd never lied—told me from the start he wasn't into commitment. Five years older than me, he'd admitted leaving a fiancée behind in Brisbane.

'Wanted to travel, not settle down. Flew to London, did the city, then took the ferry from Dover to Calais. I've been back-packing through France and Spain and here I am, down south.'

I blew on the citronella candle and stood for a while, leaning on the balustrade. It was almost dark and lights were coming on in the scattered houses. There were only a few. The developer had bought the land from my grandparents some years ago, but had built very little. My immediate neighbours to the one side were an elderly Dutch couple. To the other, a young French man and woman—about my age, I guessed. They didn't seem to spend much time together and I heard them arguing on occasion. He went out early in the morning, walking, judging by his boots. Most evenings she drove off and usually got back just as I was locking up for the night.

It didn't bother me too much though. The land and *finca* had been in my *abuelo's* family for generations and when the orchards got too much for him, he'd sold most of the land. Granddad had been savvy enough to keep the *finca* and maintain a good-sized plot around the house. My Spanish father was already working in the city. When he met my English mum, they set up home in the U.K. and that's where I was brought up. I loved my holidays in the sun though. Now I was living in this part of the *campo* where rural charm still existed. The new buildings were in keeping with the Spanish style—small roofs at various angles, abundant chimneys and hidden sun terraces.

Time to go inside. The mosquitos were beginning their nightly rounds. I slapped at my arm as I heard the low droning heralding a bite.

Then all hell broke loose. There was a loud shout next door and then a scream pierced the night air. I froze. Seconds later, the French guy was at his gate, waving and yelling 'Ambulance vite…*glissé sur le carrelage mouillé…*'

I caught 'Ambulance, quick'. My next thought, as I rushed indoors to dial 112, was perhaps I should call the police as well. Had he hit her? I gave the directions to the emergency services but couldn't fill in any details. I went back out, phone in hand, but he'd disappeared.

Taking my first-aid kit, heart in my mouth, I made my way to their villa. Giving myself a mental shake, I strode up the path. I lifted my hand to knock and was almost bowled over by my neighbour rushing out.

'*Merci, venez, elle ne bouge pas.*'

Oh God, let her be alive!

Feeling my heart beating in my throat, I followed him into the kitchen. The woman lay on the floor but thankfully, I saw her eyelids flutter. She gave a low moan but didn't open her eyes. He knelt down beside her, touching her head. There was blood on his shaking hand and he looked at her fearfully.

Using English and a little Spanish, I explained the ambulance would be here soon. He replied in perfect English.

The paramedics, after assessment, proclaimed all vital signs were good but they would admit her for overnight observation.

The man went with her and I made myself a cuppa in the tranquillity of my own home.

The following morning there was a gentle tap on my door. I must have forgotten to lock the gate. He stood there, quite dishevelled, but smiling. I shook his outstretched hand.

'*Je suis Jacques.*'

'Claudia,' I responded.

'It is a good morning, is it not? Amélie is fine. The knock to her head when she slipped made her *inconsciente* but no permanent damage. I warn her always about the wet tiles but still she cleans and walks before they are dry.'

I nod.

'I'm so glad. Is she home?'

'*Oui*. She asks if you would come to tea—just tea and cake. Her head still hurts a little but she wishes to thank you.

I hesitated. He looked straight at me. His smile was in his dark eyes and I found myself agreeing.

'At four then.'

What was I thinking? He kept popping into my head throughout the day. I could hear that cute French accent and see those curls of black hair trailing over his collar. I made a note to self—once tea was over—to keep my distance.

I liked Amélie and still do. We see each other most days. We go to town shopping or pop to the village for coffee or a glass of wine.

Jacques and I were married within the year and she's a wonderful help with Louis and Élodie, the babies.

Amélie? Oh, she's his twin sister.

© **Christine Nedahl**

Christine Nedahl is a member of Writers Abroad. She has been published in four anthologies and online. She has two novels written both of which are in that ethereal state called 'editing'.

# Flat hunting
## by Jennifer Fell

The glow from the street light turns the snow in the street a cloudy yellow. Next to the light, fixed to the building wall is a small square sign with the number 38 inside.

'This is the house number.' Nick says.

'I thought you said 28?' He looks in his notebook.

'Oh right, yes, 28.' We are at the wrong house. A couple trudges past us carrying shopping bags, the wind shuffles the hem of my ankle length coat. My Doc Marten boots are unsuitable for my new life in the St. Petersburg winter and are soaked through.

'Come on then,' I say. We walk another block to the end of the street. 'There is no 28.' The numbers stop at 32. 'What time are we meant to meet Olga?'

'Fifteen minutes ago.' His beanie comes off and hands run through his hair. 'Shit.'

'Nick, this is the wrong street. Did you say *Podolskaya*? This is *Pokrovskaya*.' We barely know one other and this is not the first time we have been lost tonight. Thrown together we are, the only two students to remain in the city after the finish of our teaching course. I get out my map. 'I can't make out anything.' I shrug. A youth struts past, skinny jean legs and a jaunty step, his hands in the pockets of his leather bomber jacket. Nick calls out.

'*Molodoi Chelovek*!' Young man! Bemusement spills from the young man's warm eyes. '*Ulitsa Podoloskaya? Gde??*' Where is it? He crooks a finger toward us. We follow him around the corner. We thank him and he disappears down the street into the darkness. Nick finds the doorway of number 28 and presses the intercom.

'Allo? Nicholai?' They are expecting us.

'*Da.*' Yes, Nick replies. 'It's Nicolai.' He smirks.

'*Tretti Etazh*, Nicolai.' Third floor. The intercom plays its short melody; we haul open the door.

The stairs smell of beer and dogs, concrete and dust. We are on our way to meet Olga, an 'independent' real estate agent. She has no office as such, all she has is a mobile phone she can barely use and contacts around the city to let her know when an apartment comes on the market. As soon as one of the school secretaries put Olga onto us, she was calling non-stop day and night and even in the middle of class. 'Where do you want to live? Centre ok? What about *Vasilevsky*? *Vasilevsky* cheaper, only worry is the bridges but that is only in Summer. You'll party anyway in Summer, I know! On the Petrograd side? How much can you spend? Can you spend a little bit more?'

Halfway up the first flight of stairs, Nick's phone is ringing again.
   'Olga? We're coming now, we are right outside.' A pause. 'Where are you? Olga? ...' Nick's voice trails off as his Russian fails. Our eyes meet. 'Can I call you back?' He hangs up and walks towards me.
   'What's going on?'
   'That was Olga, our agent. She's at her house. I'm not even sure I know the Olga in this apartment.' He smiles. Lovely all-American sports boy teeth.

The doorbell pings. The padded grey security door opens. It's one of the young teachers from our school. Another Olga. She's wearing glasses and her hair in a bun. I have seen her around. Someone from school must have given her Nick's number.
   'Olga?' Nick and I say together.
   'Hi! Come in. I have a great flat for you.' Olga is standing in a small entrance way. Behind her, another lady is standing. A lady with grey wispy hair, wearing a brown coat and slippers is holding out coat hangers. As Nick hands his coat to her, his phone rings. He looks at it. 'It's Olga again. The other one.'

The Olga standing next to me takes Nick by the elbow.
   'Nick, don't answer it. Come see this apartment. This is Galina, your landlady.' To me, she pronounces the word in Russian, slowly. *Hozhyaika*. We are stopped here while we listen to Nick tell Olga on the phone that yes, we are still looking. No we haven't found something yet. Where are we now? Looking at an apartment! I can't come away now. I'll call you back Olga. He ends the call and we move across to the kitchen.

Galina sits behind the kitchen table on one side of the L-shaped bench. The table is fixed to the floor and we slide in on the other side of the table. Olga sits opposite us on a stool. Mirrors are fixed behind us on the walls, and behind Olga there is a small sink, cupboards, a fridge and an oven. An oven! Olga takes the boiling tea kettle off the stove and brings it to the bench. Cups and saucer sets are moved around the table in a ballet until one lands in front of each of us. From a packet of *Neferti*-Tea, she measures two spoons out into the teapot. Olga places foil wrapped *confetki* toffees into a bowl. '*Kushaite*!'

Eat! She says, as Galina smiles at us with closed lips. 'Help yourself.' I pluck a pink one and unwrap it.

'How many bedrooms?' I ask.

'Two,' Olga says and points down the hallway. On the walls, a portrait of Peter the Great stares down at me. There's a vase of plastic flowers on a corner shelf halfway up the wall. 'This is a lovely area. Quiet but close to the metro. Five minutes and you are in the centre. Right away but here is much cheaper.' Galina nods. I am not sure how much she understands. Once Olga is gone, how will we communicate with her?

'How much?' Nick says, popping a *confetki* into his mouth.

Olga turns to Galina and asks how much she wants for the apartment. Galina hasn't said a word yet, but now she and Olga are muttering away with a fair bit of nodding. 'Fifteen thousand roubles,' Olga announces.

'Fifteen thousand,' Nick repeats. I convert this to Australian dollars. It's a lot for an unemployed trainee teacher but I have a credit card. We finish our tea and look around the apartment. There's carpet in the toilet again. A bath. The flat is mostly clean, but there is no washing machine. I ask Olga about getting one.

'Galina? *Stiralnaya Machina?*'

Olga says that Galina has one and will bring it next week.

'It's a nice apartment isn't it?' Olga says to me as I am looking out the bedroom windows to the *produkti* below. The falling snow catches the light outside, the windows are taped up to keep out draughts and there are radiators in each of the rooms. In one of the rooms, there is a square green armchair. Nick tells me he has read about them before. There's a sticker on the wood underneath CCCP, the Russian for USSR. Together he and Olga turn it into a single bed.

'Genius,' Nick says. He lies down.

We go back to the kitchen table and sign the contract. There is a copy in English but we sign the one in Russian.

'It's totally the same,' Olga reassures us. We don't argue but I read it anyway. Galina says she has to leave the city tonight to be back at her country place in the morning. Can we pay tonight? Nick and I have to go the Citibank ATM near the *Vasileostrovskaya* Metro where we withdraw thousands of roubles on our visa cards. Nick has to try two cards before he finds one with enough credit. We walk through an arcade, past the cigarette and beer kiosks, the chemist, the shop selling only dairy products, the second hand bookshop that is still open at 9pm and the hardware shop. As we pass the bakery selling *khachipuri* cheese bread and sour cream buns, Nick says to me, 'I guess you're not using that return ticket home now, are you?'

'Nope,' I reply.

After we give 15,000 roubles to Galina for rent and another 15,000 for a bond and yet another 15,000 to Olga for introducing us, our tea is long cold. Before Olga leaves, she gives Galina Nick's phone number and rings it to make sure it works. We expect to see Olga around our school over the next few weeks, but we never run into her again.

We move our belongings in the next day. Before I leave I ask my landlady-*babushka* where I have been staying for my first month what *Vasilevsky* Island is really like.

'Alright,' she says. 'I have a friend there.' I pay her my rent money and pack my bags. I sit on the bed, covered with her childhood doll collection and her handmade quilt. Marsik, her round orange cat wanders in to inspect the window. I sit and cry. Where these tears are coming from? I'm tired these days. The darkness, the snow, I'm not used to it.

'Is it that man?' My landlady asks. 'The American? If you don't like this man, don't move there.'

'I signed already, I paid my money.' She sits down.

'You can stay here.'

'Thanks,' I say, 'But I need my own place.' My landlady doesn't understand this. Instead of explaining, I tell her, 'It's cheaper there.'

'Do you have your own room?'

'Yes.'

'Okay.' She raises her hand. 'Don't cook and clean for him. He's just your friend.' I wipe my tears away and shoulder my backpack. A trolleybus and a metro ride later, I am coming up the escalator at *Vasileostrovskaya* metro. From my new favourite bakery, I buy a warm *khachipuri*. Nick is moving the furniture around. I will take the monastic single bed and he, dreaming of the company he hopes to keep, chooses the sofa bed which converts to a double. A wedge of cheese, a loaf of black bread and a deck of playing cards are on the kitchen table. As I stow the vase of plastic flowers in a cupboard and stick the kettle on for tea, I notice that our kitchen has no window.

© **Jennifer Fell**

Jennifer Fell is a writer from rural Australia. She has lived in St. Petersburg, Russia, working as an English teacher and writing for a local travel guide. She returned home in 2010. She has also lived in Japan and Vietnam.

# Floating World *
## by Chris Galvin

In the flood plains and waterways of the Mekong Delta, life moves along the water. At Long Xuyên, we climbed into a low wooden boat crowded with child-sized plastic stools. With room for only eight seats, the boatman operating the long-tailed outboard motor sat cross-legged on a plank and I was happy to sit on the prow, looking out over the river.

Terri and I had arrived in Việt Nam a few days before. I would eventually move here but for now, I was a traveller, visiting the country with my niece.

Gliding between tall stands of water spinach, we passed homes on stilts over patches of built-up land, women scrubbing clothing in the river and women harvesting the water spinach. Their row boats obscured under bundles of green, they appeared to float on rafts of vegetation.

Wooden cargo boats with eyes painted on their prows crossed our path, laden with everything from sand to fruits I didn't recognize. Houseboats with potted plants decorating their gunwales chugged through islands of water hyacinth. Dogs stood on the bows leaning into the wind, noses held high like noble mascots, while laundry fluttered from clotheslines above them.

Hiếu, an American friend visiting family in Việt Nam, had invited us along on a trip through the delta with several of his friends. He pointed and the boatman guided our vessel towards a tiny, man-made island. We clambered up the bank onto a rectangle of land with a pond in its middle. A path led us all the way around from the wooden stilt house on one corner, through groves of miniature papaya trees heavy with fruit, past feathery carrot tops and patches of basil and coriander. Ducks and chickens scattered before us.

A burst of shouting drew my attention to a platform on stilts over the pond, where two men scooped up fish feed pellets with dinner plates. The water roiled with expectant fish that erupted in flashing silver when the men jerked the plates like Frisbees, launching the pellets in a wide arc over the water.

In the dark, cool interior of the two-room house, we sat cross-legged on polished floor boards. Hiếu cracked jokes and shredded a yellow-skinned chicken and purple banana blossoms for salad. The hostess rolled vermillion cubes of blood pudding in rice. Terri and I shelled snails, and Terri, grimacing and pretending to eat one, asked me to snap a photo. We ate slowly, finishing off one dish while preparing the next, and washing it all down with beer. Except for the rice, everything we ate had been grown or raised right outside the house.

I admired their self-sufficiency—something I'd long aspired to—but the simplicity of their lifestyle belied the hardships of life in the delta. Our hostess said the annual monsoons sometimes put up to half the delta under water, washing away crops, animals and roads, and keeping her children home from school. In the dry season, the river level falls so low that seawater pushes into the plains, the increased salinity kills off rice crops and even the mangroves that protect the land from the sea, and there isn't enough fresh drinking water.

I asked about the dike systems. Hiếu explained that though necessary, they also reduce soil fertility and increase water pollution and mosquitoes. Closer to the coastline, the dikes keeping the sea out of the freshwater canals are often washed away.

I later learned that the Mekong Delta, barely above sea level, is one of the eight areas in the world affected by sea rise from climate change. Every year, families along the shrinking coastline lose their homes to erosion, and many are too poor to move to safer areas.

After dinner, the family hugged my niece and I like old friends. 'Come back any time,' they said. 'Hiếu's friends are always welcome.' They stood waving while our boatman pushed us away from shore.

Streaks of orange merged into dusk as Terri and I purchased fresh rice papers, herbs, pork slices and dipping sauce. We sat in our hotel room rolling the rice papers around the fillings. I heard no other guests save a resident gecko that chirped while we ate.

We sank into sleep, only to be jolted awake by loud music and an off-key voice. Kept awake by the noise, I watched the gecko on the ceiling and thought about the people I'd eaten dinner with, how the water that surrounded them was their livelihood, their most valuable resource, and their greatest foe. I wondered if I had what it took to live in the delta, and what kind of work I could get if I did. A year later, I would be offered a job teaching ESL at Long Xuyên University, but decide instead to live in Huế, in the central region.

In the morning, I stood on the verandah, gazing at the sunlit canal. Hiếu emerged from his room.

'Were you able to sleep?' I asked.

He nodded. 'I had a wonderful sleep.'

I mentioned the music.

'Yes, it's a karaoke hotel. People rent rooms on the first floor for drinking and singing. Are you and Terri ready for breakfast before continuing south?'

On the outskirts of the city, a man in a blue apron stood grilling meat. Down the road, the river sparkled. As soon as we sat down, the man placed plates of *cơm sườn nướng* on our tiny sidewalk table. Terri frowned at her rice topped with a sizzling pork chop and a fried egg. 'That doesn't look like breakfast.'

I savoured the smoky pork. 'One of the best breakfasts I've ever had,' I said, but the next morning I'd find a new favourite breakfast at a different bend in the river. Wherever we were in the delta, the water was never far away, but the scent of grilling pork or the crunch of chicken and banana blossom salad will always bring me back to Long Xuyên.

## © Chris Galvin

Chris Galvin is a writer, editor and photographer living in Việt Nam and Canada. Her work has appeared in various anthologies and literary journals, including Descant, PRISM International, Asian Cha, and the 2012 Writers Abroad anthology, *Foreign Encounters*.

# Flowers for the Lady
## by Susmita Bhattacharya

'I'll marry you one day.'

Veeru chased her across the courtyard. She stuck her tongue out. 'I don't want to. You're too fat.'

Veeru slowed down. She vanished, flinging the string of jasmine he'd got her on the ground. He pressed the flowers inside his heavy maths book and entered her house. Most boys from the village went to Professor Sanyal for maths tuition. He had the reputation of making successful men out of boys. He also had great aspirations for Veeru, for he was smarter than the rest. He didn't know of Veeru's ambition to make his daughter, Shalini, his bride.

Shalini who could outrun most boys and skim pebbles furthest across the river, whose mental maths skills surpassed those of her father's students, who always wore jasmine in her hair and chewed her nails down to the skin.

Sometimes he'd get her a string of jasmine, sometimes a stolen mango from the orchards behind the house. She'd laugh and run. But later, on his way home, a mango-stone would come skimming down from a tree followed by laughter soaked with the sweetness of the stolen fruit.

Veeru grew up and lost interest in the professor's daughter. He had exams to sit, a career to make, a bride to find, parents to please; those lazy summer days in the tutor's garden brought only an indulgent smile on his face. Shalini grew up too. She was not a temptress anymore. She was now too dark to be attractive. Too thin to be fertile. Too intelligent to be a home-maker. Veeru returned home on holiday from his London-based job. His parents had lined up six suitable girls for him to inspect. If he accepted, there would be a wedding that summer. He went to pay his respects to his old tutor. He was told that Shalini was in Oxford, studying chemistry and maths.

So girl selected, Veeru returned to England. He landed outside Shalini's door one winter morning with a string of jasmine in his pocket. Just to tease her, he thought. She let him into her tiny bedsit. It smelled of stale cigarette. Her eyes were darker and her smile tighter. Her hair was chopped into little spikes poking out of her scalp, tinted deep red. She smoked constantly and talked of experiments and her thesis. She was having an affair with a professor, she told him. He told her of his upcoming marriage. She laughed and asked, so you don't want to marry me anymore?

In the morning, when Shalini wakes up, she will turn on the radio and call her lover; hang up when his wife answers the phone. She will light her cigarette and drink strong coffee. Then she will discover a familiar fragrance. From another world. Another lifetime. And she will find, tucked under the cushions, a string of jasmine. Wilted. Broken. But still with a promise of its heady fragrance.

© **Susmita Bhattacharya**

Susmita Bhattacharya grew up in India, but now lives in Plymouth. She received an M.A. in Creative Writing from Cardiff University and has had several short stories published. Her debut novel *Crossing Borders* will be published in 2014 by Parthian. http://susmita-bhattacharya.blogspot.co.uk

# Flying Low *
## by Nina Croft

These days, I'm just a little bit scared of flying. I tend to pick an aisle seat so I can make a run for it (not quite sure where I'd run). And at the back, because I've read that's the bit most likely to survive a crash. I can trace my fear of flying (and actually any form of moving unnaturally fast) back to a mini-bus crash on the island of Zanzibar. But I wasn't always so scared.

I'd been working in London a couple of years after qualifying as an accountant, when I realized I was bored and in need of adventure. So I volunteered (along with my other half) and we soon found ourselves living in a remote village, Munyama, on the banks of Lake Kariba, in Zambia.

Lake Kariba is a spectacularly beautiful area formed when the Zambezi river, which divides Zambia from Zimbabwe, was damned in the 1950s. We'd signed on to work with a local charity, helping the Tonga people, who'd been displaced when their homes were flooded.

The charity was run by a white Zambian couple, Ginny and Leo, who had a deep connection to the area and its people.

Leo was tall, lanky, and charismatic, with wavy black hair and blue eyes. It was rumoured he'd run wild in his youth, and spent his time hunting and roaming the bush with the locals. Later he'd met Ginny and found religion (they were Quakers) and together they'd set up the charity.

But I suspect the wildness still lurked in Leo's character. It needed some sort of outlet, and that came in the form of flying. Leo was crazy about flying.

When we first arrived, he was putting the finishing touches to a plane he had built from a kit—a small two-seater. Think Airfix models, but on a somewhat larger scale. I'm pretty sure there were elastic bands involved, and if you looked closely at the front wheel it read: *wheelbarrow tyre - not to exceed 7 km per hour.*

Leo's brother-in-law was a pilot with Zambia Airways, and he helped get the necessary paperwork through—not easy, as at that time, the borders between Zambia and Zimbabwe were still a restricted zone (after the Zimbabwean war of Liberation) and permission was required from the Zambian air force to fly in the area.

Leo purchased a bulldozer and flattened a section of lakeshore for a runway, put up a makeshift windsock, and he was ready to fly.

And he wanted to share his pleasure.

Today, I would have to be dragged kicking and screaming into that tiny little plane, but back then, I went along with a grin. I'm not saying I wasn't scared, but it was also thrilling, soaring over the lake with the fish eagles, flying high up toward the African plateau. In retrospect, I believe Leo had a sense of fatalism. A 'What will be, will be' attitude. He believed that God would look after him.

Landing was a problem, as runways were in short supply. Leo occasionally made use of the roads around town, and the locals learned to be wary and keep their eyes not only on the road ahead, but also on the sky above.

The plan was to use the plane to visit the communities along the lake, but once in the bush, there were no roads to use as makeshift runways. Football pitches, present in every African village, were the obvious alternative, but there turned out to be a small (actually pretty huge) problem in the form of termite mounds. The footballers were quite happy to dodge them during play, but they would have proved fatal to the poor plane. The goal posts didn't help either.

Leo's next plan was floats, which would enable him to land on the water. Unfortunately, the shallows of Lake Kariba are littered with the petrified remains of old Mopani trees, drowned when the Lake was filled. Naked trunks and branches, loitered treacherously along the shoreline. So floats were ruled out.

Undaunted, Leo considered the problem. He still wanted to fly, and so he took himself off to South Africa for a six-week intensive course, and arrived back in the prettiest little helicopter I've ever seen. A bright yellow Robinson two-seater.

The helicopter was much easier to land and Leo flew me on many business trips to the local communities. Though it's fair to say, the helicopter wasn't always a popular sight with the locals. On approach, we would invariably spot the women scurrying out to save their washing from the cloud of dust that always accompanied our landings.

Of course, the helicopter had its limitations. It could only carry two people whereas the boats we usually used to visit would carry ten. But all the same, it was a wonderful experience.

One of images I will always retain from our time on Lake Kariba is sitting beside Leo in his yellow helicopter, my knuckles white, the hot dusty air blowing through the open doorways (Leo had removed the doors, as he claimed it made him feel like we were really flying.) Skimming low across the water, the setting sun, a huge crimson ball, sinking below the mountains, silhouetting the black skeletons of the drowned trees as they clawed up to the sky.

We left Lake Kariba after three years, not to go home, but to move to another project two hundred miles to the north. About a year after we'd left, we heard the tragic news that Leo had been killed. He'd been flying a microlight. I like to think he died doing something he loved.

© **Nina Croft**

Nina Croft grew up in the north of England. She travelled extensively when younger, but has now settled to a life of writing and picking almonds in the mountains of Southern Spain. Meet with her at www.ninacroft.com

## Foreign Soil **
### by Jonathan Elsom

I'm tempted still to dig
beneath the soil and check the roots
of my transplanted life,
examining like some new plant
these carefully nurtured tendrils
in hope they'll one day give
fresh vigour to my softly dwindling years.
I'd made a pact when first I quit
those distant British shores
that not a backward glance would I allow,
no wistful thoughts, no snatched regrets,
no dwelt-in dreams of what I'd left behind.
And for a time these glittering sands,
blue denim skies, and endless sun-bleached days
washed clinging memories away,
supplanting them with pristine summer joys
and tempting me to say –
this new life's all I need.
But now those deeper roots which all unknown
lay dormant down the years,
have sent faint tremors through life's loam,
awakening buried, long hidden dreams.
I yearn for sodden skies,
crisp frosted dawns, and huddled winter days,
red double-deckers and the misty Thames,
bare flinty beaches and deserted piers,
and wonder, as I bask on Bondi sands
through constant summers in my new found land,
if this old plant can ever really
flower in foreign soil?

## © Jonathan Elsom

Following a successful 40 year acting career in the UK, Jonathan settled in Sydney Australia in 2000. He has continued to appear in theatre and TV while his short stories and poetry have been published in the UK, US, and Australia.

# Going Native
## by Susan Carey

Cor rolled up his knee-length shorts, unbuckled his sandals and stripped off his socks before running into the lake. The shallow, lapping water cooled him in the tropical afternoon. Shoals of tiny fish darted around his legs and damsel flies skimmed over the water's dark surface. A burst of chatter came from the shore. A bunch of barefooted Indonesian children were sniffing around his stuff. One of them tossed the sandals to his chums and waved the socks back and forth above his head, as if they were flags. The others threw back their heads and laughed. Cor shook his fist and sloshed through the water in pursuit of the boys, but they disappeared into the mangrove's shadow. A butcherbird flew overhead and squawked, joining in the derision.

Cor ran towards the trees, but as the sweat gushed off him he thought better of it. Good riddance, he thought, who needs socks and sandals anyway. It was a ridiculous school rule that he had to obey. It was just his bad luck that his dad was home on leave, so he'd probably get a hiding for losing part of his school uniform. Soon enough he forgot his cares, relishing the freedom of walking barefoot along the dirt track and stopping every so often, to wiggle his liberated toes.

The maid, Rikki, was sweeping the veranda floor. She beckoned to him as he walked up the steps. Pointing at his feet, she put her index finger against her lips and shushed. She took his hand and they went up the stairs to the linen cupboard and she found him some clean socks. Cor got his brown lace-ups from his room and put them on, going along with the charade. If his father hadn't been home, none of this would have been necessary. He clunked downstairs, missing the freedom of bare-soles and sat in the cane chair on the veranda.

Music drifted from the bungalow window. Tante Leen singing, *Diep in Mijn Hart*. Cor's mum often played the record on the wind-up gramophone before dinner. In the garden his sister, Gerda, picked a hibiscus flower and put it behind her ear. She waltzed around with an imaginary dance partner. Why are sisters so utterly ridiculous, Cor asked himself. If he had a brother they could be playing football or pretending they were knights and having jousting matches, not dancing to soppy Dutch songs. He stood up and grabbed the broom Rikki had left on the veranda. He tiptoed down the steps, watching his sister all the time. She was lost in her own fantasy world. Cor squatted down behind the rhododendron bush. He wriggled through its branches and just as Gerda danced by, he stuck out the broom handle. She stumbled but managed to save herself by grabbing the edge of a garden table. He quickly withdrew the broomstick and crouched very still while Gerda looked on the ground for whatever had made her falter. Cor extricated himself from the bush, dusted off a few spare leaves, crept back up the steps and sat down in the chair as if nothing had happened.

From the kitchen wafted a smell that turned Cor's stomach. Vomity sock smell. A while back he'd thrown up over his feet at school and tossed the sick-soaked socks in the back of the cupboard when he'd got home. A few months later he'd found them and the smell reminded him of the food he loathed. Caul-ee-flower, even the word left a bitter taste in his mouth. What kind of people lived in Holland where his father sailed to? And why did they eat a blubbery vegetable that looked like the pickled monkey brain the biology teacher had showed them, worst of all, why on earth did his father have to bring it back and insist on sharing it with them?

He banished the vegetable's wet paper taste from his memory and imagined the smell of peanut butter sauce and sizzling pork coming from the barbecue. They always ate Indonesian dishes when Father was away at sea. Mother was learning how to use all the vegetables and spices from their maid, Rikki. Cor adored the sweet and spicy tastes of the colourful dishes they prepared. Those cooking smells were in Rikki's clothes and inhaling her scent when she read him a Malay bedtime story, made him hungry.

'Dinner!' Rikki called. Cor sat down at the mirror-surfaced dining table. Rikki had kindly given him a small portion of the offending vegetable. His father sat at the head in his white Captain's uniform. In between bites, he cast a proprietorial glance over his family. Mother arranged her napkin over her oyster-coloured gown. Gerda chewed daintily like a lamb eating grass for the first time and gazed into the middle distance, the hibiscus flower starting to wilt behind her ear.

'I suppose you think that looks pretty?' Cor asked.

Gerda looked at him as if he was something dirty she'd found under her shoe. 'Your opinion is of no interest to me, little brother.'

'Stop it you two. Eat the food in front of you and don't start one of your silly arguments,' their mother said.

Cor ate his meat and potatoes but carefully left a neat pile of cauliflower on his plate. He put his knife and fork together. 'May I be excused?' he asked.

'Not until you've finished, boy.' His father nodded towards the cauliflower.

Cor put a tiny bit in his mouth, chewed it briefly then spat it out on his plate.

'Cornelis, how dare you treat good food like that!' His father's chair scraped over the wooden floor as he stood up. He grabbed Cor's scruff and pulled him from the table. As he was dragged past, Cor yanked the flower and a lock of his sister's hair for good measure.

After being frogmarched along the corridor, he was shoved in the cupboard under the stairs. Then came the familiar sound of the door slamming shut behind him, followed by the key turning in the lock. 'I'll deal with you later!' His father said.

Cor sneezed. It was dusty in the broom cupboard. The dark never bothered him much and anyway, some light filtered in through the slatted door. He lay down and rested his head on the scratchy pile of picnic blankets. Perhaps if he was very quiet his father would forget all about him and go back to his ship.

He fell asleep but was awakened by his sister whispering through the slatted door. 'Won't be long now, little brother, Daddy's going back to the ship this evening but before that he's going to give you such a belting!' Her breath whirled the dust motes that hovered in the air. Cor sat on his haunches, wrapped his arms around his body and hugged his knees to his chest. Something scrambled over his shoe. He screamed, stood up and rammed the sole of his foot against the door. Silence. Then, from the dining room, the sound of the gramophone record again. He imagined his sister waltzing across the wooden floor. He longed to be there, and really trip her up this time. Why didn't she ever get punished for anything? What was so precious about Little Miss Goody-Two-Shoes?

Footsteps echoed along the corridor towards the broom cupboard: military boots clicking in a steady, authoritative rhythm. Cor pictured his father in his white linen uniform and the minute spats of blood that had stained his neatly pressed trousers after the last misdemeanour. His heart thumped a jungle rhythm and his mouth went dry. The key turned slowly and there stood his sister, a wide grin on her face, her spindly legs looking ridiculous in their father's huge boots. Cor slammed the door back and with both hands, pushed his sibling over. She stumbled backwards, tried to save herself against a marble-topped table but her head cracked against it and she hit the floor. Blood spilled out like a soft-boiled yolk. Mother ran from the drawing room and squatted down next to her daughter. She cradled Gerda's head as blood gushed from the wound. Looking up at her son, she shook her head and let out a wail that filled the house, echoed across the island and shattered the dark silence of the mangrove.

© **Susan Carey**

Originally from Herefordshire, England, Susan currently lives in Amsterdam and teaches business English. She writes short stories, flash-fiction, poetry and the occasional novel. Some of her work has been published online and in print. Visit her blog at
http://amsterdamoriole.wordpress.com

# High Noon
## by John Dickson

ROME, August 1960, 12:00 noon, 40° C and rising.

The city quiet, as anyone with any sense escapes from the heat into the shade of a *ristorante*, or seeks refuge under the awning of a pavement cafe. The distant roar of traffic fades away as others hurry home to start their long siesta.

But not us: three English students—mad dogs who know no better—cramming in the sights during our short holiday. No time to waste.

We turn the corner into the long road toward the Colosseum. The pavement stretches away into the shimmering air above the hot tarmac.

Empty, but not quite. For fifty yards away, a slim young woman walks purposefully ahead. White sandals, white sun-dress, slim, bare arms, blonde hair streaming down her back, a large white handbag swinging from her right hand. A Nordic goddess visiting the ruined temples of her Roman antecedents.

And there, following closely in the standard strategic position, two feet behind her left shoulder, is the inevitable, inescapable, pestering Italian man. They learn it from childhood, whispering blandishments in the ears of foreign women. Eighteen to eighty, it makes no difference. Always prepared to face a hundred rejections for the chance of one brief conquest.

She stops, turns, glares, tries to swat him away like an irritating fly. To no avail: he stands his ground and shrugs.

She turns away. He follows. Whisper, pester. Pester, whisper.

Stop, turn, glare, swat, shrug, and round they go again.

We follow slowly, amateur anthropologists fascinated by this ancient ritual dance which we have seen so many times already. How will it end this time, we wonder? A slight movement hints that Round Three is about to start. But no. Without warning she strikes, pirouetting on her sandalled toes like a champion discus thrower. The handbag, straining outward from her outstretched arm, describes a whirling arc and stuns him with a mighty blow to the head. She turns on her heel and strides away, leaving him gawping in silent amazement.

We roar and cheer, clapping our hands in glee. Celebrating this magnificent revenge on behalf of all the other victims we have seen. She doesn't turn, but fades into the mirage, the handbag swinging gently in her hand again. A swaying twitch of hip and bum is all the recognition we will ever need.

© **John Dickson**

Naval architect, computer scientist, mathematician, global hitch-hiker and expat—two years in Singapore, five years in Kuwait. Would be poet and Zen philosopher. Still working on my autobiography 'Life, the Universe and Everything—a general theory'.

# Home is Where...?
## by Helen Parker

'Cairo is such an assault on the senses,' Josh had written in his blog soon after arriving. He had mentally filed its richness into cerebral recycling bins for future use. He would write poems about the colour, the noise, and the buzz it gave him. Five years ago he'd written a poem for his first girlfriend. She'd giggled, but Josh knew she'd liked it. He enjoyed writing his blog. It made a welcome change from his dissertation.

Josh thought of his blog now, as he stepped out on to the platform with the jostling mass of commuters disgorged by the metro. He liked the metro, despite the shoving, elbowing crowds trying to board before the unforgiving doors slid closed, trapping them or separating them from their family or friends. It was clean, reliable and incredibly cheap. His blog was his way of recording the impressions before they paled, and he hoped his mates back home would read it, too. Especially Emma.

Swept along with those exiting, he emerged from the stuffy, airless heat of the underground into the blazing sun of the dusty street, with its cacophony of car horns, exuberant greetings and the clunk of the gas bottle seller.

Following Ashraf's directions, Josh headed down a side street, where pedestrians vied for space with cars, motor bikes, *tuk-tuks* and donkey carts. Men wearing *galabeyas* and turbans luxuriated in their *shishas* while the warm apple smell mingled with coffee with cardamom, wet fish and *koshari*.

Josh loved *koshari*. It seemed to be the local home food. Easy to make, with rice, pasta, lentils, onions and tomato, it even suited his student budget.

Suddenly he heard someone bellowing his name, and he looked up to see Ashraf waving from a balcony three buildings further down the street. Josh stood and waited for him. Looking around, he suddenly felt conspicuous with his skinny limbs, his probably-too-long blond hair and his jeans designed to reveal the brand of his boxers. He admired the dignified woman walking with such poise, an enormous load balanced on her head. A small, barefoot girl, unafraid, was weaving in and out of the traffic, selling sprigs of mint.

'Hello my friend!' Ashraf embraced Josh warmly with a kiss on each cheek. He linked arms with Josh. Familiar, now, with the physical contact between men, Josh allowed himself to be propelled towards the flat. Ashraf apologized, 'We live on eighth floor. No lift. You OK?'

'Sure,' Josh replied, and followed his friend up the stairs.

'This my home,' Ashraf said finally, with a measure of pride. 'And this Heba, my wife.'

A young woman emerged from the flat. Josh could tell she was pretty, although her headscarf hid her hair and neck. The beautiful blue floor-length robe, intended to conceal her shape and preserve her modesty, failed to disguise an elegant bump. 'Hello. How are you? Welcome in Egypt.'

'Hello,' Josh replied. 'You speak good English.'

Ashraf chuckled. 'That all. She practised special for you. She don't speak English.' He pushed the door wide open. 'Please to come in. *Baytee baytak*—my house, your house.' He led Josh into a tiny seating area. Josh glanced around. There were two chairs with wooden arms, a coffee table and a colourful rug. Heba had already disappeared behind a door, which must be the kitchen. There was only one other door. The bedroom? Was there an en suite bathroom? The very word felt alien here.

'Please to sit down. I am so happy you come my house. Thank you very much.'

'No, no,' Josh remonstrated in faltering Arabic. 'I am very happy to have you as my language helper. Thank you for inviting me. And thank you to Heba.' He gestured towards the door, just as she reappeared with glasses of sweet mint tea. The conversation continued in a mixture of English and Arabic, while Josh tried to come to terms with his surroundings. The tiny flat was sparse but spotless. A selection of unframed family photos was blu-tacked to the wall. Josh delved into his rucksack. At his Arabic teacher's suggestion, he had brought some pictures as conversation starters, and a couple of postcards of Edinburgh, his hometown.

'Who's this?' Josh asked, pointing to one of Ashraf's photos.

'That my brother, Mina and his wife. He have two boys. My nephews. You have brothers?'

'A sister,' Josh replied, producing a photo of Alison, 'And these are my parents.' He handed Ashraf a picture of his mum and dad looking happy and windblown on a walk up Ben Lomond. He slid a picture of his home back into his bag. It wasn't that he lived in a mansion, just a three-bed semi. But the neat front lawn and pretty flowerbed seemed out of place here. He did the same with the photo of Emma. Girlfriend was something of a non-category.

'And these my parents,' Ashraf said, lifting the only framed photo reverently from its hook. The couple looked serious, distinguished and very formal.

'Beautiful,' Josh admired. 'Do they live in Cairo?'

'My mother, yes. She live with my brother, Mina. My father—he dead.'

'Oh, I'm sorry,' Josh murmured.

Ashraf nodded his head briefly in acknowledgement. 'Mina and me, we have tour guide company.'

'Great! How's the company doing?'

'Er—please?'

'I mean, is the company doing well? Is it successful? Do you like the work?'

'Yes, I like. But no, not successful. No tourists come Egypt now. Since the revolution.'

'Hmm.' Josh hadn't thought about that. He'd been a long way from Egypt in January 2011. The Egyptian Uprising had been just another piece of bad news on TV. Tear gas and barricades. Another dictator bit the dust. As wars go, there hadn't been many casualties.

But Ashraf was continuing eagerly, 'That why I want to learn English good. I need good job. Maybe I go Australia.'

'Australia? Why?'

He pointed to another photo. 'This my sister and her husband and her baby. They live in Australia now. This my niece. She have four years now.'

'So you haven't seen her...?'

'No, not never seen her. My sister go Australia five years ago.'

Australia! Josh thought of surfing and kangaroos. Then he thought of Alison. While it was true that sisters could be a pain sometimes, he couldn't begin to imagine not seeing her. She'd made enough fuss when he'd announced he'd be going to Egypt for six months.

The kitchen door opened, and Heba said something to Ashraf. 'She say we eat now.'

'Ah,' Josh said, and managed not to add, 'At last'. He still hadn't got used to eating lunch at 4.30pm. Heba brought in dish after dish of food, until every surface was groaning. He wondered how many more people were coming to lunch.

'Please, help yourself,' Ashraf said, waving a hand at the food.

'But where is Heba going to sit?'

'She eat later,' Ashraf smiled, nodding towards the kitchen door.

Josh hesitated, embarrassed, but Ashraf insisted. There was so much food. Although he'd entered the realm of stir-fries and curries at university, Josh came from a shepherd's-pie-and-apple-crumble sort of home. He didn't know where to start. Ashraf must have sensed it. 'In Egypt, we always prepare much food. Maybe other family members will come.'

'Will they?' Josh asked, not quite understanding.

'Insh-Allah. If God wills,' Ashraf said, piling his plate high.

Josh ate as much as he could, in appreciation of his hostess' hard work, and remembered finally to leave a morsel on his plate to indicate that he had finished. The conversation returned to family. 'What about Heba? Does she have brothers and sisters?' Josh asked.

Ashraf took another photo from the wall, unsticking it carefully and wiping the dust off with his hand. 'This Heba's brother. He dead in Egyptian revolution.'

Josh gasped and stared at the picture of a smart, handsome, confident-looking young man. 'You see,' Ashraf continued, still holding the photo and looking earnestly at Josh, 'I want to learn English good so we can go Australia, but Heba's mother, she not want. She said she lost one child. She not want to lose another. I understand, but there no future here for me and Heba and our child.' Ashraf had lost his warm, welcoming smile. Now his face was full of pain, and Josh's thoughts were in turmoil.

But Ashraf hadn't finished. 'No justice here. If robbers come, who can help us? No police. Now, neighbours not trust neighbours. In the past in Cairo, everyone help everyone. Now, what will happen? No future here for us.'

'But... but, when I arrived everyone was so friendly and helpful to me. You especially. In the street...'

'In the street,' Ashraf interrupted, 'men on motorbikes steal women bags. Heba afraid go out now. In the street, people very rude. Only want money. Not proud of Egypt now. No justice for football fans who dead at Port Said. Government want big rent, impossible for poor people. No money for doctors. If my child sick, how I pay? How can we live here?'

Ashraf's fixed stare seemed to bore into Josh. At every memory of how lucky he was, Josh felt embarrassed. The accident of his birth had predetermined his lifestyle, but a stinging arrow of guilt pierced his thinking. His British passport, his bank accounts in England and Egypt, his university course and his plans to travel again next summer—the security of his home, he had always taken them all for granted. Each red-hot arrow stung more fiercely than the last.

'Come on to the balcony. The sun is finishing,' Ashraf invited him. Josh took his camera from his rucksack and they went outside. The street noise was muted at this height, and the motion less insistent. Sunset was only minutes away. There was no dusk. Heba came out, and the three of them stood in silence, watching the fiery red ball slide beyond the horizon, and the muddle of ill-sorted buildings become silhouettes in the pink glow. Day ended, night began, while living, dying, fighting, loving, hoping and despairing continued in the city's organised chaos.

## © **Helen Parker**

Helen Parker has just returned home to Scotland after teaching English in Cairo for nearly five years. Addicted to words, she also made a stab at learning Arabic, joined a book group and facilitated a writing group.

# Home James
## by Peter Hawkins

'But that's the thing about foreign languages...'

James is on his second pint at 6pm, the late-spring sun setting behind the lip of the valley, burning the horizon's edge like paper.

'You never learn a foreign language. Every bit you learn becomes familiar, so by its nature it's not foreign any more.'

I'd not seen him in three years, but here he is, the author of his online adventures, sitting in front of me. He's avoiding that weight that starts to gather in your mid 30s. Neither of us knows how long he's staying. We grew up nearby: me in Moreton, just one kilometre away, but at the top of the hill, and he in Sledgeton, three kilometres of flat stumble along the green-flanked banks of the Severn.

'It's like when you dream in another language. You don't really realise it's another language, unless you can remember an exact phrase. It's only the Brits, well, maybe the Yanks and Irish, that get in a tangle over different languages. To most people on the planet it's pretty normal to speak a few.'

'What do you dream about?'

'Dunno.'

We are in the riverside beer garden of the White House, a partially-timbered pub inexplicably painted red by the new owners eight months ago. Having survived the winter both in terms of trade (snow and ice didn't render the valley inaccessible) and flooding (the defences channelling the weight of the water towards less critical farmland), the new wooden tables and benches are receiving their first patrons. The air is cooling quickly, but the sky above the valley is still bright and scored with silent contrails. In the lower shadows of the surrounding leafy hills, bats and birds are swapping shifts.

'Do they have Wi-Fi here?' asks James.

'Sure. Password's on the ashtray.'

The new owners also installed the Wi-Fi, ending the pub's reputation as shield against modern day communications. James sets his phone on the table and ignores it as it buzzes repeatedly with the first gush of messages from the open pipe.

'So, where next? No. Actually. Where've you been?' I ask.

'Sort of alternating between Burma and Bangkok.'

I have only vague knowledge of these places. I picture monks, the army and prostitutes.

'Nice,' I say—but it's more of a question on my part.

He draws his arms around himself, muttering about the cold and gives in to the obvious urge to pick up his phone.

'It's midnight' he says, lifting his head from the phone to argue with the still-blue sky, 'I'm getting all the drunk messages.'

He chuckles to himself a couple of times.

'Jesus,' he says and shows me a picture of a snake by a wall. 'My friend Vanna found this in his kitchen today. It was trying to escape the floods.'

'So, what is it you do in all these places?'

'Freelance work for NGOs.'

'Like...?'

'Some marketing, cross-promotional stuff, greasing the wheels.'

'That doesn't make me feel like my charity money is going to the people in need.'

'Rest assured it isn't. They'll keep those countries dependent for as long as they can. What else would they do? They're like multinationals with better PR.'

'Like you?'

'Well, I can't take all the credit.'

Conversations with James were often like this, be it in real life or in fleeting online exchanges. Late-evening became midnight, charities became parasites, foreign became familiar. This evening we don't have a lot of time. Debs leaves for the night shift at the hospital in an hour and I still have to pick up Laura from her gran's. She's offered to look after her for a couple of hours while I'm at the pub. Laura's only 14 months and we're careful not to impose too much on 'Gran'. It makes these last-minute appeals much easier.

'Good to be back?'

'Feels weird. Like I'm a spaceman without a ship.'

'What about going back to France? You were raving about it a few years back.'

'France can go fuck itself. I'm done with the attitude.'

I smile, remembering him gesticulating his appreciation about the French take-it-or-leave-it, don't-give-a-fuck attitude. He remembers it too.

'It's like that Italian writer, Calvino? Invisible Cities. You start off staring at the tops of magnificent buildings, by the end you're just looking at the gutter, and there's a lot of dog shit to watch out for in Nice. 'Course in Asia you need to watch where you're going all the time all or you'll fall down some uncovered manhole, or get hit by some guy driving on the pavement.'

I finally get around to it. 'How's your dad?'

'Not good. He never was after mum died. The last 15 months, the cough's got worse. He's given up... It's not if, but when, and I think when will be soon.'

'I'm sorry.'

James looks straight at me. He's upset, but I know it's not to do with his dad. It's a nostalgic hurt. He's remembering my dad. We were both 16 when he died. I honestly think it marked him as much as it marked me. And now I'm thinking how much he would have loved to have been 'Granddad'.

'To fathers,' I say and we tip our glasses at each other.

'So how is it?' asks James.

'Fatherhood? It's the future. Everything is about the future now. And security. You've got to think ahead all the time.'

'Sounds terrible.'

'Nah. It's great. When you grow up you think father is a person. But when you're a dad, you realise it's an attribute. Like you've unlocked this brand new secret level inside yourself. It's a whole new world.'

James starts to smile. He's one of the most enigmatic people I know. I've always wondered if this was him just reflecting emotions back, or absorbing them. Certainly it was one of his key business skills.

'Do you really never want kids?' I ask.

'Where would I keep them?'

'Seriously.'

'Not never. But not now. I can see myself as a father, but when I imagine it, I see myself showing kids places and things. How can you show a kid the world when they've got to be in school every day spending a year learning what could be taught in six months? I'd have to take my kid to a country where they didn't care about that stuff.'

'You do realise children only see stuff as foreign if you tell them it is. Everywhere is new and exciting. Laura just has this face of constant amazement. Well, not constant, in between, let's see, grumpy, crying, happy and attention-seeking.'

'The only people I know with babies are in the UK,' he said, frowning, perhaps realising for the first time.

'Really?'

'I guess it's because you're the "real" people. You've got lineage, or heritage, or something here. Something to keep. Hardly anyone I've met since I've left has that. In fact, I don't think they want it. We flow, we don't like to stick. Rolling stones and that. I guess if I start seeing babies around me again, then that's a sign I'm settling down.'

'*Ooo baby, baby it's a wild world...*' I sing it out. I spent several nights making a playlist of 'baby' based tunes for Debs when she was pregnant. I could do this all evening.

'I'm going to sell the house,' says James. His dad lived there, receiving care, until his admission to hospital last week.

'You're not going to let it out? I thought there was good money in that.'

'Better investment chances in Burma now. Of course there's always a risk it will all go tits up, but then...' He shrugs, clearly not expecting a 'but then'.

'So you'd be permanently based out there?'

'No, I'm not putting all my eggs in that basket case. I'll be...' He picks up his phone and wobbles it at me. 'I'll be online.'

I remember us as teenagers, lying on the roof of his family's gravel-topped garage, stoned, staring at the stars, listening to *Bowie's Space Oddity*. I was trying to talk to him but he wouldn't respond, like he'd fallen over the edge. Was he dreaming back then? Now he's leaving a thread behind, as frail or fat as the bandwidth he's connected to. *You're circuit's dead, there's something wrong.* James reads my mind, another one of his foreign-living survival abilities, and throws another line.

'This country gets stranger and prettier every time I visit. Maybe someday it will be foreign enough for me to stick around and enjoy it.'

He looks at the time on his phone.

'You'd better go get her. I'll keep you posted about dad. Who knows, one day you could come visit me out there.'

I leave him tapping rapidly on his phone, messaging hundreds of friends, catching up on the stories of a boundless friendship network encircling the world and go to pick up my daughter.

© **Peter Hawkins**

Peter Hawkins left the UK in 2006, living in Nice until 2011. After 18 months exploring Asia he has returned to France. He's a dual Irish/British passport holder, but the world's least-convincing Irishman.

## Humanitarian Aid Worker **
### by Sandra Renew

She lies at night
on the metal framed bed,
inches above
the mud floor of the *tukul*.
In the dense blackness,
left as the candle died,
she senses the scorpions
shuffling beside her,
investigating her socks and shoes.
She knows that if she
puts her foot down,
puts a foot wrong,
steps over the line,
steps out of line,
she will be walking
on scorpion shells,
and something nasty will happen.

© **Sandra Renew**

Sandra Renew is Australian and worked for twelve years for international NGOs in war affected countries. As Country Director for child-focused organisations she spent much time and energy negotiating with government officials and some military organisations.

# I Lived with the Arabs *
## by Simone Mackinnon

My first night in Jerusalem was not reassuring. I turned out the light and found a comfortable dent in the horsehair mattress then—sirens, crashes, yells.

I thought the Centre, where I had just arrived as a volunteer, was being raided. Should I hide under the bed or rush upstairs to help save the children? In the end I did what most 50-year-old cowards would do, I pulled the covers over my head and waited until the racket stopped.

The Israelis had raided a house in the street and arrested two Arab men. They wrecked belongings and frightened the family—and me! I was Australian; we were not used to such goings on. During my stay in the country I got very used to it.

Hours earlier I arrived at Tel Aviv airport and found a minibus, called a *sherut*, going to Jerusalem. Two Israelis clambered in beside me, wearing black fedora hats and black suits with fringed shawls below their jackets, and their wives with caps over wigs on their heads and long, dated dresses. Our luggage was crammed in behind the seats and off we went, taking the highway towards Jerusalem. A plain stretched away to our right and we gaped at the surreal sight of huge hot air balloons, of every shape and colour, gliding in some ghostly armada against a pale aqua, twilit sky as the already forgotten sun splashed its last orange rays along the horizon. The driver said it was an international competition and the spectacle so inspired my bearded neighbour that he began to sing in a deep, mellow voice redolent with age-old sorrow and yearning. Hebrew lullaby, someone whispered in my ear. I gaped at the singer in amazement; you wouldn't catch anyone singing on a London bus.

The road wound up through hills, where pine trees clung and remains of rusted army vehicles clutched the rocky escarpments, a reminder of the fight for the State of Israel. An hour later, noisy, chaotic traffic and lighted modern buildings—we had arrived in Jerusalem City. I had asked to be taken to the East Jerusalem YMCA but the *sherut* driver pulled into a lay-by and told me to get out. He dumped my bags on the pavement, among the stampeding feet of commuters, shouted unintelligible instructions at me and drove off. I presumed he was keen to get home to his dinner. I didn't know then, that Israeli taxi drivers are reluctant to go into East Jerusalem, afraid of Arab stone throwers. I was beginning to panic when the fourth taxi to pass actually stopped. The driver wanted to deliver a message to his daughter, who would be waiting on King George Street and we diverted into the City Centre. She wasn't waiting, which caused much Hebrew lamentation and shrugging of shoulders. He finally took me to the YMCA in Nablus Road where he asked for a kiss as he deposited me in the driveway. Talk about pushing his luck. I shooed him away and he laughed. An elderly Arab rushed down the wide steps waving his arms and shouting at me. What he was saying was 'Thanks be to Allah. You're here, welcome. Where have you been, we were worried'. I didn't know that at the time and was about to make for the hills as he grabbed my arm, smiled toothlessly at me and led me up the steps into the large lobby. The receptionist explained Abdullah's enthusiastic welcome with a grin. They soothingly loaded me into an Arab taxi and I was bounced up the road to the Mount of Olives and off loaded outside the Jerusalem Princess Basma Centre for Disabled Children.

I squeezed through partly open rusted iron gates and lugged my baggage to the front entrance, watched by a group of Arab women, some wearing veils, who were sitting on the steps. They welcomed me in English and *Ahlan wa Sahlan* in Arabic and invited me to sit with them in the warm evening tinged with a lingering scent of spices and dusty, ancient air. In five minutes they had wormed out my important credentials. Was I married? No—much tutting and head shaking. Any children? Yes two daughters, sighs and smiles. Any sons? No—much head shaking and hand patting in sympathy. Where was I from—Australia, oh good somewhere new, most volunteers were from Europe. My answers seemed satisfactory, discussed roundly in Arabic and I was accepted. Mary, a young nurse in *hijab*, white tunic and long white pants, led me into the building. The large hall was tiled and darkened doorways opened off it but we turned left through open double iron doors and down a dim corridor.

'Children sleep.'

Mary waved a hand as we passed open doors. A faint smell of disinfectant overlaid the smell of nappies. I followed Mary through swing doors and we descended stairs into a large room with wicker chairs, a coffee table strewn with old magazines, a dining table and a galley kitchen, all overlaid with dust. Mary opened cupboards, pointing to coffee and tea packets and pulled the fridge open, shrugging because it was empty. A bookcase held dilapidated novels in various languages and some cassettes discarded by former volunteers. Mary led me into another corridor and opened the first door on the left.

'Your room'.

I looked around: a gay patchwork quilt on the narrow iron bed, a small table, a chair and an ensuite bathroom. My home for six months. I had no idea what was outside the window—it was dark and I was alone in a strange, war torn country among people I had learned were terrorists.

I stayed for two years. I loved the refugee children, who never cried with their terrible disabilities. I learned a deep appreciation for the affection, generosity and laughter of the Palestinians, in the face of difficulties we Australians would not tolerate for a moment.

## © Simone Mackinnon

Born in UK, emigrated and became Australian. She has written articles, essays and a novel. She returned to the UK in 1990 but during that time lived for two years in Israel/Palestine. Simone returned to live in Brisbane in 1997.

# Incognito
## by Anita Goodfellow

Darkness falls like a curtain. There is no twilight. No warning. It's at this time of the day when I start thinking about home. I'm missing home, but I can't go back. Of course, I know that.

Yesterday we saw an armadillo scuttling in the ditch by the side of the road. It was an astonishing sight. He really did look like he was wearing metal armour, but even that didn't lift my spirits.

The exotic birds are a dazzling myriad of colours. I am still transfixed by the sight of the delicate hummingbirds hovering above the blazing heliconia flowers. We have even spotted the elusive Toucan once or twice.

I am trying to learn the names of the tropical plants. It gives me something to do. I used to love gardening, growing my own vegetables. It's impossible here of course. I did try once, but a coral snake, its red, yellow and brown body glowing against the soil as it slithered away, put paid to any more gardening plans.

Some nights Mike and I walk along the beach, the sand luminous in the moonlight. The sound of the Pacific heaving itself onto the shore fills our silences. We used to have so much to say to each other. In the Spring the beach becomes a mass of turtles as the great sea creatures come ashore to lay their eggs in the sand. It's at this time of year that visitors and conservationists flock to the area to see the hatchlings scurry down the beach and plunge into the waves. Of course those are the lucky ones; many are eaten by predators. I stay away from the beach when the tourists are here.

When the rainy season arrives the landscape is bathed in an emerald green hue and the air is fresh. This is my favourite time; there are no tourists here then. If I close my eyes it almost feels like an English Summer's day.

Costa Rica really is paradise, but for me it is a prison.

If Mike is away I find a quiet spot on the beach and bask in the warmth, pretending I am on holiday. I am always careful to wear huge sunglasses though, and I never speak to anyone.

Mike is going back again next week. Going home. I wish I could go with him, but of course it's impossible. He says he'll bring me back some M&S marmalade. That's something to look forward to then, I think, trying not to be bitter like the taste of the Seville oranges. It's been three years since I was home.

With the insurance money we, or rather Mike, bought a small villa overlooking the Pacific. To the right, far below, the Nosara River meanders its way out to sea. We went kayaking in the river, through the mangroves, their network of roots home to playful otters. A few days after our kayaking trip we heard that a local man had been attacked by a crocodile. I remember afterwards seeing a picture of the ragged scar along his side. We never went kayaking after that. Our villa has a corrugated iron roof and when it rains the drops echo like the drumming of hooves.

Our first winter here Mike persuaded me to go horse-riding. I have always been nervous of the huge beasts. We rode through the rain-forest, the cry of Howler monkeys calling overhead as they swung through the jungle. Horse-riding is now one of my favourite pastimes. Sometimes when I'm out riding I find myself gasping at the beauty of the place and I forget why I'm here. Those moments don't last long.

We don't have many friends. I guess our closest friends are Geoff and Ann, a couple of hippy types who moved here some twenty-odd years ago from the States. Their bodies are a tortured mass of tattoos and piercings. We would never have been friends with them back home. They have no television, no internet; they are cut off from the outside world. We feel safe in their company. They never ask us any searching questions and we respect their privacy. Ann runs a small riding stables and it's her horse that I take out.

Geoff scratches a living by taking tourists out on his rickety boat. He took us out once in search of dolphins. As the boat bounced over the waves and diesel fumes filled my nostrils I clutched the side of the vessel, my stomach heaving. I have never been good on water. We came across some fishermen, their limbs conker brown. One of them was attached to a rope, his shoulders huge and powerful, his chest barrel shaped. We watched as he wrapped coils of metal chain around himself and then descended to the deep. He returned moments later with several conch shells. He tossed them on board to his partner who began scooping out the slimy pink flesh with a fearsome looking knife. The fishy insides would be sold later, but the shells were being discarded overboard. I watched a shell as it slowly sank into the depths, disappearing, just like I had. I asked if I could have one. I still have that conch shell, its surface shiny and smooth. We didn't see any dolphins that day.

In the early days Mike was always saying that it wouldn't be forever. To be honest when we first came here the prospect that it might be 'forever' didn't worry me. I was happy to escape the British climate. It felt like we were on one long holiday, but things change. The heat here is incredible; it presses down, squashing the life out of you.

I don't think I'll ever get used to the insects. I've seen crickets the size of small birds. As darkness descends we scurry inside to the safety of our home as fruit bats dart through the night. I miss my cat. Mike tells me he is fine, that he found him a good home. Here I just have racoons for company. Sometimes, when Mike isn't looking I throw them scraps of food. They still regard me warily from the confines of the forest.

My Spanish isn't bad so I can communicate when I need to, which isn't often as I know Mike doesn't like me speaking to strangers. But I miss talking to people. I wonder what is happening at home. I long for my friends. The memorial service had been packed apparently. I never knew I meant so much to so many people. It's too late now anyway. I don't expect anyone even remembers me.

One of the reasons for Mike's visits to England is to see his daughter from his first marriage. I'm sure she wonders why Mike chose to come to such a remote spot in Costa Rica, but I guess she thinks it was his way of dealing with the grief. She has never shown any interest in coming here, thank goodness. I know she sometimes asks Mike awkward questions, but Mike has become very adept at lying. Sometimes I wonder if he is lying to me. I know there isn't as much money in the bank as he had told me there would be. Of course it made sense that I was the one who should disappear. I had no family to speak of, no one to ask questions.

Mike seems to be going home more and more these days. I wonder what keeps him there. He always has an extra spring in his step when he returns. I wonder if one day he won't come back. I have no access to the money. How can I? I'm not here. How easy it would be for me to disappear again. I shiver at the thought.

Mike has suggested going on a kayaking trip when he gets back. I stare out at the inky black night and wonder why.

© **Anita Goodfellow**

Anita Goodfellow has a Diploma in Creative Writing and Literature and is currently editing her first novel, whilst enjoying life in France. She is at her happiest with her walking boots on and a rucksack on her back.
http://anitagoodfellow.blogspot.fr

# Into The Moment
## by Maryanne Khan

Down on the stone plaza, the men were unloading the catch. Julian Summerrell watched the baskets passed from hand to hand, the fishermen comparing the haul to past catches, immortalised in stories that had been passed on and on down through time.

He ran his hand through his white hair. It was sticky with salt, as though he had swum in the night sea and dragged himself out of the water onto this piazza, unconscious of where he had been. He watched the sea beyond gradually light up, his shadow stretching over the flagstones, growing sharper as the light increased in the roundling sun.

One of the fishermen called, '*Oi! Signor Giuliano! Un caffè?*'

'*Certo*,' he called back.

Perhaps I have been here too long, he thought, spooning sugar into his espresso. What is it, a year now? Where has it gone?

'*Tutto passa*,' Gianni Pinti was saying.

Yes, Julian thought, everything does pass and the moment does slide backwards into memory and people like me tug desperately at the hem of its departing robe to haul it from that past into this present.

One man said, '*Un momento, pensiamoci sopra.*'

Perhaps that was what he had been doing here—thinking it over.

The fishermen put down their glasses saying, '*Arrivederci! A presto.*'

At the fishmonger's, men were severing the heads of fish, the eyes now unseeing, to be tossed into a plastic bin they would empty down at the quay. Boats bobbed on the gently heaving breast of the Mediterranean, dreaming until dawn when they would shudder to life and their grumbling engines would scatter the seagulls that sat, heads wing-tucked, on the prows.

Julian was not one to abandon himself completely to a romantic notion that he might embrace the concept of the simple life and end up living out his days as a fisherman. But then again, he was a little disoriented about why he had ever seen himself as a historian either. He walked up the steps to the room he was renting in the village and sat down to write an aerogramme.

*Dear Emily* . . .

Emily. Emily, who had laughed at him when he announced his intention to live in Florence and dedicate himself to researching the life of Catherine de' Medici.

'God, Summerrell,' she had said. 'What for?'

'I will be the first to translate this biography. No one knows it exists! Just stumbled on it in the archive. Wait till I get my hands on it.'

Emily had tipped turpentine onto a rag and wiped her paint-spattered hands. She had looked at him with one raised eyebrow.

He resumed writing the letter, trying to shake off the memory of Emily gloriously, uncompromisingly unconvinced.

*How is the painting going? Ready for the exhibition? Thanks for the invite, won't be able to make it. Sorry* .

How was she feeling? It was her first solo show.

*You must be so excited!*

He underlined the word 'so' twice.

*You would have loved the sea this morning, such lovely colours.*

Such lovely colours, he repeated to himself. Obviously.

*The village was all white and the sun picked it out bit by bit and . . .*

He slammed the pen down. He did it every time—wrote about the scenery to a painter, for god's sake!

What time was it in Australia? What was she doing now? He remembered her clock—every night he slept with her he had removed the batteries. She had laughed when he complained about the ticking and had thrown her leg over him in bed and said, 'You have to face it mate, time goes on.'

He searched about for something else to write, but the drought had struck. He was stuck in the past, remembering how he had left her place one morning, drained, as if her endless energy had sapped the life out of him. She had also been rather noisy in her lusty pleasure and left the window open, regardless of neighbours. He saw her face outlined against the window as the dawn leached upwards from the horizon into the darkness and Venus was a single, luminous stitch in the sky.

'Smell that sea air, Summerrell? *Hate* the winter. Too many clothes, the windows shut.'

He had not mentioned it, but he was rather partial to winter. He enjoyed the closeness of it: layers of comfy sweaters, breathing through a woollen scarf and the sensation of warm breath on his cheeks; the designs the frost made on grass, picking out each blade, a frozen cobweb that looked as though it were etched in crystal and hung with dew, an unlikely chandelier. He liked the way the air bit him back when he breathed.

They had stopped sleeping together, but they had remained friends, suspended in that bleak state of abandoned intimacy.

Not exactly abandoned, he thought, more like 'consumed.' That was it—Emily would have eaten him alive and spat out the bones. He'd been afraid of her, he realised. He always thought of her as 'larger than life,' always in terms of clichés that merely skirted the fact that she was the one person he knew who bit off great chunks of life and chewed them up. He shook his head, signed the pitiful letter after adding a few fervent wishes for success. He sealed the flaps, stuffed it into his pocket and went to lunch. Grilled sardines, he rather thought.

A month later, he received a letter from a mutual friend in Australia.

*Dear Julian*, it began, *useless beating around the bush, I know you guys were close, so I don't know how to tell you this, but Emily died.*

His eyes glued to the words as if they were written in blood, he leaned against the table and lowered himself unsteadily onto the chair.

No! his mind screamed. Emily doesn't just *die*!

He rambled over the words that were trying to frame an awful truth with tact.

*Must have jumped*, he read . . . *they found her on the rocks.*

He took a long gulp from last night's bottle of wine and wiped his mouth on his sleeve. He perused the letter, thinking, why? You're telling me how, but not why. Can't have been the exhibition; she'd written afterwards, said it had been a success. Sales even.

The friend obviously did not know why and had written, *no idea . . . out of the blue...*

He rambled on about *full of life* and *a shock to us all*, lame little phrases trying to mask the horror of it, make it palatable. Julian screwed up the letter and threw it across the room, where it danced on the floor in the draft coming in under the door.

Emily was dead. He found it difficult to even connect the kind of emotion that would cause despair with the person who had been Emily. He couldn't do it and obviously, neither could anyone else.

*A shock to us all.*

He took himself down to the edge of the sea, but the breeze would not take his thoughts, lift him like a sail to bear him away from imagining the state in which living is too painful, too intense perhaps, to bear.

He watched fishermen working on their boats, women striding along the footpath armed with canvas shopping-bags, dragging reluctant children along like little boats in tow; the sun striking the stucco façade of the small church that offered no solace to a man such as him, and what was his loss anyway?

Am I being self-indulgent? he wondered. Emily has done this and it has nothing to do with me.

But yes, in a funny way it had done something to him. She had.

'Come on Summerrell,' she would tease, 'Get your nose out of a bloody book and do something with yourself!'

To which he had thrown up a lame excuse and Emily would reply, 'Well it's *your* life, *your* loss.'

He saw it now—Emily had represented some alternative that he had failed to embrace.

Emily, he realised, had always inhabited a realm of which he only ever caught sidelong glances. Emily, so full of life; Emily, so creative and so frustratingly right about everything. But Emily so disturbed beneath it all, and where lay the blame?

It's hardly my fault, he thought.

He stood at the shore as millions had done before him and would do after him, and he thought back to what Virginia Woolf had said about the moment. She had written that the whole of existence—everything that was the world—was contained in a single moment, and yet there was also the one appalling moment in which identity ceases to be, and one is engulfed by an unnameable, unfathomable emptiness.

He looked at the boats bobbing in the harbour, the gulls scrabbling noisily on the beach, as if he were itemising objects in a catalogue: twelve white boats, one red, two blue; a score of gulls, cirrus clouds, gentle swell, slight northerly breeze. He saw himself for what he was—detached, an observer.

It's not my fault, he'd thought.

Yet life surged around him—life laden on carts spilling over with fleshy red tomatoes, glistening in baskets of twitching scaly bodies; life surging up the stalks of the corn as it stood ripening in the sun; life twining on the vine to produce the sudden flower, exploding.

He suddenly understood why his hair had turned prematurely white—he was dying. Over the years, he had removed himself, softly, softly, from his own life, had been in the process of doing it for years. Part of him lay amongst the scavenged books in the office in Florence, a dusty lexicon that was Julian Summerrell—a list of facts and dates that served no one. What was he doing, simply existing, drifting aimlessly around Italy as T.S. Eliot had said, *living, living and partly living*?

'What for?' Emily had said.

Perhaps you are right, Emily, he thought. What for indeed?

He would return to Sydney and take roses to her grave.

Full-blown red ones.

© **Maryanne Khan**

Maryanne Khan was born in Australia and has lived in Milan, Chicago, Brussels, Rome and Washington DC. Her short stories and poetry have been published in US and Australia. *Domain of the Lower Air* was published in the States in 2010.

# Knickers *
## by S.B. Borgersen

A pale April early morning light hovers on the window ledge. In the maple tree outside the bedroom window, the chickadees add an enthusiasm that does not match mine. Ready to stumble into yet another busy day, I fumble for my clothes. But freeze with my knickers in my hands. I've never really given them any thought before. I generally just rake them on, pull on jeans and sweater then hot-foot it to the kitchen to get things underway for yet another day.

My knickers are of the cotton variety. Pretty but comfortable. Stylish but dependable. But now I explore the seams; stitch, by stitch. The precision of the work is perfect. Not a thread loose. The lace edging is exquisitely attached. And the tiny blue satin bow, carefully hand sewn, front and centre. This is the first time I have examined my supermarket bargain underwear in such detail.

But it is the label that I look at the most. Stroking it over and over with the tip of my forefinger. 'Made in Bangladesh' in orange thread on the filmy white tag.

I've been watching the news. A garment factory in Bangladesh collapsed. Hundreds of workers are dead or missing. I look again at my fine cotton, high cut, briefs. I imagine those who worked on them; women supporting their families, working for 20 cents an hour. I can feel, through the fabric, their nimble, possibly gnarled, hard worked hands. I shiver; my finger tips connecting with theirs.

I wonder what they thought as they sweated away at their sewing machines, day after day, making hundreds upon hundreds of these garments for the Canadian market. A market that sells this underwear alongside groceries at $5 for a three-pack.

And I wonder what knickers these strong women wore themselves.

Why do we need to get our knickers made so far away? I ask myself rhetorically, knowing it's always about money. There is an underwear manufacturer right here in Nova Scotia. The garments have a reputation for lasting years. Forever, in fact. The brand is a household name. Even the name is a household name. One of the famously named family became premier of Nova Scotia in the 1940s. He was in line for higher things, politically, and I quote, 'he was the best prime-minister Canada never had'. The international airport is named after him. People joke that it's the only airport in the world named for underpants.

The company had its beginnings at a mill on Prince Edward Island, the province next door. It was 1870. The long johns were itchy and scratchy. Most men in Canada had at least one set. The wool went into the mill directly from the sheep grazing in nearby fields. In 1882 the family business moved to Nova Scotia and, initially, devoted their research to taking the 'shrink' out of the fabric. However hard they tried, apparently, they couldn't take the 'scratch' or the 'itch' out of the wool.

The history of the company and its underwear was completely unknown to me before now. Before the tragedy in Bangladesh. Before I felt the need to write this. I wonder what working in an underwear factory over 100 years ago was like. And has the rag trade manufacturing business progressed at all? I find old reprinted etching illustrations of this forward-looking maker of fine under garments, line drawings of the advanced working conditions they offered their employees over 125 years ago.

I read about spinning rooms and 66 knitting machines designed especially for this Nova Scotia company. They hired one 'girl' to each attend seven 'sensitive' machines. I learn about the cutting room, where, for greater accuracy, the garments were cut by hand to help detect any flaws.

My next discovery is best described by quoting directly from the local newspaper in 1906: The finishing is done by a long row of 54 electric sewing machines operated by 54 bright and shining girls. The garments passed on from one to another and are seamed, button-holed, buttoned, trimmed, packed, stamped, boxed and sent away, perhaps, to cover the brawny chest of some British Columbia miner.

Much as I would like, I can't let myself drift to brawny miners' chests in British Columbia; my mind is still with the collapsing factory in Bangladesh. I watch more news updates. One woman gives birth to her baby under the rubble. Does that mean she was still working with her pregnancy so advanced? I watch more bodies gently lifted from the dust and dirt. I see pink and turquoise bales of fabrics, tumbling, wafting like flags.

I am convinced the quality of the work by the women in the factory in Bangladesh was every bit as good as the 54 bright and shining girls in the local factory last century.

The local factory still makes underwear, employing about 550 people who produce garments that are sought after worldwide. One pair of knickers retails at $50.

For $50 I can buy 30 pairs of Bangladesh-made knickers at the supermarket. I don't need 30 pairs. But the very talented and diligent clothing workers in Bangladesh need this market. I understand that their garment industry accounts for 80 per cent of the country's exports. According to the economists currently spouting forth on the issue, Canada taking a guilty escape and reverting to knickers made right here in Nova Scotia is not the answer.

I slowly open the top drawer of my dresser revealing piles of underwear in many colours. I touch my hastily folded knickers. My fingers catch the lace edgings, the satin ribbons. Tomorrow I will wear another fresh pair with an additional connection; a closeness to the women workers of Bangladesh, something I could never have anticipated.

*Postscript. Since writing this piece the death toll is reported to have soared beyond 1200.*

## © S.B. Borgersen

Originally from England, S.B. Borgersen writes and makes art on the south shore of Nova Scotia, Canada, surrounded by boisterous dogs and a vast ukulele collection. Sue is a member of The Nova Scotia Writers' Federation. www.sueborgersen.com

# Le Choix du Roi
## By M.E. Lewis

Jess stood in the shade of a plane tree by the entrance to the hospital and checked her watch. He was now officially late. They'd arranged to meet a few minutes before their appointment at Hôtel Dieu. God's hotel. She was not religious but she liked the sound of that.

She put a hand on her abdomen. It was still too early to feel the baby kick but she felt a tightening that had been nagging her on and off for a few weeks. False contractions were normal in a second pregnancy according to everything she'd read. And read she did. Information was power and it was her survival kit to giving birth in a foreign country.

Although they'd lived in Lyon for four years now, it still felt foreign much of the time. People were always telling her how well she spoke French, but it was a quite another matter to express yourself in the throes of labor and childbirth.

Jess looked at her watch again. Patience was not her virtue and expecting another baby hadn't changed that. If anything she felt even more pressed for time. She looked at the plaque on the old stone wall and read about the history of the hospital—Lyon's oldest, founded by clergy in the middle ages. It was hard to get her head around the fact that everything in this city was so ancient. In Toronto, where she'd given birth the first time, the oldest building was no more than a couple of hundred years old.

Just as she was about to give up and go inside Jess saw him hurrying down the street. Computer bag bumping on his shoulder and tie flapping in the breeze. He smiled and waved. Philippe, her husband. Emotion washed over her in waves: love, relief, then irritation.

'Sorry, am I late?'

Jess gave him a tight smile.

'You're here now, let's go!'

He put his arm around her and they crossed through the courtyard to the main entrance. The way in for outpatients was familiar by now—already her third appointment in the maternity department of the vast Gothic structure—but it had taken ages to figure out the complex sequence of doors and hallways. Twice she'd ended up asking for directions in what looked like the geriatric ward. Why was everything always so complicated in France?

They were only a few minutes late when they reached the medical imagery department, a modern implant within the old walls of the hospital. The receptionist pointed them to the ugly molded plastic chairs that were so unpleasantly familiar. In fact, Jess reflected, she probably had a hemorrhoid named after one of them, she'd sat so long waiting for her first ultrasound at twelve weeks. Philippe hadn't been able to come, so she'd broken the news by phone.

She hadn't wanted to find out the first time she was pregnant. They were hoping for two children anyway, so it was all good. But this time the stakes were higher: they didn't want a third child, so the second had better be a girl. Except the technician had told her she was carrying a boy.

'He's healthy, that's all that matters.' Philippe had said the right thing, and in her heart she felt the same way. Yet she couldn't help but feel a pinch of disappointment in knowing she would never have a daughter.

'*Tu peux toujours te faire arrêter et recommencer plus tard.*' Had she dreamt this? Or had her *belle-mère* really suggested a termination when she'd told her there would be a second *petit-fils*? Sometimes the French language played tricks on her, lulling her into thinking she was bilingual then throwing something incomprehensible at her. No, that was what she had said.

'Of course she didn't mean it,' said Philippe. 'My mother is just very…practical.'

Practical? The sheer *culot* of the woman, Jess railed. How could she suggest such a thing? She felt a fierce wave of solidarity with the tiny being inside her. Boy, girl, it was their baby and it was desired. No, wanted. It had taken almost a year to get pregnant again.

*Enceinte. Grossesse.* Jess turned the words over in her mind. She loved the French words for pregnancy. To become gross with child. It sounded biblical. And it would be a Christmas baby, born in God's Hotel. Not that she believed in God. But all those years of Catholic upbringing could not leave her indifferent to such things.

She toyed with names as they sat in the waiting room: Noël. For a boy, would that work? Too corny? Perhaps Nathan. Or Gabriel. Not Rudolph, she thought with a giggle. Unless he had red hair.

'Madame Béranger?' They were calling her name. She still didn't think of herself as Madame anything, her husband's name even less.

'*Oui*,' she said, perking up and following the woman into the examining room. Philippe sat on a chair while she got onto the examining table, raising her top and unbuttoning her jeans like an old pro.

The technician bustled into the room, a petite, efficient woman with a smooth cap of dark hair. She adjusted various settings on her machine before turning to Jess and probing her abdomen. '*La vessie est bien pleine?*' Uncomfortably so, she winced. A full bladder was de rigueur for a scan. She closed her eyes while the woman spread gel on her belly and tried to think of something else. Little Noël swimming around in there, turning loop de loops.

'Are you okay?' Philippe seemed concerned. 'Fine,' she reassured him with a smile. The technician gave them a curious look. Did they both speak French? Yes, they explained, but always English together; when they'd first met Jess hadn't spoken any French. She nodded, and to both of their surprise switched to a heavily accented English.

'This is your second child?'

Philippe nodded. 'Yes, we have a son, four-and-a-half. Oliver.'

The woman smiled, absorbing this, while focusing on her screen. She unhooked the probe from the ultra-sound machine and began moving it around on Jess's lower abdomen, sending uncomfortable spasms through her bladder. Breathe, she thought, closing her eyes again.

They could hear a lot of snap and crackle, then an underwater rhythm that cut through the static with its own intense frequency: the baby's heartbeat—fast and steady. A beautiful sound.

'Your baby has a good 'eart.' She paused. This scan was called '*morphologique*' she explained, because at twenty-two weeks they could identify all of the baby's physiological development. His body, in other words, thought Jess. Why did the French always have to make everything sound so technical?

'Do you want to know the sex?'

'Yes, well, we already found out last time.' They exchanged a look, a tiny bit rueful.

'*Ah, bon?*' The technician seemed surprised. She pursed her lips and adjusted her position on the stool. It was unusual, she said, although not impossible, to identify the gender at the first ultrasound. Who did the first scan? Jess described the woman from her memory—thin, glasses, a lot of curly hair.

The technician raised her eyebrows but said nothing more for a moment, focusing on her screen.

'What were you hoping for?'

Jess didn't hesitate. 'A girl.' Not that it mattered. As long as it was healthy.

She looked at Philippe for confirmation. 'Well, yes but…' he began, then switched to French. His English was good but Jess knew how hard it was to say certain things in a second language. She nodded along as he gave the speech they'd both been repeating to themselves.

The woman shook her head and turned back to her screen. She smiled.

'*C'est une fille.*'

Jess felt her heart leap. Had she heard right? A lump rose in her throat and tears pricked her eyes. The baby's heartbeat stayed steady. Philippe squeezed her hand.

'A girl? Are you sure? Why did the other woman think it was a boy?' She had to be certain this time.

The technician responded with what Jess could only describe as a Gallic shrug, turning her hands up and grimacing. It wasn't always possible to see the sex at twelve weeks but with experience you could usually tell. They didn't usually say anything as it was easy to make a mistake. Her gesture spoke volumes, implying her opinion of the other technician.

She turned the bigger of the two screens to face them and took them through the scan in detail.

'Here you see your baby in her room.' Jess suppressed a giggle. She must mean 'womb' but with her accent… They switched to French as the vocabulary became technical with lots of numbers and words like *moyenne* and *développement*. Philippe followed along attentively but the whole thing was a bit of a blur to Jess; all she could think about was the little girl who would make her appearance in a few months' time. Would she be a tomboy like her mother? Or a girlie-girl, *une vraie petite fille* who only wanted to wear ballet skirts and play with dolls?

When the ultrasound was over Philippe held out a memory stick for the first photos of their daughter, immortalized by technology in her little womb-room. His mother would be thrilled by the news, he whispered, squeezing her hand again. So would her parents, thought Jess, so filled with joy she even felt pleased for her *belle-mère*.

The technician left to make a copy of the scan and said something Jess didn't catch.

'What was that?' she asked Philippe.

'*Le choix du roi.*' The king's choice, he explained. A boy, then a girl.

How fitting, she thought, for a baby to be born in a place where kings and noblemen had once lived and died.

*Le choix du roi*, she repeated to herself, a boy and a girl.

They were hardly royals. It wasn't even as if they'd had any choice. Yet she felt blessed in so many ways. To be living in a time and place where the past was so vividly present, yet be able to steal a glimpse of your child, patiently growing within.

© **M.E. Lewis**

M.E. (Mel) Lewis is a writer who lives in the Rhône-Alpes region of France. A Toronto native and graduate of Ryerson University's Radio and Television Arts Program (1980), she works as a communication consultant in Switzerland and blogs at www.francesays.com

## Living Will **
### by Paola Fornari

When I can no longer see nor hear
lay me on faded rug
in fig-tree shade
where I may feel
breeze on my face
and warm earth beneath

From behind my mind's shutters
help me retrieve
ice-cold streams
fresh hay scent
early morning birdsong
and flaming fireflies

And when time calls
lie beside me
let me sense
your love-breath on my face
hold my hand
and let me sleep.

© **Paola Fornari**

Paola Fornari was born on an island in Lake Victoria, Tanzania. She has lived in a dozen countries over four continents, speaks five and a half languages, and is an expatriate *sine patria*. At present she is living in Bangladesh. www.espacios.be

# Longhouse
## by Judy Darley

*The dream never alters in its intensity though the details change. I wake up in the house where I grew up, and have a sense that something is terribly wrong. I slip out of bed, go into every room in turn, but each is empty. I step into the kitchen, and it's there that I find the shrunken head I brought back with me from Borneo, grinning at me from the windowsill. I pick it up, cradle it in my hands, and I think I hear it croon my name.*

'Excuse me, do you know where this bus goes?'

Tourists. They always target me, because I'm fair-skinned, tall, so obviously not local. To them I must look like a life-ring in a dark and unfamiliar sea.

'Where're you trying to get to?' I ask.

The man pulls out a crumpled leaflet advertising a beach hotel. The photo shows a pristine white shore. They must have got a shock when they saw the litter that washes up each day, refuse from the refugee camp set a few kilometres up the coast.

'Yes, this is the right bus,' I say. 'The driver will be along soon, ten minutes or so.'

The woman leans forward, her face avid with interest.

'You live here? In Kota Kinabalu?'

I try to guess which answer will make most sense to her. She reminds me of my mum, is probably just as incapable of guessing the ages of 'young people'.

'Gap year,' I say, and paste on a smile.

'How lovely!' she exclaims, but the man looks puzzled, indicates my left hand.

'You're wearing a wedding ring.'

I've forgotten to take it off. Careless.

'Makes life easier when you're travelling alone,' I improvise.

'Gosh, must be difficult,' the woman says.

'Sometimes. I meet people, though,' I say. 'Like you.'

This helps her believe we're friends.

Her husband is watching a man passing with a trolley laden with cages; white mice, gerbils, guinea pigs—all piled up.

'Dinner, I suppose,' he says, amused, and I feel a pinch of anger.

'Pets, actually,' I tell him. 'Just like in England.'

I pretend to check the timetable.

'Listen, it's twenty minutes till the bus goes, and it takes a windy route—at least an hour to the hotel. With three of us a taxi will cost the same.'

The woman is already nodding.

'What a good idea. Where are you staying?'

'At a hostel near your hotel. Look, there's a taxi.'

I lead the way to where Miko leans against his cab, pretending not to eavesdrop.

'Hello Madams, Sir.'

He smiles broadly as he opens the door to the backseat.

'Where to go?'

The woman slides in. The man hesitates though.

'I prefer to sit in front. My legs are long…'

'I get carsick if I sit in the back,' I say quickly. 'I'll scooch the seat forward so you'll have room.'

'Let her sit in front if she wants to, George,' the woman says. 'I'm Viv, love, what's your name?'

'Becky,' I say.

I'm never quite sure why I lie at this point, but somehow it feels better, less implicated.

'Nice to meet you.'

George grimaces, folds himself into the backseat.

We set off. I pretend to give Miko directions and we exchange a few words of Malay mixed in with Miko's tribal dialect.

'Gosh, you're fluent!' Viv exclaims.

'I love languages.'

I glimpse a dapple of envy in her eyes.

'It's one of the fun things about travelling, isn't it? Listen, the driver's asked if we'd like to see the longhouse where he lives—it's just near here.'

Viv's eyes light up but George grunts.

'We already saw some at the Sabah Museum.'

'But this is a real one, lived in by families with children and chickens and goats…'

'Don't mention the guinea pigs,' Miko mutters in Malay and I fake being delighted.

'He says his grandma and the other ladies would love to show you their beading. And they have some local rice wine we can try.'

'Oh, George, an authentic longhouse! Wouldn't that be interesting? We'll have so much to tell Larry!'

Viv turns her attention back to me.

'Larry's our son—he's studying Anthropology. Borneo's just his kind of place!'

George glowers. He looks hot, pressed up in the backseat.

'Seal the deal,' Miko says to me in Malay.

'Did you see the headhunting exhibit at the museum?' I ask George. 'Gave me the shivers! The driver's family are part of some tribe that's a sub-group of the *Kadazan-Dusuns*.'

I make a show of struggling with the pronunciation.

'Weren't they headhunters?'

'More than a century ago, perhaps,' George says, but he's finally intrigued. 'No harm in a detour, I suppose.'

I say a few words to Miko and he shouts out: 'Good, very good!'

He picks up his mobile phone to warn the families we're on our way.

When we arrive, no one's around apart from a few half-naked children, stripped of their jeans moments earlier by their parents. They're playing at being warriors, smacking long sticks together with gusto. Our own kids are tucked away out of sight, their milkiness a dead giveaway even if neither forgets their role and runs up to hug me.

Miko yells to the children: 'Run ahead, make sure everyone is ready.'

He mutters to me and I tell George and Viv to remove their shoes before entering the longhouse. Viv slips out of her sandals and flits up the bamboo ladder. George slowly unlaces his heavy hiking boots. I hear Viv's happy squeaks before we catch up.

Maria is in position, boobs out, feeding six-month-old Trevor. Just behind her, Rachel and Caroline are working on beaded *sandangs*.

Miko calls to me: 'Tell them about the stories, see if we can sell some.'

He picks up one Caroline finished previously, pointing to motifs.

'Say this is the tale of a warrior vying to win the heart of the woman he loves.'

Viv is entranced.

'Becky, is it for sale? George, can we buy it?'

He snorts, unimpressed, but hands over the notes.

I spot the camera hanging from his neck.

'I'm sure they won't mind if you take photos.'

The sound of the clicking is the cue for the children to start playing picturesquely with wooden, tin and bamboo toys, anything plastic shut away in their rooms. They climb up the sacks of rice that sit outside each door, giggling and posing for George's lens.

'Are the toys made by the tribe?' Viv asks.

I shoot Miko a glance.

'John bought some from the market yesterday,' he says in Malay. 'I'll get them.'

He wanders off, returns with a selection he lays out on the floor. Viv crouches down to see them.

'Oh, aren't they lovely?'

They're little more than trash refashioned into rudimentary animals, but she buys two jagged crocodiles.

'We're hoping to see real ones in the Kinbatangan River,' she tells one of the children.

He opens his mouth to respond, sees me shake my head, closes it fast.

George turns from his photography, sees Viv popping the crocs into her bag.

'What did you get those for, Viv? It's not like we've got grandkids to give them to.'

'Not yet, my love, but Larry…'

'Larry's not ready for all that nonsense yet, you silly…'

'You don't know that!' Viv exclaims. 'All it'll take is for him to meet the right girl, like lovely Becky here.' She turns to me. 'Larry would just adore you!'

George looks so sceptical that I'm embarrassed.

John wanders in, carrying a bottle of rice wine. Maybe that'll help. Miko ushers us to sit down, hands us each a tumbler full. He drinks his own, smacks his lips. I sip mine, try not to cough. It's rough stuff, worse even than last week's.

Viv sips daintily and chokes.

'Bit strong for me, I'm afraid.'

'Me too,' I say thankfully.

'All the more for me then, eh?'

George brightens up at last.

As he works his way through the bottle, I steer the conversation round to headhunting, and Miko dictates gruesome things for me to tell them. By the time John returns with the tray of 'shrunken heads' it's almost too easy.

'Look at the way their jaws protrude!' Viv comments.

161

'Guess that's down to the way the brains are extracted,' I suggest uneasily.

The fur has been burnt off, but if they look too closely, they may notice the resemblance to a beloved family pet. I point to the one on the end.

'Miko says this one was a matter of honour—the head was severed while he was still in battle— imagine that, thwack!'
I shudder extravagantly and Viv follows suit.

'Larry would just adore one of these,' she tells me, in the same tone she used when saying how much her son would adore me.

Miko grins at me over George's shoulder.

'Tell them the heads are talismans,' he says. 'Tell them, the more the better to bring good fortune to their home.'

I shake my head slightly—it's not good to get greedy. I pretend to buy one, slip it into my bag, watch them buy one for themselves, another for their son.

And that's that—a good day's work. We pile back into the taxi and drive along the coast road. Miko drops me off in front of a hostel, swooping back to pick me up once he's deposited George and Viv. As I climb into the car he kisses me hard on the lips.

'You devious angel,' he crows, and we drive home to the longhouse.

That night I have the first of the dreams that will lead to our break up. I wake up in my childhood bedroom, only somehow it's also our room in the longhouse. Miko is snoring beside me, our children asleep between us. I hear someone calling out in the darkness: 'Becky, Becky!' The sound comes from my bag. I slip out of bed, unzip the bag, find the shrunken head inside. Only now it isn't a cavy head with all its fur burnt off, but a genuine shrunken head, with a small, wizened version of Viv's trusting face.

## © **Judy Darley**

Judy Darley is a British writer and has lived in California and Spain, as well as travelling widely. Judy has had short fiction published by magazines and anthologies including Litro, Fiction 365 and Cease, Cows. Judy blogs at SkyLightRain.com.

# A Land of Luxury and Wickedness
## by Craig S Whyte

The Bay of Thumbs. The Hill of the Monkey.

I awoke suddenly, startled by the clarity of my recollection. It was raining outside: the lashing of hard-baked ground, the scent of crisped gum leaves soaking. Lorikeets screeched, outraged by the downpour, bonnie to the eye but harsh on my Highland ear. I longed for the pleasant piping of redshank, the looping melody of song thrush on Bunessan's rooftops.

There was a brown face at my window, supplanting the view of dripping gums and grey sky.

'H'llo, boss.'

A broad, white smile, a fine nose, twice the breadth of a European's. And the hair, lacking all civility, rejoicing in its freedom from colonial fashion.

He wore a filthy linen shirt and the grey waistcoat I had given him, the one I'd worn on my voyage around the globe and scrubbed fortnightly in the seawater we pumped daily under the scornful scrutiny of the Mate. The Mate was a bitter Lowlander who held the Highlander in high disdain, and he drove us to our chores like the slaves he had once overseen in the Caribbean.

'You come to work, boss, o'you go'n sleep all day?'

I sat up, returned the smile self-consciously, knowing mine lacked his breadth and brightness.

'Today's the Sabbath,' I told him. 'I will not work.'

'Aw, yeah.' He looked thoughtful. 'Seventh day… Seven day to make Country.' The grin reappeared slowly. 'Not much of a Dreamtime, eh?'

I smiled despite his irreverence. Back on Mull I would have been affronted, but if my travels had taught me anything it was that there are far worse things a man can do than blaspheme.

He was getting wet. He glanced upwards, assessing the sky.

'Maybe I don' work today, like you, boss… Reckon them rocks be there for us to crush tomorrow.'

'Aye,' I agreed, reluctantly. Fletcher the quarry foreman was a brute. He had just enough of the fear of God in him not to deny a man his Sabbath, but I feared for my friend who seemed fair game to Fletcher on any day. I did not wish to see him beaten again.

As I pondered, my visitor entered my doorless shack and made for my chair, my only furniture. It was in the Hebridean style, crafted by a Lewis man who'd turned his hand to local materials, guided by the Aborigines by the creek. Beyond my need for meat and meal I had put aside every penny during the parched summer. The chair was my only luxury in a place where luxury abounded... or so it seemed to me whose eyes had grown accustomed to want and famine.

And there was wealth here, for sure: the rich who'd grown richer on native land and working men's toil, who dashed about in white waistcoats and shiny boots on tall horses, surveying their new kingdoms. They played polo or hunted by day, dined, danced and drank by night, and flattered one another that they were doing the heroic work of colonisation. There was new wealth, too, men who were once humble. There was racing on the Sabbath and intemperance of the highest order, and free houses spewed their brawls onto byways like bile from dogs who'd gorged on grass.

But it was gold on which these rogues had gorged. Returned from Victoria with pouches full and desires ablaze.

I, too, had tried the diggings, but the gold had gone by the time I got there and men were killing each other for dust. I returned with six sober Scotchmen, drawing modest safety from our number. But we were set upon by bushrangers, and though we had not an ounce of Victorian gold between us, they stripped Jock Smillie of his pocket watch and Willie Shaw of his shoes. We would have perished in the scorching sun were it not for the muddied rainwater that pooled in bullock prints on the trail.

As my uninvited guest sat, I could have resented his brazenness, the creak of the fibres as he settled, but in truth there were few in this wicked colony I would have rather seen sitting there. His trousers were grubby but so were mine.

I studied him curiously. I had given him my waistcoat because he had taken a shine to it, because I had pitied him after his beating, or perhaps because I was ashamed of my race, of Fletcher's brutality. But now I wanted to know more.

'Why do you live among us white fellas and not with your people by the creek?'

There was the white smile again. 'Aw, they not my people, boss.'

'But...' My ignorance had tripped me.

'You're a white fella. But you don' talk like them Prussian fellas up in Hahndorf.'

I understood. 'Different language.'

He nodded. 'Dreaming different too.'

I would have quizzed him further but he was sharper.

'So, what your story, boss? Your people got a Songline?'

I thought about this. I had songs in me, stories I had once shared with others—the Bay of Thumbs, the Cave of the Dead—but my voice had grown quiet in this faraway land. We used to sit around the peat fire, I recalled, with the ocean wind around us, a comforting roar. There was my grandfather, tales of heroes, giants and water horses, and my father shushing him, fearful for our Presbyterian souls. But the Lord fed us well on ling and herring, and potatoes grew well in the seaweed-sweetened soil. Ma weaved on a clanking loom and sold her wares to Lowland merchants. Pa and I had work at the quarry, and the granite there was rich red and mealy and sparkled in the sunlight like the waves around Iona. So we had some money to spend when the trading smacks sailed north from Glasgow, and we crowded the shore in rowdy chatter like the lorikeets in the gums. I had purchased the waistcoat with my first month's earnings.

'There was famine,' I told him simply. 'Once we had plenty, we were stout, but then the potato blight came and we grew thin and weary.'

A pause.

'What 'bout bush tucka, boss? Country look after you, eh?'

I gazed through the small window at the gums, their lanky limbs, grey and graceful, reaching towards a sky that was not mine. The air smelled sweetly, gum oil and wet grain, fruit ripening in my landlord's orchard.

'This is a good land,' I told him. 'Food abounds. My land is harsh and challenging. But it was beautiful and was once ours.'

I glanced at him, saw interest in the warm brown of his eyes.

'The Duke said the land was his,' I continued, 'though he had never set one buckled shoe in the place. He said he wanted sheep instead of people. We begged him consider that we had lived there for many generations, that we always paid our rent on time and were no burden to him. But he bade us wander. I left my family beneath Glasgow's grime-grey clouds, told them I would send money. But I've been here two years now, and…' I showed him empty hands, with them my bare home.

Yet he was looking around with something akin to envy. I felt ashamed.

165

'You?' I asked quietly.

He looked me in the eye for a long time, measuring me, I supposed, for trustworthiness.

'Aw, you don' wan' know 'bout me.'

But now it was my eyes that encouraged.

'I come from Country, far, far...' he waved his hand eastwards. 'My people had bad times with the white fellas. The Overlanders. They come through Country driving sheep as many as stars, tramping and eating, scattering emu and kangaroo. They took our hunting. They took our women. They promise food and good things but give nothing. Laugh in our faces. So some of older fellas scatter them sheep, spear some 'stead of kangaroo. But them gentle men of Adelaide town come riding with horses and long guns, and some of us fellas got shot... my father... And they took my mother and I never seen her again.'

I looked away. I, at least, had a mother and father. Unless Glasgow's grimy squalor had claimed them.

'But how did you come here?'

'Next year more drovers come and I go with fella called Lamb. Like the sheep.' His smile bloomed briefly. 'I go look for me mother, but.... We live among them hills and he treat me kind, give me work growing watermelon and tobacco. Till brown snake bit'm hand and he die. So I come to Adelaide town, work for any white fella who pay.'

I studied him, perhaps frowning, for it seemed he had sold himself. Yet he was alive with good health and kept a coin or two in his European pocket. I looked at my waistcoat on him, wondered if I had been complicit in his prostitution.

I thought about the people by the creek. Those who had clung to fading ways, who still camped in their *wurlies* by the waterfall gully. They were fewer now; European sicknesses were taking them. Their land had been stolen, the annual shift from coast to foothill curtailed.

My own folk had once done something similar, driven black cattle from the coast to summer *shielings*. But the southerners and their sheep had taken our hill ground, and our enforced reliance on impoverished potato beds led to privation. I had fled the demise, left kin and homeland, come to find my way among the foreigners. Just as had he.

'Reckon you 'n' me's no friend of them sheep,' he said, smiling.

'Aye,' I agreed.

'Reckon we survivor, though.'

And this I agreed with, too. We had travelled far, left the lands of our Dreaming behind us. We sat together in a far-flung land of foreign men and foreign notions. A land of luxury and wickedness.

He stood up; my chair relinquished him with a soft spring of its well-woven fibres.

'See you 'morrow at work, boss.'

I nodded and smiled at him. As I watched him go, Henry Halls-Winterton's children threw stones at him and one struck him on the back.

I hoped my old grey waistcoat afforded him some protection.

## © Craig S Whyte

Craig S Whyte is a historical fiction writer from Scotland who, for three years, has lived with his family in Adelaide, Australia. An education presenter at the Maritime Museum, Craig's writing is inspired by both Scottish and South Australian history.

# Mamasan
## by Stella Chan Pasteur

I squint and lean hard against the steering wheel. I draw back and sigh. Snow, snow, snow. Thick and fast.

I love snow cloaking every fir and pine around the chalet, sparkling diamonds in the sun especially when I'm nestled inside with a fire roaring and a good book half-lying, half-sitting in the *mamasan*, a huge white, round cushion cradled in wicker. I push, stretch and snuggle and the cushion makes a niche for me.

I fell on the chalet in the summer, walking lost in the mountains of St Cergue. A path, trees and there it was. All wood, all geraniums, all Swiss. At the *épicerie*, five kilometres away, I got the number and booked the chalet for the winter.

The only thing I dragged from Geneva was the *mamasan*.

I locked up the house, left plants and keys with my spinster neighbour. It felt strange at first, this picking up and going, no longer sitting, watching, waiting.

Tick tock tick tock, my heart had counted each second, each minute, each hour, each day. Staring out the window from the rocking chair, dawn seeing pink, then orange, then fire on the white mountain peaks. Then dusk kissing them red and purple. The same colours on the mountain are in the picture on the wall above the bed, above the white head on the pillow. His hair had not been as white as the starched white pillowcase. He had always liked to sleep on starched white things. I could never be bothered. Until then.

He had slept. He had often slept. Up, down, up, down the sheet covering him went and my heart fluttered to its silent beat. One day the sheet above his chest moved no more.

I sat in my rocking chair and stared out into my mountain-of-many-colours. A long time. A very long time.

The day came, the day for turning the house from holding two to one, and as closets and drawers emptied, as tears no longer came, one last thing remained. The attic. And there it was. The *mamasan* where two twenty somethings had spooned themselves into one, its round emptiness waiting to enfold me.

It has been in front of the fireplace of the chalet ever since. Now only three kilometres away, waiting. I squint in the snow, change gears, drive up the steep mountain road. The tires skid on ice, I brake, the car dances and flies.

I struggle to open my eyes. It is dark. It is quiet. I am in my *mamasan* at last, a *mamasan* of snow.

## © **Stella Chan Pasteur**

Stella Chan Pasteur is Chinese, born and raised in the Philippines, and has been living in Geneva, Switzerland, for 22 years. She won a prize for one of her short stories and is a published author.

### Manger, Manger Glorieux *
### (Food, Glorious Food à la Française)
#### by Patricia Feinberg Stoner

My father shot me a dubious look over his spectacles.

'But what do you actually do, down there in the south of France?'

My father was American, Jewish, hard-headed. His idea of a holiday was to shoehorn in as many 'sights' as could be crammed into a week or a fortnight. His idea of the rationale for buying a property was its investment value. Lollygagging, as we call it, was a closed book to him.

'Well,' I answered slowly, knowing how he would react, 'we do spend a lot of time eating.'

There was a pause. Then, simultaneously, we burst out laughing.

But it got me thinking. We'd been living in the Languedoc for six months by then, and were beginning to come to grips with the lifestyle.

Food in France is, if you'll pardon the pun, an entirely different kettle of fish. To say 'we spend a lot of time eating' does not carry the same sense of urgency—you might say gluttony—that it holds in our colder climes. Lingering late into the evening, even over a meal as simple as bread and cheese, is only paying your dues.

The French respect food, in a way that we do not. Take the words '*Bon appétit.*' Quite untranslatable. 'Good Appetite' means nothing (and sounds faintly Germanic) while 'Enjoy your meal' just doesn't cut it. Yet *politesse oblige*, as you pass someone's table in a restaurant, to utter the phrase. When it's said to you—or to me at any rate—you feel a little glow of comradeship: we are sharing the love, sharing the respect.

And the French are not the slightest bit shy about it. I still become hysterical when I remember the day we were sitting in a roadside picnic spot, feasting like royalty on *saucisson* and cheese, fragrant olives and walnut bread. A Land Rover slid to a stop nearby and the driver hopped out. '*Bon appétit*' he called, and disappeared into the bushes for a pee. No Englishman I have ever met would call attention to himself with such cheerful insouciance while bound on such an intimate mission.

Then there's the lunch hour. In England it's a strict hour, if you're lucky. At the top of the corporate ladder you may find the fat cats lunching at leisure in their clubs, although that's more a myth than a reality these days. But for the less exalted—and especially middle management—a quick sandwich at their desks is a clear bid for brownie points.

Not so in France. *L'heure du repas* is likely to extend to two hours, for the lowliest shop assistant or office minion right up to the chief executive herself, and the workers return refreshed and relaxed to renew their attack on the day's labours.

And then there's the question of where this feast takes place. Take a bunch of men in an English office. One o'clock rolls round and they head for the pub. And while they may shovel an unregarded pork pie into their mouths for sustenance, the main business of the hour is liquid. Their French counterparts will gather at a local café or small neighbourhood restaurant. There won't be an extensive menu; it may be a case of 'You'll eat what we've got.' But it will be proper food, properly cooked and properly served at a table, with certainly an entrée and a main dish and often a dessert and/or coffee—and it will be treated with due regard. The French on the whole don't tolerate shoddy food, and will vote with their feet if it is not up to standard.

Things are no different on the road. If you're driving in France and the hands of the clock are creeping towards lunch, keep your eyes open for the café or service station with the largest collection of lorries outside. Good plain food and plenty of it will be the order of the day.

French truck drivers are no fools where their stomachs are concerned.

Even when it comes to the humble picnic, the French have a certain flair. There was
the day when, on the road to somewhere or other, we stopped in a leafy *aire* for a spot of lunch.
Four men whom I can only imagine were commercial travellers had had the same idea. Their suit trousers were pressed. Their suit jackets were carefully hung over the back of their picnic chairs, the sleeves of their immaculate white shirts neatly rolled up.

There was a checked cloth on the table. Plates, glasses and cutlery were set out, a baguette sat on a bread board and there was a selection of cheese and *charcuterie* on the table before them.

They looked so happy, relaxed and carefree that I just couldn't resist.

'*Bon appétit, Messieurs!*' I called out.

My father is long gone now. But every time we sit down to a slow, self-indulgent Languedoc meal, as the sun sinks behind the olive trees and the first bats flutter out into the blue dusk, I find myself explaining it to him all over again. In France, you spend a lot of time eating.

© **Patricia Feinberg Stoner**

Patricia Feinberg Stoner is a retired journalist and publicist. Between 2001 and 2005 she and her husband lived in a small village in the Languedoc.

## Mango Orchard at Chapai **
### by Rilla Nørslund

Ancient mango trees
breathe sun-kissed air
in cathedral tranquility, hints of an echo
where living light descends in dancing beams,
stained and strained through sun-soaked leaves.

Beneath high domes and mighty pillars
feet tread hard-packed soil,
sacred space where village women harvest fallen foliage
bowing low and bowing low to sweep up crackling leaves,
fragrant fuel for simple meals

Monsoon heat caresses swelling treasures,
branches sigh with heavy growing green,
mangoes grow and glow in golden light as hot days linger
with nostalgic scents of nature's sweet delights,
gifts from ancient trees to those who dream.

© **RillaNørslund**

Rilla lives in Bangladesh and has previously worked in a number of African countries. She writes poetry and short fiction and tries to add a little poetry to life through weekly poems and poetic twittering.

# Meeting Abinaya *
## by Danielle Lalonde

Ten years ago I began sponsoring children through a Canadian charity called Chalice. It started out with one child that my Mom and I 'shared'. His name was Gift and he was from Africa. Soon I took on another child myself—Jocelaine from Haiti. Then a third—in India. And so on. It was easy... sign up, send a cheque and feel good that I was making a difference in a life of a child somewhere.

It wasn't until I got the first card from one 'my kids' that I started to think more about wouldn't it be great to meet at least one of them someday?

In 2006 I was posted in India for work and one morning I decided I was going to find out how far it was to each of the two girls I had sponsored there. I was told that both were very far off and were not on easy routes of travel for foreigners. I determined that the next time I had a chance I was going to go for it. By March the following year, my dream came true. I was being sent to the Chennai office for two weeks and one of 'my kids' was about 350 kilometres to the southwest. I contacted Sister Maria who ran the convent that was the local partner for Chalice. She was excited that I was coming and she arranged for my sponsor child to come to the convent to meet, someplace private, away from the crowds of the village.

I wondered how we would communicate as I didn't speak Tamil and I doubted she could speak English or French.

Saturday morning I jumped out of bed early, packed a few small treats, a couple of picture books, and two little dresses. The charity had warned me that taking expensive gifts was discouraged as not all the other children get extra gifts from their sponsors.

When my driver arrived we quickly figured out that I neglected to specify that I needed a driver that could speak English. Once you get away from the city there are no street signs so directions of 'go straight then turn in a few miles' are very vague... better to stop regularly and check. My driver was good that way. We didn't say much because of the language barrier, but I pointed and asked and sometimes he said a word and I would repeat it. He'd smile. As we got closer, the paved road became gravel, then dirt, then tire tracks through tall grass, and finally a single track. We were met by a guy on a motorbike who offered to take me the rest of the way while my driver followed slowly and carefully behind.

As the bike came through the last of the tall grass I saw the Good Shepherd Convent. Sister Maria and several others were waiting for me. They greeted me warmly and took me inside to wash up after my eight-hour journey. I was then led to an outdoor patio and that's where I first laid eyes on her. She was so beautiful, so tiny. Abinaya. She wore a purple dress and had two pigtails wrapped around her head with bright orange flowers twisted around them. She was surprised when she saw me —I don't think anyone had told her I was Caucasian. Next to her sat her sister… just as beautiful—a little older, a little taller, wearing a red dress. She smiled at me and I winked back. And next to them sat their Mom. I could instantly see where they got their beautiful looks from.

I walked over to the Mother and wasn't sure if I could shake her hand or hug her, but when she stood she hugged me. Question answered. Then I walked over to Abinaya and her sister and squatted down between their chairs, facing them. Abinaya leaned back, not sure what to make of me… a full figured, red-haired, freckled, white woman. Her sister just kept smiling. I slowly put each of my hands over the top of their hands on the armrest and they didn't mind. What an amazing feeling it was—to have come all this way to see the little girl who sends me hand drawn pictures once a year. Who (because of my small monthly donation) could afford to go to school (and her sister too), that the whole family had food, and had even managed to save enough to buy a goat for milk and put a deposit down for bricks to build a better house than the one that blew down or washed away each year during monsoon season. Sister Maria explained that their father had not made the 5 km walk with them because he was building the house that weekend so it would be dry before monsoon season started in a few weeks.

The time flew by. I showed the picture books I brought (about Canadian animals) and I made sounds that the animals make. The girls (and everyone else) laughed and laughed. We had such a good time, but it ended so quickly. Sister Maria advised that it was a long walk back for three women in the dark and I had a long journey back as well. I asked Sister Maria if my driver and I could drop them at their village. She said that it would be difficult on Abinaya and her family if others were to see them getting special treatment, but she agreed to send them in the convent car.

As I hugged Abinaya good-bye, I squeezed her tightly and told her I loved her. She hugged me tightly too and I knew we understood each other. As they got in the car and drove off into the dusk I found tears streaming down my face... my heart filled with a peaceful calm. My little angel with the halo of orange flowers.

© **Danielle Lalonde**

Danielle is a Canadian, currently living in Bangladesh. She has worked or lived in over 27 countries. She is married and has two adult daughters, and a cat named Lola.

# Middle-Earth Sea **
## by Richard King Perkins II

Air of airs on the shores of the middle-earth sea,
the mother binds her child in North African blankets
like scorpion death hidden in tarot.

Hanging bubbles are the tears of a dying deity.

A cloth suspended on bamboo poles is The House of God
for the red eagle princeling.
She is the Empress of White Sands,
sapient powder on the heel of a boot.

Italians lounge on the beach, basking in the occult
when Aleister Crowley walks out of the sea
and the waves settle into a potent milk
sucked warm from the villa doorway.

The spiral universe is entirely placid
for a mother and son closer than Gemini replicas.

© **Richard King Perkins II**

Richard King Perkins II was born in Tripoli, Libya, North Africa and grew up playing on the beaches of the Mediterranean Sea while living in Italy. He then came to the U.S, where he has lived ever since.

# Missionary Dress
## by Sally Robinson

Jody steps out from the throng of well-wishers at the airport and presses a small brass-coloured metal box, like a miniature pirate's chest, into my hand.

'For those difficult moments,' he murmurs.

I thank him and toss it into my handbag. We continue with our goodbyes.

I first saw Jody as he sat hunched up in a corner of the Amsterdam office of Amnesty International, where I worked as a volunteer. It was the end of a warm day and everyone was keen to get home. He was wearing an imitation sheepskin coat in the height of summer and looked pale and exhausted. He seemed hardly more than a boy.

'Who's the lad in the corner?' I asked the secretary.

'His name's Jody. He arrived from the sleep-in this afternoon. He needs somewhere to stay.'

'Sleep-in?'

'Yes. You know, one of those places where the young ones kip down in rows for practically nothing a night. There's one in that old warehouse on the Rozengracht.'

'Where's he from?' I asked.

'South Africa.'

It was 1975. Apartheid, war in Namibia, sleep-ins and dope in Amsterdam.

My maternal heart began to pound. 'You mean he has nowhere to sleep tonight?'

'No,' she said. 'He just turned up about 10 minutes ago. I guess we'll have to turn him out and tell him to come back in the morning.'

What could I do?

What would you do?

I offered him a bed for the night. I could always bring him back next morning. Ignoring the gasps of surprise, Jody and I set off home.

'I'm a conscientious objector from South Africa,' he said grandly over supper that evening. 'The war against Namibia is all wrong and I refused to fight. So here I am.' He eyed us both challengingly. And he stayed.

'My mother's a manipulative bitch and my father's a fascist pig,' was his answer to our entreaties to at least tell his parents where he was. 'And my brothers and sisters just toe the line.' Worse was to come.

Afterwards, he disappeared into the kitchen. Some time later he emerged bearing a steaming, aromatic quiche. The pastry was perfect, crisp and nicely browned, the cheese light and fluffy, perfectly risen, its dark contents spaced evenly throughout like small flowers.

'My speciality,' he announced. 'Mushroom quiche. Magic mushrooms!'

Magic chocolate gateau followed.

So of course, I should have known what was in the little metal box. Meanwhile it nestles snugly in my handbag, as we set off into our new future, working for the German Lutheran Church at a Christian university in the Far East. I have studied my unfamiliar role with elaborate care, and there has been no shortage of advice.

Mother-in-law: 'The mini-skirts will have to go. 'I'll take you to my dressmaker. She'll know what you need.'

A team of maiden missionary aunts willingly joined in the project.

Aunt Miep: 'Wonderful! You'll be carrying on the family tradition.'

Aunt Truus: 'Missionaries get 10 kilos extra baggage allowance for bibles. I can help you there.'

Aunt Beppie: 'You're so lucky!'

And finally Aunt Hilda: 'I'll come with you!'

The dress that I finally chose for the journey combined modesty with sweetness. It was made up in two colours of crisp Laura Ashley cotton print. The bottom part was dark green with small white fresh-looking flowers, ending mid-calf; the top part, bosom upwards, dusky old-fashioned pink with puffed sleeves to just above the elbow, again with small white fresh-looking flowers. The bodice consisted of a V-neck wrap-over with a high neckline. I called it my Missionary Dress.

We are well into the night, and everyone around me is asleep, open mouths, faint snores, not so faint snores. The gentle rattle of a stewardess wheeling along the cold drinks trolley. For me, though, the moment is too precious to waste in sleep. I look out of the window and far, far below I make out small scatterings of twinkling lights. I imagine oases strewn across a vast desert. Above us the stars shine brighter than I have ever seen them.

Encapsulated in that unreal state of being projected across the world, I remember Jody's little metal box. Opening it carefully I see that it is filled with tiny, flat seeds. I begin to dream of my new garden and the small fertile plantation that I shall visit in those 'difficult moments'. Mentally I place it between the bougainvillea and the hibiscus, or among sweet-smelling jasmine.

My Missionary Dress is feeling less crisp now, and rather tight beneath the arms. Heads loll uncomfortably around me and we start the descent to Abu Dhabi, our first stop-over.

Out in the transfer hall, even though it is three o' clock in the morning, all is noise and bustle. We seem to have entered a vast oriental market. Bright chandeliers hang from the ceiling throwing down their light onto glass kiosks that overflow with what seems to be every kind of contraband, flashing gold and precious stones. We move in a cloud of exotic scents—sandalwood, patchouli, frangipani. Dark-skinned Arabs crouch behind tiers of Rolex watches, flashing their golden smiles, urging us to buy, buy, buy. Plastic dummies dressed in burkas, Scottish tartans, even fur coats, stare ahead with static smiles. There is excitement around me and gasps of surprise and delight from our fellow passengers. My thoughts hark back to childhood readings of the *Arabian Nights*, and all fulfils my every romantic dream of the gateway to the East. My greedy gaze falls upon a pair of golden curly-toed Arabian slippers, sequined in ruby red and emerald green. But then I remember my Missionary Dress, crumpled now, its sweet flowers wilting. In the Ladies a group of burka'd women spit lustily onto the marble floor.

Smart young soldiers stand around, brand new Kalashnikovs slung with almost casual elegance across their shoulders. They smile indulgently as we pass them by with our two wide-eyed children. Our sense of freedom is exhilarating after the confines of the plane, and we wander in delight as if in a land of dreams. Even Aunt Hilda— yes, she has come too—is enchanted.

'Well, I never,' she exclaims, waving her crutches dangerously, 'How times have changed!'

Our flight is called and it is time to re-board. We gather up the children. Strangely, we are all required to pass along this trestle-type table that has suddenly appeared. Lined up behind it, the smart young soldiers we saw earlier, seemingly so relaxed and benign, now look different.

'Mum, what's he doing with his gun?' my son asks.

Suddenly I remember the little metal box, sitting so snugly in my bag. I stop in terror. I freeze. Visions flash before my eyes of public execution, orphaned children, my bereaved husband and parents, an unmarked grave in the desert; the past and the future—my home, my childhood, my children now grown-up, my husband happily remarried. My Missionary Dress cuts painfully into my flesh, constricting my breasts, and under my arms, where a rush of dampness spreads, spoiling the scents of the Orient with my sour sweat. Now we are being shepherded into a queue. More soldiers appear and their faces stiffen. Now their Kalashnikovs are no longer strung elegantly across their shoulders, but held firmly at the ready. Handbags are opened, their contents strewn onto the table, and cries of protest arrogantly ignored. An officer comes forward.

'I'm so sorry,' a woman cries out nervously, struggling with her bag. 'It just won't open.' The officer leads her away. Everything has gone quiet. Just the sound of footsteps as the queue moves slowly forward, more relentlessly now, it seems, and the click of handbags being opened and shut. The odd anxious murmur. Just a few more people to go.

I see my husband, tall, fair-haired, purposeful, on the brink of a new life; my children gaze in wonder in Aladdin's Cave, never dreaming of danger. Aunt Hilda stands tall, leaning on her crutches, her face alive in happy expectancy of new conversions ahead. Then it hits me.

Carefully, almost casually, I take the little metal box from my handbag. I can feel its smallness, its sharp edges like little teeth biting into my hand. Gently I slip it down the ample front of my Missionary Dress, amidst its fresh white flowers. Now it nestles safely, deep in my damp, matronly cleavage, where I can feel its welcome coldness. I feel safe, buoyant, righteous even, in my Missionary Dress, its generous folds protective against my skin. I move forward, my two children walking demurely by my side. I am even spared the handbag routine, and serenely return the handsome soldier's gaze as we sail through.

## © Sally Robinson

Sally Robinson is a member of Writers Abroad. She lives in The Netherlands. She writes short stories and flash fiction.

# More Rakia for the Amerikanski *
## by Dominic Carrillo

I hung out with a fifty something year-old Bulgarian bus driver named Boris the other day. He had taken one of my classes on a field trip and I'd offered to buy him and the tour guide a drink at some point later that day. It was a gesture. I didn't think they'd really take me up on the offer.

The three of us sat at a table on the sidewalk in front of a bar just outside of Sofia. Boris didn't speak much English. His voice was deep and his accent was thick. But my Bulgarian vocabulary, about twenty-five words, was much worse. So the tour guide, Lukas, served as the translator most of the time. Before our beers arrived, Boris pulled out a plastic water bottle with a gold-colored liquid inside. He smiled so widely that his eyes became narrow slits.

'You have my *Rakia*?' he asked and pointed to the bottle. 'I make. Try.'

'Yes,' I said. It was still early in the afternoon, but I didn't want to be impolite and reject an elder Bulgarian's friendly offer of homemade *rakia*.

Boris poured a tall glass half way full and rambled something off in Bulgarian.

'He says that *rakia* bought in stores is probably 30 to 40 proof power,' Lukas translated. 'But this homemade stuff is close to 70 proof.'

'Wow,' I said.

'*Nazdravey*,' Boris said and held his glass out to mine. Lukas did the same.

'*Nazdravey*. Cheers.'

We all took big sips. The *rakia* was strong.

I made a pained expression and Boris chuckled like a Mafioso as he leaned back in his chair. But the smile was soon wiped off of his face when two teenage boys ran by our table yelling at each other, almost bumping into us. Boris shook his head and grunted like an angry bear.

'This problem now...' he said, and trailed off in his native tongue.

'He says that there is no order in these days,' Lukas explained. 'He misses this about the Soviet times. There was order then. No crime. No teenagers running around like that. No problems.'

'No problems?' I asked.

'Well, yes, there is always some problems,' Lukas admitted, 'but comparatively it was a good time.' Lukas was speaking for himself now. 'I don't agree, but he is much older than me. He was in the army too.'

'What else did Boris like about the Soviet era?' I asked.

Lukas translated my question and Boris concentrated on him, then me. He paused before responding.

Lukas translated. 'He says things were more equal in Communist times. Everybody could go to the mountains in the winter and to the beach in the summer... Nobody was poor and hungry. We didn't have much, but there was no excess... Also, the leaders led and there were no questions. It was simple and direct.'

I took another drink of *rakia* and added another cube of ice. Even though I knew the basics of Soviet history, I asked Boris more questions because this man had lived it.

'What was worse about the Soviet times, compared to now?'

Lukas didn't need to translate my question because Boris understood me. Lukas listened to Boris's response and then explained. 'He says that if you wanted to buy a car back then, you had to save up for fifteen years. Then you could only buy Russian made Lada... Now we have more choices, but only the rich can make whatever choices they want.'

'Is that the only thing that's better?' I asked.

Lukas listened to Boris's response and then translated for me. 'He says that you couldn't talk about the government in a bad way. If you did, they would find out and put you in a prison camp.'

I nodded my head indicating that I understood, but knew that I hadn't absorbed it in any real sense. My only knowledge of political prison camps was what I'd seen in the movies.

'You like?' Boris asked me in English, pointing to his glass of *rakia*.

'*Da*,' I lied. 'It's good.' What else could I say? He'd made the drink himself and it was clear that he took great pride in it. 'It's strong.'

'*Da*,' Boris said and laughed. 'Very strrrong.' He grabbed my glass and poured more *rakia* for me, with apparently no regard for our waiter or the bar's policy on bringing your own liquor.

I drank that glass and the next one he poured me because I was being polite, which was a mistake. It turns out that mixing *rakia* and beer doesn't work. But I loved the experience—sitting and drinking with a former Soviet soldier, hearing about his nostalgia and mixed feelings about past and present day Bulgaria.

And there was my self-actualizing again—at an outdoor bar in Sofia, Bulgaria, unintentionally getting drunk at four in the afternoon off homemade *rakia*, a liquor I didn't previously know existed. I had left San Diego a little over a year before with a sense of urgency. It was now or never, I had thought, and maybe I was right. If I had stayed in my hometown and continued to work and socialize in the same, comfortable, contented environment, then I'd probably be doing it for the rest of my life. I'd always wanted the challenge and adventure of life abroad, but the timing never seemed right. There were always commitments: relationships, family, security, steady salaries, but no savings. There was also fear of the unknown. It may sound dramatic, but somewhere into my early thirties, I began to feel that life was too brief to wait for your dreams to be realized someday in the distant future.

So I left San Diego, and I'm glad I did.

*Rakia* might not be my favorite drink, but Sofia feels like the right place for now.

## © **Dominic Carrillo**

Dominic Carrillo, author of *To Be Frank Diego*, is a freelance writer and teacher from San Diego, CA. He began creative writing during graduate school at UCLA. He currently teaches English in Bulgaria and is working on his next novel. http://americanoabroad.blogspot.com

# On Teach-Big Street *
## by Sabine Chai

Do you remember when we first met? I don't think I saw much of you that hot, humid afternoon. I was concentrating on accomplishing three tasks.

Number one: do not lose the friendly student who was helping me find a new apartment. The street was full of fast-moving people, half of whom seemed to be wearing white button-down shirts and navy blue pants. While trying to keep up with my new friend, I was wondering how all these white shirts managed to stay so crisp and dry. Do Taiwanese people not sweat? I remember looking forward to a long, relaxing shower.

Task two: keep track of my own movements on the increasingly crinkled and soggy map of Taipei City I held clasped in my hands. I suspected I was walking down a street called Shi Da Lu—Teach-Big Street? New friends are great, but some degree of control is better. I could do this on my own if I had to, right? After we got lost twice trying to identify lane 128 of Roosevelt Road, I was not so sure about that anymore.

Finally, task three: avoid stumbling on the unpredictable, creatively distributed pavement. Yes, that was my first impression of you. Later that year, I learned to appreciate the sudden crevices and other traps for sandaled feet as part of your character—your way of inviting the rushing crowd to take a breath and slow down. That first day they were just one more obstacle to be overcome, and I admit I may have disliked you just a little for adding bruises to my toes.

We were properly introduced the next day when my landlady explained, 'Just follow Shi Da Street all the way and you will run right into your university, Shifan Daxue, Teachers' University.' Ah, so you were named for my school. From then on, we spent a lot of time together.

Morning or night, you were always teeming with people running in all directions, honking cars, the omnipresent hordes of motorscooters, booming K-Pop beats streaming out of open storefronts, food stalls with crowds waiting for some unknown delicacy, and endless other sounds and smells. Walk—do not run into people—do not stumble over the curbs of the numerous side streets—avoid stepping on cockroaches—keep up the speed—try to remember landmarks; the grocery, the 7/11, the bakery—recognize and greet any recent acquaintances. I felt like a juggler with always one more ball than I could handle.

After a while, some details became more familiar. A visit to the bookstore set me up with a number of excellent dictionaries. How I wished just owning them could transfer all these Chinese characters into my head! Then, there was the corner store whose bewildering mix of goods offered new surprises every day—from fluffy Pikachu slippers to leopard print underwear. And after walking up and down your sidewalk for a few weeks, my feet learned to avoid all those opportunities for bruises.

As my toes healed and I got to lift my eyes from the pavement, though, I was met with an unpleasant surprise. I was foreign! You say I should have known that? Of course, a new place, a new language, a new culture, all require learning and adapting. I was not prepared, however, for the relentless staring; people changing cars in public transport to get a better look at me, children giggling and pointing, students talking about me assuming I did not understand—'Look how big her eyes are! What do you think her hair feels like?'—Like an animal in the zoo.

Did you notice how my eyes returned to the pavement, trying to hide my foreignness behind a fast pace and deep sips from my Guava juice box? Thank heaven for cooler winter temperatures bringing coat pockets in which to hide my map—the ultimate sign of the insecure newcomer.

Winter came and went and I began to remember names and faces. The friendly lady selling warming egg pancakes for breakfast. The family running the corner restaurant with the best fried rice on the street. You could hear the roaring of the fire and the clanging and scraping of the spatula in the wok before you saw the rice flying up, down, and around until it had combined perfectly with your chosen meats and vegetables. I got busy, spending endless hours in all those fashionable little coffee shops in your side streets, moving from basic survival Chinese to discussions of philosophy and religion, talking and laughing with new friends in the little park along your busy lanes.

Then, one day I observed an old gentleman so busy staring at me and my friends that he ran into a street sign. People around giggled. I giggled. I smiled. And my heart was laughing because he was free to look and so was I—free to observe the people passing by, free to peek into the pots and pans of the food stalls popping up every evening and to join the most promising queues, free to have tea and chat with tea store owners and choose my favorite Gaoshan Oolong tea, free to explore every facet of life along this street and beyond.

I never got to ask how you feel about all those new people arriving every year, stumbling around, dazzled and confused until they gradually make you their home. Do you welcome us? Do you cheer for us when we find the grocery store without detours for the first time? Are you glad to see maps disappear in backpacks and smiles return to faces? Do you miss us when we are gone? Do we leave a trace in your memory? Or is every day a clear slate for you, to be filled with the chatter, laughs, and tears of all who come along?

If you start every day anew, I look forward to our next first meeting. You may not recognize me but I will come with your trace in my heart.

© **Sabine Chai**

Sabine Chai earned her Ph.D. in Communication at the University of Maryland/College Park. Her teaching, research, and writing focus on intercultural communication. She has lived in Austria, Germany, China, Taiwan, and the U.S., and is now located in Dhaka, Bangladesh.

# One Percent
## by Jane Downing

They didn't talk anymore. Leo said he was busy at work and he was tired (they said things to each other, they just didn't talk). Kim sat in the silence after he'd left that morning with her third iced tea and watched the banana tree outside the kitchen window. There was a new frond, furled tighter than a pre-dawn flag. Seven older fronds swayed on the slight breeze Kim could not feel because the window was closed and the air-conditioning on. One, the one that had been furled the day before, was crisp and green and inviolate, the rest were shredded by the elements, as they all would be in time. She stared at the new, tight pole of a leaf. If she had the patience, she told herself, one day she'd catch one *in flagrante*. She took another sip of her tea. Nothing happened. Nothing unfurled.

Yesterday, Sunday, Leo had taken pity, his words, and taken her off the island. Saipan was larger than a cabin but was small by anyone's standards, not only to someone with Australia as a template. He diagnosed a fever in her pacing, in her silences, in her unhappiness, and he prescribed a daytrip.

'To another island?'

'A different island.'

Tinian was a ferry ride away. They hired a car at the other side and followed a road into the jungle of *tangan tangan*, an interloping plant that was seeded after the war had scraped the island bare. They seemed to be the only tourists on the island, because who else would want to remember the events of 1945 on a daytrip? When the *tangan tangan* got too vigorous—a tunnel of green drawing in on them, mutant claws clutching and threatening the side of the rental car—it was easier to drive on the former runway. At one stage, two B29 Superfortresses had taken off from here every forty-five seconds, and the history got into Leo and he put his foot down. There were no speed limits to transgress: he sped toward the horizon. Kim clutched her seatbelt across her chest but stopped herself saying anything. She reminded herself she was happy to be out of the condominium.

Their destination would have been easy to miss if it hadn't been for the other car. It was a silver sedan, a twin to their own (part of the rental fleet of three). Leo headed towards it at a more sedate pace then drifted to the left.

'We'll go to the second one first,' he said.

Kim watched the three Japanese men by Bomb Loading Pit 1 turn to watch them pull up next to the second bomb loading pit. Then they all politely ignored each other.

Out of the cocoon of air-conditioning, Kim was instantly wet. Sweat welled under her breasts and at the back of her knees. Leo was already reading from the guidebook, getting the names and the dates sorted. This was where Fat Man was loaded, readied to fly over Nagasaki. There wasn't much to see. The pit had been filled in, there was no B29 fighter in the vicinity; the only shadow was cast by a collared kingfisher flying overhead. Kim tried to imagine men down there going about the mechanics of war. She tried to work out how small the bomb must have been judging be the dimensions of the loading pit. So small to have killed so many.

The roar of the car's engine spared her from thinking about all the Japanese dead. The three Japanese businessmen as old as her father drove off, and soon enough she and Leo were following them down 8th Avenue and Broadway. The American Marines had noticed Tinian was the same shape as Manhattan and scattered their names accordingly (another droned snippet from the guidebook. Leo only used the written words to fill the silences). The vines worked their way across even these wide avenues. Let the jungle take it all, Kim thought. I'd rather be in Manhattan. I'd rather be anywhere.

This time she had to make Leo slow down, and then stop. She got out quickly. The sounds of The Eagles blasted over the plain before her car door was pulled shut from the inside—to keep the cool air in, Leo gesticulated. Kim ran into the undergrowth, pushing aside a veil of vines, before doubling over and vomiting. Ants were instantly swarming over the chunks of pawpaw and watery bile.

Kim made herself coffee this time, to test the nausea she still felt. The coffee grains fizzed in the limestone-loaded water. She tried to remember how funny this had seemed when they first arrived. Everything was bright then, and not just because of the startling sunlight.

The coffee tasted foul. She poured it down the sink.

For the first year of their marriage, as part of the ritual as Leo left for work each morning, she'd asked him 'How much do you love me?' And he'd let his lips linger on hers before forming a rounded 'One hundred percent.' She hadn't asked him that morning, or for many previous mornings. She wondered what his answer would be down to now. Fifty percent some of the time, on a good day?

She should have looked for a job as soon as they'd arrived on Saipan, but it hadn't seemed worth it for a year. And, truth be told, she'd been looking forward to time for herself. If she'd been able to raise a laugh now, it would have been sarcastic. Today she could drive down to Garapan, get some money from the bank then some tuna fresh enough for sashimi, in all this time for herself. She wouldn't make the mistake of popping in to the hospital to suggest lunch again. What had she seen? Leo, a local woman, a look. Nothing more. He hadn't seen her as he lent toward this woman, as she'd toyed with the stethoscope around his neck.

Kim splashed her face and buried it briefly in her musty towel. Her restlessness drove her out the door into the heat. Her headache only kicked in as she drove along the waterfront. The red of the flame trees burnt her retina, then a coconut grater started gauging out the back of her skull.

'I want to go home,' she sobbed in the car park behind the Bank of Hawaii. She meant her kitchen, to watch the banana leaf open, she meant their little house in Melbourne, she meant the past when any talk of warmth was emotional, and any talk of heat was sensual.

There was no way she could get out of the car and face people so she drove on, heading to the east, experimenting with the accelerator on the straight road, but pulling back from Leo's Tinian speeds as the mountains loomed up.

Where the green of the sea met the blue of the sky, clouds were anchored like far flung islands. Kim knew they were illusions. There was nothing in that direction until Japan. Only one percent of the entire Pacific Ocean was land. She lived on a tiny part of this one percent.

Kim got out of the car and walked closer to the edge of the land. The drop was sheer, onto jagged rocks and frothing sea. Her stomach lurched even before she imagined the scenes here after the Americans took the island. Some of the Japanese went to the cliff now called Suicide, others stopped here at Banzai Cliff. *Banzai*: an exclamation, ten thousand years. She imagined they shouted this as they leapt to their deaths. Men and women, and also women holding children.

Kim could feel the breeze on her face. She wrapped her arms around her belly. She didn't need a doctor husband to tell her there were changes and how to interpret them. She swayed. That breeze. A step back, a step forward; either way felt like a leap of faith.

After the Americans took Saipan and Tinian (and the mothers took their children onto the cliffs) the Marines built the airstrips from which to bomb Japan and eventually, famously, the cities of Hiroshima and Nagasaki. The B29 about to deliver the world's first atomic bomb had no name until the last moment when the pilot named it after his mother. Leo had read this too from the guidebook on Tinian after the three Japanese men left and they swapped bomb loading pits. A palm grew out of this one: nature was determined to take the island back. Kim had asked why an aeroplane needs a name and Leo had kept reading. Kim asked herself now how Enola Gay felt about this honour, that within her namesake's belly sat Little Boy and tens of thousands of deaths.

Kim wondered too why these were the only images of motherhood she could conjure on a quiet Monday with a perfect sun directly overhead. She lifted her eyes from the rocks to the horizon. The clouds were moving in. If she waited, they'd bring rain and wash the sweat—because it was not tears—out of her eyes.

The banana leaf unfurled as she sliced the tuna for dinner. She put down the knife to watch each roll of supple green loosening and letting go its grip until it flopped clear like an elephant ear.

She decided she'd ask Leo tomorrow when he left for work. Not anything new, just the old question: how much do you love me? At least then she'd know.

The air-conditioner kicked in and thrummed loudly in the next room, or perhaps it was the sound of his car coming through the condominium gates.

## © Jane Downing

Jane has over 140 stories published. Her novels *The Trickster* and *The Lost Tribe* are set in the Pacific. She lived as an expat child in PNG, Tanzania, Ireland, Indonesia, and as an adult in Russia, China, the Marshall Islands and Guam.

## Postcard from Benares, India **
### by Bruce Louis Dodson

Ganges
Early morning
Sun comes pale pink
Out of dust horizon
Long warm days before monsoon

Stone and concrete reflect the dawn's new light
Gold temple tops cast
Daytime stars onto this timeless river
People bathing, praying
Working
Dugouts float past
Barely moving
Oars creak
Temple bells toll
Voices over water . . . hushed

A trail of laundrymen beat shirts, and sheets and saris
Against rocks worn smooth
So many lives ago
No one remembers
Songs and whopping
Echo
Krishna! Whop! Om Shanti! Whop! Jai Rama! Whop!

Vultures soar patiently
Without effort
Gliding above blue fog mist
Mingling with smoke from burning ghats
Along the shore
The end and the beginning.

© **Bruce Louis Dodson**

Originally from San Francisco, California and Seattle, Washington, Bruce Louis Dodson now resides in Borlange, Sweden where he continues to practice photography, sculpture, fiction and poetry.
http://brucelouisdodson.wordpress.com

# Pretty, Jittery Indian Girls
## by Justin Petrone

I'm not sure what the latest progressive male's code of conduct has to say about the seduction of women indigenous to the Western Hemisphere. I suppose we're just supposed to eye them from afar, and leave them to their Pacific Northwest *pot-latches* and tribal dances and make sure they are married off to strong Native men together with whom they will breed 10 prolific children, who will somehow undo the hundreds of years of genocide visited upon them by the so-called white race.

Racism. It's how the West was won. Go read Jack London, he'll tell you. Only now that we Europeans have plowed North America over with highways and fast food restaurants can we glance sometimes with unease in the rear-view mirror. Then, like a bout of indigestion, we try to ignore it and drive on.

But, hey, Vancouver is beautiful anyway. I always went there in March when it was its wettest. The late-winter moisture would knock a man down on the way out the door. Water everywhere. It was sponged up in your cheeks or beading down the taxi windows. You would see big brick houses downtown, covered to the roof with dripping green ivy. At night, the office and apartment buildings spiraled up all around the futuristic metropolis, like a cross between Tokyo and Star Trek. But the water reminded you that Vancouver was still a wild place, a place for plants and animals.

And pretty, jittery Indian girls.

It really is hilarious, the women you find attractive. *Cosmopolitan* leads the ladies to think that if they apply enough make up and make use of enough sex tips and put cucumbers on their eyes, then they'll stand a better chance of catching a dude. Not so. This woman looked like she had been born in her raggedy black clothes. Her hair was dark and dense—there could have been an owl in there. But she did have on a pair of fetching, gold-colored shoes. And gentle features. And there was kindness in the motions of her slender body, a mother's kindness, because she had her two sons with her.

I was instantly smitten when I met her at the bus stop in North Vancouver and then just as instantly ashamed that the thought of liking her, because Indian women were OFF LIMITS. Could you imagine? Me and her? Back in my room at The Cosmopolitan? No, no, no, no, no, no, no. Not done.

Her kids were like two-thirds of the Three Stooges huddling and bumbling and elbowing each other. One of the preteens was asthmatic and was coughing all over himself and others. His face was pallid and grew a shade whiter with every wheeze, 'Kah-hah'. I wondered if his father had been a white man like myself, he was so gray. Maybe a trucker from the steak joint across the way, where guys named Bruce and Mitch sit around, drink, and watch hockey and say, 'Eh.' Maybe he met the mother right here at this very bus stop.

The sturdier son was darker. I had him pegged as one hundred percent native. This kid was Squanto, Geronimo. He was that exotic. Both looked like they had been thawed from Ice Age ice blocks. These were faces you never saw. You saw Scottish faces and African faces, even South American Amerindian faces, were trained to recognize them. But the faces of the Squamish Nation of British Columbia?

That's what they were called. You should have heard the golden-shoed Native woman's sad lament.

'We've lost everything,' she told me at the bus stop. 'We've lost our land, we've lost our language.'

A passionate lady, she was. Couldn't sit still. And all the time, fumbling with plastic bags filled with rolls of quarters. Her two sons held them, too.

'What's with the quarters?'

'Oh, these? We're coming from a *pot-latch*. It's kind of like a big party. And we're supposed to spread the wealth. We don't have much, the Squamish people, but we give quarters as a symbol of wealth.'

'What did you give each other before you had quarters?'

She shrugged. 'I don't know. We've always just given each other quarters. That's our tradition.'

Her chocolate eyes trained in on mine because she could tell I was actually listening to her with my heart. I'm not sure if she smelled my intent, or even what my intent was at that point. Even if I could negotiate her past the front desk at The Cosmopolitan, what was I going to do with her two kids? I felt tenderness for her, for her situation. I had seen the Squamish First Nation Reserve when I came down the Lion's Gate Bridge at dusk. Dilapidated houses, dirty streets, kids bicycle here, street hockey net there. And all the time that pristine Pacific sadness. O magnanimous Canadian fathers, how kind of you to build a massive bridge right over the heads of the Squamish people. That way it would be easier for them to walk from North Vancouver to Stanley Park and Burnaby Island. Thank you, Canada!

We weren't the only people at the bus stop, you know. There was another man standing away toward the posted timetable, looking only occasionally at us over his beige raincoat. He was dark, too, big bushy mustache, thick eyebrows, bulldog jowls. I couldn't tell if he was French or Indian or both, but he seemed to keep his nose up in the air, monitoring our conversation. And the golden-shoed woman said nothing to him, didn't even look at him, so he must have just been another passerby, I thought. North Vancouver at night, full of surprises and weirdos.

When the bus came, we all got on, me and the Native woman sat in the middle, her two sons, Wheezy and Geronimo behind us, and the other gentleman all the way in the back, standing. There were a lot of questions I wanted to ask the woman, about where she had grown up, or where the father or fathers of her sons were, or where she was going. All I managed to ask her was her name. Esther.

She got a lot of me though. My life of international travel. Genetics conference to genetics conference.

'Sounds exciting,' she said.

'Actually, it's kind of lonely.'

Then she took her hand in mine. 'I understand,' she said. It had a calming effect on me. I looked over my shoulder at the man in the raincoat with the mustache. His dark eyes said something, but what? I eyed the quarters again.

'What are you going to buy with them?'

'Dinner.'

We rode the bus downtown, watched the city through dark bus windows and beads of dripping rain, stared out at the Asian neighborhoods where the Korean and Japanese and Chinese restaurants stand right next to each other and Eastern faces hang outside of nightclubs or zoom around on mopeds. The Squamish had once owned most of British Columbia, Esther had said. This around us was what had become of it. All they had left were a dozen reserves, like the one under the bridge. That and her quarters. Her son wheezed, the other one elbowed him, and all the time, her calming hand in mine, like a friend's. Forget all about a midnight tryst in The Cosmopolitan hotel, I was ready to marry the woman, adopt Wheezy and Geronimo, get her out from her home beneath the Lion's Gate, give her a proper home, a proper life, but let her keep her quarters and her *pot-latches*. Anything to save the culture! Where is the line between pity and affection? Are they the same things?

When we got off the bus in downtown Vancouver, the man in the beige raincoat punched me in the face. He had good aim and it hurt, but since I didn't fall, he punched me again. Then I went down on my knees. I'll never forget that shriek, the scream as Esther stooped down and held my face in her hands.

'Stop it, you ass, stop it!' she cried out, while the man started kicking me in the gut, grunting, 'Keep your hands off of my sister!' Then I heard someone yell, 'Somebody, get the cops!'

The party of Squamish disappeared into the streets after that. When the polite Canadian police officers arrived a moment later, they told me they had caught the man a block away, asked me what had happened. I told them to let him go, that it was a misunderstanding, and that I had deserved it.

© **Justin Petrone**

Justin Petrone is a New York-born author and journalist who lives in Estonia with his wife, the author Epp Petrone, and their three daughters.

# Priorities *
## by Doreen Porter

Shortly after the end of the war in the former Yugoslavia, I travelled there with Tony, a photographer, to write about the work UK civil servants were doing to help rebuild the area. They were mainly experts in procurement, contracts, and general admin who worked alongside the military.

We began by spending a few days in Split, Croatia, where NATO had its headquarters. At any other time this would have been an idyllic spot, overlooking the sparking blue Adriatic. Yet even then, normality was beginning to return to the town as restaurants and cafes opened for business again and locals strolled along the promenade, sweaters draped casually over their shoulders.

Afterwards, the plan was to go by helicopter to Banja Luka in Bosnia, where the UK contingent had made itself at home in the shell of an old metal factory.

The helicopter duly took off, flew around a bit and landed in a field of potatoes. An elderly man appeared from nowhere, refuelled it and off we went—back to Split. The weather was apparently too bad to fly over the mountain range between us and Banja Luka.

We were told we could have a lift to Banja Luka with a brigadier who was going that way. Tony and I quickly bundled into the back of an Army jeep, one each side of the armoured guard. We clutched our Army ration packs and settled in for a long, uncomfortable journey. Our ration packs each contained a sandwich, a packet of crisps, a carton of orange juice and a Crunchie. We made short work of everything. After a while, I noticed with pleasure that the brigadier hadn't eaten his Crunchie, so suggested to Tony we share it. When the brigadier felt peckish later and started to look for it, we managed to convince him that it had fallen out of the jeep as we went over one of the many potholes the driver had to negotiate.

After a few hours, the brigadier told us he had to stop at an Army outpost to make some phone calls. 'Go and find something to eat,' he advised, unaware we were full of Crunchie. Later, replete with the standard Army fare of sausage, beans and chips, I needed the loo. 'I definitely remember seeing some earlier,' said Tony confidently. Amazingly he was able to lead us to a couple of portaloos he'd spied while we were making our way to the canteen. As I emerged comfortable after using my pristine portaloo, Tony whispered to me urgently, 'Run!'. 'Why?' I gasped once I'd got my breath back. 'I have an awful feeling the loos have been put there ready to be transported somewhere else,' he replied.

The rest of the journey was long and tiring but the countryside was beautiful. We drove past lush, rolling green hills, dense forests and fast flowing rivers that were dotted with historic towns and villages. Full of character, once they were bustling centres boasting colourful markets and thriving shops selling local specialities. One day that life would return. Armies of fireflies frequently escorted us on our way. Sometimes they were the only light once dusk had fallen as there were no working street lamps anywhere.

Sometimes, you would look across at what had once been a smart house, to see a makeshift grave in the garden. Some were just mounds, others decorated with flowers. It was too dangerous to stop and get out of the Jeep to stretch our legs because of the risk of landmines. We saw very few other vehicles. If people moved around they used a horse and cart or sometimes rickety old bicycles. We saw signs to what were once thriving ski resorts that had obviously buzzed with tourists in the past.

Banja Luka had been badly damaged in the war. The infrastructure was shot to pieces. The British civil servants mostly lived in run-down apartments in the town—preferable to the metal factory, it seemed. Or indeed the four-berth portacabins we slept in, mix and match with military personnel.

One day one of the civil servants asked, 'Do you want to watch the football on TV this evening?' I wondered how that would be possible as there was no electricity, but said nothing. Watching football is not my favourite pastime, but when in Banja Luka... So, intrigued, I replied, 'Yes, please!' with a commendable show of enthusiasm that almost, but not quite, matched Tony's.

We watched the football by candlelight on a TV powered by a generator. It was in German as that was the only station they could get. At half-time, someone asked, 'Fancy a pizza?' He speed dialled a number on his mobile and 15 minutes later some pizzas (with a variety of toppings) were delivered. Priorities.

On the flight home we sat behind journalist Martin Bell who'd been out to do a piece for the BBC's Holiday Programme to encourage tourists to return to previously popular resorts such as

Dubrovnik. What a difference a decade or so has made as Croatia joined the EU in July this year.

© **Doreen Porter**

Doreen is a former journalist who moved to SW France with her husband and three cats six years ago. She enjoys writing about the quirky side of life, which includes helping Rupert, a Standard Poodle, write his blog: www.adoginfrance.blogspot.com

# Queen for a Day *
## by Jayme Wills

Shaking his head in amazement, my husband John swears I'll eat anything that doesn't eat me first! Traveling around the world and living as an expat in various countries has fueled my passion for exotic produce and I have absolutely no qualms about sampling weird-looking selections.

Initially the five-hundred foot warehouse structure looks intimidating. My first trip to the vast farmers' market near our new home in San Isidro de General, Costa Rica, promises to provide ample selections of previously unknown gastronomical delights. In an air of mixed aromas from fruit to fowl, sellers stack produce to make the best use of tight space between stalls. Dotted with restaurants, bakers and fishmongers, the *feria* serves as the weekly place to meet and greet. Surveying the huge expanse, I wonder, 'Can I eat my way through the whole building?' Armed with a purse full of change and suspended pre-conceived notions of what good eating looks like, I happily peruse the aisles seeking my next delicious discovery.

Clamoring for business, vendors present their wares in natural splendor. Contrasted against juicy black seeds, the bright orange flesh of artfully carved papayas resembles large flowers. Enticed by juicy slices of red melon, buyers enjoy a brief respite from the morning heat. Using a mixture of skill and showmanship, a farmer wields a razor-sharp machete to whack the tops off coconuts. Inserting a straw in the green ovals instantly provides awe-struck tourists with refreshing cocktails *à la* Mother Nature.

Reminiscent of southern boiled peanuts, odd orange baubles bob in a steaming gas-fired cauldron. The seller fishes out a plump one and uses his complete English vocabulary in a single sentence. '*Pejibaye* is good, OK?' Inside a slick outer hull, the pale inner flesh presents an inviting challenge. From a condiment dispenser the smiling young man squeezes a splat of mayonnaise on top of the beige fruit. Akin to chewing a mealy raw potato, a bland report from my taste buds propels me toward more exciting conquests.

Suddenly a vendor and I lock gazes. He walks from behind his table and presents me with a deep purple, plum-like orb. '*Señora*, please accept the food of royalty.' Brown stem and outer shell removed, the delicate white pillows of the *mangosteen* look like cloves of garlic, but the heavenly taste tickles my tongue with a hypnotic flavor that sends shock waves to my brain. Legend holds that Queen Victoria offered a sum of £100 to anyone who could supply her with the fresh fruit. I gobble two and John promises me a new pair of earrings if I can pry myself from the spot.

In my haste toward a foot high pile of furry red balls, I become aware of an extra appendage. From under a cute pink sunbonnet, a roly-poly toddler grins up at me. 'I go wif' you!' Relieved to spot the frazzled mom at the other end of a baby carriage, we attempt to jockey a spot in front of the amusing food. Like a street corner magician, the seller mesmerizes the crowd by demonstrating the proper technique for eating his exotic offerings. Navigating through the prickly hull with ease, he pulls it apart to reveal an inside whiter than snow. He explains that fresh *mamón chino*—rambutan—are only available a few months of the year.

Watching the proceedings from her father's shoulders, my newest acquaintance squeals, 'I want to eat a spider!' With the ease of snake oil salesmen, the savvy vendor and his assistant manage to get one of the prickly prizes in every hand. Amid a buzz of excitement and smiles, shoppers shake, rattle and take pictures of the strange fruit. Natives cut to the chase and quickly enjoy their free treat.

During the trip home, we munch on my latest finds and discuss our adventures at the *feria*.

'Speaking of fun, your 60th birthday is rapidly approaching and you haven't given me any idea as to what you'd like.'

Nonchalantly I reply, 'Some fruit would be nice. I'd like a jackfruit from India, a *pepino* from South America and an African cucumber.'

Amused, John asks, 'Is that all?'

'Well, once I shop for the fresh fruit in the various countries, I'm sure there'll be a few other sights we'll want to see. Detecting some hesitation, I attempt to reassure him. 'Don't worry about a thing, dear. I'll arrange the travel plans.'

Determined to get the last word, John quips, 'I'll be behind you with a stomach pump, just in case.'

© **Jayme Wills**

Professional storyteller, fabric artist and musician Jayme Emily Wills is originally from Augusta, Georgia, USA Currently residing in Costa Rica, her latest works can be found at Amazon.com.
http://www.jaymeemilywills.com/

# Reaching out in Africa *
## by Helen Moat

Your head was sleep-heavy on my shoulder, my boy with his porcelain skin, autumn hair and grey-pale eyes. Africa was there for you outside the truck window but you had opted out.

When you awoke, I told you about my own first encounter with Africa, crackled and faded and covered in spidery lines: an old cine film of Joy Adamson projected onto a screen. I was your age then. 'Yeah,' you said in a distant voice and returned to your own screen, Africa ignored, thumbs twitching at speed.

The cine-projector had whirled and clicked in a dim 70s living room, my soundtrack to Africa and a silent movie. I had no idea what Africa really sounded like—or how it smelled. I had to go.

And now there, I was still viewing Africa through a screen—a window screen. I gazed out at a blurry panning of shanty shops with dirt floors and makeshift corrugated tin roofs, rusty tins and faded plastic jerry-cans, earth-coloured fruits and bundles of twiggy firewood.

'Look out the window,' I said. You glanced up briefly, your eyes far away, before returning to your game. I looked at you and sighed, remembering the night after you were born, how I had woken up to find you gone, an impression on the hospital cot mattress where your small body had been. The midwife had taken me to intensive care where you lay behind glass, hidden under layers of clothes and a woollen hat despite the summer heat.

The flashbacks were overlaid with the more immediate but transient images of Africa: a wobble of bicycle, a sway of hip, the flailing limbs of running children, grins as wide as the Rift Valley.

I took you home. You fed painfully slowly just for the milk to ooze back through your mouth and nostrils. A few days in and you were back in hospital.

We had left the Kenyan town of Kisii behind and were climbing through tea plantations, smudges of wet green vegetation on the landscape. Between the rivulets on the windowpane, I glimpsed flashes of brightly patterned fabric and the weave of basket among dark, rain-glossed tea leaves.

At night I left you alone in the hospital, exhausted from trying to nourish you. Did you hold it against me? There was so much anger inside you.

Our reflections in the window were superimposed onto hunched figures in anoraks, standing on the roadside waving bags of tea in the drizzle. Our eyes met in the glass and you gave me a Mona Lisa smile.

We had travelled hundreds of miles already—from the coast at Dar-es-Salaam through Tanzania and the Serengeti Plains before reaching Lake Victoria and the crossing with Kenya. But Africa had sailed by in a sea of red dust before I could reach out and touch it. The continent's singular smell was that of diesel, its soundtrack now the growl of engine. Then I realised, I too felt a kind of detachment, encased in metal and glass.

That is, until Lake Naivasha. On the shoreline, I lay in our tent, slowly breathing in the scent of woody smoke, paraffin and yellow fever tree. So this is what Africa smelled like. Through the darkness, I could hear the faint munching of grass; a hippo behind thin wire, just yards away. And somewhere beyond that, the stark cry of a fish eagle.

We rose before dawn. The hippo was gone and there was a black silence. We reached the rim of Crater Lake as pale primrose light began to soak through monochrome. At last, the feel of solid ground beneath my feet, the dew on my boots and the cool early morning air on my skin; the aroma of damp bark and earth filling my head.

As we walked, I heard the dull rhythmic sound of hoof on earth. I looked up to find we are surrounded by zebra. You gripped my arm and walked close beside me. Neither of us spoke. The zebras moved ahead and disappeared into the horizon. We crept on through shrub and tree until we closed in on five giraffes, close enough to see their long, rough purple-black tongues and the dribble of saliva as they chewed the cud, the slimy green paste reeking like chewed tobacco.

'Look,' Daniel, our guide said, hunkering down by a large hole, 'An aardvark hole. Other animals could be using it though—hyenas, jackals, warthogs, lizards or snakes.'

We belly-flopped onto the ground, our laughter bouncing round the aardvark hole. I breathed in the sour, dank odour of African earth and felt your breath on my cheek. This was as close as it gets.

© **Helen Moat**

Helen Moat lived and worked in Switzerland and Germany before settling in the Peak District of England. When not travelling, she's out walking or cycling the hills and dales. Her writing has appeared in newspapers, on-line and in book form.

# Saintes **
## by Lesley Ingram

I'd like to say *Remember when…* but you
were not there. I was alone when they forced
red meat down my throat, strange words in my mouth,

a stretching on my bones. I was alone
when she said *you don't know your mozzer tongue,*
when she sprayed *yessssss* in my face to show me

and I slipped a sharp sliver of myself
into the heart of *L'arc de Germanicus*
as the *Charente* flooded my teenage blood.

> Forty years on, and I leave again,
> but with you. We focus on the problems
> of too much furniture, of transport costs,
>
> of storage, of sentimentality
> over a teaspoon, a table, a clock.
> We bubble wrap everything. Every thing.

The sliver from the chipped child is still wedged
in stone, its edges weather-beaten smooth.
I cannot reclaim it. It no longer fits.

## © Lesley Ingram

Lesley Ingram moved to France to teach EFL in 2000. She now splits her time between France and England. Her first poetry collection will be published by Cinnamon Press in 2015. She won the 2013 Ludlow Fringe Poetry competition.

# Security
## by Jody Callahan

Retiring to the Caribbean island of St. Lucia had not yet brought the tranquility Jill had anticipated. Before finishing much needed renovations to the beachfront house on the northern tip of the island (the roof was leaky, the septic tank a nightmare, the electricity spotty) she'd had to redirect her savings to better secure the property after a middle-of-the-night burglary pointed out how vulnerable it really was. Though she lost her television and beloved laptop she considered herself lucky for having slept through the burglary unharmed.

Perhaps it was a blessing that her hearing wasn't what it used to be! What would have happened if she'd awoken to confront a man or men inside her house?

In Massachusetts she had been feared as principal by the students, their parents and the entire school faculty of the Henry Whittemore Junior High. Her dominance had carried over into her residential neighborhood where it had been rare for anyone to intentionally aggravate the thick-waisted woman with the spiky, gray hair. Her home had never been egged on Halloween. The newspaper boy had always got off his bike to place The Boston Globe directly on her doormat. It was unnerving, now, to think of herself as a victim. She wanted to move quickly past this stage, secure her home, and establish to the locals that she would not tolerate being burglarized a second time.

No, she wasn't lonely, she assured her daughters. She was too busy having an adventure! Living her dream of moving to the place where they'd had so many happy vacations when the girls had been young and their father still alive. She didn't mention her sickly feeling of buyer's remorse, that a home in the Caribbean was nothing like staying in one of those all inclusive resorts, that maybe she'd made a mistake. Why hadn't she used her money to take longer holidays and stay in the safety and comfort of a hotel with pool and beach access? No, she shook her head at the thought. She was adjusting. Anyone would be shaken after a burglary, and now she was safe. Her yard of mango and coconut trees were newly surrounded by a barbed wire fence. The house was armed with an alarm system complete with cameras and laser sensors. Should anyone open a door or window or even cross the outside patio, armed guards would be dispatched immediately to her house and to her rescue. The guards came even when she accidentally tripped an alarm one morning, having forgotten to shut it off. Arriving in a big, red truck, they wore navy-blue, long-sleeved uniforms and enormous black boots that must have been unbearable in the heat. Though she felt foolish seeing the guards arrive unnecessarily, it did lessen her anxiety about the house.

The most comforting security upgrade though, was the dog. Security was a good guard dog. A little too good. He barked at the barefoot fisherman, spears slung over their backs, walking past the driveway to the rocky shore. He barked at the Rastafarians, tending to their horses in the open field next to her yard. He barked at the geckos. He barked at the giant toads. He barked at any living creature that walked within his sight. Just the other day, Jill caught Security barking at a red and yellow striped caterpillar inching its way across the patio floor. Jill picked up the caterpillar with her bare hands and flung it into the bushes.

'Shut up!' she yelled at the dog.

Security barked back at her, as if defying her, and then dove into the bush to hunt for his caterpillar friend.

It was to be a joke, to name the dog Security. She had pictured, dimly in her mind, a new burglary attempt. She would be sitting outside on the patio one evening, a cold glass of beer in her hand, when a shadow would form behind the light of a *tiki* torch. 'Security!' she would yell and take great pleasure as the dog would instantly answer her call and with his enormous brown bulk, scare the shit out of the intruder.

This morning the dog's barking had been incessant. Jill walked out onto the patio, remembering at the last minute to shut off the alarm, and without having yet had a sip of her morning coffee, began the first of what she expected to be countless times that day, to shush the dog.

'Security!' she yelled. 'Will you please stop barking!'

Security stopped, perhaps not in response to Jill's command but merely to catch his breath, and then launched into a fresh barking fit. He shot Jill a look which, if the dog could speak probably said, 'Whadda ya an idiot? I'm working my ass off here protecting you!'

Security, though a St. Lucian stray, found as a puppy wandering the beach, spoke in Jill's imagination with a hell of a Boston accent.

Okay so today the dog wasn't crying wolf. There on the opposite side of the gate, standing by Jill's tipped over trash barrel, stood an enormous, brown horse. He appeared to be enjoying discarded mango peels and cantaloupe rinds. Jill unlocked the gate, careful to keep Security from following, and righted the barrel. The horse watched her, feet planted, mouth chomping away.

'Hello there, big boy,' Jill said, speaking in the no nonsense tone she had successfully used for years to underscore her authority within the school's walls. She held out a fist for the horse to smell as she would if it were a strange dog. Could horses smell fear the way that dogs could? The horse watched as Jill collected her trash, securing the lid once again. Shipped over from Massachusetts, the barrel had served her for many years as raccoon-proof in the Back Bay. Did they sell horse-proof trash barrels on the island?

Jill retreated into her yard, backwards, careful not to show the horse her backside in case it decided to charge her like a bull. As she was focused on the horse, Security managed to slip behind her legs and out the gate.

'Security, no!' Jill yelled as the dog lunged for the horse.
The horse kicked up and ran out of Jill's driveway and down to the open field. There in the field stood a herd of horses that scattered with the new arrivals. Security, acting as a lion would among wildebeests, changed direction, zeroing in on the weakest target.

'Cut it out!' Jill screamed at Security who was jumping up now to nip the tail of a skinny gray foal.

'Come here right now! Come!'

Security never failed a command when Jill held a beef treat in her hand, inside the house. Without a treat and off his leash, Security picked and chose which commands to follow.

'Security!' Jill yelled again, enraged by his disobedience.

A large gray mare, probably the foal's mother, decided that the deranged woman, not the dog, was the enemy. Yes it was true, Jill found out, a horse, at least an overly protective one, could charge at a person, like a bull. Jill turned and ran, arms above her head, screaming, back to the safety of her yard. Sweat poured down her face. She felt the prickly heat of a rash erupting across her chest.

'Security!' Jill yelled in the general direction of the dog.

'Come! Home! Right now!'

Home. Was this really to be her home? For good? Like hell it would be.

'I give up!' she screamed, kicking the base of the barbed wire fence like a child in the midst of a tantrum.

'Do you hear me? I give up! I give up!' she yelled to the dog, to the horses, to the field, to the whole stupid island.

'Uncle!' she cried, remembering it said by children on the losing end of schoolyard fights.

She had a sudden vision, remembered pushing her way through a group of students. A kind, weak, little boy was held down by an older, habitual troublemaker that Jill would suspend and eventually expel from her school.

'Get off him right now!' Jill had yelled.

The bully, drunk with power, refused to release the hold on his prey. Jill pulled and twisted the larger boy's arm with more strength than an adult had any right to lay on a child. But not until the little boy had cried 'Uncle,' admitting complete defeat in front of the collected school assembly, did the larger boy release his grasp and allow himself to be dragged into the principal's office.

'Uncle!' Jill screamed one last time, closing her eyes and releasing some of the sorrow and the fear that she kept contained within her itchy chest. She dropped to her knees and sobbed with a helplessness that would have disgusted her had she come across a cry-baby doing so in her school. When she was done, when she had completely dehydrated herself in the heat, she opened her eyes and took a deep, noisy breath. She noticed that Security had returned. He stood on the opposite side of the fence, waiting to be admitted into the yard. Jill calmly got up, opened the gate for the dog and latched it closed behind him.

'Sit,' she told the dog and the dog did.

Security sat and looked at Jill as if he were awaiting further instruction.

'Well, what do we do now?' Jill asked the dog.

The dog, even in Jill's imagination, failed to come up with a response. Jill stood and the dog sat as they considered their options. A mosquito buzzed around Jill's head in a circle like a halo. A bluish, long-legged bird walked past them on the other side of the gate. An overripe coconut fell from a tree onto the lawn with a cushioning splat. Amazingly, the dog did not bark.

'Let's get ourselves some cold water to drink,' Jill suggested.

She turned, no longer waiting for a consensus, walked across the patio, up the stairs and into the kitchen of her own home. The dog followed, closely, guarding her back.

## © **Jody Callahan**

American expat Jody Callahan lives on the Caribbean island of St. Lucia. Her comedic pieces have been used throughout the U.S. and by Liars' League London, Liars' League Hong Kong, and at the Wilderness Arts Festival in Oxfordshire.

## Sensing Africa in Hong Kong **
### by Celia Claase

For eyes weakened by the southern sun to forget
the shade of blue that compliments a sky
and search for a headdress in the lava-suit flow.

For manicured feet once cracked by pure dirt to miss
the sting of stepping in a thorn
and the feel of dry dung floors.

For a nose that could mix Lavender with apricots to smell
fossil-gas carbon-dioxiding mildew crawling along tile-seams.

For ears that could rhythm on taxi sounds to hear
spur-of-the-moment singing and African drum-calls during midnight
traffic-breaks.

For fingers that became accustomed to pushing buttons to lift
a page by the wet of a tongue
or maroon their tips with mulberries from the highest branch.

For a mind nurtured to emotion freely to contain
itself under non-reactive rules of saving-face
and interpret sensory-stimuli with Confucian-modesty.

© **Celia Claase**

Celia was born in South-Africa, studied at the University of Johannesburg and has been teaching English in Hong Kong for the past five years. Previous publications included: poems and flash fiction in LitNet.co.za and memoirs by Sarie.com.

# Separated by a Common Language *
## by Katie Dickerson

*Elevator* was the first to go, I think. It became *lift* so easily I didn't even have to think about it. Or maybe it was *pants*, which became *trousers* out of sheer necessity since *pants* now meant *underwear*, and that wasn't a mistake that I wanted to make. Before I knew it, I was watching the *telly* and carrying a *brolly* like they were the most natural things in the world. When I said *cheers* instead of *thanks* to a bus driver one day, I knew that it had happened.

Scotland had become my home.

When I moved to Scotland from New York, the Scottish accent was an almost unintelligible jumble of strange words spoken with a guttural brogue. I spent a lot of time saying, 'Sorry?' to people, which seemed to go over pretty well. Scottish people are always apologising for things that aren't their fault, like when someone else bumps into them or opens the door on them while they're in the toilet. They are polite to a fault, forever worried that they're inconveniencing someone simply by being there.

My co-workers at my new job made sure I understood the most important Scottish and British words. *Fitba* was the sport that I always knew as *soccer*, except *fitba* seemed to have more swearing and sectarianism. *Chips* were like *fries* but fatter, covered in vinegar and served with pretty much everything. *Dreich* was the best way to describe the permanently wet and grey Scottish weather, except maybe for *pish*, which also means *urine*. *Pishing it doon* means raining heavily, as though God is taking an angry pee on your head.

It's not as though I decided to replace my American words with Scottish and British ones. They simply slipped in one by one until I sometimes forgot which was which. One time when I was visiting my parents in New York, I suggested to my father that we get *takeaway* for dinner.

'Don't you mean *takeout*?' he asked.

Did I? I wasn't sure anymore. But take out or away, it doesn't really matter. You take the food with you and you eat it at home.

British spelling and grammar started to slip into my writing. My *Z*s disappeared and I replaced them with *S*s, which softened words like *antagonise* and *agonise*. The *U*s came next, sneaking their way into words where they weren't really needed. *Colour. Neighbour. Flavour.*

Before long my double quotes became single quotes and my sentences ended with full stops instead of periods. On paper I could easily be mistaken as British, but in person my accent betrayed me for what I was—someone who had taken something that wasn't really theirs.

My friends and family said that I was becoming Scottish. I don't think I'll ever stop being American, even if I live in Scotland for the rest of my life, but each Scottish or British word that I adopted took me another step away from New York. My hometown became just another place that I went on *holiday* instead of *vacation*, where people talked so loudly that I felt like they were shouting at me.

If I ever move back to America, I'll have to remove those unnecessary *U*s and remember that I watch *movies* at the *movie theater*, not *films* at the *cinema*. My shoes will cease to be *trainers*, which suggest a certain level of athleticism, and become *sneakers* again, shoes with a decidedly less noble purpose. When someone bumps into me I will not say 'Sorry', but rather 'Watch where you're going' and maybe give them a little push, since I won't need to be so polite anymore.

© **Katie Dickerson**

Katie Dickerson is a New Yorker who moved to Scotland in 2004 and never looked back. She works as a web content developer and spends her free time writing and cooking vegetarian food.

## Sepilok Rainforest Virgin **
### by Mairi Wilson

Green dripping canopy,
luscious creeping tapestries
reeking of mulch and crushed leaves;
stifling silence but for creaking feet
and the ear-drumming beat
of quickening blood.

The leech dropped; a snip of string,
blades sinking in like fish-hooks
latching onto this fish out of water;
you'd warned me of the dangers of naked flesh
but still I'd come sleeveless and in shorts.
Khaki-clad and clever as a leaf tailed gecko
you attracted no attention from under-hanging scavengers,
shrugged your shoulders and sighed
at my recklessness.

I dangled my arm like a broken branch
and held my breath at the threat suspended.
You rummaged for cigarettes,
pulled your lighter from the pack.
A click, a hiss, a flame tongue flicked,
a tickle of heat grazed my skin
and clean as the crack of a mousetrap snap
the bloodsucker furled and fell.

No mark left behind, no itch to scratch,
no badge of honour to mark my ordeal;
a burst of anaesthetic, Wikipedia said.
Nine pairs of testes you also read;
you hadn't needed to tell me that.

© **Mairi Wilson**

Mairi Wilson was born and lives in Scotland, but spent her formative years overseas. She draws directly and thematically on this experience in her work and continues to travel extensively, using her TEFL. qualification to support this

# Sirocco
## by Louise Rockne

A slight breeze rippled the surface of the sea. November, the beginning of the Sirocco. The old women believed the wind blew insanity into the minds of those who listened to it. But listen one must. The Sirocco was a relentless, dry wind turning the green to brown.

By the time the woman reached the small inlet, the fishermen had already moored their boats. They knew when the sea became thick, like yoghurt, the Sirocco would soon blow. They would use this time to repair their nets and gossip at Georgos' little taverna.

The fishermen sensed the woman's approach but avoided looking at her. They knew she would be staring straight at them. Her black eyes unnerved them, unnerved most people. Some of the old women whispered 'Gypsy—eyes', others said she had the eyes of owls.

Unlike other tourists who came and went to the small island, she'd stayed. The locals, used to strangely dressed foreigners in search of summer romance, noticed her and gossiped that she was one of them. But when the tourist police questioned them, no one could remember when she had come to the village. She'd mostly kept to herself. She was always pleasant to shopkeepers and spoke in simple Greek. She wasn't liked, but she wasn't disliked either. She didn't belong, but she could stay.

'*Yassou* Yanni,' she called as she ambled past them towards the little jetty.

'*Yassou*,' Yannis mumbled without looking, keeping his eyes on his net.

One of the fisherman smirked, another made a lewd gesture. Yannis tried to ignore them and continued mending his net. The woman arranged a large towel on the rocks next to the jetty.

Yannis was flustered after his strange encounter with her the previous evening. He had sold his day's catch to Georgos who had given him a good price, so he'd had money to spare. He decided to stay on for a drink or two and listen to some bouzouki before going home to his mother's cooking and complaints about his continuing avoidance of marriage.

'Hello,' the woman had said, suddenly appearing out of nowhere. 'May I sit here?'

Yannis, startled had motioned towards a chair across the table.

'I have seen you in the village; perhaps you have seen me too,' she said in a low voice.

'Okay.' Yannis finally managed to reply to her first question.

'Would you like drink? *Retsina*? Ouzo?'

'*Nai, efharisto, retsina*,' she replied in Greek.

Her pronunciation amused Yannis as he jumped up to get the *retsina*, eager to leave the table. He motioned to Soula, Georgos' wife, to bring a small plate of dips, olives and bread, and he filled a large anodised carafe with *retsina* from a wine barrel suspended above the bar. He left 50 drachmas on the bar and returned to his table. The woman had lit a cigarette and offered one to Yannis. Yannis fumbled with the packet. The woman took a cigarette and lit it and passed it to Yannis.

He felt his face redden. He knew Georgos and Soula would be watching them from the bar.

'You come from America?' Yannis asked as he poured *retsina* into two small glasses.

'No, I come from nowhere. I come from here now.'

Yannis didn't understand her answer.

'You like Greek music?'

She smiled at him and nodded. Soula nudged Yannis when she brought the *meze* to their table.

Yannis had been thinking all day about last evening and about the woman. They'd talked in broken English and Greek and had had many carafes of *retsina* and Soula had continued to replenish their plates. She'd asked Yannis lots of questions but all he found out about her was that she didn't have any family. Yannis didn't ask her what had happened. She seemed too remote for him to pry.

Very late the woman got up from their table and had said something to Petros, the bouzouki player, who'd struck a minor chord. Then she had sung a low song in a language Yannis didn't recognise. The few people still in the taverna fell silent. She had stared at Yannis throughout and Yannis had stared back at her. When she sang her third song, Yannis danced in front of her. He'd grown bold. When he returned to the table, he looked for the woman but she had vanished. Yannis slowly made his way to his mother's house.

One of the fishermen hauled a plastic bucket from his caïque and shouted, 'Soula, *marithes*'. Soula hurried from the taverna to collect

219

the whitebait to fry for their lunch. Old Petros slapped Yannis on his shoulder and gestured towards the woman. Yannis shook his head.

'*Ohi*', he muttered.

Through more silent language the fishermen warned that if he didn't invite her, they would. Yannis glared at them and they winked. Yannis slowly rose from his net and walked towards the woman.

'You want to eat?' Yannis asked, aware of his reddened face. 'We have *marithes*. Too little to sell, but good to eat. You come?'

The woman shaded her eyes with her hand and looked up at Yannis.

'You danced beautifully last night.'

'You want to meet my friends?'

Yannis felt the eyes of the other fishermen on him and he could feel himself blush again.

'I want you, Yannis.'

The woman's voice was low and soft.

'We have nice fish. We have *retsina*. Soula made for us.'

He turned back towards his friends and didn't wait for her reply.

The woman stood, as if to follow him, but turned and dove off the jetty instead. She turned to look at Yannis. He watched her briefly then returned to his net. The woman swam, arm over arm, towards the horizon. Yannis and the others watched until she was a white speck of splash. White caps had formed on the dark water.

'*Po, po*' the men muttered shaking their heads.

Soula brought the fried whitebait, a plate of olives, bread, soft cheese and a large carafe of *retsina* to the men sitting in the shade of a tamarisk.

The men ate with their hands, mopping olive oil with the bread and occasionally cast their eyes towards the horizon. They were sleepy from the heat, the food and the wine, and hauled their nets into the shade. They would nap, then continue mending.

The tamarisks began to whine in the increasing wind. Soula brought clamps to secure the plastic tablecloth. Overhead wires moaned like Aeolus' harp. Sirocco.

The fishermen muttered. 'Stupid tourists.' Each wondered if he should go search for her? But in this weather? Crazy.

Yannis was silent. His eyes scanned the horizon. Dust had turned the sun red. Yannis remembered the haunting melody the woman had sung the previous night. He remembered her hand, hot on his.

Without speaking, Yannis poured a full glass of *retsina* and tossed it back. Then he took another before leaving the table and un-tying his boat. The others shook their heads and watched as Yannis started the small motor and steered his boat towards the horizon.

Soon he too became a speck and then could be seen no longer.

The Sirocco blew. No fishing boats went out. The people of the village stayed indoors and listened to the wind. It blew for seven days. A hot wind bringing red dust from Africa.

© **Louise Rockne**

Louise Rockne is a writer of stories, poetry and occasionally non-fiction articles. She has published in several Australian literary magazines. She grew up in Minnesota, lived for 2 years in Greece and now lives in South Australia.

# Sisters of Mercy *
## by Denise Gibbs

India has always fascinated me: the promise of vibrant colours, spices and noise, holy men with orange smudged foreheads, beautiful women with beautiful children, laughing, touching. Slim boys with coal-coloured hair, olive skin, sultry eyed, holding hands. The throb of life and death is palpable. India is not a place to be ignored.

Arrival at the Motherhouse of Mother Theresa in Calcutta was the reward of persistence. The chaos; the heat, dirt and rubbish dropped everywhere; the deafening noise of car horns. Complete families on bikes, mopeds; people pushing, touching, children pulling at me, staring up with old eyes. Pleading mothers thrusting their babies forward as if to prove their need was greater than the next.

Once inside the Motherhouse it was cooler, but not tranquil. The Sister, small, round and smiley, welcomed us volunteers. She gave advice on dealing with beggars—if giving food, unwrap it, or it would be sold on. Most children were part of organised gangs and any money would be taken from them, so better not to give any! India, in the name of survival, seemed ruthless and unforgiving to my western eye. Sister asked us where and with whom we wished to work; apparently everyone wants to work with the babies. I enrolled to work with 'destitute women', women who had been in prison, prostitutes or mental health cases discarded by their families.

The journey to the complex in Shanti Baan was by bus and on foot, through a shanty town of huts and make-do tents. Radios blaring; naked, brown bodied children with bangles on their wrists and pierced ears. Pigs playing in the same pools of dirty water. School children, in contrast, looking smart in spotless uniforms. Everyone staring, wondering what I was doing there.

I met my Sister of Mercy. No first name, just 'Sister'. Tall, black and hostile, she looked uninterested: 'So here's someone else who thinks she can change the world'. The 'ladies' surrounded me and I felt totally at their mercy. They prodded me in the most inappropriate places. I was the latest curiosity to be inspected—and I was white, blonde! Sister took charge with a bark, and they released me. Inspection over, I was asked to paint fingernails and toenails with varnish; no polish remover was available, as Sister informed me the ladies would drink it. In some cases the chipped polish seemed an inch thick. Woe betide me if I missed a bit: I was rewarded with a swift slap—only once though; I'm a quick learner.

Next was the medication queue. Sister handed out handfuls of pills, which were downed quickly. I asked Sister when the ladies were given a medical to ensure the dosage was correct. She ignored me. The effect of the medication was to induce calm. I was pleased that I'd taken the advice to wear a headscarf—not my best look—as the ladies were covered in nits. I watched mesmerised as the nits crawled down the hair, looking for escape. Our family motto is not to sit on strange toilets, so the communal facilities were, for me, a leap too far. I asked Sister if I could use her toilet. She reluctantly agreed.

A barren, damp, cement-floored room served as a meeting place and dining-room. Lunch was a large urn of rice and something floating in liquid. The ladies sat cross-legged on the cold floor. I sensed this was the norm and not an opportunity to socialise or enjoy a good meal. I experienced an overwhelming sense of sadness. Who was I kidding? I left feeling I could not return. Sister was right. India, all of a sudden, did not feel quite so exotic.

There's nothing like a good night's sleep to put things in perspective; after all, I had something to prove, if not to Sister, to myself. I arrived wiser and with more realistic expectations. Nails polished, headscarf in place—nits beware! The day began. I came armed with coloured pencils and paints; today we would become artists. Four of the ladies showed a fantastic ability in arithmetic. Dancing was the next activity, thanks to a reluctant loan of Sister's radio. The ladies thought my dancing was worthy of roars of laughter and applause! Over the coming weeks the ladies became individuals with their own personalities. Molly would draw dozens of butterflies, so I suggested to Sister we display the artwork on the walls. The look on Molly's face when she viewed her work, displayed and admired by others, was a joy! Molly shared with me her most precious belongings—two pieces of paper buried deep inside her bedding: one a food voucher, the other her assessment form from the doctor who had admitted her to the centre. Together we re-buried these items for continued safety.

Dancers, singers and practical jokers emerged. Sister actually smiled more than once. Confirmation that I was okay arrived when another Sister asked if I could work with her group.

Sister's response was 'No, she stays here!'

The seven weeks flew by. My daily journey was greeted with smiles and waves. The routine at the Centre was now well established, the walls covered in colour, not only with Molly's butterflies, but flowers in every shape and colour, and lists and lists of mathematical additions. The biggest delight was the dancing; they all joined in, swirling arms mirroring the beat.

My lasting treasured memories of my time in India are the roars of laughter; chipped nail varnish; smiling faces, and particularly Molly's toothless grin. But the greatest joy was the big hug and thanks from Sister. To leave was painful. I do not pretend that I made a difference to the lives of my ladies, but for sure I will never forget them and they will live in my heart forever, as will the Sisters of Mercy who fill the void of no hope.

© **Denise Gibbs**

After a career as a company executive, Denise Gibbs retrained as a social worker, and practised for several years before emigrating with her husband to South West France. She has travelled extensively in India, China and South East Asia.

# Sunday
## by Desirée Jung

The port has big ships, with piled-up containers, of different colors. North Vancouver, from a distance, watches over him. On his walks, he often asks himself if there are others like him journeying through the streets of the city. In the park, the benches are still empty, despite the sun coming out from the clouds. Spring is near, but the wind and the air continue to be cold.

A Chinese family gathers in the large extension of green grass. The child is small with thin hair, black like crow's feathers. She wants to run away from her parents but soon loses her balance. He observes them from a distance. He's gotten used to the loneliness of living in a foreign country. Sometimes he imagines stories and they occupy his mind and heart. In this case, he fancies that the woman wants more attention from the man, asking him to work less, but he cannot stop fidgeting with his phone.

That life is left behind when he enters the Sea bus terminal station, a gateway to downtown. He's going to the cinema to watch a movie about the dictatorship in Chile. Many people walk on the footbridge to catch the boat. There are a lot of foreigners in Vancouver, of many nationalities, an interesting mix accentuated with the passing of the years. They speak many languages.

His own Portuguese begins to fail, for lack of practice. He doesn't know if that is a problem or a characteristic of his life history. It is Sunday, and Sundays carry a bit of melancholy. He feels abandonment in what surrounds him, the culture, and dreams with a place where there is less demand for consumption and information. He enters the cinema and hopes that the fantasy will fulfill him, even if for a while.

© **Desirée Jung**

Desirée Jung is a writer and translator. She received her M. F. A in Creative Writing and her Ph.D. in Comparative Literature from the University of British Columbia. She has published translations and poetry in Exile, The Dirty Goat, among others.

# Sweet Shop *
## by Rilla Nørslund

'How long would you stay away this time?' my mother asks over the phone.

'Perhaps two or three years,' I say, trying to make the length of months of my proposed contract extension seem less solid and substantial, not only to her, but also to my mum-longing self.

No matter how I skirt it, decision time is here. Having the job offer is a relief, of course, but there are days when a sinking feeling engulfs me. There are so many things I miss, there are plans I have for the middle years of my life that seem never to get any closer; to live in a place with theaters and orderly traffic, to work with people more like myself, to have a job where I would not always have to make the hard decisions and be the one who says, 'No, that is not allowed, that is against the regulations, no, no, no.'

I go for a field-trip to shake off the gloom and help make up my mind. It is my first chance to get out of Dhaka after weeks where political unrest has prevented travel on the highways. Driver Ali and I, back on the road, staring death in the face, hooting and swerving our way through mango markets that have taken over the highway, playing chicken with village poultry and adding our bit to the general confusion. It is the hottest time of year, everything is green and streaming and from the car I watch the fascinating anthill of life that is the Bangladesh countryside. The dry paddies where goats gaze on the stubble of recently reaped rice, field after field of harvest bustle and land being cleared in preparation for the monsoon floods.

'Shall we stop, Madam?'

I see we are passing a poor thatch-roofed village and recognize the low, open-fronted sweet shop.

'Yes, yes, let's stop and have tea.'

'Maybe you buy something for your family?'

'No, but I will get something for the people in the office,' I say, eager to buy and knowing where it will be most appreciated.

We park on the roadside. Inside the shop there are six or seven people sitting at plastic-covered wooden tables, drinking steaming tea and eating round shiny syrupy sweets from small aluminum bowls. Two unshapely dogs lie near the entrance, one with a fine dusting of sugar on his muzzle.

I make my customary detour to the attached sweet factory where huge silver pots of milk are bubbling over strong fires. The pulsing heat and sweet lactic smell are nauseating and fascinating at the same time. The small space is filled with the glistening dark bodies of two men dressed only in *lungis* tied carelessly around their waists, and stirring the boiling milk with metal scrapers. After the cool of the car the heat is shocking and as I walk into the dark interior of the shop I feel the tickle of a trickle of sweat down my back.

The cheeky-faced serving boy grins when he sees me.

'Red tea, no sugar,' he shouts at the tea maker who is sweating with his kettles and cups near the front of the shop.

I grin back, and appreciate how much service a 10 *taka* tip can get you in the countryside.

Ali takes care of the purchase of dripping white and brown balls of sugar and boiled milk, arguing cheerfully with the shopkeeper as he weighs the chosen sweets on hand-held metal plates with worn brass weights.

'I get a good price today, too cheap, half of Dhaka price,' he stage whispers, joining me at the table for his cup of tea once the packing of the purchases into hand-made cardboard boxes is underway.

'You don't take milk tea today?' he asks disappointedly. 'It is very fresh.'

He never can understand that no matter how fresh the milk I prefer my tea without, and seems slightly offended on behalf of the cows we see grazing behind the shop.

The shop owner sends over fresh sweets for us to try, and then we are forgotten in the hustle of new customers arriving, as two motorbikes and a Dhaka car stop along the roadside and a dozen people bustle into the shop all at once. A bus roars past, hooter held down but no one reacts or even looks up except me. As usual I tremble at the lack of attention paid to near-miss disasters.

Madam comes in from the back of the shop in a bright sari, bare feet moving quietly across the stamped earth floor. Her papery skin is smooth and shiny between the wrinkles. She comes over to the dark corner where I sit and wordlessly offers me two sugar-coated biscuits to taste. 'Thank you—I have two already,' I say indicating the sweets on my plate, but Ali will not let me refuse. He leaps up to receive the proffered biscuits and takes them to be packed with the other sweets.

'I take them for the children of the cook at the training centre,' he assures me, when he notices my raised eyebrows.

The serving boy comes over to wipe the table and leans on the table edge so he can scrutinise the tea-drinking habits of a foreign lady.

'What's your name?' I ask in Bangla, and he laughs in delight, despite my poor pronunciation.

'Ami Johnny,' is his surprising answer, if I heard right.

He nods when I repeat it and grins widely when I slip him a tightly folded 10 *taka* note as I get up to leave. We collect our neatly wrapped parcels and pay for the purchases and tea.

As I settle in the car for the next few hours of the drive I feel reconciled to Bangladesh, its sweaty sweet smells and sweet shops will be my life for a while yet, and that is not so bad. I can live with that.

© **Rilla Nørslund**

Rilla lives in Bangladesh and has previously worked in a number of African countries. She writes poetry and short fiction and tries to add a little poetry to life through weekly poems and poetic twittering.

# Taxi Rides with Aysha *
## by Jillian Schedneck

Around 3:30 every afternoon, Aysha and I would slip out of our offices, past the dozing guards protecting empty corridors, and descend the steps onto Abu Dhabi University's male parking lot. With her black *abaya* trailing behind her like puffs of smoke, her silky *sheyla* covering her hair and neck, she shuffled ahead of me alongside rows of Range Rovers and Porsche Cayennes.

Sometimes a solicitous young man with his eyes cast down would approach her, saying, 'Sheikha, is your husband not here today? Can I bring you somewhere?'

Aysha always told them no, claiming that her husband was meeting her just around the corner. We continued our walk over patches of sand and newly laid pavement, past South Asian laborers toiling in the afternoon sun, until we reached the dusty road of the highway. We stood on the shoulder as cars zoomed by, waving at any approaching gold and white taxis.

The search for a cab in the middle of the afternoon frustrated me and humiliated Aysha. Superficially, there was the blazing heat; when the weather cooled in the winter months, a sandstorm often swept into our faces. Although the male students' intentions were chivalrous, their offers for rides also presented a problem. It would look peculiar, possibly scandalous, if Aysha, a well-respected teacher and devout Muslim, accepted a ride from a male outside of her family. On a deeper, more significant level, here was a thirty-eight-year-old Iraqi beauty now stalking around in the desert heat. By walking with me—a young, American woman who left her hair uncovered—it was evident that Aysha had no reliable male protection and couldn't afford a driver. It was evident that her options were limited, that she had, somehow, fallen.

We stood on the shoulder for stretches of fifteen to twenty minutes, cursing the university's relocation to the desolate desert, where taxis rarely ventured. A cab with its backseat full of male laborers might pull over, and the driver would motion for us to squeeze in and share the fare back to the city. Predictably, Aysha waved those cabs away in disdain, and I laughed at the thought of the modest woman before me pressed between male construction workers. When an empty taxi finally stopped for us, I would exclaim,

'*Al hamdulilah*,' praise God. I said this to please Aysha, but she wasn't ready to shout for joy yet; we still had to negotiate. Once out of Abu Dhabi city limits, the meter was up for grabs, and Aysha would agree to no more than twenty dirhams, about six dollars. When they refused our price she let them carry on to the city alone. For all the discomfort, she wasn't about to pay a cent more than she deemed reasonable.

Once we finally got into a cab, though, that world of sand and desperation fell away. Scooting onto the plastic-covered backseat was like pulling off an itchy wool turtleneck and slipping on a favourite pair of loose pajamas. Our mode of travel may not have been glamorous or even respectable for a woman like Aysha, but we were content in those back seats, sharing more of our lives than we ever could have in the university hallways. Aysha generated her own world with her own logic; we stood above our measly circumstances as underpaid English language teachers and our true, splendid selves shone through. Yet on some afternoons, something would turn inside Aysha, and she would become silent, reflective.

'When you die, you will be asked two questions: "Who is your God?" and "Who is your prophet?"'

She repeated the correct answers twice in Arabic. I nodded, and she stared at me.

'I want you to practice the answers, because you'll need to say them in Arabic.'

'Yes, of course!' I said, finally understanding.
She smiled, relieved.

'It's just that I don't want you to get left behind. I'm so used to travelling with you.'
After a few tries, Aysha pronounced my accent perfect.

On weekend nights, I would wait for a taxi outside Aysha's building, across the street from mine. On those nights, the cloying students and my uncertain future, the question of why I came here and where I would go next, could be left behind. It was enough to feel adrift on the collective buzz of the packed bar, alongside my equally bewildered expat friends. I felt lighter, happy to put on another self, the one Aysha wouldn't condone.

One night I ran into Aysha exiting a taxi with her daughter. She kissed me on both cheeks and ushered me into the waiting cab. The driver cocked his head at me in the rearview mirror, and I told him where I was going.

'You know her?' he asked. 'Are you a local?'

'Of course not.'

As an uncovered white woman with fair skin, I looked nothing like a local Gulf Arab, like Aysha.

That Sunday, back at work, I told Aysha about the driver.

'They find it hard to believe that a Western girl and a covered Arab would be friends.'

Magazine and billboards regularly featured beautiful covered women and their Western girlfriends, clutching shopping bags. They looked so pleased with themselves, so content in their easy friendship based on nothing more than Chanel purses and Dolce and Gabbana sunglasses. But such couples almost never appeared together in the malls or on the streets of Abu Dhabi.

That afternoon, when the cab stopped outside her building, Aysha handed the driver our twenty
Dirhams.

'*Masalama*,' we called to each other, parting ways.

As I crossed the street and walked the block to my own apartment building, I looked out among the high rises of Abu Dhabi city, feeling a quiet buzz rising in my chest, and smiled. No matter how frustrating this school or this city could be, I thought, I will miss those rides when I am gone. I will miss this unlikely friendship and our peals of laughter. I will miss Aysha.

© **Jillian Schedneck**

Jillian Schedneck lived in the United Arab Emirates for two years, working as a university lecturer in Abu Dhabi and Dubai. Her travel memoir, Abu Dhabi Days, Dubai Nights, was published in 2012.
http://www.jillianschedneck.com

# Tectonic Plate Shift *
## by Bev Henwood

In the early seventies an affair of the heart took me to live on the Gazelle Peninsula of Papua New Guinea. Stormy and doomed as that relationship was, the experience shifted, broadened and deepened my perspective on the world.

A committed anti-racist, as yet unaware of feminism's promise, I was in need of a Black Knight. I found one. I planned to be his handmaiden in the struggle for justice.

Not everyone on the Gazelle was pleased at my arrival. The white community saw me as batting for the wrong side. My Knight's family would have preferred him to choose one of his own for partner. We seemed to be the only ones pleased with our arrangement.

The Gazelle offers sensory overload at every eye-blink. I lurched along, alternately gasping in wonder and reeling in shock.

The township of Rabaul nestles on the foreshore of a harbour consisting of a vast volcanic caldera. At one point two spears of rocky outcrop rise out of the deep crevice below, a plug holding the molten innards of the earth down. Tectonic plates struggle for supremacy down there. At another a jet of steaming water simmers. Scrub turkeys' eggs, lowered into that water in woven baskets, cook within minutes: mid-harbour snack.

Vegetation is lush, each colour vibrant in brilliant sunshine and a gloriously blue sky. Everything grows. A fence built from sticks will become a hedge within weeks. A saucepan of stock left standing overnight will be fermenting by morning. A scratched mosquito bite will become ulcerated within hours.

Turquoise ocean, pumice-laden volcanic soil. Overwhelming heat, torturous humidity. It can be amusing at first, halfway through wiping yourself after a shower, to be unsure which parts of yourself you have dried. Every part continues to drip.

I took a job in a town school. My Knight was engaged in community development.

The Australian Administration's behaviour towards Papuans and New Guineans had been clumsy at best, brutal and offensive at worst. Men, called *bois*, had been denied the right to wear trousers, lest they think themselves the equal of the *Maste*. A twelve-year-old child, held back after school one afternoon, had been gaoled. He had been unable to get through town and home before dark, thus breaking the native curfew.

People were getting very tired of being subjected to foreign laws and practices. Over the century since the colonisation process began, traditional ways had been interrupted, replaced by western systems. Now powerful movements were springing up, determined to restore practices that were compatible with Indigenous values. Pressure for Self-Government and Independence was building.

The Australian Administration was fiercely resistant to this move. 'Not in my lifetime,' was the remark made by Sir Paul Hasluck, then Minister for Territories.

The heady steam of community determination and expectation compounded the environmental humidity. The atmosphere became electric.

Two massive earthquakes, followed in quick succession by an assassination, had the Gazelle at explosive fever pitch. The violent rocking of the earth, the roar emitting from the ground, the great surge of the water back from the harbour's edge then up onto the ground where we stood, roiling back and forth like a slopped cauldron, the fear and panic in the township, the cry of extreme and prolonged outrage represented in the assassination, all left me reeling. From that day to this I have never used the term 'solid ground'.

In contrast, a visit to the family's village would find people going about their business, calm and orderly, at peace with the process of life. This was the place I wanted to be at those times, for all that our village was sited on a shaky little island which had emerged from the harbour only two centuries before. People knew the land, understood its processes, accepted its might and unpredictability. Sitting on a bamboo bench, watching women scrape coconut for the evening meal, young men out on the water hunting for fish to throw in the pot, I could absorb some of that calm, acknowledge the power of the earth as pre-eminent over puny human demands. As dark fell and people set up their sleeping mats, perhaps brewing one more pot of tea before settling for the night, I would leave for town, restored and peaceful.

Self-Government, with attendant elections to form the first representative Parliament in the nation, followed shortly. My Knight was deeply involved in these developments. He was away for long periods, leaving me to keep the home fires burning. At first it didn't matter.

Gradually cracks appeared in our relationship. I was left alone too much, managing business that was not mine. His vision was vast. The national stage beckoned. The limitations of my handmaidenly role became apparent. The rose-tinted glasses which had concealed our conflicting value systems, lost their glow. His vengeful sexism constrained me. My unaware racism offended him. The differences mattered more and more. The time came for us to part.

I returned to Australia. I saw it through different eyes. Everything I loved about the place remained. The most recent wave of refugees was offering us alternative perspectives, tastes and sounds. Feminism and multiculturalism were emerging, opening exciting new understandings of the ways we could be in the world.

Yet I had seen how we could casually, sometimes without noticing, dismiss a people as lesser human beings, deny their right to live their own lives in their own ways, be astounded when their outrage became apparent, sometimes violently.

We continue in that cycle to this day: decades later we make a breakthrough in our capacity to embrace humanity in all its diversity. We begin to adapt ourselves around those new awarenesses, then lose it all in a cloud of resentment and self-preservation. We find ourselves unwilling to make the unforeseen yet inevitable adjustments.

If only we could see ourselves as others see us.

## © Bev Henwood

Already committed to anti-racist work in Australia, Bev spent several years in an interracial marriage in Papua New Guinea in the early seventies. The experience transformed her view of the world. Its influence percolates through to the present day.

# The Beautiful Tent
## by Eileen Dickson

Our sturdy white *Bedu* tent has become our home and salvation from flat life since we came to Kuwait. Bought after hours of haggling in the tent *souk* in Kuwait City, it flaunts a purple- and orange-flowered lining, the least lurid of those on offer. And you can stand up in it. It's our passport for escaping to the beach with friends. We build driftwood fires, cook, eat, swim and flirt a little. Precious gin is drunk at sundown. The thick central tent pole may well have been hauled by elephants through Indian forests, but now sticks out of the back of our Impala, as we drive down the Trans-Arabian Pipeline towards Jordan.

*28th December, Kuwait-Saudi*

'I do envy you having an adventurous husband, Di,' Alice whispers as we leave. 'The most I can do is to get Andrew to the Golf Club on Fridays.'

She should not envy me. We'd started five hours later than planned, and Mike had a hangover from too much blackberry wine. The fan belt broke shortly after we'd crossed the Saudi border at around seven o'clock that evening, and the garage men were more intent on getting their supper than repairing it. Ramadan is not a good time to be travelling. Ten years of marriage stopped me from saying we hadn't got very far.

After Hafar Al Batin, the road became a thin black ribbon. There were no stars and the only lights came from oncoming lorries looming from, then disappearing back into dark. The ground either side of the road was strewn with boulders. It was not inviting to tents.

'Right, early night I think, darling. Shall we get the tent out?'

For the first time I heard a note of uncertainty in my husband's voice, or was it entreaty?

'No, let's pretend we're on our honeymoon and sleep in the car. Remember that time in Bantham when we tried to make love but the gear stick got in the way?' I wasn't rejecting the tent, but I just wanted to sleep.

'Well if you're sure, but I'm happy to put it up.'

'Thanks Mike, I'll take my headscarf off in that case.'

*29th December, Saudi-Jordan*

4am. Wake and eat Arab bread, cheese and cucumber for breakfast with oranges. Mike's gone off with the only loo roll into the wide, flat scrub. I shout at him but only attract a passing goat that leers at me through its beard. The black bitumen track follows the Trans-Arabian Pipeline. It's great for direction but does little for a marriage. I read from *Verse and Worse* to keep us awake, then recite bits from *The Ancient Mariner*. We argue about the *Wedding Guest*, so I count saltbushes, which has the same effect as sheep. My obligatory headscarf itches.

Late in the afternoon I saw the clouds. Huge shapes drifting in the distance. Except they weren't. They were mountains, rising into impressive heights from the flat desert. In Kuwait, we had the Zor Hills on the Iraqi border, home to desert foxes, rabbits and ravens. The Jordanian landscape was different, it had little yellow flowers and grey-blue spiky bushes and contours that went on and on like the Highlands. The air smelt of thyme and oregano, and I fully expected stags and rhododendrons.

Tent was at home in the landscape. We camped in the Wadi Mujeeb and I washed my hair in the River Jordan. Our *Bedu* neighbours wandered by and gave Mike advice on how he'd pitched the tent in the wrong place. My admiration grew, as he nodded and smiled and took no notice. We were invited to their tent for goat's milk cheese, which he kindly accepted on my behalf. 'My wife loves it,' I think he said as they pressed more of the curds, grass and grit mixture into my clenched hand. Their return visit was not a success, as they spat out my tea, not fooled by saccharine instead of sugar. But they did it outside the tent.

Over the next two weeks, we explored historic ruins, castles, forts, towers, caravan inns, fortified palaces and a memorable bathhouse with naughty frescoes of nubile young women.

'They certainly liked their pleasures,' I remarked.

'So would I if I was a bloody caliph.'

There seemed no end to history, and Mike's enthusiasm was undimmed as he sprang around the rocky countryside. It was colder at night, and the desert wind whipped around the tent pegs as we snuggled down inside the beautiful tent. There was sand in everything, and I was tired of tuna and rice mish-mash for supper. As my mood dropped, so Mike's had risen. Poring over the guidebook by the light of the Gaz lamp swinging from the tent pole, he asked, 'Did you know Di, they built these palaces in the desert to escape plague in the big cities?'

I didn't care where they built them or why. I wanted to go home. I wanted to eat dinner in a restaurant with real wine and a tablecloth. To have a hot, running shower and sleep in a bed. And I was getting my period. 'Could we, do you think stay in a Rest House for a change? The guidebook says there's one at Azraq.'

'Why on earth would we want to do that, Diana, when we've a perfectly good tent.'

Sometimes I hate my husband.

The Al-Azraq Hotel and Rest House looked warm and welcoming with lights blazing out over the courtyard as we parked the car. When we got nearer, we saw the glass-plated front door had a jagged man-sized hole in it like the brick wall in a Desperate Dan comic. Reception was empty so we pressed the bell on the desk. No one came. There was a sound of breaking glass followed by loud laughter from the bar to one side.

'You're sure this is what you want, Di? We can still change our minds.'

A Saudi in a grey *dish-dasha* lumbered through from the bar, and his face broke into smiles when he saw us.

'Ah, welcome, come drink with us,' he beamed, and held out his hand. It was covered in blood, which dripped onto his *dish-dasha*. A glass of cloudy orange liquid was clutched in the other hand, and he obviously hadn't noticed the blood.

'That's very kind of you,' Mike said, 'but we need to book a room first. Er, your hand?' He pointed to the blood, which was slowing its flow a little.

'No problem. Just a little drinking game with friends. Have you tried gin and blackcurrant? Or whisky-orange? Come and join us.'

'Perhaps when we've had dinner, *shukran*.'

'You come here for dinner?' Our new drinking friend threw his head back and laughed.

Mike unearthed a small, dark man having a smoke outside the kitchen. There was no pretence of it being a normal hotel, as he followed us from room to room with a Flit Gun. 'Which you want? Any one you can have.'

'No other guests?' I asked.

'They not come now. But we have good swimming pool. No many mosquitoes.'

There were several rooms full of beds. I looked at them and could smell months of unchanged bed sheets. In another, the bath was full of ants. Eventually we settled for one, marginally better than the others. There were small, black flying insects on the ceiling, and I pointed to them.

'No problem.' He aimed the Flit Gun over the ceiling, and they dropped like confetti onto the beds. He smiled happily. 'All OK now?'

We agreed all OK, and went down to the restaurant. It was very cold, and there was a lone diner sitting at a table reading a book propped against an HP Sauce bottle.

'May we join you?' Mike asked.

'Not much choice,' he replied, 'but I'd welcome your company.' John Sutherland was a water reservoir engineer working in the desert, and used the Rest House as an occasional base. 'Though after one night here, I'm glad to get back to my tent.' I ignored Mike's triumphant look.

'Why don't they repair the door?'

'No point. The Saudis just fall through it again next time, though they do sometimes paste brown paper over it. Actually, you get used to it, and they're a friendly bunch, just want to have a drink in peace, though their choice of cocktails is a bit bizarre.'

'Expect they're just trying to find one they like,' I said. Dinner was disappointing, but red wine helped us get through the athletic chicken. Upstairs, more black insects had dropped onto the beds.

'We could always sleep in the car, Di.' I ignored him and slept fully dressed on top of the blankets with my mouth closed.

At the Kuwait-Saudi border, the car was taken apart by a gang of Korean labourers looking for drugs. I was led off to a room, where an old woman with incredibly strong fingers prodded at me.

'Clothes off,' she demanded and attacked my shirt buttons. We had a staring competition and I won. I noticed a single sinister flip-flop by a mattress in the corner. She hadn't said she was a customs official, but I still wouldn't have undressed. Emerging into the sunlight, I found bemused young men trying to fit my precious Tampax back into their cardboard holders strewn over the ground. Mike's imperfect Arabic, 'They are for my wife, once a year' had failed

238

to convince them. But worst of all, they were kicking the tent. My guilt for deserting it was so strong that I sprang forward to stop them.

'Enough, Diana, remember where you are. Time to go home.'

Driving again along familiar roads, Mike put his hand over mine.

'Thank you for putting up with me. I know it wasn't what you wanted, but it wouldn't have been the same without you.'

I turned my head to see the reassuring sight of the tent pole sticking out of the back of the Impala. The Beautiful Tent was safe and sound and so were we.

© **Eileen Dickson**

Eileen plundered five years of living and working in Kuwait for her novel, *New Under the Sun*, published this year. Her second novel, *The Governess* competes with full time work. Bring on the Fairy Godmother. She writes short stories. http://www.jeevestories.co.uk

# The Encounter
## by Pamela Felton

Dusk was descending over the vast empty landscape, devoid of trees, road signs and any visible habitation. Except there on the horizon arose a mirage—tents, turrets, steeples and that oh, so inviting blue water.

Wisps of mist appeared as the sun sank, casting a strange purple, orange glow over the terrain before it disappeared, leaving in darkness what had so recently been bathed in blinding sunlight. Overhead was a sliver of moon with thousands of twinkling stars, all gathering for what seemed a nocturnal fiesta.

As Nursing Officer for one of the first interior hospitals of Northern Oman, I was returning from a visit to a remote Health Centre. There had been the usual protracted leave-taking. Much help was offered by all the staff to pack the Suzuki Jeep. Everyone knew, or thought they did, just what went where. This needed close supervision, otherwise I ended up with a clanging and a banging as I drove, then having to stop to readjust the boxes. The goodbyes had to be completed, all very formal, because the staff, being either local or Indian, set great store by this—that all was done correctly.

I drove homewards, on the endless bumpy road, just a track really, with no markings to guide you, unless you counted the multiple tyre tracks of vehicles that had passed before. With some way to go, I was thinking blissfully how I would be sleeping tonight in my own bed.

A slight breeze caused eddies of sand to dance and swirl like dervishes in the beam of the headlights. Closely behind, never faltering, was a dense cloud of dust. As I drove, a shiver escaped me, more of apprehension than chill, as it had been very hot. But then rarely was it otherwise in this Gulf State.

Then without warning the jeep faltered, the engine hiccupped and with a long sigh, it died. Searching for my torch in the inky blackness—even the moon had deserted me—I was now well and truly alone.

Or was I?

A flicker. The merest of movements. I could detect something emerging and edging towards me through the rising ground mist. Small forms of ghostly white, antelope-like, slowly inching forward, snuffling and shuffling, and the distinct though somewhat faint tinkle of a bell.

I sat mesmerised, motionless, the torch lying idle on my lap, watching…waiting…they would soon surround me. Slowly, as if I was not there, they veered away, still snorting and snuffling. The musical tinkling drifted away with them and the silence returned.

This was Oryx territory. That wild, shy, graceful, creature that sadly had been hunted to extinction. Now re-introduced into this demanding habitat, they remained elusive and rarely were they seen.

Rousing myself, I again tried the ignition. There was a pause as I held my breath. Then with a jerk and a prolonged wheeze, the engine leapt into life. I was heading once more for home—dreaming?

© **Pamela Felton**

Pamela Felton emigrated to Australia in 1960, having completed her nursing training. Bar 2 years, she has lived outside the UK. She did nursing for 22 years in Saudi Arabia and Oman, before retiring to live in Spain in 1989.

# The English Wall **
## by C. R. Resetarits

Morgue and meadow, spent season, hollow lane. All Saints commons where dead poets and druids lie. A village churchyard of broken bones, of headstones stacked like uneaten toast so the mowers from Hursley IBM can better turn upon the green. And I'm out each morning to walk my dog who loves everything here, especially the green and the wood and the underbrush, the creeping vine that won't let me be but point and stare. The green suggests itself, so feck all lovely in winter, the huge, whispering yews and the weeping jasmine tumbling up the ancestral crypt, tiny yellow twinkle-star blooms and the white ghost flowers on honeysuckle runs, the pink clematis in the dead of winter with the constant whitewash of English brumebane air. The brutal brilliance of this postcard world pulls me in spite of disavowals, disembowels. Only in the wood, the brown bare wood, am I free of this thought-crippling green in my oasis so temporal, brief, before the wicked bluebells appear to sweep green the muddy wood floor. I enter the comforting brown each morning, let my traitor dog off lead to trail the creek, and I admire the shades of bark and mud and rock. Here the old manor wall is unkept, fallen, frosted, the texture of dried rivulets, a reverse verdigris of copper and bronze, a topography of want and loss but then I see that red weed vine. It spills and runs the stones and gaps of brown brambled woods and wall and I see just how strange my strangeness is made anxious by that red against that map against my best futile attempt not to sense the threat of this bloody winter on this bloody English lane.

## © C. R. Resetarits

C. R. Resetarits' poetry has recently appeared in *New Writing*, *ARS Medica*, *Stoneboat*, and *Dirtcake*. Her essay on 'Emerson in Paris' will appear in Paris in American Literature: On Distance as a Literary Resource (Rowman & Littlefield, 2013).

# The Interloper
## by Colin Hodson

The olive farm stretched across the hillside, facing south over the little port in the distance, to the Aegean beyond. The farmhouse was built of stone, rendered and white-washed like all the other houses on the island. A covered verandah ran along the western side giving shelter from the fierce summer sun. Stefanos had inherited the farm from his father and his father's father before him. It had been in their family for as long as anyone could remember. A dutiful son, he cared for his mother and three sisters until they left him, one by one, two to husbands and two to Thanatos.* The work was hard, leaving him little time and energy for his own needs. When he was finally alone, unskilled in the ways of the world, he had asked the Papas to help him find a wife.

Elena was nearly 20 years younger than Stefanos. If she was not pretty, she had a strong back and took willingly to the work on the farm. She had raven hair, a full figure and there was an animal quality about her that excited him. She cleaned the house, mended or threw away things that were broken or worn, and made curtains for their bedroom from a length of blue and white striped cotton that she found.

She wanted children, both of them did, but they never came. There were some who blamed her, for it was never the fault of the man. Eventually, resigned, they got on with their life together that was governed by the seasons—and so the years passed.

One day, after they had been married for eight years, Elena was sitting on the verandah making *dolmades* with the vine leaves that grew in their garden, when a young man walked up the dusty track that led to their house. Stefanos was in bed, had been for over a month, having fractured his back falling off a ladder replacing a tile on the roof. The doctor had said it might take time, but how long he couldn't say.

The young man said that his name was Giles and he was looking for work. He was English, blonde and brown-skinned by the sun, and he spoke Greek in an old-fashioned way. It seemed to Elena that he was some kind of gift for, without her husband and the harvest due, she would be overwhelmed. They couldn't pay much, she told him, indeed they couldn't pay him at all, but she could feed him and he

243

could sleep in the little room over the donkey's stable. He said that he could stay for a month, just to help out. He was in no hurry to return home. He had lost his job, he told her, and things were bad in England.

Elena cleaned out the little room for him and he scrubbed the clay tiles on the floor and mended the door that was broken. She had some of the blue and white cotton left, enough to make him a curtain for the small window, and found a patchwork bedspread to cover the mattress on the floor. Within just two weeks it knew both of their bodies. Driven by lust, they lay together in the heat of early afternoons, moments snatched during siesta before going back to work on the farm. Moments only, for Elena had to feed and bathe Stefanos. Stefanos, who lay in his own sweat, in a room like an oven, complaining of neglect, pain and the sores on his buttocks. Life gradually became intolerable.

Winters were mild on the island, and the February sunshine was warm on the small group as they tumbled out of the church and down to the *taverna* by the port.

It had been barely three months since Elena and Giles had stood apart at the graveside, careful not to betray their secret by any hint or look. It had been an accident after all. Hadn't the doctor agreed?

Today, released from religion, the party drank *retsina* and the dark red wine from Paphos; but the toasts, when they came, were in the sparkling *Athiri* from Rhodes. The tables had been laid with bowls of *tzatziki* and *taramolosalata*, *hummus* and Elena's own *dolmades*. The bouzouki player began to pick out the notes of the *White Rose of Athens* and some began to dance, their arms around each others' shoulders. But there were others, mainly the women, who thought the wedding had been too hasty, that nothing good would come from a second wearing of the bridal gown, especially one that had a few stitches let out at the sides.

\* The Greek God of Death

## © **Colin Hodson**

Colin Hodson is a retired architect living in the Languedoc. He has been writing short stories most of his life, recently completed a Creative Writing course at UEA and writes regularly with a local group. He has published one novel.

## The Old Turkish Garden **
### by Susan Riley

Black iron railings hid it from our view,
plumbago blue and orange trumpet vine,
cloying jasmine urged us trembling through
into that garden never to be mine.

Sprinklings of black pepper made me sneeze;
I never knew it grew on trees so feathery and fine,
red peppers laid out drying in the sweet Aegean breeze
in the garden that's not mine.

Chickens scratched on knobbly, scrawny knees,
their rare exotic colours mixed so feathery and fine,
seed full figs sweet dropped down beneath the vine
in a garden that's not mine.

Sage and tall sorrel tall seize the near spent soil,
aubergines atop marigolds so feathery and fine,
white vine-tumbling grapes foretelling next year's wine
in the garden that's not mine.

Here is the turning of the year displayed
in golden maize heads feathery and fine,
I only wished I could stay forever
inside that garden never to be mine.

© **Susan Riley**

Susan Riley is a poet, linguist, teacher and writer. For several years she lived with her husband in Bodrum, Turkey. She draws on both her experiences as an expat and citizen of the world for inspiration.
http://www.sujenuity.com

# The Other Paris *
## by Ingrid Littmann-Tai

A multi-coloured well-stocked spice stand caught our attention. Ochre-tinted Indian curry powder in a massive bowl next to blood-orange hewed paprika, neighbouring earth-brown colombo from the French West Indies, next to hunks of fresh ginger and Italian nora pepper powder. Interspersed amongst these foreign exotic spices were dried French lavender and pale Camomile flowers from the Anjou region. It was Sunday morning sensory overload at the market.

The next stand comprised of massive white bins stuffed with fresh olives in all shades and sizes: red, brown, amber, green, ebony, avocado, alabaster, large, small, pitted, stuffed, their skin glistening in oil and spices, luminescent from the fluorescent lights above. The skin colours of the hurried shoppers jockeying for position in front of the olive stand were as varied as the fragrant wares being offered. Multiculturalism was alive and well at the Saint Denis *marché*.

It was a warm bright March day, a welcomed change after the grey days of Paris winter. My daughters and I had boarded the metro early that morning for the one-hour ride up to Saint Denis. We were venturing beyond the *périphérique*, the ring road of Paris, and were outside Paris proper, something we rarely did. We would also be outside our comfort zone. This neighbourhood was known for the world famous Cathedral Basilica of Saint Denis. I had recently read about the Sunday market in Saint Denis and how varied and vibrant it was. The area was known as one of the most multicultural in Paris with 80 languages spoken daily. You could catch snippets of cultures and countries from around the world while simply walking through the market. It was like traveling while staying in your own city, only 21 metro stations away.

Although only eight and eleven-years-old, I knew my well-travelled daughters would see the differences and I wanted them to experience the many sides of Paris including the less-affluent neighbourhoods where everyday life could be struggle. I wanted them to realize that more Parisians lived like this than like we did. As with our privileged lives in Canada, we were spending much of our time in Paris living in a comfortable bubble.

Leaving the olive stand behind, the odour of brine and salt was quickly replaced by the smell of raw meat as we approached a substantial meat stand, chunks of cut up meat arranged in neat piles. Pointed pigs feet, tails, ears, tripe, hunks of dark-red liver, hog's heads, roasts; any cut of meat was available and the selection was impressive. Hanging above were skinned *gros lapins*, large rabbits, cut open from their chest to their legs, their livers flopping out and hanging down, their delicate front legs dangling together not quite shielding their bulging eyeballs. Five months ago this meat display, especially the bunnies, would have produced squeamish squeals from my daughters. Now they just looked at them and shrugged in a classic Gallic fashion as if, oh well.

With my purse slung tightly across my shoulders, my daughters hovering close by, I had pulled out my camera as I did on many of our Parisian adventures, wanting to record the life, colour and movement around us.

'Hey not allowed, no photos,' I heard someone yelling at me in broken Middle-Eastern accented French. An unshaven worker at the meat stand was hovering above me on a raised platform, looking down at me, his minute jet-black dagger-like eyes boring holes in me. He did not look happy.

'What are you taking pictures for? *Pourquoi?*' he demanded.

Shocked at his reaction, I quickly dropped my camera, letting it hang by my hips.

'I'm a Canadian taking pictures, just for me, for my enjoyment,' I replied.

His expression softened slightly, yet he was not impressed.

'I'm not in any of these photos, right?'

'No. I was just taking pictures of the meat and the rabbits, not you,' I said.

A larger man, obviously the *patron*, the boss, stepped in front of the worker and tried to intervene. Taller, with the same rough accent but more amiable, he said grinning, 'He is not paying his child support payments to his wife and he is worried that she is sending spies to find him.'

'I'm just taking some photos of the meat. Your selection is amazing,' I said, trying to throw in a compliment.

'Ok, just don't take any pictures of us.'

I nodded and we swiftly moved onto the next vendor, both my daughters no longer just hovering next to me but rather their small hands gripping onto the front pockets of my jeans. The sting of the yelling and the smell of meat were quickly forgotten as we were drawn to a long brightly-lit stand at the side of the market, nestled up against the wall. The sweet buttery lemon scent of fresh *madeleine* pastries being pulled out of the oven lingered in the air and was a welcome change from the pungent beef odour that had filled my nostrils. My younger daughter's eyes lit up, *madeleines* being one of her favourite pastries. Immediately the three of us were standing at the bakery counter, our senses absorbing the fresh delicacy that awaited us.

'*Une douzaine s'il vous plait*,' I asked, believing that one dozen would suffice.

As I bit into the spongy soft cake, visions of lemon trees danced in my head. The melt-in-your-mouth warm pastries were gone in less than two minutes. Our fragrant selection of multi-coloured olives and supply of Indian curry would make it home with us back to our apartment but I knew the *madeleines* would not last past the market entryway.

'Another dozen please,' I asked quickly back at the counter.

They were outstanding, the best we had ever had—a slice of classic French familiarity in amongst the multitude of languages, the head scarves, the rainbow of skin colours, the fish monger and the gruff butcher. It was a gentle reminder that we were indeed still in Paris.

## ©Ingrid Littmann-Tai

In 2010 Ingrid Littmann-Tai moved to Paris, her young daughters in tow. While the children attended the local schools, Ingrid rediscovered her love of writing surrounded by the inspiration and beauty of Paris. They are now back in Canada.

## The Road to Trail Creek Summit **
### by Jennifer Saunders

We knew the summer road, the fall,
leaves turning on the cottonwoods
and the trout running.

Now it is winter on the road to Trail Creek Summit.
It is still and you are small, so small I can carry
all the coarse grains of you with one hand
and wonder where the rest of you went.

Ketchum, Idaho, 1975 –
you have one hand raised to shade your eyes
from sunlight on the riffles
and with the other lead a child up the bank.
The leaves are yellow on the cottonwoods
and we are smiling at the camera.

Now it is winter on the road to Trail Creek Summit.
There are no leaves on the cottonwoods.
The snow has closed the road.
It is still and you are small
and I loose you grain by grain
into the riffles.

The road is closed
but the creek runs free,
even in winter
on the road to Trail Creek Summit.

## © Jennifer Saunders

Jennifer Saunders is a US native living in Switzerland with her Swiss husband and their two hockey playing Swiss-American sons. Her poetry has appeared in *Literary Bohemian*, *Literary Mama*, and elsewhere. She blogs about writing, hockey, and life at www.magpiedays.com.

# The Surprise
## by Kavita Bedford

Tell me, what has happened, he asks.

He is sitting in his favourite black leather armchair, which has rocked him to sleep each night since I can remember from my youth. I used to tiptoe past on late nights coming home only to hear the baritone reprimand coming from its leather folds. The chair has now lost its former intimidation tactics and swallows up his shrunken frame so the effect is almost comic. His beige pants are hiked up high to his waist with his shirt, freshly ironed, tucked in tight. He is slumped in the centre, as his bent body can no longer support his once-proud stance. He wears the cap on his head he bought from a trip to Cuba in his younger years. His 'high rolling' cap he calls it. He puts it over his balding head so he can forget the black locks are disappearing; the remaining vestige of his glamour. He gives an impatient shuffle in the chair causing it to rock back and forth and he demands again, tell me, what has happened?

I came in to bring her usual tablet rounds in the morning I say; one blue, swallow, two red, swallow, and one black—swallow. She always imagined the colours swimming in her belly forming different shades and heightening her changing emotions: the basement blues, a green-eyed monster, or erotic mauve. However, this morning she did not stir when I gently shook her and called for my fiendish purple to arise. She had passed away in her sleep during the night. I watch him digest this. His face crumples. It amazes me how his already creased face finds room to welcome fresh etchings. These ones cut deep. His hands reach up to cover his face. He sits there for a long time, unable to move, the chair slowly losing its momentum.

This is the thirty-third day I've told him and each day we go through the same emotions. My father suffers from short-term memory loss and he is unable to recall from one day to the next that his wife, my mother, has passed away. I am living in the old house and each morning I awaken with dread knowing that we are both going to have to grieve anew, as if for the first time. I am aware that I am losing him too as each day goes. Each day we are feeling hurt and irritable, making it harder to push on. I realise this can't continue.

The next morning I have set the alarm and I am up before him. My father has always been an early riser from his strict upbringing, a trait he did not pass on to me and that he would always tell me was a sign of my apathy. When he comes into the lounge room I have the floor covered in tissue papers and I am cutting out giant semi-circles from a piece of card. Blown up balloons are bobbing around in the hallway.

Tell me, what has happened, he asks.

I admonish him for getting up so late, especially when there is so much to do. I can see his poor mind flipping various threads of thoughts over, but nothing stays long enough that he can grasp hold of. It is your wedding anniversary I say, unable to look at him. She will be back at the end of the day expecting a party of some kind or she will be disappointed. We must make a surprise for her I say—something she will love. I wait a moment and he doesn't say anything. I am scared he will shout at me, or worse, call me a liar. Then he hitches up his pant legs in the same way he used to when he was about to get down to some serious business, and tells me the first thing we need is some decent music. He walks over to the old record player he brought from Chile when he immigrated here and sifts through the papery jacket sleeves of his old recordings. Since his memory has gone we have heard the same album over and over and it seems we have to re-discover this anew as well. He puts on his favourite *Queca* song and gives a little hop, which sets off a small bout of excited wheezing. My mother and he used to love re-enacting the festivities, including doing the traditional *Queca* dance. In the dance, the male pretends to be a rooster and my mother would play the coquettish female hen who is wooed. Then they would hop around each flourishing a handkerchief that they wave about.

My father was a 22 year- old law student when he first met my mother in Chile. At that stage he spent his time viewing life through the lens of his camera and would go away on secret trips to be alone with this craft instead of studying. On one such get away he had travelled down to small sleepy village south of Santiago, snapping the villagers going about their usual day unaware of this lurking paparazzi. His eye fell on a young woman who had dropped a bag of shopping, bags of flour, maize and potatoes rolling down the street. He snapped her; chasing the potatoes, brushing flour out of her skirt, removing strands of hair out of her face, her lips, the curve of her neck—and her gaze up close and upon him. He realised he had been sprung and to redeem himself he collected and then carried the food back to her family house. He found an excuse to visit every month, each time disarming her further with a click of his shutter.

I turn and see him fussing in the kitchen. My father has always been a wonderful cook, even now he will want to cook for us both and his hands seem to do all the remembering. He pulls out the avocadoes from a wicker basket we have hanging in the kitchen and feels along their dark olive ridges for ripeness. He selects two and then reaches in for several bursting, waxy red vine-ripened tomatoes. He arranges them methodically on the wooden cutting board alongside a red onion, a clove of garlic, a small deadly chilli and a fresh bunch of cilantro that fills the house with a piquant freshness as he dices the leaves.

I sit outside in the living room cutting my semi-circles, wrapping them around to tape into cone shapes as we used to do for my childhood piñata parties. I have a stash of his favourite caramels gleaming in their enticing gold wrappers that I pour into the cone. I then begin the job of reinforcing the base. I have bought tissue papers in oranges and yellows to cover the cone so finally by the end it looks like an Australian sunburnt desert hanging askew from our doorway. After some time he shuffles slowly into the room, swaying to the beat of the music and carrying his *pebre* salsa and loaves of white bread. He tells me to get the bottle on the table. I return carrying a bottle of *pisco*, a fermented spirit that is notoriously strong. He is not allowed alcohol as a rule but neither of us cares today. I pour two crystal-cut glasses for us and hand him one mixed with lemonade. He picks up a paper serviette from the table and shakes it at me. I gently loop my arm through his and slowly turn him, both of us giggling and sipping from our drinks. He looks up at me, his eyes shining through his ravaged features, and I know he knows: all of it. And we keep dancing slowly.

© **Kavita Bedford**

Kavita Bedford is an award-winning Australian writer. She worked for the Santiago Times English newspaper in 2009. She recently completed her Masters of Anthropology, whilst working in Indonesia as a research associate for the World Bank.
http://wherewindowsmeet.wordpress.com/

# The Tell-Tale Divided Heart *
## by Gillian Bouras

Migration was not my idea. At the time of my marriage, my Anglo-Celtic family had been in Australia for more than a century, and the only reason for departure had been two world wars, in which my grandfather and father did their bit. Against many odds they were spared, returned home with a deep sense of gratitude, and later encouraged me to think that anyone born in Australia had won First Prize in the Lottery of Life.

This being the case, why have I have been in the Peloponnese for three decades? I met and married a wistful and homesick Greek migrant, that's why. In Melbourne, which used to be a very Greek city. But Greeks pine, Greek villagers pine more than city dwellers, and I had married a villager.

And so it was that after some years I found myself setting out on a six-month holiday, which soon got out of hand when George found a job in the nearby town. He was desperate to stay and to return to remembered happiness in the bosom of the original family, and to be in his village, the place where he knew the rules and attitudes so well that he never had to think about them. And by that time he had the added bonus of two little boys, aged seven and five, who would automatically learn to love the *patritha* and the extended family as he did.

While I was still young enough to have a sense of adventure, migration turned out to be a salutary shock. George had been a migrant, too, but he became part of Melbourne's large Greek community; I think that in his head he never really left Greece, while I formed an Australian community of one. A major problem was that I had to live with my mother-in-law, the quintessential traditional woman, and the widow of a priest. Another difficulty was the fact that the redoubtable Aphrodite, the cultural continuum who measured five feet nothing in her black-stockinged feet, was illiterate, and so could not understand my need for books and writing. Nor could she understand my ignorance: I had never made cheese, could not milk a goat, and knew nothing about the harvesting of olives, and not much more about the rules and regulations of the Orthodox Church. The day I asked her which end of a garlic bulb goes in the

253

ground, she turned her basilisk and incredulous gaze on me: the silence that followed was long and thunderous.

I was willing to learn, and did not regard the learning as an obstacle. There were, however, other obstacles. I suppose language was the main one, for as I had had no childhood in Modern Greek I was humiliatingly reduced to the language level of a three-year-old: I was 35. I also realised before too long that in migrating I had crossed almost every conceivable boundary and divide, those of education, religion, culture and class. And I was largely a product of Melbourne suburbia.

I was continually translating in my head and had myself been translated. As saints' bodies are often lugged from one sacred spot to another, so my far from saintly being had been removed to a place I could not regard as being sacred, although I know countless philhellenes would disagree. And much was lost in translation. But much was also gained. It was at that stage that I began to write about the daunting experience of being foreign, and I remember thinking and writing that the whole business was like trying to fit a new key into an old lock, or vice versa. Something like that: at least one shape had to change.

I also thought and wrote about the death of the old self; now I think the pain of this comes about because simultaneously the new self is experiencing its slow birth pangs. Of course we die many times in our lives and our essential selves are continually being added to and reshaped, but migration accelerates the whole process. In the end, one of the satisfactions of migration is the knowledge that you have used part of yourself that would have remained unused otherwise.

It is sometimes said that being a foreigner is not a matter of location, but of temperament, and it is probably true that I have always had a sense of separateness common to the one the literal foreigner has. I was a quiet child, but my head was a noisy place to live in, and my ears were always at full stretch, as I observed continually, and tried to make sense of my observations. As an adult foreigner in a Greek village, I found that my senses were sharpened by the enthrallingly different landscape, by my close contact with the natural world and the turn of the seasons, and by my slow learning about a way of life that had changed little in a thousand years. And I drove people, especially Aphrodite, mad with my questions.

My first-born son found migration at the age of seven difficult. He was tormented in the school ground for being Australian, learned quickly about the burden of the divided heart, and for years felt he didn't fit anywhere. Aged eleven, he said bitterly to me, 'Why did you two have to marry? If you hadn't, then I wouldn't be suffering now.' At one stage he had spent half his life in Australia and half in Greece, but he eventually settled in Australia. When questioned, he replies simply that Australia suits him better. But I don't think he regrets his early years. Nor do I think he has ever read a line of Tennyson in his life. I know, however, that he would agree that he is part of all he has met, and that he can now regard being foreign as a positive state.

© **Gillian Bouras**

Gillian Bouras has been resident in the Peloponnese since 1980. She is a mother and a grandmother; she has had eight books published, and she continues to publish short pieces. She visits Australia irregularly. http://www.gillianbouras.com

# The Temple of Isis
## by Louise Charles

Isis rises with the dawn; a heaviness rests in the pit of her stomach. She kneels before the sun until the skylark sings its wakening call and then bathes in water scented with incense and lavender. She murmurs quietly, reciting her spells she knows by heart but can never divulge except to those in need. She massages her thick jet-black hair with aloe vera until it moves as one. She dresses simply in a silk sarong tied at the waist, her breasts left bare.

Standing before the temple Isis pauses and basks in the golden light reflected from the temple walls. Her gaze moves over the painted scenes, figures picked out in emerald, azure and crimson, like precious jewels. The pyramids of Pharaohs—long gone—loom in the background like silent warriors. The huge circular columns cast shadows as Isis advances with tiny steps, the skirt restricting her movement. She counts the stairs as she climbs. She is aware of the daily crowd of people who gather hoping for her help. It is not easy, there are choices to be made and some are not always the right ones.

Isis lowers herself onto the stone throne and adjusts her tall headdress which trembles and threatens to fall. Her neck aches with its weight and sometimes she wishes that she could remove it. But that would not please the Gods and not please Horus. She checks the leather knot which hangs from a strap around her waist. Evil is never far away and always ready to catch her out.

She takes three long breaths and then nods to her chief priestess.

'Isis, there are many who need your protection.' The tall young woman spans her arm across a sea of bowed heads. 'Who shall be first?'

Isis does not hesitate, she always chooses the person standing in the same position whether it be man, woman or child. Her gaze roams across the room before she fixes on the fifth person to her right.

'You,' Isis commands. 'What is it you require protection from?'

The small figure stands up slowly and raises his head. Isis catches her breath as the eyes of a child flash with red and orange. Demons. Not wanting to alarm the child, she beckons him forward. He is helped by his mother with a gentle push from behind.

'We will need to retire to the inner chamber,' she tells the priestess. This is not a ritual she can perform in front of others. The priestess turns to the crowd and dips her shaven head as a slow moan of regret swells from the floor.

'Come child, do not be frightened.' Isis takes his hand in hers. It is cold and heavy like that of someone whose soul has left for another world. 'What is your name?' she asks as she leads him to her chamber. The room is shaped like a star and a shaft of light spills to the floor from a small opening in the ceiling. A bronze bucket sits in one corner and a wooden container in the other.

'Jabari,' the child speaks to the dirt floor.

Isis lifts his chin with a finger. 'Ah, Jabari. You are brave then, like your name?'

He shakes his head and Isis sees the opaqueness behind his eyes.

'Have you been having dreams, Jabari?'

The boy nods and chews at his bottom lip.

'Dreams that frighten you?'

Another nod.

'Whom have you told?' Isis indicates to the priestess that she should leave and locks the door behind her. She stands within a circle of stones and waits for his answer.

'I've told my mother a little but not everything. She thinks I am lying and has brought me here to be cleansed.'

Isis breathes in and almost recoils from the stench of decaying flesh. The demon is gathering its strength, using the child's inner energy. She must act. Now.

'I know you're not lying, Jabari. There is an evil presence within you.' Isis puts her palms together and chants until the boy falls into a trance. She steps out of the stone ring, removes her headdress and places it at his feet. She kneels before him and calls to the evil spirit within.

The demon is aggressive and the child reaches out to claw at her cheeks with long dirty fingernails and then spits in her face. The air cools and the shaft of light is extinguished, plunging the room into darkness. Isis continues to cast the spell, her voice becoming lower and lower as her powers fight with the evil. Isis knows that if she falters for a second, the demon will win and possess her. Calling on Horus for strength, she battles, closing her hands around the child's neck as the demon forces her to squeeze. She does not stop, nor open her eyes even when the child whimpers and falls limp into her arms.

The chill wind leaves and she hears the snapping shut of her rosewood box as the demon is contained. Isis relaxes her grip. The room floods with light once more and the air is sweet.

The boy lies on the ground, his skin the colour of slate. She reaches for a glass phial from her belt and releases the stopper, wafting it under his nose. From the bronze bucket, she splashes his face with holy Nile water that she herself has blessed.

His hand twitches and he coughs, spluttering like a new-born baby. His eyelids flutter then open.

Isis sees her smile reflected in the clear brown eyes of Jabari.

## © **Louise Charles**

Louise is a member of Writers Abroad. She lives in rural Italy and writes short stories, flash fiction and several longer works, in varying states of progress. She plans to self-publish her first completed novel— *The Duke's Shadow*—in 2013. www.louisecharles.com

# The VIP Latrine *
## by Desley Allen

'Where am I supposed to go?' I asked my African husband.

'You do like so,' Sam replied.

'Like so? Like how?'

'Like everyone else, Debbie. Squat in the bushes.'

I had just arrived back in Kenya from an extended visit with my family in Australia. During my time away, Sam was to supervise the building of our new house behind the main homestead on his parents' farm; a conglomeration of crumbling mud walls, thatched roofs and rickety lean-tos. The design of the house would incorporate a sound studio, Sam's proposed business venture.

Grand plans? Castles in the air.

The farm had no electricity. And no water; apart from what the women brought back from the river in brimming plastic buckets balanced precariously on their heads. Sam agreed to attach guttering to the galvanized roof to harvest the rainwater and purchase an exceedingly expensive water tank. He promised me that the house, complete with a bath and toilet room, would be ready for occupation by the time I returned.

I was not sure what to expect, whether to believe Sam's assurances from our brief phone calls that our new home was well on the way to completion. What I found rendered me speechless. Piles of rocks, sand and rubble surrounded the site. The builders had concreted the floor. However, the stone walls were unfinished and a good 50 centimetres short of the makeshift tin roof.

'Well, what do you think?' Sam asked, hardly concealing the pride in his voice.

'I thought it would be finished.'

'Ah, well. The money ran out.'

'But when I left there was enough money to finish, even buy the water tank.'

'Ah, well, you know how it is. Everything is twice as expensive as you think.'

I followed Sam nimbly picking his way through the rubble. He helped me clamber up the pile of rocks, a substitute for front steps, to the raised floor of the house and ushered me through the open entryway. Sheets of yellow plastic hung over the window holes in an attempt to keep the rain out.

'See, this is our bedroom. There is enough room here for our bed and wardrobe up that end, my desk and chair down this end. The men should be back one day to finish the walls and then we will move the rest of our furniture in. Meanwhile, we'll eat over at the main house with the old people.'

That was when I asked Sam about the sanitary arrangements. He told me Baba had exclusive use of the long-drop toilet dug behind the family graveyard. Flattened kerosene tins, nailed to four palings hammered into the ground, surrounded the latrine on three sides in an attempt to provide some privacy. A wooden handle nailed to a square sheet of tin covered the small hole.

By late afternoon, I was desperate. I sneaked over and tentatively lifted the lid. I stepped back, stifling a scream, as a buzzing cloud of irate blowflies engulfed me. Fighting hysteria, I positioned myself, hanging on to the handle of the lid for support, making sure of my aim so that my feet didn't get splattered. I had no idea how I could manage number twos. I would die of mortification if I missed the hole.

Before we locked ourselves in that night, a scowling Sam stood guard, armed with his long cane knife, throwing stones at a rustle in the bushes, as I squatted at his feet. I did not waste a second to marvel at the stars.

'Tomorrow, I will erect a shelter in the yard where you can bathe. My sister will bring a bucket of water across from the main house for you. Nobody passing will see you behind the reed mats.'

'What about my loo?'

'The men might come to dig the hole next week, if it doesn't rain. Meanwhile, I'll ask Baba for permission for you to use his long drop.'

I explained my predicament about squatting and lack of balance. Sam gave me a jam tin. You can put it beside the hole and perch one side of your back end on that to do your business. How humiliated I felt trotting across to Baba's toilet, toting my tin and toilet paper. Not to mention the amusement of the neighbours.

Work began; the 10-metre hole dug in the black soil without incident. Now it was Sam's job to build the structure; each step watched with avid interest by the passing community. After two days of toil and sweat, two broken hammers and a few choice Swahili words, his masterpiece looked like it was nearing completion.

My hopes began to climb.

The old man arrived to give it the once over. Many instructions given. Submissive nods from Sam. Baba didn't stay to help with the deconstruction.

My hopes floundered in the puddle at the bottom of the pit.

Finally, the VIP Latrine, encased in galvanized iron, was finished. A mat of reeds, nailed under the roof, gave some insulation from the heat. Sam spread gravel around the base of the structure in a vain attempt to keep the smell in and the blowflies out. He sawed a rough hole in the wooden box that served as a seat, with the customary tin lid. Baba contributed a sturdy door, a bolt screwed on with a padlock.

The VIP latrine was mine exclusively.

I fashioned a toilet paper holder from a wire hanger and suggested that we have an official opening: speeches, guest of honour cutting the toilet paper ribbon, that kind of thing. Sam did not appreciate the joke.

Within days of completion, my beautiful loo had become the local tourist attraction. People walked long distances to marvel at it. I should have charged a viewing fee in hindsight.

Our work took us on safari to Tanzania for a few weeks. While we were away, torrential rain flooded the district. The pit caved in.

My heaven-sent loo sank majestically into the abyss.

© **Desley Allen**

Desley Allen lives in Brisbane, Australia. Her inspiration for writing, depicting her life experiences and relationships, comes from living in Kenya for over a decade. Two of her short stories have been published in anthologies.

# Upriver
## by Valerie Cameron

The Englishman looked back at a wicker cage full of skulls. It had been put there in the Second World War as a warning to Japanese troops not to venture upriver. His machete lay under his seat wrapped in a tea towel. He had been on the river since early morning travelling towards Keningau and the hill people. At a fork, the river narrowed and the boat entered a gloomy corridor of towering trees. As nipah palms closed behind them, the outboard whined louder.

Before leaving town, he had mentioned his plans in the staff room.

'I'm going to meet the Murut family of my fiancée.'

'Mr. John. You are going to marry a tribal girl! Why?' The geography teacher gulped his tea in astonishment.

'It's so far. And the journey upriver. It is full of dangers.' Now the Chinese maths teacher had to get her tuppence-worth in. What did she know? She never ventured further than the town's only supermarket.

'The Murut are not educated. They are not like us. Not civilised.'

'Mr. John, they are very fierce.'

Secretly he knew more than they did about indigenous peoples. Deep down everyone was the same and he was tired of being alone. He wanted someone to take care of him. They offered him tea and bananas and tried to dissuade him with improbable tales.

He leaned over the side of his narrow canoe to soak a handkerchief for his head. Hoping that a bottle of Chin Sau would ease his hangover, he cracked open two beers and offered one to the boatman. Five minutes later, torrential rain drummed on the surface of the water, drowning out cicadas. Thunder rumbled in the distance and fork lightning lit the darkening sky. They would have to camp soon, erect a shelter from branches and leaves. The boatman was Murut and had the skills.

They pulled the boat onto a sandy embankment. Within an hour, the Murut had lopped some lengths of bamboo, lashed them together with strips of rattan and constructed a sleeping platform. He laid some palm leaves over the A-frame. As darkness fell, the forest came to life with deafening insects and childhood monsters.

They broke camp before dawn and by late afternoon had reached a longhouse on stilts, the only settlement for a hundred miles in either direction.

Naked children in the shallows screamed, '*Orang Puteh! Orang Puteh!*' White man.

As the boat eased into the side, two young boys helped John out. Shouldering his pack he climbed a greasy pole to the house, feeling for notches along the sides. Everyone laughed as he slipped and slithered towards the headman.

'*Selamat Siang*, a blessed Good Day,' he panted.

He offered his hand to the small man whose body was covered in blue stars, one for each head taken.

'*Selamat Datang*. Safe arrival.'

Children climbed the pole in seconds and followed him, a Pied Piper. The chief waved them away ushering him through the first door. In darkness, John could make out another senior tribal member and a young man who introduced himself as the translator.

He began, 'My chief is happy you come our *kumpong*, our village.'

'Good. Good. I am happy to be here.'

They continued for a few minutes, asking about family health and running through social rituals. John longed for some fermented rice wine. The old man uttered short, sharp sounds like a squawking macaw.

'You want marry my daughter, Rose. What you give her?'

'She can live in the town. You know, shops, restaurants. My house is very comfortable. Running water, electricity, air-conditioning.' He spoke to his feet. 'We will have many children, *anakanak*.'

The place was a cultural minefield but he knew the game. He remembered the skulls stacked like cricket balls.

John rummaged around in his bag and felt for the gold bangle and heavy necklace. Luckily he didn't need to bring a head like the old days although he could think of a few such as the ex-wife, nit-picking manager and rip-off mechanic.

'You won't be disappointed with this. It's from the Emporium in Orchard Road, Singapore. And a buffalo for the wedding feast.'

The old man held the jewellery, turning it over, feeling its weight.

His translator continued. 'You good man to daughter. She youngest, she favourite. She happy very important, understand?'

These people were losing their land to logging companies and needed money.

'I will take care of her like a father.'

His own daughter, a few years older than his bride-to-be, had recently graduated from university. She had sent him a photo with a curt note: *In case you still care, from Brenda your daughter.*

He produced a bag of glass beads and laid them out on the mat.

A teenage girl in a batik sarong and T-shirt entered carrying a clay jar which she placed in front of the men. She greeted them and shook hands with John with lowered eyes. Was she shy or nervous? She seemed out of place here, not cleaning his floor or dusting. Her long hair made her look like a child. He made an effort to keep smiling although his future bride ignored him. She whispered to her father, then glanced at John. The old man nodded, then turned to the Englishman with hard eyes. John mopped his brow, rubbed his cramped leg and mentally counted to ten. The room was suffocating.

Rose returned briefly to leave a roasted monkey and sago. The Muruts tore strips off the carcass and wound gluey sago round their fingers, laughing at John's attempts. When a cockroach ran across the matting, he whacked it with the palm of his hand.

'You drink.'

The translator passed him the jar which he held to his mouth.

'You like our food?'

John nodded between sips.

Finished, they rose in one movement. He lumbered along the verandah past a row of doors. Each room housed a family. About halfway along was the largest room, reserved for the tribal chief and gatherings. As the sun sank like a penny in a slot, women hung kerosene lamps from struts. Waving away flying ants, John sat with the headman and elders. Villagers took their place on either side of a carved hornbill, chanting a welcome. When they stopped he heaved himself up to lay a bundle of notes at the totem.

He longed to bathe but the river was a slippery climb away. Wearing a head-dress of black and white feathers, an old woman twirled like a child playing airplanes in the hornbill dance. How could he take such primitive animists seriously? The monotonous tone of a sape lute reminded him of a primary school concert.

To keep himself awake, he spoke to the translator.

'Interesting tattoos.'

'You look sky now. See many stars. This mean you go to good place when you die. If many on your body, it protect you. Light like stars across big bridge to special place. They make light in dark to show you way. That boy over there you see?'

John peered through the gloom. They all looked the same, crouched in the dark.

'He have many girlfriend. He sleep with them but not like this.'

The boy rubbed his forefingers together. John coughed and shifted his legs.

'And if do bad thing with girl before marry, then very big problem for boy.'

He spat and swaggered over to his friends.

After endless twanging, the women were satisfied that the bird's spirit would protect them by attacking the enemy. John sang *Old Man River* several times then mimed sleep. He was led to a room where he staggered and fell against the wall.

He dreamt about a water buffalo in a clearing, tethered to a stake, its head held down by a short rope. While a Murut sharpened a knife, four men held its horns steady. The boy stepped forward and with one movement, slashed its neck. As it sank to its knees, villagers crowded round jeering and laughing.

'*Orang Puteh, Orang Puteh.*'

Their grinning faces were the skulls from the wicker cage he had passed downriver.

Awakened by his own shout, he tried to sit up. He needed to get down to the river, to sluice himself with cool water. But he couldn't move, immobilised like the bull. The only sound was his rasping breath. A shadow moved across the room. He could not mistake the child's hair and the small mouth bending over him.

'Rose, help me.'

'Mr. John, this good. You drink.'

Liquid dribbled down his chin. She tightened her grip and forced the rim against his lips.

'Mr. John, you drink!'

He coughed and forced it down. Almost immediately the constriction around his throat increased. He began to choke. A hand was crushing his windpipe. He gasped and looked into face of the tribal chief.

'Rose. Where are you? Rose, Come back!'

But she had melted into darkness. The chief stayed for a long time as his breathing became more laboured.

'Help! Help me, please!'

He had no energy to beg the old man. Heavy notes of the gamelan xylophone banged next door. Surely someone would soon come and see what was happening? Above him swirled a Milky Way of starry tattoos. Gradually they faded until the only light left in the room was a flickering candle. Shadows danced across the walls, but not the one he wanted to see.

He remembered Dayang Noriah's warning.

'Be careful, Mr. John. The Murut are poisoners.'

© **Valerie Cameron**

Valerie has been teaching overseas for 30 years in Borneo, Sri Lanka, the Middle East, Europe and latterly North Africa. Following a two-year posting in post-revolutionary Egypt, she has relocated to peaceful Dahab on the S. Sinai coast. http://valcam55.wordpress.com

# Walking Barry Island Beach **
## by Glyn Pope

Eyes,
the houses watch,
never sleeping.
Tides turn
out and about.
How many days
since you played
mother, sister, brothers?

I walk now on the beach,
glass of time
beaten blind.
Nothing ever changes.
The children still run
dancing on the waves.

You are still here
as you were there.
My body walks your path
with your soul,
weary of death.

My Father,
we only die
but never fade away.

As the tide
we return
each dawn
each dusk,
to remember
our passing
of days

© **Glyn Pope**

Glyn Pope is resident of France. His Father was taken for days out to Barry Island. Glyn was the founder of the St Clementin Literary Festival, France. He has a novel and poem published and has signed a new contract for two new novels.

# Walking in the Afternoon II **
## by Jennifer A. McGowan

*for my parents*

The world turns. Ages past
these hills were islands, this path
not even, perhaps, a track, being too close to the sea.
Now every November
we take refuge from the Severn in flood.
Those same rains
run down the hills and feed the springs.
For ten, twenty, two hundred years,
kestrels hover, buzzards stoop and cry,
larks cast their song through the greenery.
This is my time. My feet
tread in dappling shadow. My hands
paint the foxglove
and the tiny blue flowers no one
I know can identify. My mind
presses them as if in amber.
No tread is too slow,
nor gaze too lengthy,
here where seasons trip and tarry.
Quiet enfolds my mind.
I remember how to smile.
I come upon the well
like a pilgrim; seeking only water,
I am granted every wish.

## © Jennifer A. McGowan

An expatriate New Englander living in Oxford, England, Jennifer A. McGowan writes poetry that reflects on her current situation and back on her formative years in the American Northeast. She has many publication credits on both sides of the Atlantic. www. jenniferamcgowan.com

# Walking the Streets of Hong Kong *
## by Laura Besley

Noise and the lucky colour red for the Chinese, are synonymous with Hong Kong. Tung Choi Street, in the heart of Kowloon, is crammed with red lampshades, red shutters, red awnings. I hear people shout, talk on mobile phones, deafening traffic, drilling—the endless drilling—as I shade my eyes from the orb of the sun. The air is hot and gloopy and the humidity makes being outside away from air-conditioning a necessity rather than a pleasure.

As I saunter down the long street lined with tiny shops no bigger than cupboards, and market stalls even smaller, I wonder again how I found myself living in this little part of Asia. Of course, the real explanation is that my husband and I decided we wanted "an adventure". We'd been living and teaching in Germany and applied for various jobs in Asia, and accepted those offered to us in Hong Kong. But more often than not these days, I wonder why I am so far from home.

Swarms of tourists flock to the cheap goods on sale, like bees to pollen, and in many ways I am similar to these people with their backpacks and cameras; I am obviously not from this world. I am tall, Caucasian, non-Cantonese speaking and nearly always feel like an outsider in a place I've chosen to call home. And yet I do know more than the average tourist. Haggling is a game the Hong Kongese like to play and many tourists pay full price for the goods unaware that you shouldn't be paying any more than half of what the original asking price was. They can afford it though, and the sellers know it. Things are only worth what you're willing to pay for them.

'Missy, missy.' An old man, with deep wrinkles ingrained in his wide pale face, holds a fake Chanel bag in front of me. His outstretched arms tremble slightly, but his eyes are dark and fierce, challenging me to buy it. Should I? Will my conscience rest easier if I do? I can afford the asking price, let alone the price I would make him drop to, but you can't keep buying. You can't keep trying to rescue people from the poverty that prevails in the lower classes of this region.

'No, thank you,' I reply, moving on swiftly before he thinks I'm even remotely interested. Racked up one above another his stall has hundreds of bags in all shapes, sizes and colours. All are fake. He calls after me a couple of times, but eventually gives up and has, no doubt, picked someone new to try.

A young Indian man with a thin moustache steps towards me. 'Copy watch? Copy watch?' he asks.

'No, thank you,' I reply again. I can feel a trickle of sweat working its way down my back.

Despite the zebra crossing I look extremely carefully before I cross. British-enforced black and white stripes on the road are certainly not a guarantee that the traffic will stop. I didn't give Hong Kong much thought before I moved here, but I had expected it to be more colonial than it is: eighty to ninety per cent British, and the remainder Asian. I couldn't have been more wrong. There are snippets of British influence, like the zebra crossings and sign posts being in English as well as the traditional Chinese characters, but mainly it's a different world.

Ambling past the food stalls something attacks me; my eyes water, my throat contracts and I involuntarily take a step backwards. That smell. In all my years here I haven't been able to figure out what it is. Could it be fish balls? Stinky tofu? The hunks of raw meat hanging from hooks in the open air?

I move as swiftly as possible in this thick and clinging heat to the relative calm of the air-conditioned shiny shopping centre beyond the market where my husband is waiting for me.

© **Laura Besley**

Laura is a member of Writers Abroad and currently lives in Hong Kong. She teaches English as a foreign language and enjoys this connection with her students. She has been published in several anthologies, online and also enjoys blogging. http://www.laurabesley.blogspot.hk/

# When Only Rain Will Do *
## by Cynthia Reed

You move somewhere. Somewhere different. Somewhere alien. There are things you like and things you won't ever deal with beyond a sort of begrudging acceptance that comes from reminding yourself I'm only here for this assignment. Then I'll be gone. On bad days you add: They can't make me stay. We have a contract.

You love England. Even New England. Both have been Home. The crispness of an autumnal morning makes you long for the colours of the fall and wellies and fallen leaves and woolly dogs on long leads. Even the way Brits say 'autumnal'—ahhhhh-tum'-nuhl—makes you ache for it.

And the promise of snow. Always the promise of snow, whispered when white rimes the road and then shouted when the winter winds make promises come true and deposit infinite wonders—or even a single solitary wonder—in the form of a snowflake on your nose.

You own snow dogs, for heaven's sake. Adaptive creatures meant to withstand temperatures to 60 degrees below zero. That's cold. Great happy smiling wooing woolly beasts look into your face every day and howl as if to howl you to that other home and never let you forget the bite of winter on your cheeks, the numbness that seeps in through your boots, the breath that catches on the frozen hairs in your nose and makes you tingle and itch.

They remind you they're in Malaysia now. Three degrees north of the Equator. It takes more than three degrees north of the Equator to summon a snowflake, you remind yourself.

You sigh. Short of living with your head in a deep freeze, your best hope here is the 'rainy season'. Or one of them. You've learnt there are several—and that they are inconsistent and different depending on where you are and the time of year. Or perhaps it's a state of mind. You're not sure yet.

Yesterday you received a letter from a friend in Massachusetts who walks her dog on some wondrous four-mile trail that Paul Revere allegedly traversed in order to warn the Colonists that the British were coming. In her jealousy-invoking dog-walk tale-of-the-week she is out with her German Shepherd, Stoney, on a bright apple-crisp freezing cold day and meets a woman wearing a purple hat and walking five goats on a joined-up leash contraption.

A confrontation erupts. Stoney, you are told, would like to get himself a goat or two. Chaos ensues. It makes for a fine tale and you laugh but feel self-consciously sullen. You resent that running into a woman with a purple hat and five goats on one leash is so superior to your fate: sulking on a marble floor under an air conditioner with two slumbering Alaskan Malamutes.

Eventually your British husband comes home and you regale him with the goat tale. He likes Americans like you because 'they chatter a lot', he reminds you, and then appends the proclamation with 'it's a silly story anyway'. You agree.

To your surprise, he adds 'But not about the goats!' You then listen to him tell you that the 'silly' thing about this tale is that 'The British were already there and all those Colonists were, in fact, themselves British—and terrorists at that.'

You remind yourself that the English don't forgive and forget easily. But you still long with all your heart to be in Massachusetts on that icy-cold trail with your dogs—colonist, terrorist or otherwise.

You look up, dejected. The sky has closed in, now near-black. Something rumbles. The scaredy-dog, Solo, shoots by on his way to hide in the shower. With no warning, a *crack* as big as the world erupts. In an instant, the clouds throw down an absolute deluge of water.

You know if you went out it would throw you to the ground and wash you away with the detritus rushing down the gutters and broad, concrete drains. You remember that just last week it rained so hard that the back patio flooded and the lawn was inundated. You braved the torrents, clearing the patio drain of dirt and dog fluff, finally opening the cover and watching in awe at how rapidly the vortex of water swirled away.

Today's downpour is perfectly perpendicular. You watch, mesmerised. The drops are massive; you can't stop looking at it, wondering if you could drown in it. How would one breathe in all that water?

Suddenly, the thunder is gone, the rain lessens and you hear something akin to a Brahms lullaby no longer the 1812 Overture at full volume. It hasn't been twenty minutes and now it's just a steady rain, almost regular rain, you think, though the gutters still gush into the drains.

Oh! It will be cool when it stops, and make-you-gasp fresh. The humidity and closeness will disappear for a while. You take a deep happy breath and think, 'I could go for a walk and wear a hoodie if I wanted'. Just that minor possibility renders you giddy.

Suddenly, you abandon resentment and feel gratitude for the reminder from a faraway friend. All that longing for cold climes, well-seasoned with envy and sprinkled with fond memories, enables you to see that there are things everywhere to love—when you remember to stop and look.

Ah, so this is home now. You sigh, put on your shoes and wonder where you left the other leash. It may not be snow but, you admit, each homeland is remarkable and beautiful in its own way. The Malaysian rainy season will not lavish on you pine cones or blankets of snow—but there is delicate beauty in the rain-kissed frangipani and strength and awe in storms like the one just passed.

You smile. You welcome the bliss of this cooler air that kisses the skin and the glistening flowers that feed the soul. You walk the woolly dogs and watch for goats and purple hats. It was only rain. But it will do.

**© Cynthia Reed**

Cynthia Reed lives in Malaysia with her husband and two Alaskan Malamutes. Originally American, she's been UK resident since 1999. After a career in technical writing, she's now completing her first novel; she's passionate about dogs and photography.
http://cynthia-reed.blogspot.com/

# Wild Dogs of the Middle Atlas
## by Sophia Gorgens

There were three things Joan was told before she went to the Middle Atlas. One: always stay hydrated. You need more water in Morocco than in America. The sun was the same in the whole world, but in Morocco, it wove heat into skin like a carpet, from the fraying beginning to the tasseled Alhamdulillah.

Two: don't go hiking in the mountains in the Middle Atlas. The mountains belong to the shepherds and the wild dogs.

Three: and this was the most important thing. Never go anywhere alone in the company of one or more Moroccan men. When you agreed to be alone with a man, you agreed to everything that might follow.

Joan didn't mean to disregard any of this advice, but somehow Leah convinced her that hiking would be fun and safe. It really wasn't her fault that Leah called only that morning to say that she was sick or that John and Elise both overslept. So it was just her and three Moroccan guys they'd all met yesterday at a café and who said they knew the trails. They were already past the town of Ifrane and striking off across a rock-strewn field before Joan realized that her friends were, indeed, not with her.

'So where exactly are we going again?' It was still early in the morning, but already the sun was causing a thin line of sweat to set in on Joan's forehead. She wondered when they would stop to take a break.

'La Vallée des Roches,' the man in the lead replied. Yassine, Joan thought, and he was twenty-two or maybe twenty-three. And so were his friends, Mehdi and Youssef. 'You're not tired yet, are you?'

'Of course not!' Joan would rather not be the stereotypical American. 'I hope you're not either. Or are you out of shape?' she added, because Yassine had stopped at a low ridge running alongside a small lake. He said something in Arabic to his friends, and they laughed. Joan wondered if it had been such a good idea after all to be alone out here with them.

'No, no,' he explained, '*wa-lakin*, I haven't had my breakfast yet.'

They sat and he offered her some, a yogurt and a sandwich with cheese, but Joan had already eaten at home. She pulled out her water and took a sip.

'That's not all the water you brought?' Yassine asked around a mouthful of bread.

'No, I brought another two bottles.' But as she put the first bottle back in her drawstring backpack, she saw that apart from her sunglasses and disposable camera, her bag was empty. The two other bottles, she now remembered, were still on her bed. That and her pack of gum. She could really do with a piece of gum just now.

'Well, come on then!' Yassine had sprung to his feet and was rocking back and forth on the heels of his feet impatiently. Mehdi smiled and said something in Arabic. Youssef kicked him in the shin and held out a hand to help Joan up.

She took it and his hand felt warm and soft and it was drawing her closer to him and she felt her heart beating backwards but then he had let go and they were on their way again.

'Watch out for the needles,' Youssef told her as they picked their way across another field. Joan didn't see how this was hiking. All they seemed to be doing was crossing field after field, and she hadn't even seen any sheep yet.

'You mean spikes,' Yassine provided helpfully and Mehdi nodded.

'Burs?' Joan asked.

'No, spikes,' Yassine said and picked one up to show her. Joan didn't know what she would have called it, but she didn't think spike was the word.

'Aha! Look at this rock!'

Youssef, who had wandered ahead considerably, came bounding back, his bag bouncing against his back. He was tanned, and he didn't even wear sunscreen. Joan wore SPF 50.

They all stopped and gathered around the proffered, fist-sized rock. The sun was hot, and Joan was thirsty. She wondered what Leah, John, and Elise were doing at that moment. She wondered what they would do if she died out here. All alone.

'It looks like Africa,' Yassine finally said.

'Right?' Youssef held it out to Joan. 'You should have it. The Africa rock!'

'The Africa rock!' Yassine and Mehdi shouted and thumped each other on the back in a burst of laughter.

Joan didn't know what she was supposed to do with a rock. 'Find me Morocco instead, and maybe I'll keep that,' she said, shaking her head.

'No, no, Morocco's right here,' Youssef explained, and his shoulder was touching hers as he traced Morocco on the rock's surface with his finger. 'See it?'

'Sure, I guess.' She took the rock and dropped it in her bag and quickly pulled the strings closed again. 'Thanks.'

'Is that a camera?'

Shit. He'd seen her camera. Her awful, disposable camera.

'Yeah.'

'Digital?'

'No, disposable. My digital one broke in Tangier.'

'Aren't you going to take it out?' Youssef was at her side, tugging at the drawstrings. 'Want a picture of you with the sheep?'

'What sheep?'

'Over there.' Youssef's hand was on her shoulder, turning her in the right direction. He pointed.

'Aw, you two look so cute,' Yassine interjected, wiggling his eyebrows. 'Come on, a picture of that.'

Joan handed him the camera rather reluctantly. Youssef took his hand off of her shoulder for the picture, but she could still feel it there, warmer than the sun. Her nostrils flared and she could smell the sheep now and she wished they'd move and click, there was the picture, camera back in the bag, and they were walking again. Hiking, supposedly, but it was so hot.

'See the shepherd?' Yassine asked. 'Wave!'

Joan waved. The shepherd—was it only a boy?—shouted something back.

'What did he say?'

'Oh, nothing nice.' Yassine shrugged.

'What, though?'

'Swear words. You don't want me to repeat them.'

Joan did, but, 'I know a swear word. I think, anyway.'

Yassine moved closer to her. Youssef, too, and Mehdi was picking up pebbles and throwing them in the direction of the sheep.

'What?' Yassine asked.

'*Ibin al hamar*. Son of a donkey.'

A smile tugged at Yassine's lips, and Youssef let out a bark of a laugh. 'That's not a swear word. That's just shameful to say.'

'Well, an insult then,' Joan defended herself. 'That still counts.'

They fell into silence and walked past the sheep, which were, like so many rocks, scattered haphazardly across the field. Then the sheep and the shepherd were out of sight, and there were occasional trees that grew like gargoyles from the barren landscape. Their trunks were twisted and gnarled with the ancient lore of the earth, and the leaves were shriveled reminders of water from the sky. Joan had seen rain once since her arrival in Morocco, and she thought of those trickles of water in the cracking seams of the earth. Where was the water now? She was so thirsty, but her bottle was already half empty.

Youssef's hand brushed against hers while they walked. She jerked away.

'Tired?' he asked.

She was, but she said no.

'You sure? We can rest if you want.' He was looking at her, staring at her. Mehdi and Yassine were a few steps ahead, and suddenly, Joan felt terribly alone. A dull pounding had started between her ears because of the dehydration.

'I'd rather not,' she said, and it was true. Even her ear lobes hurt, and now Youssef's body was only a hairbreadth from hers.

Then he had stopped and he was grabbing her shoulder and pulling her towards him, and Joan felt her heart shrivel in the sun.

'Let go of me!' she screamed, but then she saw the dogs. Feral dogs, five of them. Teeth snapping and jowls glistening, they came down the side of the sloping hill, right at them. They were running and jumping in their excitement, barks and growls and scrambling claws on rock mixing into a deafening cacophony.

She would have frozen, but Youssef didn't let go of her. He dragged her further down the path, and then there were Mehdi and Yassine, rocks in both fists, yelling right back at the pack of fur and diseased patches and frayed ears and flies.

She tripped and went down even as Youssef continued to try to lead her back. Her calf scraped against the sharp edge of a stone, but she didn't care because one of the dogs was lunging right at her until—

Yassine's rock hit the wild dog right on the cheek, and the dog skipped sideways two steps before coming to a stop. It growled and eyed Yassine warily. He threw another rock, and this time the dog yelped and backed up a few steps.

'Get lost!' Yassine yelled and then fell into a tirade of Arabic. Mehdi threw a rock, too, at the big gray one, the one with the white patch on its chest. And another, at the small female creeping forward with an open maw. Arabic words and rocks that flew, and the dogs put up a fight. If someone got bitten, they would die from rabies, Joan thought. Of thirst. She wondered if she'd been bitten.

But then the dogs were gone, or nearly so, slinking away with yelps and whimpers and stones tangled like burs in their fur. No one had been bitten.

'Like spikes, not burs,' Youssef said and helped her to her feet. His hands were warm and soft, but this time, she didn't mind. The sun was very bright and very hot.

'Thanks,' she said, and Youssef gave her some of his water.

'A photo?' he asked jokingly as he took the bottle back.

Joan's legs were still trembling but she managed a laugh. Her calf was bleeding from being scraped against the ground, and she wished she'd brought more water, but she supposed it was alright.

'Maybe.' They were only halfway through their hike. She sighed. 'Or maybe not.'

## © Sophia Gorgens

Sophia Gorgens is of German nationality and spent four years in Bonn, but for the majority of her life, she lived in the United States. She also spent two years in Ankara, Turkey and two months in Ifrane, Morocco.

# Worth her Weight in Gold *
## by Paola Fornari

'I was seven years old, *sonamoni*, when I got married.'

I loved it when my grandmother called me *sonamoni*. Golden one. But it was she who was golden. I never tired of listening to her stories, as we sat in the verandah of her big house in Dhaka in the evenings. In winter she would pull her *achol* snugly round her shoulders. The crickets and starlings screeching their cacophony from the nearby banyan tree nearly drowned her soft voice.

Her eyes glowed. 'My father held me tight as I sat on one side of the scales. I felt his tear-damp cheek on mine. My future father-in-law, Karim, piled up the other side with gold hair clips, necklaces, bangles, brooches, and anklets, until the scales balanced. That was my *denmohorana*. All for me. Karim was so rich, he could buy anything in the world. He even imported slaves from Assam, in India. He wanted me for his son, Jalil. You see, a fortune-teller had spotted a lucky line on my hand…he said it would bring good fortune wherever I went.'

'Show me the line, *dadima*…'

I took her right hand and gently stroked its creases. I was afraid it would crumple.

'Tell me about your wedding, *dadima*…'

The crinkles around her eyes were like curtains, hiding her secrets, but she opened them wide in excitement.

'It was 1930. I wore a sparkling sari with gold fibres woven between the red silk threads. My hair was decorated with sweet-smelling jasmine—you know, *sonamoni*, my name, Zahura, means flower lady. My eyes were blackened with *kajohl*. My in-laws arrived on horses, and Jalil on a decorated *palki*, carried by four men. Oh, he was so handsome in his high white turban and his red *sherwani*. He was 13. I loved being the centre of attention, though I didn't understand what was happening.

'I was taken back to their home in the *palki*, through bamboo groves and paddy fields, and then on a boat to their village on the other side of the river. They had a luxurious two-storey house, so different from our mud hut with chickens and goats running around.

'My sister-in-law Mariam took me under her wing. She was 10 years older, and taught me to light the mud hob, and cook lentil dal and rice and vegetables for our everyday meals, and delicate *hilsha* fish and sweet *rosho gollas* and *jelabis* for special occasions. We girls lived, played and ate separately from the boys.

'You know, *sonamoni*, I was a bit naughty...' A mischievous smile crept over her face. 'Household chores bored me. I wanted to play all the time...Mariam used to scold me, but my father-in-law pampered me like a doll. Whenever I was sad, he took me to see my parents on horseback. I remember my long, ribboned braids swishing in the wind as we rode. I felt like a princess.

'This was my life, for six years. I only did two years of schooling, and learnt to write my name. I used to love reciting the traditional *shloks*...'

Here *dadima* began to recite a sort of repetitive mantra, her voice wavery and comforting. Then she jerked herself back to her story.

'When I was 13, I moved in with Jalil, and we began our life as man and wife. Jalil was clever. He studied homeopathic medicine in Kolkata. You know, he was quite a character. Let me tell you something.'

She whispered in my ear.

'His mother went mad, *sonamoni*. She did some crazy things. These days they call it Alzheimers. It was a disgrace for the whole family. One day she wandered out of the house stark naked. Jalil tried to defend her from her husband's rage. His father was furious with him, and threw him out. Jalil moved to Dhaka without a *paisa* of his father's wealth. That was around 1950. He left me behind with our four children while he started building up his medical practice from a friend's verandah. He was very successful, and soon he bought some land, built a house, and we joined him. Over the years we had four more children. He launched his own business importing medicines from Germany. His patients came from all over Bangladesh and as far afield as India, Pakistan, Burma, Bhutan, even England. Today people still remember him.'

Sometimes *dadima* spoke late into the night. Through the trees I could see the silver new moon, which made me think of a saucer filled with shiny stories ready for her to pluck.

'It was not all milk and honey, *sonamoni*. In 1971 the Pakistani army attacked Dhaka. Jalil sent us back to the village to hide. He stayed behind, with two vicious dogs that kept the soldiers at bay.'

Whenever she spoke of the war, she trembled.

'My father and uncles were freedom fighters. But they refused the certificate after the war. "We did not fight for recognition," they said, "but for the honour and freedom to speak our minds". My heart was filled with joy when we were reunited afterwards.

'We had a happy life together though Jalil was harsh sometimes. He liked things to be just so, and if I made a mistake he would beat me. I understood that it was because he loved me and wanted to improve me, so I tried harder to please him.'

I will never forget the last time *dadima* spoke to me. She must have been 80.

'I missed him so much after he died. He loved me, and I loved him. I still love him. You know, *sonamoni*, all my gold was buried near the village before the Pakistani soldiers came. After the war, we never found it again. It was stolen. So you see, *sonamoni*, his success did not come from his family.'

I took her right hand in mine. This papery-thin hand had been so powerful; it had changed her life, but now it felt fragile. She opened it, tracing one of its deep lines with her left index finger.

Barely audibly, she murmured: 'I like to think that perhaps this had something to do with it.'

'You're worth your weight in gold,' I said, as I kissed her closed eyes, sealing in her memories.

© **Paola Fornari**

Paola was born on an island in Lake Victoria, Tanzania. She has lived in a dozen countries over four continents, and is an expatriate *sine patria*. At present she is living in Bangladesh where a good friend told her this story. http://www.espacios.be

# Index of Authors

Adams, Cathy ............ 83
Agar, Anton ............ 30
Allen, Desley ............ 259
Ascroft, Dianne ............ 91
Barick, Pamela ............ 88
Bedford, Kavita ............ 250
Besley, Laura ............ 270
Bhattacharya, Susmita ............ 114
Borgersen, S.B. ............ 149
Bouras, Gillian ............ 253
Brown, Gillian ............ 12
Callahan, Jody ............ 208
Cameron, Valerie ............ 54, 262
Carey, Susan ............ 74, 120
Carrillo, Dominic ............ 182
Chai, Sabine ............ 185
Challender, Margaret ............ 70
Chan Pasteur, Stella ............ 168
Charles, Louise ............ 256
Claase, Celia ............ 213
Couchman, Vanessa ............ 42
Croft, Nina ............ 48, 116
Darley, Judy ............ 158
Davies, Mary ............ 38
Dickerson, Katie ............ 214
Dickson, Eileen ............ 235
Dickson, John ............ 124
Dodson, Bruce Louis ............ 192
Downing, Jane ............ 188
Eames, Susan ............ 23
Elsom, Jonathan ............ 119
Feinberg Stoner, Patricia ............ 170
Fell, Jennifer ............ 106
Felton, Pamela ............ 240
Fornari, Paola ............ 157, 280
Galvin, Chris ............ 111

| | |
|---|---|
| Gibbs, Denise | 222 |
| Goodfellow, Anita | 140 |
| Gorgens, Sophia | 275 |
| Hammick, Marilyn | 87 |
| Henwood, Bev | 232 |
| Hilbourne, Alyson | 63 |
| Hodson, Colin | 243 |
| Howie, Elisabeth | 51 |
| Ingram, Lesley | 207 |
| Isiminger, Andrea | 97 |
| Jennings, Taylor | 55 |
| Johnson, Frances | 75 |
| Jung, Desirée | 225 |
| Kendig, Diane | 68 |
| Khan, Maryanne | 144 |
| Lalonde, Danielle | 174 |
| Landini, Claudia | 100 |
| Lewis, M.E. | 152 |
| Littmann-Tai, Ingrid | 246 |
| Mackinnon, Simone | 137 |
| Manandhar, Mary | 78 |
| McGowan, Jennifer A. | 269 |
| McMaster, Vesna | 27 |
| Moat, Helen | 204 |
| Mumford, Leanne | 9 |
| Nedahl, Christine | 72, 103 |
| Nørslund, Rilla | 173, 226 |
| Nyman, Mikaela | 1 |
| O'Neil, Chris | 20 |
| Parker, Helen | 126 |
| Peter Hawkins | 131 |
| Petrone, Epp | 94 |
| Petrone, Justin | 194 |
| Pope, Glyn | 267 |
| Porter, Doreen | 198 |
| Reed, Cynthia | 272 |
| Renew, Sandra | 136 |
| Resetarits, C. R. | 242 |
| Richard King Perkins II | 177 |
| Riley, Susan | 245 |

| | |
|---|---|
| Robinson, Sally | 178 |
| Rockne, Louise | 218 |
| Rosenberg, Tracey S. | 47 |
| Saunders, Jennifer | 249 |
| Schedneck, Jillian | 229 |
| Seman, Patricia | 6 |
| Stewart, Alison | 60 |
| Sullivan. Kimberly | 33 |
| Whyte, Craig S | 163 |
| Wills, Jayme | 201 |
| Wilson, Anne | 17 |
| Wilson, Mairi | 216 |

Made in the USA
San Bernardino, CA
13 January 2016